THE SNAKE PIT

"Long ago they lowered insane persons into snake pits; they thought that an experience that might drive a sane person out of his wits might send an insane person back into sanity."

The
Snake Pit

MARY JANE WARD

RANDOM HOUSE   NEW YORK

THE SNAKE PIT

CHAPTER ONE

"Do you hear voices?" he asked.

You think I am deaf? "Of course," she said. "I hear yours." It was hard to keep on being civil. She was tired and he had been asking questions such a long time, days and days of incredibly naïve questions.

Now he was explaining that she misunderstood; he did not mean real voices. Fantastic. He was speaking, he said, of voices that were not real and yet they were voices he expected her to hear. He seemed determined that she should hear them. He was something of a pest, this man, but she could think of no decent way to get rid of him. You could tell he meant well and so you tried to play the game with him, as if with a fanciful child.

"You can make water say anything," she said. That should appeal to the childish fancy that leaped from pebble to pebble, dancing in the sun, giggling in the sparkle.

And now the water rushed from the quiet pool of his voice to a stone-cluttered bed uneasy for fishes. The song of the brook soared to a rapid soprano and his voice was changing him into a small boy. Dreadful. She tried not to look, but at last her eyes turned irresistibly and, with horror, saw him a girl. She had suspected him of magic and now she knew.

For once he was not asking questions; he was letting gibberish flow from his lips and you would have far more difficulty making sense from it than you would have in imagining words from a genuine stream. Suppose it was not he.

She turned her head. He had a peculiar habit of crouching behind you. Was he in the bushes? And just who was he? You met so many people and they came and went before you got them sorted out properly. A moment ago he was here and speaking seriously of voices that were not real voices and you knew he would be sad if he discovered that you did not know his name. Never mind. The sun is the chief thing.

The sunshine was a warm almost hot bath of thick gold. There had been no intermediate period, no saying, But it really is getting warmer. You were freezing and then you were warm. Does it happen that way in New York too? New York has so many things over Chicago; I hate for it to have Chicago's ability to make a twinkling change from winter to summer. Maybe I am back in Chicago.

But no. He asked where I was and how pleased he was when I said New York. He said fine, fine. I said I was in Chicago recently for a visit and he said fine, fine. It was as if he was the teacher and I, the student, had given the correct answer to a complicated problem. Yes, he did not ask for information. He was testing me, though God knows why.

He was gone now, at least he was out of sight, out hunting voices that are not voices, poor man, and on the bench was a young woman. She was a pretty girl. Her light curly hair stuck to her forehead in baby rings and her lashes were thick. She might be beautiful if she was not so pale. If I knew her I would suggest liver; perhaps she hates it

4

as much as I do. Robert likes it. I should fix it for him oftener. I can eat the bacon. I could suggest shots. Expensive, though, and she looks poor. Only a very poor girl would go to a public park in a hoover apron. For that hoover? No, that would be collars.

Dear Emily Post: Is it proper to go out park-sitting in a hoover apron? Answer: This is a custom entirely unknown to me, but if it is the general practice in your community it would be well not to be conspicuous. I assume the hoover apron is always fresh and that you would not lap the clean side over the soiled side and attempt in that way to maintain a false front.

Complacently enjoying her advice column in the *Virginia Quarterly,* the *Virginia-Drawn-and-Quarterlied,* Virginia-the-wit looked down at her own garment. Not this old rag. Virginia Stuart Cunningham, Mrs. Robert P. Cunningham to you and Miss Stuart to a minute section of the reading public—the section of literary persons who get their books free. . . . This young writer from the very proper and intelligent city of Evanston, Illinois, where intelligence is second to nothing but propriety. . . . Look, Ginger, you wouldn't wear this old thing out to the park, even a New York park.

What was I thinking when I dashed out? I must have been in a rush, but then why sit in the sun? She wore this wreck of a dress only when doing the most revolting of household tasks and she certainly had learned by now that you cannot go out on New York streets looking any old way. You were always running into someone from Evanston. Funny how you could go down to the Loop at home and never see a soul but just step out of your New York apartment and the city swarmed with Evanstonians done up in their most proper and intelligent costumes.

However, the fair girl on the bench was not an Evanston person. She was not anyone you had ever seen before. You had not been introduced, but she appeared to be talking to you. This city full of people who talked to you at the drop of a hat knocked your hat off. Even so, Virginia Stuart Cunningham was not the type to pick up strangers in the park. Oh, these New York parks. What next?

Yesterday or the day before, I saw a cat on a leash. He was walking along as sedately as a Doberman. Probably they had not let him know he was a cat. Like Margaret. Margaret, when I called kittykittykitty. . . . "Stop that, Virginia," she said. "He doesn't know he's a cat." And the day of the cat on the leash there was a dog in a little plaid coat and he had a plaid cap like Sherlock Holmes' and he was carrying a pipe in his mouth. They had not got him to smoke it, though. Good for him. And good for Mag's cat. That one not only caught on to being a cat, he also had kittens. And Mag always so careful to call him He and she even named him Coolidge. After the kittens Robert said she should have taught him to choose to run. Family fun, not funny to anyone but family. I've seen them all recently. No reason to feel this way. Think about that pipe-carrying dog or you'll begin to bellow.

The poor beast hung its head but marching behind him in oozing pride were a man and woman. . . . No dogs in this park. You wouldn't know you were in New York, the place all bad dogs go when they die. And spend eternity wearing damnfool coats and caps and carrying pipes.

She stirred her shoetips in the dust that lay thick on the path and secretly, not to disturb Miss Hoover, began to look for her groceries and her pocketbook. It was possible that she had not gone to the store yet but not possible that she had come away from home without her purse.

6

Her eyes were acting up. From the sun. The park might be familiar but the sun flattened the colors and blurred the shapes. It was as if she hadn't her glasses on.

She put her hands up to her eyes and her glasses were not there. "Is there any danger of her ever losing her sight?" Mother asked the doctor. You were ten then. "Well," said the old coot of a doctor, "well, I don't—think so." For years you felt as if you were committing a crime when you read anything that was not Required. And reading was the only thing you cared much for. Well, softball. Yes. What ever became of all those kids, I wonder. Let me see . . . David is a priest, Fred runs a laundry, Kate teaches school . . . Did Edgar end up in jail? Mother said he would. He was a good ball player, though. So was I, in spite of the bum eyes.

Then as you grew older the lenses were changed less frequently and now that you had reached a great age you bought new lenses simply because the old ones had become scratched. Somewhere you read about the possibility of the middle-age farsight correcting the youthful nearsight. Then you are not middle-aged, dearie; still you can't see a foot in front of your face. What are you doing going around without your glasses? Trying to be pretty?

Didn't wear them much in college. Not at a school where there were four or five girls to each boy. I always had more dates than time, though. From going without glasses? Sitting here on this bench she could think of six girls who never wore glasses and who never had dates, except for the political kind got through fraternity blackmail. It is a fine thing for an almost middle-aged woman to sit in the sun and feel smug about having had a lot of dates in college. Where are my glasses?

Where was her pocketbook? Where—this was the real

question that gnawed through the artificial frivolity—
where exactly was she?

ii

It was hazardous for her to go out alone, even with her
glasses. She had learned how to get to Wanamaker's and
she could find her way to Bleecker Street where the vege-
tables were cheap and she seldom went many blocks out
of the way to reach the French bakery for baba au rhum,
so wonderful, with just a touch of nastiness to make you
appreciate the wonder. That nasty taste, said Robert, was
rum, but that could not be. The medicinal flavor was
something they had not been able to overcome yet. Each
time she bought the cake she thought now this time they
will have got rid of the bad taste. Robert had another
explanation that had to do with water poured from stewed
flypaper. Quite fresh, unused flypaper, he insisted. But
enough of this. You will have to ask the way home.

She hoped Miss Hoover was not a New Yorker. They
never know anything. Oh, they know how to get there
themselves but blessed if they can tell you. They take a
crack at it in their own language. Remember the time the
taxi man took us to Pearl Street when we had so dis-
tinctly asked for Pell. They and their pell earrings and
their store cheese. Half a pound of American cheese, I
said, and the grocer said he hadn't any. Well, what do you
call that? I pointed to the cheese he was leaning on. That?
he said, why, that's store cheese. . . . A few days later I
asked this same wiseacre for cottage cheese and he said he
had never heard of it. Standing there practically up to his
elbows in it. But no, that was pot cheese. Well, where I
come from, I said, they call it cottage cheese. He asked
where I came from and I said Evanston, Illinois, and he

8

said he had never heard of it and then I betrayed the Athens of the Middle West and said it is a suburb of Chicago. You musta been glad to get away from them gangsters, he said. And when I got home and opened up the carton of cheese it was less than three-quarters full.

If she would just stop talking a minute. A New Yorker, all right, this Miss Hoover. Can't understand a word she says. Pardon me, but could you tell me how to get to . . . ?

How to get to where? Where?

The sun is too warm. Am I going to throw up? Where is the apartment? We have lived so many places. Robert and I. The family and I. After Margaret was born we didn't move so often, but there have been many many places for Robert and me. He lived in the same house all his life until he married.

Since they had been in New York she and Robert had lived in three or four or four or five places. She could say exactly if she put her mind to it. Maybe it was six. It was not that she did not know, it was the sun. She would be able to say their present address as soon as she recovered from this touch of nausea. Even the most familiar things can slip from your head momentarily. You always know where you live. Once someone telephoned Mother and asked her address and Mother said, "Excuse me a moment, but there's something on the stove." She went to the front porch and read the house number and came back to the telephone and said, "There. Now what was it you wanted?" Yes, anyone could forget his address for an instant. Nothing to get excited about, but it would be convenient to have the front porch along—and your glasses to read the number. But my glasses are here somewhere. A person who puts glasses on before getting out of bed is not likely to leave the house without them.

Maybe I am waiting for Robert. He has told me to wait. I almost remember him saying, Now you wait here and I'll be right back.

She pushed her hair from her forehead, no baby rings for this hair. Being without glasses made you feel as if your brain could not function. Her thoughts seemed as blurred as her vision. She sat up straight. She must not become ill.

When she lowered her hands she saw that they were trembling. I am afraid. I wonder why. I am terribly, terribly afraid.

iii

. . . my name. In any conversational clatter the sound of your name will ring out and even though you have a common name you cannot help pricking up your ears. Miss Hoover, you assumed, was speaking of the state. She did not know you. The state of Virginia. Carry me back. Gran's quavering voice, Carry me back to ole Vuhginny . . . and tears rolling down her soft, carefully creamed and powdered cheeks. Sentimental as all get out about her native state, but when Mother gave her money for a good long visit there she said she guessed she had better things to do with her money. "Vuhginny, of all places," she said. "Why, I married your father to get away from there, didn't I?"

It was lucky for Virginia Stuart that her grandmother was not always so frank. Otherwise the first Stuart girl would have been Pernissa, Gran's name. Patent medicine. "She was set on having you named for her," said Mother, "and we sure enough thought we were going to have to. But then we got the idea of making a big fuss about her home state and first thing we knew she was bragging all over about how she had named you Virginia."

"Virginia," said the girl on the bench, "Virginia, I said when was it you worked on a newspaper?"

Someone gave me a pin once, a wood carving that said Virginia and I wore it for about two minutes. Before I got ten steps from the door a man said, "Hi, Virginia," and a second later another was yelling, "Morning, Ginny." But I am not wearing that pin now.

Question to be answered. *On* a newspaper, not *for*. Miss Hoover one of the profession? "I never worked for a paper," said Virginia. Never having been paid for her work, she was darned if she would say *on*. "Just reviewing. Books and tickets none of the regulars wanted. For a while I did edit a short-story feature. Without pay, of course. For prizes I gave my review copies."

That was a lot of talking for a hot day. She was too tired to talk. This dress indicated that she had been working hard in the apartment. . . . That short-story feature was a laugh. Town where literature was more popular than bridge, town where the minute you had something published literary ladies swarmed to offer chances to collaborate. Fine offers. You do the writing.

Miss Hoover said to tell her about the short-story feature. She was as persistent as that man. Is he in the bushes? "Well, the town was full of women who wanted to write. When they had time. What they wanted most of all was someone to take down their ideas and whip them into shape. They talked about how the money meant nothing to them and the thousands the *Post* paid out and if they just had a private secretary. Very few of them bothered to send anything to the newspaper. I usually had to fill the space. Used different by-lines, of course."

11

"I can't get over it," said Miss Hoover. "You are so young."

"I'm not so young," said Virginia. "I'm. . . ." How old am I? What year is this? What month? Her birthday was in the summer; had it come and gone? Quickly she selected an age that was substantial and uncontroversial. "I'm thirty-five," she said.

Miss Hoover sucked her breath in and said that wasn't old, not really old. The way she said it you knew she was astounded to learn that she had been talking to a thirty-five-year-old just as if that antique was a regular person.

"Thank you," said Virginia. Though why you were obliged to thank people who said you did not look your age was something she did not understand.

"I'm twenty-five myself," whispered Miss Hoover.

"I never would have thought it," said Virginia dutifully.

"I'm afraid I show it," said the girl. "Now." She sighed. "But I'm not going to worry about it. . . . When I read *Afternoon of a Faun* I never dreamed I would meet the author. And here, of all places."

This was the first time Virginia had met a stranger who had read something of hers. As a rule new people had never heard of you. If it came out that you were a writer they always offered to read something you had written, that is, they said they certainly would like to but they were afraid they were pretty busy and anyhow they didn't exactly go in for novels. They rather went in for the serious stuff, you know. They always read the *Reader's Digest*.

Virginia, though tired, was set to listen to Miss Hoover's praises. They would be brief. Then would come the pay-off. Any writer knows he has to pay for his compliments. As soon as he has said, Why, thank you, that's very generous of you, the other person clears his throat and dives into his own writing experiences. Miss Hoover did not wait for the gratitude. Her compliments about *Afternoon of a Faun,* Virginia Stuart's heart blood, were condensed into a statement that the book was about the length of the projected Hoover opus. It could not fail to be a hit. Virginia had listened to this sort of talk often enough to know when to cluck. She would, she supposed, go home with a thick manuscript written in longhand. For a frank and honest opinion. I can take it, so don't try to pull your punches—if you honestly don't think it is good. But I have spent years on it, you know, well, months anyhow, I have such a little time. It's all based on fact, by the way. I understand there's a rage for historical novels. Personally I loathe them, but I thought a novel based on my grandfather's diaries. . . . If you have any comments just jot them on the margins. It's such a nuisance not to be a typist. Maybe you could tell me someone who might be willing to type my book. I suppose you . . . Naturally I'll be glad to pay for it, after the book is published. And by the way, if you think of a title, something catchy, you know, that they can use in the movie.

Take me home, find my glasses and I'll read the fictionized histories of all your second cousins. If I had my glasses I could walk directly to the apartment. It is not seeing that makes me believe I am not thinking. Without my glasses things look so different; hardly look at all.

In connection with the word apartment she thought of the word house and then of a large house where many young people milled around and talked at the top of their lungs. They argued and they sang and they laughed. God in heaven, do we still live with all those young people somewhere outside of Manhattan? This I am not enduring.

13

She closed her eyes. No, we went from there. They were too noisy and too young and too always. "You are lovely tonight, Virginia," the tall one kept saying. He was twenty. At first I thought it was marvelous to have a young, very handsome boy telling me every night that I was lovely but after a while I wanted to slap his face. Isn't that shameful? We unco-operated and went back to Manhattan. I am positive of that. Yes, I remember that as soon as we got back to ourselves, all the co-operators came to see us and the tall boy said I was lovely and his great black eyes were swimming. I called it a conquest, but Robert said it was a mother complex. Somewhere not far from here—I would not go far in this dress—we have a little apartment. It has to be little. The money was getting low, and anyhow, Robert said, This time there won't be any extra room for running a hotel for the city of Evanston. But just where is that little apartment?

The thing was to wait until Miss Hoover came to a breathing space. Her first theme in English at high school. A. Everything A. College. Everything A—well, not science or math, but everything that counted. Virginia clucked. Job on a newspaper. Virginia clucked. Reporting job gave no time for the real writing and there was no money without the job. "Do you wonder I ended up here?" asked Miss Hoover.

That gave you the cold chills, a girl ending up as a bum on a park bench. "Don't be discouraged," said Virginia. "Obviously you have talent or you never would have got the job in the first place."

Miss Hoover shook her head. "It's being here that gets me."

"You musn't feel that way about it," said Virginia.

"I'd a lot rather feel that way about it than think it's something in the family," said Miss Hoover.

The sentence had no meaning. No wonder the girl had lost her job. It was going to be difficult to get adequate directions from her. She seemed not quite . . . There you go. Pretend to be so social-minded but the minute you rub elbows with someone who has lost her job you think it must be her own fault and that she isn't quite all there.

"Look," said Virginia. She was going to ask Miss Hoover to dinner. She didn't want her but you had to prove to yourself that you were practically as well as theoretically social-minded. Robert would not mind as soon as he was told that the girl was down and out. He isn't wild about women who talk as much as Miss Hoover does but he is very good about people who are down and out. "Look. . . ." She can help me get back home and then we'll start dinner. "Look, how would you like to . . . ?"

A new voice interrupted. It was a shrill voice. No water, deep or shallow. It was a sharp knife that cut you away from the sun. The creeping fear returned. Like cold wet sheets it wound around and around your body and made you its prisoner.

CHAPTER TWO

"All right, ladies."

You had awakened from a bad dream and almost torn yourself from the memory; the dream itself was obscured by depression which would remain until you were fully awake. But you had no chance. The sharp voice ordered you back into the horror. What am I thinking? The voice has nothing to do with me.

However, it had something to do with Miss Hoover. The girl sprang from the bench and pulled at Virginia. "Hurry," she said. "Hurry."

Blobs rose from other benches and gathered into a large smear. "What's the matter?" asked Virginia.

"Please," said Miss Hoover. She said please, but she gave Virginia no alternative and the pallor was deceptive; there was no anemia in the tug that stood Virginia up, nor in the grasp that urged her across the lawn. A group of women in faded cotton comprised that dull smear of color. "What's the matter?" asked Virginia. A fire? A riot?

Miss Hoover paid no attention. The women were scrambling into a two-abreast line. There was a determined sort of frenzy in the way they shoved. It was as if they were little children who had learned the urgency of responding to the bell but who hadn't as yet discovered how to form

16

a neat line. "Where are they going?" said Virginia. "Why do we have to stand with them?"

"Sh," whispered Miss Hoover. "You mustn't talk. It's against the rules."

Leave it to a chatterbox to put down a rule against talking. It was rather funny. The whole thing was rather funny. Only rather. It will be really funny when I tell Robert. Things that were not amusing when they were happening could be made very funny when you told Robert. He laughed and laughed. Sometimes she wondered if he laughed entirely at what she said; sometimes when she was having especial success she caught a look in his eyes that made her wonder if he might be laughing at the way she told it and not it. And there were all those queer women, she would say to him, and this girl who had picked me up kept insisting that we had to stand in line. It was a zoo, you know. At first I didn't notice the cage but then I saw it and I smelled the animals.

There seemed to be no animals in the cage just now. There was a blue-and-white something but it looked more like a person. "All right, ladies," said the blue-and-white something. There, that will make him laugh. Not having my glasses, I'll say, I assumed the thing was an animal and my goodness when it spoke. . . .

The door to the cage was open and the blue-and-white creature appeared to expect them to enter. A tour?

"Virginia," said Miss Hoover, "you've got to come." She looked about to weep. "It's no use, you know. Keep it up and they'll just put you back."

Recess was over and now if you got P in deportment you would be put back. How silly. Miss Hoover was absurd but inasmuch as she seemed on the edge of hysteria you had to humor her. A few more minutes would not spoil the dinner and anyhow you had to get your bearings and your glasses. How had you come to be mixed up in a tour? Undoubtedly one of those government things. Adult education. See your city. Study conditions.

"Enjoy the sun, Virginia?"

Blue-and-white had solidified into a large woman dressed to look like a nurse. Oh, these New York zoos. It is a peculiar city, not really American. The potage not melted. "Yes, thank you," said Virginia. How does she know my name? Strange she calls me Virginia instead of Mrs. Cunningham. Fresh. What do I call her? Kiddo?

The group did not loiter. Nothing to see. The guide made no remarks about the cage. She said to step along, ladies. She spoke as if they had to do what she said. For all her calling them ladies she hadn't very good manners. Maybe it was the last tour of the day and she was tired of having to recite her piece over and over. Or maybe she had a pull, daughter or cousin of an alderman, and could get away with anything.

You expected to find cages inside the building, but there was none. Inside was a large room with wicker furniture, the sort typical of public waiting rooms not yet advanced to chromium. The smell of the zoo was unmistakable, and so the animals were not far off. You would know that musky, fetid straw smell anywhere.

The room was oblong and the floor was covered with brown linoleum that looked very clean. No gum wrappers or cigarette ends. The walls were painted a dark brown to the height of a tall man and then a lighter brown up to the tan ceiling. At the narrow windows were stringlike curtains that were brown or dirty, maybe both.

"You want to get anything?" asked Miss Hoover. She spoke aloud now as if a ban had been lifted.

"I'd like my bag," said Virginia.

"You stay here and don't move," said Miss Hoover. She pushed Virginia down into a wicker settee. "I'll get it when I get mine."

There were no cushions on the settee. Virginia picked at its scaling paint and thought how fortunate it was that Miss Hoover knew where the pocketbook was. If I weren't so tired I would be glad to take her home. But we have been having so much company. . . . Anyhow I take back what I thought about her not being quite all there. She is very sweet and I would be lost without her.

"Grace, you wait your turn," came the razor voice of the guide. Most of the women were now crowding around blue-and-white.

"I am," said Miss Hoover. "I am simply trying to get Virginia's bag for her. Really, Miss Hart. . . ."

Two names. Miss Hoover is Grace. The guide is Miss Hart. Looks more like a wildebeest.

In a few minutes Miss Hoover, no, you must call her Grace from now on, came back. She handed over a bag Virginia had not expected. It was the small overnight bag Mother had given her. It was a bit small for a practical overnight bag but it was enormous for a pocketbook. I must look a fool, carrying that thing. "Thank you so much."

She was going to apologize for having such a queer sort of purse when she noticed that Grace was carrying a Dobbs hatbox. It was a nice hatbox, but Grace did not look as if she had been hat shopping. When she opened the box you saw no hat; it was full of the miscellany you carry in your purse, except, Virginia guessed, money. Grace must have pawned her pocketbook and now she carried everything she owned around in a hatbox and lived on park benches and went on city tours just for something to do or maybe for a chance to get under a roof. How dreadful. It would make a good story but I could never bear to write it. And look at that woman over there, with a shoebox. Perhaps this was a picnic. That would explain why I brought this bag. We have taken it to the beach several times. It isn't like me to have got mixed up in this sort of affair. I suppose it is for a Cause. New York is so full of Causes.

Squinting at the women she decided her True Trotskyite friend must have got her into this. It would be like Helene. She was always saying if they would just have open minds. Robert and Virginia tried. They went to a True Trotskyite banquet once. Photographers were there and popping pictures and once when one pointed his camera at Virginia she turned her head and saw that behind her was a huge sign, Defend the Soviet Union. Oh! This was at a time when you didn't say Russia aloud in Evanston and she thought suppose our pictures get into the Chicago *Tribune* and we are elected to Mrs. Dilling's club. How dreadful Mother and Dad will feel. And all during this the speakers were yipping about defending the Soviet and how we must abolish Stalin. Helene said this was logical to anyone who had an open mind. Well, now she's got me into some sort of True Trotskyite picnic. Robert will have fits.

"Do you want to go to the washroom?" asked Grace.

"No, thanks," said Virginia. Her glasses would be in the bag. No thanks, no park restroom for me. I'll find my glasses and hurry home.

She unzipped her bag and began to rummage for the glasses. Someone had been into the bag. She never would have left it in such a mess. She started to say something

20

about this to Grace but then decided not to. Grace would think she suspected one of the comrades. Like Helene, Grace would insist that everyone who was under the Heel of Capitalistic Oppression was as virtuous as the field lilies. Helene suspected only those who had money and this was very amusing because Helene had quite a lot of money herself, money she was using to bring on the Revolution.

But thoughts of Helene and her very special kind of revolution, a strictly invitational affair, were interrupted by the discovery of a large box of powder. Now you do not take a large box of powder to a picnic; you take a compact. Nor would you take a large comb and a hairbrush. Don't tell me I've got into an overnight project.

It was so difficult to think. The sun did things to you. She should have known better than to sit in it so long. Remember the girl back home who had a sunstroke and was really very strange for a long time. . . . Pack of letters. Why take a pack of letters around with you? She picked up the letters, forty or fifty tied into a bundle with a bit of darning cotton. Mrs. Robert P. Cunningham. Robert's writing. Why does he write when he sees me every day of the world?

"Don't look at them," said Grace. "Put them back. They'll take them from you if you don't watch out—like they won't let him write any more because you cry every time you get one."

"I can't imagine anyone crying over Robert's letters," said Virginia stiffly. Somehow she and this Grace had got rather more intimate than she cared to get with someone she had barely met. She thrust the letters deep into the bag. First thing you knew, the girl would be wanting to read them. "Robert writes a very amusing letter. People always say so."

Our address will be on the letters. When she isn't looking I'll take them out and then I'll ask her how to get
there. And when I see Helene I'll tell her I did not think
much of her rally-in-the-zoo. I understand why you gave
me your ticket, I'll say to her.

"Never mind," said Grace. She patted Virginia. "Never
mind," she said. "It won't be much longer."

ii

When the women who had accepted Miss Hart's invitation to the washroom returned to the large room where
Virginia and Grace waited, there was a good deal of pacing
up and down. There was little conversation. The room
had the restless, railroad-station feel.

"What are we waiting for?" asked Virginia.

"You'll be transferred before you know it," said Grace.

"I can't imagine anything here happening after I know
it," said Virginia. "Are there to be speeches?"

"After all," said Grace, "you have come a long way in a
very short time."

"I have never said New York transportation wasn't wonderful," said Virginia. "But I do hate the subway."

"You couldn't get here on the subway. You know that."

"My dear, what I know about the subway. . . ." Virginia
laughed a little to cover up her ignorance of how they had
come to this place. Chartered bus, no doubt. Financed by
Helene in memory of The Old Man.

"You mustn't be discouraged."

Nothing like getting encouragement from someone who
had not yet started a novel. Like Cassie. I tried to impress
her. I rewrite and rewrite, I said. It takes me two years to
write a novel, I said. And Cassie was sympathetic and she

said it would take her a long time too and that she bet she would have to rewrite. Later on, she said, you may get on to it and make some money on your writing.

Now Paula is different. Paula is pleased by my not making any money. It proves that you are too good, she says. Oh, it is fine to listen to Paula, but I can't help wondering if Cassie is nearer the truth.

"I have worked hard," she said now to Grace, "but I have never been ambitious. I write for fun." What are you going to do while I paint? Robert asked when I said he would paint while we stayed in Paris. Will you paint too? he asked. No, I said, maybe I'll write a book. Well, he said, I don't see why you couldn't write a book here. Not quite all of the American writers are doing it in Paris. "I thought Robert was making fun of me and so I had to start to write, to show him. That's really how I got started."

"All right," said Grace, "if you don't want to talk about it."

"But I am talking about it. As soon as I started writing I knew that was what I wanted. I had thought I wanted to go to Paris or somewhere for a year but when I started writing I knew that was it. About a month after he asked what I would do in Paris I told him I had to have a typewriter. A typewriter, he said. Why? You never write letters and anyhow you don't know how to type. Well, I can teach myself, I said. I'm writing a book, I said, and when you are writing a book you want it to look like a book, not like a letter or a diary. . . . Writing a book? he said. What about? It's not about anything, I said. It's a novel. . . . We were poor then. I mean, we thought we were. Really we were quite rich, but you never know it until afterwards. I had bought a piano and a vacuum and some other things on the installment plan and that made Robert nervous.

23

Robert, I said, you know how my handwriting is. I always got the worst marks of the class in Palmer Method. . . ."

Was Grace listening? Why bother to tell all this to a stranger?

. . . a long time ago we went to a party where there was a man who had studied handwriting for a hobby and the hostess made him perform. When he got to me I wrote a sentence and my name in my best Palmer Method and he looked at it and said this and that about my character, the sort of thing you could say about anyone, just to look at them. Then he lowered his voice so that no one but me could hear and he said, "I think that someone very close to you has died."

This was about three years after Gordon.

"Cheer up," said Grace. "You'll be transferred soon."

All this about transferring. Do you have to go to that terrible place where people run wildly from one train to another, place where I got stuck once without a nickel? Left the dress shop with five cents and that seemed all right; get anywhere in New York for a nickel—wonderful transportation—Chicago ought to be ashamed. Had to transfer at this rabbit warren and they wanted another nickel from me. . . .

"I wasn't going to tell you," said Grace, "but I'm being transferred."

"I hope you have a nickel."

"What did you say?"

"Just a family joke," said Virginia.

"I'm going next door," said Grace. "Maybe I'll leave from there. I thought you had to go to One first but he said there is no rule about it. He explained it to me."

And then Virginia knew where she was. It was some sort of training school for underprivileged and delinquent girls and she had come to study Conditions. I must be doing a novel with Social Significance. All these new friends of ours always pestering me about why don't I write something that has Social Significance. I wish Robert had put his foot down. I get enthusiastic about something but it wears off. I wish he wouldn't take me seriously. Like that about Paris, my God, we would be there now if they'd not got messed up in a war. Wonder we were not there and caught in it. If Robert had decided just a little sooner to make the break. . . .

"Supper, ladies!"

"Before long," said Grace, as she got up from the settee, "I'll be out shifting for myself—wondering where the next meal's coming from, maybe."

"You must feel free to come to our house any time," said Virginia. You had to watch out in New York when you said something like that. At home you said to call you up some time when you meant you didn't care if you never saw them again and you were perfectly safe; they didn't care if they never saw you again and they said oh, you must call me. But here in New York you said to call you up some time and they did; you said to drop over for dinner some time and they said they were free tomorrow and what time should they come. But it was a relief to discover that Grace was getting her meals here at the industrial school. Undoubtedly she slept here too and surely they would find her a job when she had finished the course.

"It would be funny if I looked back and wished for some of the slop they serve here, wouldn't it?" said the girl.

"The bread is good," said Virginia. She had been taught to say something kind, if possible. That was Gran. There is always some little good thing, Gran always said. Like all great talkers, Gran wanted to cramp everyone else's

25

style. If there is anything I dearly love, she used to say, it is a good listener. . . . I wonder why I mentioned bread. I must have been thinking of that twenty-five-cent kind that infuriates Robert. He thinks nothing of losing a quarter but just let me spend twenty-five cents on a loaf of bread and he says what are we coming to.

"Man cannot live by bread alone," said Grace. "And I am not being funny."

"No," agreed Virginia, "you aren't." I'll order a steak and let Helene pay for it. Even if this isn't a Trotskyite, pardon me, True Trotskyite picnic I am certain that Helene is in some way responsible. I had forgotten that Robert isn't coming home to dinner tonight but of course he isn't. I would not be staying here otherwise. His new schedule is so baffling. I better say medium rare because if you say rare you often get it raw.

She and Grace went to where the women were lining up. "No pushing, ladies," said Miss Hart. She spoke as if they and she were separated by a thick wall. "Ladies! We'll wait until this pushing stops."

The pushing stopped. Miss Hart took the key that swung from a long chain at her waist. She unlocked the door. She opened the door and they marched into a hall that was curiously familiar. The floor was brown linoleum and the walls had that same institution combination of paint. The floor sloped gradually and something about the bobbing heads of the women who marched in front made Virginia think of horses. "Rosa Bonheur," she said.

"I see what you mean," said Grace.

"No talking, ladies!" said Miss Hart.

She treats the women as if they were criminals.

Criminals? That is it. The key. The locked door. That cagelike porch through which we entered the building.

26

One of our friends has roped me into doing a prison novel. That would be Gus. Being a newspaperman he could manage to get me in, I suppose. But I will not go through with it. I don't care how many notes I have taken, after dinner I am going home.

They halted at a door that was guarded by another woman fixed up to look like a nurse. This one waited until there was respectful silence and then she unlocked the door. The feeling was that you were about to go into a chapel to view the remains of a great saint.

The new guide had a board and clipped to the board was a sheet of paper. As the women filed past her she made checks on the paper. There will be a special notation after my name: writer, here to observe.

The new guide, no, you must think of them as guards now that you knew this was jail, was rather nice-looking. She was not pretty, but she had a sweet face and that was a change from Miss Wildebeest Hart.

"Cut the shoving, ladies," said the sweet-faced one out of the corner of her daintily rouged mouth.

iii

The dining room was not so large as the waiting room but it was oblong and painted in the same dull way. There were four rows and in each row were four tables and at each table were six chairs.

"No," said Grace, when Virginia very naturally accompanied her to a table. "Please, Virginia, don't make any trouble. You have to go to your own table."

Make trouble? My own table? Virginia shrugged. Grace definitely needed a psychiatrist. It would be kind to tell her, might save her much trouble later on. But how can you suggest to a person that she go to a psychiatrist? People go to a psychiatrist as secretly as they go to an abortionist.

At the moment it was best to humor Grace. If she didn't want you to sit with her, very well. Perhaps she thought she would be stuck with the check. I'll have to sign for my dinner, come to think of it. Someone cleaned my bag of money. I wouldn't mind the money so much if they had left my glasses. . . . Here was a vacant chair. As Virginia hesitated beside it a woman shoved her roughly. "Get away from my chair, you," said the woman.

"I beg your pardon," said Virginia. "I didn't know it was yours."

"I'm reporting you the next time," said the woman fiercely. "Watch out or you'll be sorry."

The more I watch, the sorrier I am. Well, you didn't care to dine at that table. She went to another one but here again she paused at the wrong chair. Another woman, quite as outraged as the first but not shoving, bawled for Miss Hart. "Miss Hart! Virginia will not take her own place. She is on the wrong side again."

"I'm sorry," said Virginia. "I didn't see the seating chart. Not having my glasses. . . ."

"Alibi Al," said the woman. "Glasses yet."

Miss Hart had not heard, or had not cared to interfere. Virginia got around to the other side of the table where she took the remaining empty chair. Nobody objected. The woman at her left even smiled. "Hello hello hello," she said. "Hello, Virginia."

"Hello," said Virginia.

"Hello," said the woman. "Hell's low and heaven's high."

"Huh," said the Alibi Al woman, "that's what you think.

28

If you knew what I know, you would laugh on the other side of your face."

"Not being two-faced like some I could mention," said the cheerful woman, "I say hello again."

"No talking, ladies," shouted Miss Hart.

"You see," said the gloomy one.

The other two women opposite said nothing. The woman at Virginia's right breathed hard through a most aristocratic nose.

Where were the waiters? There were no menus. I would have preferred the European Plan, but in a prison even a visitor can't expect de-luxe service.

Then Miss Hart and the other blue-and-white one came with a steam wagon. They put two bowls on each table. One bowl held what looked like a stew and the other was a mess of sliced beets fixed in a rigid gelatinous sauce as bright and inedible-looking as store cherry pie. The instant the stew touched the table, the woman on Virginia's right, the Nose, began to remove chunks of meat from the bowl. She selected the pieces with finicking care. During this process the woman on the left kept saying to save some for Virginia. It was thoughtful of her but also embarrassing. Really, you should treat me as one of you.

Finally Virginia's champion took the bowl from the Nose and Virginia leaned back. The Champion was going to serve her plate for her. How kind.

But the Champion, once she had prized the bowl from the Nose's fingers, served herself. Then she passed the bowl across the table. "Save some for Virginia," she said to each of the three women on the other side of the table.

Eventually the bowl came to Virginia. There was perhaps a full tablespoon of pale gravy left in it. In the gravy were a piece of potato, two slices of carrot and seven peas.

29

Virginia counted them to make them last longer. The flavor of the gravy suggested that the meat had been sheep. Goat, really, but surely this was not a ceremonial meal.

The leave-some-for-Virginia procedure was repeated with the beets. "Never mind," said Virginia. "I don't care much for them." She thought she said this aloud, but no one paid any attention. The Nose stirred her beets into her magnificent portion of stew. She did an excellent job of blending the brown and the red and then she took a piece of bread from the plate in the center of the table. She ate the bread. She did not eat even a thread of the meat or a droplet of the raspberry-shaded sauce she had labored to achieve.

Virginia took a piece of bread. She was not quick enough to get in on the butter. Several of the women ate the butter as if the little squares were candies. The bread, as Virginia had said, was good. I must be sure to tell Robert the bread is good. It will cheer him up. She had no idea why, but she felt as if Robert needed cheering up. Why? He was happy. He had wanted to stay in New York and they had stayed. Only this morning, or another morning not long ago, he was saying, wasn't it wonderful to be in New York.

Queer how far away it seemed. Queer she felt as if not so long ago she had been lying in a coffin and Robert had been standing near, weeping. Crazy dream. For a minute she toyed with the idea that she had died. She had read a book like that once. For a long time the character couldn't figure out where he was and then it developed that he was dead and in heaven. This place, however, this place of the zoo smell and the locked doors could not be heaven and Virginia's church had renounced hell some years ago.

My trouble is the need of a good meal. Even another piece of bread. . . . She reached and was successful.

"Leave some for the Countess," said the Champion.

"By all means," said Virginia. To show that she had caught on to the playful spirit of the thing she stuffed the bread into her mouth as fast as she could. There were two good bites left when the crust was snatched from her.

"Thank you, dear."

She turned and saw a great black hulk. The old woman looked exactly the way a countess should look. She was fat and dressed in rusty silk that went down to her heels. Her hair was built into a beehive of yellowish white and the hand that had taken the bread was grimy. There was an expression of affability on the large flabby face. "Thank you one and thank you all," she said.

She held the bread in a basket made of her jutting bosom and one of her hands. After going the rounds of the tables she waddled to one of the narrow windows and threw the bread out.

"Why does she do that?" asked Virginia. I could have eaten it.

"Questions yet," commented the cross one.

"For the birds," said the Champion. "They are her little children. Save your spoon."

The dishes were being sent at great rate down to the end of the table. Dessert. Virginia hoped it would be substantial. Apple pie à la mode. She helped slide the dishes on and Miss Hart came and put them on her wagon. Then she gave each diner a dear little aluminum pan. Virginia hadn't much time to see what was in her pan. She hoped it was lemon custard; she had never been fond of lemon custard.

The Champion swept the pan from her, emptied the

31

custard into her own pan. "There you are," she said, as she returned Virginia's dish.

Virginia started to say something sarcastic, but then she noticed the Champion's eyes. "Thank you," she said. She said it sincerely because she realized that her champion wished her well and labored, though obscurely, to that end.

"That's all right," said the woman. "I've got children of my own." Her words were thickened by custard but there were tears in her eyes and Virginia was ashamed of herself.

It is vulgar to be so concerned about your stomach. Especially when you can have anything you want as soon as you reach home. These poor women are stuck here until they get their diplomas or until they have served their time or whatever it is they are here about. It isn't right to spy on them. I cannot believe they are hardened criminals . . . Well, that one directly across—she might be a lifer. I wonder if I have jotted down the jargon. The wrong language would make the book a phony. Let me see, you say rap for sentence? Or rap for what you did to earn the sentence?

What crime would Grace have committed? Libel? Dared you ask her? But she might be here for an investigation. They do such sneaking things to get their stories. I won't. I'll tell the person who put me up to this that I will not do it. I will not betray those poor women. Why, they give up their bread, the only decent part of their meal, to feed the birds. More than likely nothing more than sparrows.

"All right, ladies," shouted Miss Hart.

That would be something a modern penologist had thought up, that calling them ladies. Call them ladies and they will act like ladies. I should think somewhat better

32

food might be more encouraging but of course that would cost money. It costs no money for Miss Hart to blat out *Ladies*.

Find a telephone and call Robert. Look, darling, I'll say, it wasn't such a hot idea. You were right. I don't want to do that sort of book. And listen, honey, stop at Gristede's and pick up a steak before you come for me. I've been watching them eat and it's given me a terrific appetite. And, honey, get some of that twenty-five-cent bread, will you? Just this once.

iv

They lined up in front of the dining-room door. When the door was unlocked they marched out. Miss Cut-the-Shoving was checking on her board. To see if any of them had died of the meal?

They marched up the brown hall and stopped at the door at the end of it. Miss Hart unlocked the door and they went into the waiting room. They crossed that room and paused at another door. Miss Hart unlocked the door. They went into another hall. They stopped at another door. When it was unlocked they went into a room that was stunningly different.

It was a large light room. There was tile on the floor, tiny octagonal pieces of tile charmingly fitted together and so white and clean. The walls had the two-color paint job but they seemed more cheerful. It was a lovely room. Virginia studied the floor as if it was an exceptional mosaic and she thought suddenly of her beautiful Kelim rug and had then to suppress a ridiculous and unexpected sob. Don't be a baby. Suppose you had to stay here.

If I had to remain in this prison I would choose this room, she thought. But presently her enthusiasm waned.

33

There were four booths. The women stood and waited for their turn. Anyhow, that was the idea. Your turn wasn't necessarily when you thought. It depended a good deal on where Miss Hart was. The pushing was done quietly and with no hard feeling. Virginia changed from line to line but it was no use; none of the booths had a door.

When at last it was her uncontested turn she discovered that an even more vital accessory was missing. There was no wooden seat and the old joke about not falling in was in this case no joke. But she forgot how frightful this was when she saw there was no toilet paper, no toilet tissue as you would call it in Evanston. There wasn't even an empty container. Nor any holes to indicate that there had ever been a dispenser. She was about to call to her next neighbor, but then she remembered the cleansing tissues in her handbag.

When she left the booth she peered at the walls of the other three. None of them had paper. This must be reported.

As a rule she held back and let others do the reporting but now she was angry and she went to Miss Hart to say what is the idea of not providing these women with toilet paper. When she reached Miss Hart she saw that the woman was providing toilet paper. Miss Hart was the dispenser. If you required paper you asked her for it in advance and she doled it out to you. She was the judge of how much you needed. It was a curious and humiliating procedure. Hadn't they gone deep enough into a woman's privacy when they removed the doors from the booths?

You had to admit, though, that the floors were cleaner than the floors of any public washrooms you had ever had the misfortune to be in. The usual public toilet is strewn with paper and of course that must exasperate the clean-

34

ing women. The system here seemed a bit drastic, though.

"Virginia," said Grace, "could I bum another cigarette? I'm ashamed of the way I'm always asking you but . . ."

"Don't be silly," said Virginia. She opened her bag. "Here are cigarettes but I haven't any matches."

"That's what I like about you," said Grace. "No matter what, you always have a joke."

"I'd rather have a light just now," said Virginia. What a nuisance it is to be one of these unconscious wits. You have always to pretend you meant to be funny and that you see the point.

"That's rich," said Grace. She laughed as she took three cigarettes from the pack. "Come on."

They and the other women clustered around Miss Hart. Miss Hart had exchanged the toilet paper for a handful of kitchen matches. When she struck a match the women tried to get four or more lights from it. Did they think three could bring them worse luck than they already had?

When they had got their lights they sat down to enjoy their smokes. It was cozy. There was a chair and Miss Hart sat on it and watched. The others sat on the nice white floor and leaned back against the brown wall. It was something like being at a studio party, except that now and then the hostess would scream for them to watch their ashes. "Watch your ashes, ladies!"

"Make me one of your cute little ashtrays," said Grace.

Virginia reached into the ratsnest of her bag and found a piece of paper. She tore the paper in two and she made a cone of each piece. She tore a latch to hold each cone together and this seemed to be what Grace had wanted. When she had given one of the cones to her friend she noticed that Miss Hart was looking at her with affection. Perhaps Miss Hart had to scrub the floor.

The smoking was a chain proposition. You were allowed three cigarettes but only one light. When Virginia had lit a fresh cigarette from her stub she dropped the butt into the cone and gave it a quick squeeze. You did this expertly and neither you nor the cone became scorched. Vaguely you remembered times when you hadn't had any paper, when you had had to put a cigarette out in the palm of your hand. You could spit into your hand first. I must have dreamed this nonsense.

Miss Hart got up. When she had gone from the washroom one lady, the daredevil of the group, perched on the chair for a moment, but she was back on the floor when Miss Hart returned.

The guard was shoving a sort of rack that dress shops use for Special Values. Swinging from the rack were white sacks. Miss Hart put the rack in the center of the room and the ladies stopped smoking and began to undress. Virginia started toward Miss Hart to ask where a telephone was but somehow she didn't go through with it. She had a feeling that she was not a free agent and that she had to stay overnight. This was absurd. She was no criminal and no one could keep her shut up. All she had to do was say she was leaving; she would not have to say it if she knew the way out, or if she had one of those keys.

"Forty-three," said Grace. "You've got to remember it. I don't know what you'll do when I leave. You never remember your number."

Forty-three. The hangers on the rack were numbered. I am forty-three. She found the hanger and took it from the rack. The white sack was supposed to represent a nightgown. It was enormous and made of material suitable for tents. The number forty-three was stamped on the gar-

36

ment as a sort of trim. The neck was deep and wide and the sleeves were butterfly.

The system was simple. You hung your clothes on the hanger and put your shoes under the place numbered forty-three. Remembering athlete's foot Virginia hurriedly put her shoes back on. No one had bedroom slippers but she noticed that several of the women used their shoes. The majority, however, braved fungus.

There were four washbowls and you waited in line to brush your teeth and wash your face. Virginia found soap in her bag and so could ignore the questionable piece that lay beside the bowl. Next to her a woman sat in the washbowl to give herself an intimate bath. Virginia rushed through her washing just in case the plumbing should collapse. She supposed they wouldn't blame her but it was as well to be in another part of the room.

"Meditation, ladies," announced Miss Hart.

This was too much. You would not join them in evening prayers. Virginia had nothing against prayers, but she did not care to be included. She was extremely tired. The others could run along and pray if they wished.

But the ubiquitous, mind-reading Grace spoke up. "You've got to take medication, Virginia. You have got to take it as long as you are on the list."

"Medication? I thought she said meditation."

"Sue," said Grace, "you take Virginia to medication. I'm not on the list any more."

"Sure," said a woman who was almost fat enough for the prison gown. "Come on." She had a Dutch bob, always the favorite cut of square-faced, dark, fat women. She looked as if she might make trouble if you didn't come on, and although Virginia felt she would almost rather meditate than medicate, she came on.

They and several other women went through the hall to a room they called the office. At a desk was a woman in white uniform and cap, just as if she was an R.N. She was serving something in lilycups.

Sue graciously let Virginia go ahead but fortunately she was not the first in the line and so was able to watch the procedure. The guard poured something into a lilycup and the prisoner drank it down. While the victim choked and sputtered the guard refilled the cup from another pitcher and this was drunk gratefully. One woman just ahead of Virginia knocked the cup from the guard's hand, but the white uniform simply filled another cup and said, "'You drink this." The prisoner drank it.

And so did Virginia drink what was handed to her. It was a worse drink than she had expected. "This beats Martin's gin," she gasped. The guard wouldn't know who Martin was or how he had made such awful gin during prohibition days, but the remark was wrenched from your stinging throat.

"Virginia," said the guard as you drank the water chaser, "you are a card."

"What is that stuff?" Virginia asked Grace when she met her in the hall a moment later.

"Formaldehyde," said Grace.

"Jesus," said Virginia. If she hadn't been so weary she would have gone to the washroom and put her finger down her throat.

She and Grace went to a sort of dormitory. Grace got into one of the cots and Virginia got into the one next to Grace's. No one threw her out and so it must have been the right cot. She had put her bag under the bed but now she leaned over and dragged it out. It was getting too dark to read but she did not intend to try. She slipped one of

Robert's letters from the packet and put it under her pillow and then she felt safer. They are doing their best, but it will take more than formaldehyde.

Outside of the dormitory someone was screaming. The dormitory, like the toilet booths, had no door and so you heard things easily. Drowsily Virginia imagined running down the hall to rescue the screamer. But then there was quiet.

"Grace?"

"Yes."

"How long have we been here?"

"You mean here in Three?"

"No, just here in general."

"I came in January. You came around the first of February."

February? I'd thought it was summer. "What month is this?"

"August."

Just like that. August. February to August. No use trying to fool yourself now about this being a survey in the interests of an Important Novel by a Proletarian Writer.

Was my crime so great?

v

"Good morning, ladies."

Who had got into the room? Stealthily she groped for Robert. I must put my hand over his mouth so he won't speak out. But the bed was narrow and she was alone. The room was dark but she saw pale shapes rising up. One of the shapes said her name and then she remembered that she was not at home. February to August.

"Yes," she said. She got out of the cot, fumbled for the bag under the bed and then put on her shoes.

39

"Hurry up."

"I am." Always the command to hurry and you hurried nowhere, you arrived nowhere. The shoes were cold and clammy and they squished up and down when you walked.

After she had followed Grace into the hall she remembered the letter and so she went back and took it from under the pillow. When she returned to the hall Grace had vanished but there were other ghosts that rushed in the dimness. It was far too dark to be morning and she wondered if this might be a fire drill.

She followed the shapes into the washroom. Although it was the same room it had been moved to the other end of the hall. She would not give them the satisfaction of commenting on the change. She found her hanger and began to dress.

"Virginia! You don't take breakfast this morning."

Then why not let me stay in bed, fool? She turned and there was another guard, not Miss Hart, a smaller one but with a big voice. Not that I took dinner last night, but thank you just the same for saving me the bother of the trip. "All right," she said. Perhaps Robert is coming to take me away. She continued to dress.

Now this one that was not Miss Hart came over to her and took her by the shoulders and shook her. "You put your clothes right back on that hanger." This guard had puffy cheeks and her rouge was in purple splotches and her hair was scooped into a black-silk net and she looked as if she had been up all night. "You know you go for shock. Hurry up or you'll be late."

It was quaint of the guard to think you had to go elsewhere for a shock. But Virginia put her clothes back on the hanger and again got into the grotesque nightgown.

"You'll have to concentrate," whispered Grace. "It

makes her so mad when you forget. And it counts against you."

"Where am I going?"

"For shock. You remember."

Do I? I remember it no more than I remember the house where I was born and the little window. Going for shock. An odd, foreign expression. Sensation seekers go to be shocked; I never heard anyone say go for shock, as if it was a commodity like the morning milk.

Presently she and the guard were the only ones left in the washroom. The guard handed her a gray terrycloth robe. "Put this on," she said. "Put your nightgown back on the hanger. Hurry up."

In the hall the guard turned her over to another one in blue and white, one who hadn't put on any rouge this morning. Virginia and the pale one went through the large room and they reached the outer corridor in time to trail along with the last of the breakfast ladies, but they did not go into the dining room with the breakfast ladies.

As they turned at a door just beyond the dining room door Virginia noticed a third door. It had gold letters on it. It looked familiar but she was unable to make out the letters. The pale one unlocked the door she had selected and they went into a cement stair-well and started to climb. After several flights the pale one unlocked another door and they went into another brown corridor. The pale one escorted her to a small room and left her there. All of this was done without any comment. Well, I don't feel like talking before I've had my coffee either.

There were wooden benches around the walls of the small room and there were two windows. Virginia tried to open one of the windows and was surprised to find that she could. The window opened down the center to make

41

two slits. They might as well have had bars. It was beginning to get light. The sky had a sick, lemon cast at the horizon.

Three robed women were ushered in. One of them sat down; the other two stood in the center of the room. No one said anything.

After a while a guard came and took one of the robed women away. There was pink in the sky now. The pink was turning to red when another woman was taken away. It was nearly light when Virginia was taken.

She was taken down the hall to a little room and the moment she saw that room she knew she had been shocked previously and that she did not care for another helping. The room smelled like her old electric egg beater and there was a dull red glass eye in the wall. "I think I'll go back downstairs," she said.

"You go right on in," said the guard.

"Good morning, Virginia." This was quite a different voice. It was so pleasant that it was silly. It dripped the sort of cheery good will that is hard to take any morning, especially a morning when you have a formaldehyde hangover.

"Good morning," said Virginia in a tone which she meant to indicate that she wished not to discuss it further.

There was a high table, like an operating table, and she knew she was supposed to get up on it. She got on it and the woman with the silly voice fussed around her. This woman was in an R.N. uniform and the room had somewhat the appearance of an operating room. I'd forgotten I was to have an operation. You don't eat before an operation, of course. I should have remembered. I wonder what I am being operated on for. What haven't I had removed? I believe I still have my gall bladder.

"Well, Jeannie. And how is Jeannie this morning?"

It was he, the Indefatigable Examiner, come out from the bushes. He was wearing a white coat. He had blue eyes and a hawkish nose and a very slender face and his hair was fair and curly, like Grace's, only shorter.

"And did you enjoy being outside in the park yesterday?" He said this with a heavy accent that you had never been able to place. It wasn't German, French, Italian or Scandinavian. Polish, perhaps. He began to talk at great rate but you could tell he didn't care if you translated or replied. He and the silly woman were busy with their hands. Evidently it was to be a local anesthetic.

They put a wedge under her back. It was most uncomfortable. It forced her back into an unnatural position. She looked at the dull glass eye that was set into the wall and she knew that soon it would glow and that she would not see the glow. They were going to electrocute her, not operate upon her. Even now the woman was applying a sort of foul-smelling cold paste to your temples. What had you done? You wouldn't have killed anyone and what other crime is there which exacts so severe a penalty? Could they electrocute you for having voted for Norman Thomas? Many people had said the country was going to come to that sort of dictatorship but you hadn't believed it would ever reach this extreme. Dare they kill me without a trial? I demand to see a lawyer. And he—he always talking about hearing voices and never hearing mine . . . He, pretending to be so solicitous of me and not even knowing my name, calling me Jeannie. If I say I demand a lawyer they have to do something. It has to do with habeas corpus, something in the Constitution. But they and their smooth talk, they intend to make a corpus of me—they and their good mornings and how are you.

Now the woman was putting clamps on your head, on the paste-smeared temples and here came another one, another nurse-garbed woman and she leaned on your feet as if in a minute you might rise up from the table and strike the ceiling. Your hands tied down, your legs held down. Three against one and the one entangled in machinery.

She opened her mouth to call for a lawyer and the silly woman thrust a gag into it and said, "Thank you, dear," and the foreign devil with the angelic smile and the beautiful voice gave a conspiratorial nod. Soon it would be over. In a way you were glad.

CHAPTER THREE

SHE was walking down a sloping hallway. At the head of the procession bobbed a white cap. When the cap stopped moving the women stood still. They were standing near a door that had gold letters but when they turned they entered another door.

"Come along, Virginia," said the White Cap. "This way."

"But that's my door," said Virginia.

"He's not there now. Come on. Come on, ladies. Make it snappy. We haven't got all day."

Why not? What comes next? I have all day. He said so. He said I had nothing to worry about, no meetings to attend, no parties to give, no house guests coming. But I have been in this room before. It is a dining room. It is where we eat. I am wise. I know things.

But do I know the plan of the tables? If you select the wrong chair something awful happens. Oh, wisdom, guide my feet.

She shut her eyes and when she opened them she was beside a chair and a woman was saying hello. The woman continued to say hello and soon she was saying to save some for Virginia. Yes, this was familiar.

The bowls swam past. "No, no, please," said Virginia. "Please. I don't want any."

"Sh," whispered the woman at her left. "I'll take care of you."

And when the bowls came to Virginia she remembered that it was an axiom. To get the others to eat you said to save some for Virginia. A proverb, a law. Your share of the process was to take what was left and they were kind and left you only enough to soil your plate. You spread the dabs to make them look like the last bits you hadn't been able to finish and thus you avoided punishment. The kind woman at your left had arranged this.

The woman on the right was not eating. She was stirring a plateful of food around and around. A wave of nausea washed through Virginia and she took a piece of bread and crumbled it into her plate.

Across the table a brown-eyed girl smiled. "I am Margaret," she said.

It was a shock to hear Mag's name. "Margaret?"

"I just came today. From Four."

"I'll remember your name. It is my sister's." Virginia bent her head to hide the tears that were starting from her eyes. She cleared her throat and blew her nose on the paper napkin. "I've not seen her for a while. Silly of me, but we've always been quite close."

"No talking, ladies," called out the woman who was pushing a cart toward their table.

When the plates were collected the waitress gave each of the women a pan of something that quivered. I would rather die than eat it. But then the woman at the left took the disgusting stuff and dumped it into her pan. "Oh, thank you," said Virginia. "You're the best friend I have here."

"Don't mention it," said the Champion. She turned. "You are late, Countess, but I saved it." She opened her napkin and displayed a collection of bread scraps.

46

"Thank you, dear," said the collector. "They appreciate your kindness."

Virginia wanted to ask who they were but she had a feeling she had asked the question before and she did not want the Champion to become impatient. Without that one's good will you would have to do your own eating. They served execrable food here and like all bad cooks, expected you to eat heartily. They became vindictive if you did not eat. They mashed the food into a mush and pushed it up your nose. No, I have dreamed that. That could never happen.

Across the aisle was a beautiful girl. Of course without your glasses you couldn't tell from here but you had seen her close up and you knew she was beautiful and that her name was Rosa. Rosa had cried in the washroom. Someone had broken her bottle of perfume. She kept saying that her brothers gave it to her and that it cost five dollars.

Now Rosa pushed her chair back. She stood up and started to make a speech. I wonder if I'm to make one. He said not to worry about having to make any more speeches; he said I never would have to make another one. But if there are speeches I am sure I am one of the speakers. If I could only remember my subject. I must listen carefully when they introduce me. Rosa is the chairman.

But this is awkward. Rosa was speaking in Italian. Virginia did not understand Italian but she could recognize it. And knowing that Rosa was an Italian helped.

The girl spoke brilliantly and she used magnificent gestures. She raised a fist and beat her chest. Almost at once you caught on that she was imitating Mussolini.

The two white-capped waitresses didn't reach the speaker right away. They scurried around their steam wagon and ran into each other. One of them knocked a stack of plates from the cart and they stopped to pick them up. The plates did not break. They were metal. They made a frightful clatter and Rosa had to raise her voice. Rosa was not simply imitating Mussolini, for the time being she was Mussolini. Everyone was much impressed and they frowned at the waitresses. The Nose, the aristocrat who dined at Virginia's right, tapped impatiently on the table and said, "Quiet, you fools."

When the waitresses reached the speaker they did not apologize for their rudeness. Great strapping women that they were, they laid hands on the delicate Rosa and took her from the dining room so rapidly that you were not certain if they carried her or walked her.

For the first time in history we are alone. Now my speech. Ladies! Now is our chance to organize. Unless we organize we are lost. Are we going to continue to accept this oppression? United we have great strength. Let us organize. Can we sit here and let them do God knows what to Comrade Rosa? They broke her bottle of perfume and pretended one of us did it. Next, they will be blaming us for the poor quality of the food. . . . (You have to work a joke in somewhere.) But all joking aside, ladies, do we not owe it to those who will come after us to. . . . The speech was clear in her mind. It was somewhat adapted from Helene but she felt that in general it was not communistic. She prepared to rise.

Before she was on her feet, one of the waitresses stormed into the room. "All right, ladies," she squalled.

ii

There was no conversation in the washroom. The women sat on the floor and smoked and when the White

Cap said to watch their ashes, they watched the White Cap. I would be afraid if I were that one, but I suppose she carries a gun. Packs a gat, she would say. She is a tough one.

The tough one smiled. She was smiling at Virginia. Virginia looked down at the paper cone she was using for an ash tray and then she remembered that the White Cap was Miss Hart. I have done her the favor of watching my ashes and the ashes of others, she can do me a favor now.

"Miss Hart?"

"Yes, Virginia."

"I wonder if I might have my glasses."

"Glasses?" Miss Hart wrinkled her brow.

"Eyeglasses. Spectacles."

"I didn't know you wore glasses. You haven't had any since you've been here in Three."

"I have never been without them before," said Virginia. "I always have two pairs, in case one should break. I am very nearsighted." And without them I can never figure out how to escape, my friend.

"Why don't you ask Miss Graves? Go to the office now, if you like. She might know something about them."

Virginia left the washroom and after a while she found a room that had a desk in it and she supposed this might be called an office. "Miss Graves?" she said to the woman who was sitting at the desk.

"Well, Virginia, what can I do for you?"

There were two pitchers on the desk. White-enamel pitchers. There was a package of paper cups. One of those pitchers contained water, the other held poison.

"You want your nightcap now?" asked Miss Graves.

That was supposed to be a joke and so Virginia forced

49

her lips into a curve. "I wonder if I could have my glasses. I'm very uncomfortable without them."

"Glasses? I didn't know you wore glasses."

"They have to be somewhere around. Robert—my husband wouldn't let me be without them." Yes, but what can Robert do for a person who is in the clutches of the Law? He had got the reprieve, that much was certain. They had not completed the electrocution. You were unconscious when the papers came. It had been a close call.

"I'll inquire at the main office," said Miss Graves. "Not all of your things were sent to this ward. I'll make a note of it."

"Thank you," said Virginia. "I really think if I'm without them much longer I'll go crazy."

She hadn't spoken loudly, but the word, that last word, bounced from one wall to another. Miss Graves stared down at her papers. "I'll get them for you," she said in a strained voice. "You go back to the washroom now and get ready for bed. You couldn't use them tonight. Tomorrow. Yes, I'll have them for you tomorrow."

iii

Slowly Virginia groped her way back to the washroom. She knew now. She really had been knowing it a long time but now she had to admit that she knew it.

All along she had known that the electrocution and crime idea was nonsense. All along she had known where she was. Oh, she did not know the geography of it, but she knew, she knew.

As she started to undress she thought about how carefully she had invented the prison fantasy. All along she had known where she was, but she had invented a setting that was easier to endure. Anything else would have been easier to bear, anything but what it was. I knew, I knew, but I tried to close the door on my knowing.

In this ward was a woman who every day went out on the cage porch during the brief airing period. She went out there and yelled swear words at the bushes and benches of the courtyard, but she never used the terrible word that Virginia had used when she had spoken to Miss Graves just now. It was one of the words that were not used here, words that were common enough outside and never considered blasphemous but words that were never said here, even by the most foul-mouthed. You could say anything here so long as you did not say the truth.

Around you in the washroom were women who were shut up with you, women who were far more wretched than criminals. I was trying to glamorize it. What it is, is the one thing I can not take. I could face the prospect of blindness, of cancer, but this, no. Never this.

How had it happened? She remembered now that her friend Grace had said she was glad that it was not something in her family. What about my family? My people. I never heard of anything like this in my family. Mother's side or Dad's side. There was old Aunt Essie but she wasn't a blood relative; she was Gran's second cousin's wife. But even Aunt Essie wasn't this way. Peculiar, that was all. When Grampa said she ought to be shut up he didn't mean it. He only meant he wished she would keep out of his way.

How, how can Robert endure it?

When she got into her cot she realized that she had neglected something that was very important. Robert must get a divorce. It was possible in some states. Any good lawyer could manage it for him. He must be the way the

Jacksons are about Don. Mrs. Jackson told me last time I was home that she doesn't go to see Don any more. *He doesn't know me now and it just does me up and finally Mr. Jackson put his foot down and said I couldn't go to visit him any more. I try to think of him as dead and he is. My real boy is dead. He's happy. Yes, he's happy. They take good care of him and he's happy.*

Lying there in the fading light Virginia remembered Don Jackson, the way he was before. He was older than she but she remembered him clearly. Such a nice-looking boy and so smart in school. They said, when it happened to him, that he was too smart, that it happened to people who were too smart. Was that any consolation? Could you say to yourself that you were too smart?

You were never any quiz kid, Virginia. Don't add delusions of grandeur to whatever it is you already have.

For about two years, said Mrs. Jackson, *he knew us. I never went through such a time. It was much worse for us then, really, though of course then we still had hopes.* Will I know Robert for about two years and then . . . ? He must get a divorce right away. I might live to be eighty. Look at Gran and Grampa. I might not be lucky enough to take after the Stuarts who died young, and anyhow a lot of them lived to be seventy or so.

"Grace. . . ."

But Grace had gone away. She had been happy about leaving and she had said it wouldn't be long before she would be back at work on her newspaper. They had promised to hold her job for her, she said.

Does it mean I might get well? I know someone who did. Mary Someone. Silly Mary, they call her. Harmless graduate of an institution, but they call her Silly Mary. I would rather be Silly Virginia shut up than Silly Virginia at large. Robert, Robert, Robert. *Happier there than he would be at home*, said Mrs. Jackson, *even if we could take proper care of him. Better off with his own kind.*

Someone was talking. Is this a voice the Examiner desired me to hear? Last night, I'll say to him, last night in the dormitory I heard your voices.

"They can't do it to me," said the voice. "I'll get the Law on them. I've got friends. They better watch out how they treat me."

"Shut up," said another voice. "Shut up and go to sleep."

"You can't talk to me like that," said the first voice. "I'll have the Law on you. I got friends. You watch your mouth when you talk to me."

And then someone began to weep. Virginia decided these were not the voices he sought. She was reminded, by the weeping, of an article she had read. It was an article about a place like this. No, not a place like this. The writer had pretended to be speaking for all such places but his description would never fit this one. When I read the article I was glad. I was thinking about Don. The writer made it sound fascinating. A group of interesting people living in dream worlds. Every one of the people he wrote about was engaged in something important. There were men who thought themselves great lawyers and they were busy writing, or thinking about writing, briefs that would make history; there were men who thought themselves financial wizards with millions and billions of dollars under their control; women who thought themselves famous beauties; women who thought themselves historical or mythical characters. Everything in the way of comfort was provided these dreamers and they hadn't a worry in the world. The author made a gentle joke about his envy of their lot. They dwell in dreams, he wrote.

"There are also nightmares," said Virginia. She had spoken aloud. I spoke aloud and not to anyone within hearing. I am one of them.

Here in this bare dormitory that had no door, here on the narrow cot, clothed in a numbered nightgown, she lay with women who were insane and she was one of them.

CHAPTER FOUR

MRS. ROBERT P. CUNNINGHAM, Juniper Hill Hospital. It was there on the envelopes, in Robert's writing. All you had had to do was look, which was of course why you had not looked. Though you had known without looking, it was far harder when you knew and looked at the same time. You were horrified and ashamed, as if it was something you had done on purpose.

She tried to dig out her memory but it was swathed in wet gray chiffon that stuck to the very part she wanted most to examine. You needed to get inside of your head and clean the place up. It was easy enough to remember things that had happened a long time ago, even a year ago. It was about a year ago that we moved to a suburb. Without much effort she recalled the names of the young people with whom she and Robert had lived for several months. I remember the kitten that used to ride on the trail of my housecoat every morning when I went down to get breakfast.

It was a co-operative house, set up according to rules and regulations. Everyone had a chore. Robert was superintendent and I was cook. As cook I was queen. The others gaped and marveled at the most simple achievements.

This was after Robert had taken a job, just after he had decided it was time to call the vacation over. Virginia had assumed they would go back home at the end of the long vacation, but Robert wanted to stay. She was fond of New York but it wasn't the same when Robert was working. That was why Robert accepted the invitation to the co-operative. "Then you won't be alone," he said.

No, she was never alone in that big old house. It was a house rule that when your bedroom door was closed you were safe but always, no matter how loudly she pounded her typewriter, someone tapped at the door. Ginny, are you too busy to let me come in a minute? Something I want to show you. Something I have to ask you. . . . No one takes a writer's business seriously. It is something to be done at odd moments when there is nothing else.

It wasn't so much that she was eager to be at her work; it was mostly that she could not endure always being at a party. The co-operative was an endless house party. Although the members were all employed there was always at least one who was having a day off, a week off, an hour off. Ginny, I suddenly remembered that you might be left alone today and so I brought my work home. . . .

They were all so young. I hadn't known until then that Robert and I had stopped being young. They were always talking, laughing, singing, dancing. They were always quoting. Their erudition was appalling. Though they seemed never to read, their supply of brilliant quotations was endless. They spoke patronizingly of the authors whose vocabularies they used casually, and for all Virginia knew, correctly. They were sorry for Virginia and said it was too bad she couldn't do a novel with Social Significance. They themselves would do surveys and essays when they found time; they would write documents which would bring the world into co-operation—when they had time. But there was time for laughter, time for song. It was marvelous for three days.

It may have been marvelous for Robert a bit longer. He was seldom there. His job was a conglomeration of days and nights and split shifts, but before long he said he wondered if he and Virginia exactly fitted in. He and she agreed, though perhaps with less enthusiasm than they had had before, that if they were to live with anyone it would be with these young people who were so bright and so loving. "But it's the sort of thing you keep thinking you should go home from," said Robert, "and then you realize that you are home."

Virginia's mother had been writing frantically. She did not understand why they were staying in the East; someone had told her that co-operative house was almost entirely Jewish—not that she minded but she did wish Virginia wouldn't tell other people things and not tell her; it was such a shock to hear things like that from other people; only the other day someone had asked her if it was true that there were Negroes in the house also. At least you can come home for a visit, she wrote. You absolutely must come home for a visit. If Robert can't come you must come without him.

"You should go," said Robert. "It will give you a rest from these maniacs and then we'll see."

He said she must have a new coat. She shopped and shopped and finally she found a good bargain. She adored a bargain. She never really liked a dress or a coat or a hat that hadn't had a price marked out and a lower one added. The new coat was a silvery shade of green and the collar was real beaver. It was a very small collar but it was real beaver. When her mother saw the coat she said it was the kind that absolutely had to have a matching hat. She took Virginia to her milliner and had a hat made and it cost more than the coat had cost.

Virginia planned to stay in Evanston two weeks but she was too tired. Every time she got on the bathroom scales she weighed less. And she was having trouble sleeping. This wasn't entirely new trouble but she thought when she got back into a regular routine it would be different. So she returned to New York and when Robert met her he said they were moving back to Manhattan. "We'll take such a small apartment that we can't have any company from home," he said.

I can't remember that little apartment, but I know we found it. We moved from the co-operative house to a little apartment in Greenwich Village. Strange not to be able to remember your home. You are coming near. Grace said February.

We decided not to have the furniture sent on. Just the rugs and dishes and silver. We bought furniture. We bought a large studio bed and I made a cover for it and that was our davenport. We had a terrace and a wood-burning fireplace. I remember that we had them but I can't visualize them.

On our wedding anniversary Robert gave me the muff. January twentieth. *You came in February,* said Grace. On the twentieth of January I was with Robert and he gave me a dear little round ball of beaver and I made him tell me how much it cost. "You and Mother!" I said to him. He had paid more for the muff than I had paid for the coat.

And thinking we were nearing the end of our money I had shopped myself limp for furniture and got the apartment fixed up on next to nothing. Such a practical man.

That is what they always say about Robert. My, they say, it's a good thing Virginia Stuart married a practical man. She hasn't got a grain of sense.

As soon as the apartment was finished she got down to her book and worked eight hours a day. Sometimes these work days were at night, when Robert was working. One week his schedule was one way and the next week it was another way. She never got it through her head. She tried to match his schedule but she was never able to sleep in the daytime. She was beginning to be unable to sleep at any time.

They had become involved in a number of organizations. Robert was on numerous ways-and-means committees and she was on committees of fine arts and program and things like that. Through their organization work they met very interesting people, writers, painters, musicians, teachers, social workers, newspaper people and so on. They entertained a good deal and they went many places. Robert assured her they weren't spending much more than he was making.

For the first time in her life she began to wonder what the tired housewife would like to read.

It had been weeks since she had had a full night's sleep. She kept telling herself it made no difference. She would make it up eventually. Get tired enough and you would sleep. Some days she was so tired that she couldn't work; she sat or lay and looked into space. She was never sleepy.

Robert was beginning to worry about her. He kept saying she should go to a doctor, that she was too thin, that she didn't eat the right sort of food. He said why not knock off writing for a while. He was not in the least concerned about what the tired housewives of America were buying for their reading material.

She hadn't told him about not sleeping. Sometimes she

thought she must imagine the sleepless nights. You could not lie awake all night. An hour or so, yes, but not all night. All night, night after night. It was impossible. Something would happen. What? You would fall asleep. What else?

She counted sheep. She pretended she was molasses being poured out of a brown jug, poured from a brown jug into a thick stream that was inching slowly toward February, February, February. . . .

It was February then that morning at five when I got up from bed and took the little beaver muff to the bathroom to look at. In the concealed pocket was a matching set, a coin purse, a compact and a lipstick. I wanted to weep when I saw how beautifully the pieces were made. Had I known he was going to take that much money out of the bank I would have made him give it to me for curtains.

I crept back into the bedroom that was also the living room. On the desk was the manuscript of my new book. It was the next-to-the-last draft and I was working it over in pencil. Even if the tired housewives did not become enthusiastic I felt sure it would do a little something for the bank account. To be poor in New York, though living was far cheaper there, seemed a more wretched prospect than poverty in Evanston. At home I wouldn't have cared about the housewives and their literary tastes; I would have been laughing with Paula at Cassie. Cassie—now I was trying to *be* Cassie.

The alarm rang and I hurried back to the big room. I slipped the manuscript under the bed so he wouldn't know I had been working.

"You up already?" he asked.

I knew then that I would have to tell him, that it was

time. "I didn't sleep very well," I said. I was dizzy and I had to catch hold of the chest of drawers. I remember it. It had a pink-marble top. "Robert," I said, "I think there is something the matter with my head."

ii

No matter how often she went back she was unable to get beyond that time which had not been time but past, way past the time. It was impossible to imagine what had happened; you had nothing to go on. You had heard so much about Don Jackson but you had never heard exactly what happened just before he was taken away. You hadn't even wondered. Poor Don lost his mind, people said, and they had to take him away. At first they thought he would get over it but he never did. Poor chap.

Before, just before it happened, did he say he thought there was something the matter with his head? Did he have that moment's warning? Mary Lamb. She and Charles making the sad journey. She had ample warning—eventually. Perhaps I had also; perhaps the not sleeping was my warning but I did not recognize it.

I sleep now. I would sleep longer if they let me, if they didn't come and roust me out before dawn. I sleep, but there is still something the matter with my head. So it is more than a matter of insomnia.

She was sitting in a wicker chair and she had been sitting there since lunch or dinner as they called it here and she was willing to keep on sitting. She was always tired. But Miss Hart came over to her. "How would you like to use the polisher, Virginia?" she asked.

Polisher? Virginia had no desire to use a polisher, but obviously the question required an affirmative answer.

Miss Hart, you knew, approved of you. It had something to do with not dropping ashes on a white-tile floor. And so now Miss Hart was going to let you use a polisher.

It was a thing that had a long handle and at the end of the handle was a heavy weight wrapped in gray blanket material. The idea was to push the polisher slowly over the linoleum. This was considered a privilege.

Whenever anyone took the polisher away from Virginia she was grateful. For days Miss Hart's chief concern was to give Virginia exclusive right to the polisher. When the nurse was occupied elsewhere some patient would snatch the long handle from Virginia, but as soon as the nurse returned she would shout, "You give that polisher back to Virginia," and the wretched task would be resumed. Virginia had never had any strength in her arms and in order to make any progress at all she had to push more with her stomach than with her arms. It would have been a splendid reducing exercise for anyone needing reduction.

Some of the women, she noticed, had regular duties. Some of them mopped the halls and dormitories. They had buckets with wringer attachments and they had a collection of mops. And there were women who worked of a morning at making beds. The scrubbing and bed-making were finished soon after breakfast but the polishing was never ended. It was tempting to believe the woman who boasted that she used the polisher all night long, every night.

Miss Hart complimented Virginia extravagantly. "The best little polisher we ever had." Oh, the nurse was devoted to Virginia; sometimes she crossed the washroom to light Virginia's cigarette and sometimes she gave her toilet paper without being asked.

Next thing they will promote me to bed-making and

then I will be in a fix. I can never learn to turn a hospital corner. Sorry, I'll say when they give me the assignment, but I never could turn a hospital corner.

She looked at the slippery floor and giggled at her pun. The sound of the faint laughter startled her. She looked around apprehensively to see if anyone had noticed the alien sound.

iii

There had been days, outside, when she had longed to make her mind blank. It wasn't that she had ever had tremendous problems—that might have been stimulating—but sometimes she had wished she might stop thinking about the committee agenda, about the Evanstonians who had to be taken to see Battery Park and the Empire State Building, and about how long you can continue to spend more than your income. Here at Juniper Hill she got her wish and she learned that having a blank mind while awake is a terrifying experience. She would be sitting in the large room—they called it the dayroom—and it would be early morning and then suddenly it would be time to go to bed. What had happened between morning and night? She would not be able to remember having gone to the dining room but she would know she had been there twice since breakfast; she would not remember having shoved the polisher but she would know she undoubtedly had been shoving it. Being teacher's pet, she never had a day free of polishing.

Being teacher's pet was a sorrow she hadn't had to contend with in school. Although she had been a good child she hadn't looked it. The hair was responsible. A child with red hair automatically was considered a devil. Often she had laughed at her mother's stories about what

63

a false reputation the older Stuart girl had got, but the laughter was never entirely mirthful. A favorite story was about Virginia's first stage appearance. She was six years old. At a signal she and a dozen other first graders marched to the stage and stood in a row while other children, more favored by nature and teacher, did tricks. Mrs. Stuart, not in the least dampened by the walk-on role, was in the audience and probably dreaming of a theatrical future. Virginia had on a new white ruffled dress with a wide blue sash and around her head was a blue-satin ribbon with a rosette just above each ear. The color was an unfortunate choice as it made the straight fringed bob look far redder than it actually was, but, once reconciled to the hair, Mrs. Stuart stubbornly played up to it.

"That's Virginia Stuart, that one with the red hair and the blue ear-bobs," the admiring mother heard someone say. "You know, Margaret Stuart's child. She's the meanest kid in town."

"And I turned around," Mother would say, "and I saw it was Madge Anderson, a sorority sister of mine! I gave her one look and I never spoke to her again."

Virginia would laugh. Everyone would laugh, but Virginia knew they were thinking Madge Anderson had been penalized for stating what must have been common knowledge.

The only really wicked thing she could ever remember doing was putting a large angleworm down the back of an enemy. Her hatred for this girl was based on jealousy. The girl had braces on her legs and Virginia coveted those braces. Later it was tooth braces that she coveted. It seemed to her that all the top-flight children had braces on their teeth. She used to watch Libby snap her braces

64

in and out of her mouth in a most affected way and she would long to be rich like Libby and have braces. Her mother's telling her that she didn't need braces did not fool her one instant. All the rich kids had braces.

At first glasses gave her a swank feeling and she made a great to-do about polishing them and waving them around under the noses of children who hadn't glasses. But glasses soon came to be a nuisance, albeit a very essential nuisance.

Several years before she and Robert came to New York for the long vacation there was a fad back home for curing poor eyes by exercises. There was a man in Chicago who made a specialty of this and Virginia went to him. It was very expensive. You sat in a darkened room and watched a series of lights flash about. The doctor—he called himself a doctor and maybe he was—said it was a matter of time. He was all in favor of her going without her glasses but of course she never could have found his office without them. All she got out of the exercises was a chain of headaches that came to an end shortly after the course was finished, but several of her friends discarded their glasses and for quite some time went around looking as if from mouseholes.

They promised to give me my glasses. Days ago.

"I wonder if I might get my glasses soon," she said to Miss Hart.

"Glasses?" said Miss Hart.

Again Virginia went through the weary story of how she had worn glasses since childhood and how dependent she was upon them. Miss Hart was fascinated. She had a friend who had worn glasses a long time. She asked why Virginia hadn't mentioned the matter before. Sometimes it was difficult at Juniper Hill to remember which were the sick ones.

Miss Hart boomed for her to come along to the office. They went to the office and a moment later Virginia had her glasses. "You see," said the nurse, "all you have to do is ask. Don't be shy."

Virginia put the glasses on and the walls of the room whirled. "Oh, but these aren't mine," she said.

"Got your name on them."

Yes, there on one shaft, on a bit of adhesive was *V. Cunningham* in fine black printing.

"Try them again," said Miss Hart. "Maybe being without them so long. But if they aren't right you mustn't wear them."

Virginia put the glasses on again. "Oh, they are fine," she said quickly. She pretended they felt fine. "I suppose Huxley is right, though. At least partly."

"Huxley?" Miss Hart was arranging papers into a pile. She had a passion for neatness and no doubt everything about her person was scrupulously clean. She was, however, one of those dark-skinned individuals who always look slightly dirty.

"Not Julian," said Virginia. "Though you would expect it to be him, wouldn't you?" Yes, a nurse would think of Julian Huxley first. "But Aldous had poor eyes and became interested in. . . ."

"I know you are glad to have them back," said Miss Hart. "Come on back to the dayroom. Let me leave a minute and the place is a—mess." The oily skin reddened. "I forgot to tell you that you're going to Petey this afternoon," she said quickly. "Isn't that swell?"

And who is Petey? My doctor? Miss Hart is great on calling everyone by first name but would she dare call my doctor by first name, even behind his back? At least she might say Peter.

In the dayroom the floor tilted but did not revolve. There were no blurred edges now. Already your eyes were responding to the old discipline. You knew that if you saw a good eye man at once you would be able to get weaker lenses. Maybe I should mention this to Petey this afternoon, before the adjustment to the strong lenses is complete. I can't call the man Petey and I cannot remember his last name.

And in the past you had thought half blindness a burden. At Juniper Hill it was a blessing. How ugly the dayroom was. How much browner and plainer. How hideous the curtains were and how dreadfully the paint was checking from the wicker. You could see that the furniture had once been green and deep under the green was yellow. But the inanimate part of the dayroom was beautiful in comparison to the ladies.

You bathed twice a week. You lined up for the showers. There were two stalls for the forty or fifty women who lived in Ward Three and in order to speed things up you were told to soap yourself before you got under the water. You reached a hand into the spray and caught enough moisture for a lather and in that way you could spend your bath time in rinsing. You might almost get completely rinsed before the nurse would tell you to get out. Virginia had not, as yet, ever had a shower stall to herself even for a moment but she understood that this could happen. It was indeed rarely that she had only one other woman in her bath.

Once a week was fine-comb night. You squatted at Miss Hart's feet and she went through your hair with a fine comb. Beside her on a stool was an enameled pan of some clear fluid that you hoped was a strong antiseptic. She dipped the comb in that pan. The same comb was used on everyone. She combed you quickly and efficiently, if roughly, and that was that.

These two processes, the showers and the fine combing, were the only organized efforts in the direction of personal cleanliness. Otherwise you were on your own. You did not have to wash or comb at any other time unless you chose. As far as Virginia could tell, all of the ladies chose. The four wash basins and the strip of mirror above them did not give much chance, though. When the way was less crowded you washed your pants and bra and stockings. You hung your washing on your private hanger and if it was not quite dry in the morning, well, there was nothing else to wear.

In the little black bag Virginia had make-up materials and bobbie pins but she seldom had enough time at the mirror to fix herself properly and there was no mirror in her bag. Not many of the ladies did anything about make-up, not many of them owned so much as a can of talcum powder. Several of them did work on their hair. Rosa, the Italian girl, had spent much time on her curls. What had they done with Rosa? Virginia had overheard someone say that Rosa had been sent to pack but she did not believe this. You wouldn't be sent home when you were worse. "That's silly," she had said. She had turned around to join in the conversation about Rosa. "They wouldn't do that. You have to get well before you can go home."

The women who had been discussing Rosa stared at Virginia. They must have been very sick. For a while after that incident Virginia felt much better; at least she knew she was not so sick as two of the patients.

She had learned a good deal. She had learned that this

was not an insane asylum; it was a mental hospital. The ladies had not lost their minds; they had had nervous breakdowns. This last was a surprise. You had thought only the wealthy and the very brilliant had nervous breakdowns. It was impossible to imagine that any of these ladies had ever been either.

She felt shy in her glasses, as if the other women could see her for the first time now. Some of them looked at her but most of them paid no attention. A lady who was shoving the polisher gave her a touch-me-if-you-dare look and Virginia said, "You are welcome to it." The lady was too far from her to hear, but your glasses made you feel as if she was in your lap. It was like looking through binoculars.

You were sickeningly reminded of drawings you had seen in a large book on the history of insanity. Once Virginia wrote a short novel about a man who had a nervous breakdown and after she had finished the book she thought it might be a good idea to read up on the subject. She really hadn't thought of this herself. Someone had said how in the world would you know anything about such a subject and did you do an awful lot of research. So after the book was finished she did some research. There really was no time before. She read maybe a dozen books on the subject and she decided that a thirteenth opinion might get by. Her book was not published but the reason given was the bad length and, as writers always believe what is pleasant to believe, she believed that the length of her breakdown book was the only thing bad about it.

Her hero's breakdown was artistic and private. He did not go to an institution. Never having been inside of that sort of place Virginia felt she could not invent such a background. So her man went about his business and had his breakdown inside of himself and of course, broken-down, was a far more attractive person than he had been before. It was a romantic book. She knew this when she was writing it. What she did not know until she came to Juniper Hill was that the dozen scholarly volumes she had read on the subject were also very romantic.

Looking at the ladies of Ward Three she was again conscious of the terrible odor that always clung to the place. The room was very clean and so the smell must come from the ladies. They did not look so very dirty but on the other hand they did not look so very clean. How could they? If there was any laundry service Virginia had never heard about it. She did not know how long it had been since she and Grace had sat in the park or how long before that she had worn this old dress but she did know that the dress had not been washed since that day in the park and that it certainly had not been clean then. She had worn it every day since then. She had tried to wash off several spots she had got when the Nose in the dining room had flicked gravy at her but the dress needed more than a sponging; it needed throwing away. All of the ladies needed washing and ironing and something done to their hair instead of fine combing. Why fine combing? Was Miss Hart hunting something when she ran that comb through your hair?

. . . something Robert said. It was queer the way she often would remember something he had said recently. She could not remember that he had ever been here. "It's one of the best in the country," he had said. "I wrote home to Charles first." Charles was their doctor at home and also their good friend. Charles had said Juniper Hill was absolutely one of the best. Also, doctors Robert had consulted in New York had said it was one of the best, if not *the* best.

Slowly she looked around the room. "It may be the very best butter," she said, "but it won't lubricate the works."

"Were you speaking to me?" asked a lady who was standing near by.

"No," said Virginia. "I am afraid I was talking to myself."

"A bad habit," said the lady. "Miss Hart says you are going to P. T. with us this afternoon."

She had said this as if it were two initials. Parent Teacher Association? But I am neither a parent nor a teacher. "Yes," she said. I'll have to write to Hortense. I'll have to tell her she's not the only one who goes to P. T. A. Only here in the East, I'll write, we just say P. T.

Hortense was always writing about the P. T. A. now that Scootie was in school. He had become a problem child. In nursery school he learned to call everyone damn stinks and now, in first grade, he complained about having to dance with the old bags from second grade when he went to dancing class. Hortense was doing something about this in P. T. A. She was working on getting a certain teacher fired and a certain Bad Influence sent to another school. Well, I'll write to her about the meeting this afternoon. I won't need to say just where it was held.

What is Robert telling people? That I have gone away for a little rest? I am not getting any letters, not even from Robert. And when has he ever come to see me?

At first we went to see him regularly but after a while the doctors decided it only upset him. Then, later on of course he didn't know us and so there was no use.

Progressive myopia was what you had wrong with your

eyes. Was your head trouble progressive? Head trouble. She tried to think of scientific words. There was dementia praecox, but that sounded too young. Precocious. There was manic something but you were pretty sure you were not a maniac. There was schizophrenia. That was a beautiful word, as a photograph slightly out of focus sometimes is very lovely. It means split personality. When I wrote my book I said that was what my man had. He didn't think he was Napoleon or anything like that but he was aware of being two decided personalities, one very proper and righteous and the other something of a rake.

But that can't be my trouble. I am just me, Virginia Stuart Cunningham. There is only one of me and it is having a hard enough time thinking for one, let alone splitting into two

CHAPTER FIVE

NOW the gold letters stood out in a clear string of con-
sonants. The letters, she knew, comprised her doctor's
name. Russian, perhaps. Senja, Virginia's pupil, had explained that it was impossible to turn a Russian name into
English. She said she had changed her name to the nearest
German equivalent and then turned that into English.
Of course Virginia knew this was not true. Senja lived in
constant fear of being caught by the Bolsheviks. She had
escaped from a Russian prison where, she told Virginia,
she sat a long time with lice. She never told how her
escape was managed but Virginia was certain of one thing,
the name Senja used was nowhere near the one she was
born to.

Not long ago, well, some time during the first of the
New York period, Virginia told Helene, the True Trotskyite, some of Senja's experiences. Helene said it was all
bosh, that Senja had invented the whole thing. Helene
knew everything about the Revolution. From books and
from being a True Trotskyite, a party that was the leftwing split of a leftwing split. Helene was an authority;
she had met The Old Man once and for a long time afterwards had not washed the hand that had touched His.

Virginia could have believed that she had never washed that hand again.

Helene was an interesting person to have known; it was nicer to have known her than to know her. Until she graduated from college she was like everyone else. She was born and reared in Evanston, and her family was the sort that sheltered its girls. They had plenty of money, not a great lot, but plenty. However, Mr. Bodford, Helene's father, had a sister who did have a great lot of money and this sister was fond of Helene. When she died she left everything she had to Helene and the young heiress immediately turned communist and fled Evanston. Now she lived in a ramshackle Village building and ran the infant split. She had joined, worked in and resigned or been fired from a half dozen parties before she organized one of her own. The True Trotskyites were not to be confused with the Untrue.

The self-appointed custodian of the creed of The Old Man had a long dark apartment that was stuffed with oriental rugs and antique furniture from her aunt's beautiful old Evanston house; it was also stuffed with cockroaches. In addition to the cockroaches Helene housed a varying number of True Believers. Her money, to her great disgust, was done up in a trust fund and she would not be able to get at the principal until she overthrew the government.

Virginia promised herself that she would memorize the doctor's name and ask Helene how to pronounce it. I'll be seeing Helene before long. Yes, once you had your glasses and got a good look at this hospital you knew it was impossible to remain here.

I suppose I have been in his office many times. It has a black couch. The leather is fastened down into deep dimples. I used to lie there while he skulked somewhere behind and asked questions. Silly questions. But Robert said Charles said the doctor with the odd name was one of the best. Oh, Charles and his amiability. As far as Charles was concerned everything was just lovely. I went to see him when I was home on that visit and he said I was wonderfully well. You can't, of course, have a very high opinion of someone you went to school with. Dr. Thompson? you said. Charles Thompson? He can't be much good. Why, we were in kindergarten together. Robert, however, was not in kindergarten with Charles and so thought he was good.

It was dreadful what glasses did in the dining room. For the first time Virginia noticed that four of her table companions lacked important teeth. The Nose was anything but regal-looking now; she was a haggle-toothed blonde whose hair was black at the roots and whose face was latticed with dirt-filled wrinkles. The Champion wasn't so ugly but she had the look of a person who isn't right in the head. "Hello hello hello," she said to Virginia.

Directly across was the new one, the one named Margaret. She grinned at Virginia and asked did she remember the time Bobby caught the rabbit.

Virginia knew a collection of Bobbys and sometimes, in a teasing mood, called her husband Bobby. She did not, however, know any rabbit-catcher Bobby, at any rate not in common with this brown-eyed Margaret. "Mmm," she said.

Margaret accepted the sound as an affirmative answer and continued to speak of Bobby and the rabbit until Miss Hart issued a No Talking Ladies.

When the unpalatable meal was finished Margaret

waited for her in the aisle. "You are my sister, aren't you?" she whispered anxiously. "You said so."

Virginia was ashamed of the revulsion that was in her. "No," she said as kindly as she could. "I said my sister's name is Margaret. You and my sister have the same name."

"You said," whimpered Margaret. "You said."

"Well," said Virginia, "perhaps for the time being we are sisters of a sort. Yes, there is a sort of relationship."

Margaret perked up. "I knew," she said. "I recognized you right away even though you have been dead so many years."

It was no use to talk to these women; they were crazy. Virginia stalked back to the washroom determined never to speak to any of them again, but in a moment two or three of the ladies were asking her for cigarettes and she was doling out her last.

She not only was out of cigarettes now, she was out of cleansing tissues. But Miss Hart gave her a deal of toilet paper without being asked; Miss Hart gave her more than she gave the other ladies; Miss Hart made no effort to hide her preference for V. Cunningham. This afternoon at P.T. meeting I'll make a motion; I'll move that toilet paper be provided in each booth. If they will not pass the motion at least they will be forced to discuss it.

"Not smoking?" asked the nurse chummily.

"I'm out."

Miss Hart clacked her tongue and said it was a pity she hadn't saved any for herself. "I'll be taking the store orders tonight right after supper," she said. "You can order some more then."

"That's right," said Virginia, as if she knew all about store orders.

In the dayroom, while waiting for the P.T. meeting,

she ran into difficulty in connection with her black bag.
She had had that bag with her almost continually and
never had any trouble about it, but this afternoon one of
the ladies decided Virginia was a doctor. This aroused
the interest of another lady and then another. The three
hung on Virginia and called her Doctor and begged to
know when they would be allowed to go home. When she
said she was not a doctor they pointed to her little black
bag. It did look like a doctor's bag.

The incident reminded her of the time she had told
Gordon she was thinking of being a doctor. She didn't
like to recall this because Gordon had laughed at her.
He had thrown back his head and howled.

She was not in the habit of comparing Gordon and
Robert. Such comparisons were as wicked as they were
futile. She had a vague memory that the doctor here had
asked her to make such a comparison and again she felt
the dimples of the leather couch. "Gordon died a very
long time ago," she had said. "He was a wonderful young
man and I was very much in love with him. But you don't
love a dead man, if that's what you are driving at. You
can remember that you did love him but you delude
yourself if you think it can continue as before."

Gordon laughed when I said I was thinking of studying
medicine. Robert would not have laughed. No, Robert
always takes me seriously. He would have started to figure
out ways and means to send me to medical school. It
would have been good if Gordon could have had a bit
of Robert and Robert a bit of Gordon. Gordon might
have taken her a little more seriously and Robert a little
less seriously. That Paris business. She had just been talking, the way you talk about what you would do if you
suddenly got a million dollars. How astounded I was when

he said it would have to be New York instead of Paris. I had forgotten my chatter about a year's holiday.

"How did you ever browbeat Robert into it?" Mother asked when she found out that Robert was throwing up his job so that we might go off to New York for a year or so.

"It's his idea," I said.

"You ought to be ashamed of yourself, Virginia," she said. "A steady ambitious young man like Robert. What will the Cunninghams think?"

That was Mother. She was always in a dither about what the Cunninghams were going to think. "I'm so embarrassed about all this that I can hardly look Mrs. Cunningham in the face," she said later on. "When Robert worked so hard and saved up all that money and got such nice promotions and now you take him off and plan to fritter everything away."

When the Stuarts told Robert not to pay any attention to their foolish daughter, Robert said Virginia had taught him to enjoy life. They had enough money to knock off for a year and so why not?

Before she met Robert, Gordon told Virginia about him. Robert was one of Gordon's closest friends. "There's something so substantial about Bob Cunningham," he said. "You know where you stand with him. He's a lot of fun but at the same time he's old business."

Excuse me, my beloved Gordon, while *I* laugh.

If Gordon's shade could tell what she was thinking she hoped it would not mind learning that she was attracted to Robert from the start. It wasn't love at first sight, as it had been in the case of her and Gordon, but it was strong attraction. So strong that she decided at once that Bob must marry a dear friend of hers, Isabel Dawson. She arranged a double date and Bob and Isabel seemed to take to each other. Gordon, who was convinced that Isabel was a halfwit, became disturbed. Oh, Gordon, if you could only see Isabel now.

Robert and Isabel went around together a good deal but when Gordon, very worried, spoke to Robert about it Robert said there was nothing serious. He said Isabel was awfully cute and a very good dancer and all but—but he guessed he would wait until he found someone like Virginia.

"Were you in love with me then?" asked Virginia once, not long after they were married.

How shocked Robert had looked. "Of course not," he said. "You were Gordon's girl. I really was quite smitten with Isabel but I didn't dare let him know."

After flunking out of two colleges Isabel Dawson settled down to study law at a third and now was partner in a good firm in Chicago. When she came to dinner she would clap Robert on the back and say, "How's my old flame?" and Robert would blench for fear that she would kiss him. Which she always did.

"You used not to mind," Virginia would say after her friend had gone. "Have you forgotten how *quite smitten* you were?"

Manlike, Robert would say the only reason he had ever gone with Isabel was to please Virginia. "Besides," he would add plaintively, "she's changed."

If Isabel Dawson could turn out to be a lawyer I most certainly could have been a doctor. Virginia looked down at the little black bag. Thank heaven she had never mentioned her medical ambition to Robert or sure enough that bag would be brimming with scalpels right now. I never would have stuck to my writing if he hadn't kept telling me how good I was.

Unaccountably she thought of a conversation she had overheard years ago in the ladies' retiring room of the Country Club. She was in one of the booths, trying to pin a broken shoulder strap. Her slip was very plain and so she had hidden away for the repair work.

She was about finished when she heard someone say Robert's name and then hers. "Isn't Robert Cunningham here tonight with that Virginia Stuart?" said a voice. The accent on the *that* advised you to remain in the booth.

"He married her," said another voice.

"So her engagement to Gordon Timberlake fell through. I knew it would."

"But, darling, didn't you know? He died."

"My God."

"Yes, isn't it awful? He was so good-looking. It was while you were abroad, I guess."

"I don't know why no one ever told me. Honestly, you'd think I didn't have any friends. Did Bob think he had to marry her just because he and Gordon were pals?"

"It looks like it."

"I never could see her. Of all the girls Gordon might have had. Me, for instance. Oh, sure, I admit it. My God, I can't believe he's dead. How did it happen?"

"I don't know. Some terrible disease, I guess."

"And she up and married Bob. Poor Bob."

"Well, it was a couple of years later. Maybe more. I never knew her very well."

"Heavens, neither did I. But I used to run around with Gordon's cousin some and you should have heard *her* on the subject."

"Well, I guess there's nothing wrong with her."

"My dear, I know for a fact that she stayed all night at the Zee Zee house."

"Oh gee, I don't believe that. I've never liked her especially, sort of a cold fish, but . . ."

"Gordon's cousin told me."

What did you do in a case like this, rush out and say you damned liar, I'll sue you for slander?

"And besides . . ."

"Watch it. Someone coming . . . Darling, I just love your dress. Pink is divine on you."

"My dear, do you think so really? Personally I think it makes me look like a hag. . . ."

There had been no use for Virginia to try to figure out which of the numerous pink dresses it might have been. She stayed in the booth until everyone had left the dressing room. It was a large party and pink was popular just then. If she had been putting this episode in a book she would have recognized that girl's voice some time or other and then polished her off beautifully. However, she never had the least idea who the person might have been. Perhaps what burned her up most was that Zee Zee was a very second-rate fraternity. If Gordon's cousin, a little rat who had tried her level best to catch him for herself, had had to invent such a story, she might at least have made it the Beta house.

ii

"Peee Teee, ladies!" shouted Miss Hart.

The call shook Virginia from a pleasant dream in which she was telling off a girl in a pink evening dress. Hurry, hurry. She ran over to the nurse who was surrounded by clamoring ladies.

Miss Hart clapped her hands. She could make more

noise with her voice than with her hands, but when she was especially excited she clapped. "Quiet, ladies," she roared. Then she read from a paper and said that only those whose names she had read were to go to Petey. The instant she finished this pronouncement there was a frantic howl and her assistant, Miss Forderly or some such name, came slapping her white shoes on the linoleum. Virginia, cautious when wearing her glasses, stepped to one side. Brown-eyed Margaret was shrieking that her mother had said she could go anywhere her big sister went, but Miss Forderly dragged her off and soon the honored ladies filed into the corridor.

They went past the dining room and the doctor's office to a door that led to the stair-well. Was this Petey a trick, a new way to get them up to that electrical place? But you always had an empty stomach for that, and it was always in the morning. When they said you were not to take breakfast it meant you were to go for shock. That is a professional phrase. Shock treatment. Something rather new in the treatment of mental illness. You see I know a great deal about these things when I set my mind to it.

Instead of going up they went down and then they went out of doors. Virginia's heart beat faster. They were going out of the hospital for the meeting. I should have worn a hat. I look a mess. But so do the others look a mess. But what will the real people think of us? Will they take our votes seriously?

Off on the horizon were hills and between the hospital and the hills were fields and woods. This was country. There was no sign of the city anywhere. Of course Virginia had often looked from the narrow windows, but without her glasses the view might have been anything from Times

Square to the Skokie marshes. Often of an afternoon the ladies were allowed to go out to their cage but the cage gave onto a sort of park that was surrounded by high red buildings. How had they spirited you out of town? Did Robert know? Those letters. Yes, he had known.

There wasn't much time for admiring the landscape. Miss Hart turned to the left and soon they were back among the red cliffs. "They have a lot of buildings," Virginia said tentatively to her marching partner.

"Hundreds," said her partner.

They turned again and went into a one-story building that had no cages. Just inside the door they were met by a gray-haired woman who was wearing a black bloomer suit, long black cotton stockings and black gym shoes. She looked like a physical education teacher of the Twenties and her hair was cut in what in the Twenties would have been considered a smart boyish bob. There were several other groups of ladies in this foyer and several other nurses.

"Well," said Bloomers to Miss Hart, "I thought you weren't coming."

Miss Hart grunted and then she and the other nurses went away and Bloomers took the ladies into a large gymnasium. The floor was marked with black painted lines and there were basketball hoops at either end and over to one side was a volleyball net.

"Fall in," said Bloomers.

"Fall in what?" gasped Virginia's partner.

"Line, I imagine," said Virginia. How very clever I am. P.T. It stands for Physical Training. But this was a letdown when you had thought you were going to a meeting where you would make a radical motion and get even with Hortense and her old P.T.A.

Virginia had managed to avoid most of the physical training offered in high school and college. She had had an old-fashioned doctor. He wore a morning coat and a white carnation and he thought exercise, beyond strolling in the park, unthinkable for young ladies. Charles Thompson would have had you going out for football, but Charles was still in school himself in those days and hadn't a word to say. Oh, Charles, even then, had words to say, but no M.D. to back them up. Anyhow, the old doctor wrote out papers to demand that you be excused from physical training.

You had to take the swimming examination, though. In order to graduate from college you had to swim the length and breadth of the pool—just what this had to do with a degree in Liberal Arts Virginia never knew. But she managed it. She used a breast stroke part of the time and part of the time a sideways version of the dog paddle. She kept her head high out of the water and the swimming instructor moaned while she took her examination. But he had to pass her. The rule simply stated that you had to swim the length and breadth of the pool without stopping. It said absolutely nothing about the style to be employed. "It's a crime, that's what it is," said the instructor when he checked Virginia's card. But at least she had passed her own examination. A friend of hers had taken the test seven times, each time under a different name and bathing cap. You had to get a date for her in return. Virginia had tried to get a date for this professional test-passer but finally had decided it would be easier to take the test herself.

"Ten—shun!" said Bloomers snappily.

Virginia stuck her stomach out. It must be Therapy instead of Training. This being a hospital. She was so engrossed in working this out that she missed the command to squat and was spoken to personally by Bloomers.

They squatted, hands on hips, ho; they stood up, hands outstretched, ho; they leaned over and touched the floor without bending their knees, ho ho, and more or less copied what Bloomers was doing.

Bloomers seemed to be having a grand time. The old girl was nimble and expected the ladies to go through the tricks quickly. Virginia wished she had Senja's nerve.

One summer Senja got it into her head that she must learn to swim. She had had a dream about being chased into Lake Michigan by the Bolsheviks and so she and Virginia went to take swimming lessons from a woman who once had been champion at that horrid stroke, the Australian Crawl. The teacher probably knew no other stroke because she was determined that her pupils should master the crawl. She lined them up at the shallow end and had them wave their arms and make fish mouths. She had them cling to the side of the pool and kick their legs. Senja endured this until the middle of the second lesson. That was when the teacher told them to put their heads under the water. "Ya ole beetch," screamed Senja then. "Ya ga ta hal!"

Virginia was Senja's language teacher for over two years. By the end of the second year Senja could make herself fairly well understood, which was a shame inasmuch as her vocabulary contained much that Virginia had never taught her. You had to be grateful for the few times when Senja had failed to make herself clear, though. Virginia would never forget the time her Russian pupil told a floorwalker he was a bastard. "Loook, ya buster," she said to him. When her volatile attention was captured by a display on a nearby counter the floorman giggled to

Virginia that it had been a long time since anyone had called him Buster. "At first I thought she was sore, but then when she called me Buster. . . . What great charm these Russian women have."

It was impossible to make much headway with Senja after that. Senja used the floorman as an example of how you have to treat the lower classes. Properly kicked around, she said, they are willing and obliging.

Now Bloomers had had enough. During the last exercise her enthusiasm had sounded mechanical. Now she said wearily that they would skate or play volleyball. They could choose. "If you choose to skate, remember to stay on this side of the gym. All right, Volleyball Ladies."

Not being a volleyball lady Virginia stayed with the skaters. They went to a large box and hauled out roller skates. You had to sit on the floor to put your skates on and as there was only one key the volleyball game was well under way before the first skater wobbled out to the rink.

Virginia did not wobble; she was an expert. She had not been on skates since she was fourteen, but she did not fall down. She was the only skating lady who did not fall down.

"You skate very well," said Bloomers when P.T. was over.

The teacher looked bushed and Virginia was sorry for her. Back in the Twenties she had probably taught at a good school and now in her old age she was driven to teaching crazy ladies. "I skated a lot when I was a child," said Virginia.

"One never forgets," said Bloomers.

"No," said Virginia. "Like riding a bicycle." This is

the first time in my whole life that I have had a chance to say this first.

"That's right," said Bloomers. "It is a good deal like riding a bicycle, that is, the sense of balance. . . ."

Miss Hart and the other nurses had come. "Well, Virginia," said Miss Hart, "how did it go?"

"I'll be stiff tomorrow, I expect," said Virginia.

"Nothing like exercise," said Miss Hart happily. Then she changed her expression. "Ward Three Ladies!"

The Ward Three patients gathered around their nurse. The treat was over.

iii

The smell of Ward Three, after you had been out in the open, was overpowering. When they stepped into the dayroom Virginia identified the smell. Paraldehyde. One romantic book she read while doing research into mental ailments stated that the stench of paraldehyde has vanished from our mental institutions. I remember I wondered what paraldehyde was and I looked it up and it said hypnotic, a hypnotic.

So it is paraldehyde and not formaldehyde. Grace knew a lot, but she did not know that. I have worked it out for myself from the sound and from the stench and also from the memory. I am therefore not so sick as Grace was when she left us. I am therefore ready to be transferred, more than that, I am ready to go home. What is the matter with that doctor who is one of the best? Months since I saw the man.

"Miss Hart," she said, after she had given her store order, that is, after she had said yes, she would like some more cigarettes, "when am I going to see my doctor again?"

"Wouldn't you like to order some candy too? You have a five-dollar credit at the store," said the nurse. "Have you heard the news? There's going to be a movie tomorrow night and you're on the list."

"I never will be missed."

"What?"

"Oh, I was just thinking about that Gilbert and Sullivan thing about having him on the list and so on."

"Say, I'd forgotten that show," said Miss Hart. "Hitchy-Koo. My goodness, I was just a child then, of course."

"Of course," said Virginia. "You think it won't be long before I get to see my doctor again?"

"Aren't you feeling well? It's probably just from Petey."

"There are some things I want to ask him."

"Can't they wait until next week? You saw him just the day before yesterday, you know."

Another patient pushed up to Miss Hart to give a store order. Virginia went off to a corner and sat down. She tried to think, but the gray chiffon wound closer.

iv

By noon the next day the word about the movie had got around, and some of the ladies whom Virginia had considered hopeless spoke sensibly about the coming adventure. Virginia and a woman who appeared to know nothing at all were the only ones who showed no enthusiasm, but when Virginia thought about a movie she thought about going with Robert. She never went without him.

It developed, when the time eventually came, that not everyone was invited. More ladies were honored than had been included in the P.T. expedition, but fifteen or so were dosed up with paraldehyde and put to bed. Virginia would not have minded going to bed but it was something, of course, to get out of the paraldehyde.

The theater-bent marched away. No slicking up had been indulged in and Virginia decided that the show was to be given on the hospital grounds. The campus.

They went to a building near the gymnasium. It was a pleasant evening. The sun was nearing the horizon and the gold-red light made the distant hills pretty. . . .

The theater was a great hall that had a stage at one end. There were many rows of folding chairs and nurses were stationed at intervals to direct traffic. When the women were seated only half of the hall was filled. Then came men.

Virginia had got used to knowing that many women were in this hospital but she had not thought about it having men patients. The long lines of shuffling men made her throat hurt; she wondered if Don Jackson might be among them. She had never thought before about what institution he was in; it could be this one, couldn't it? I doubt if I would recognize him.

Perhaps the reason the men roused her pity even more than the women did was that they did not look nearly so bad. This is something to remember when you are sorry for men on account of their dull way of dressing. When they lose their minds they look less lost than women. They looked like ordinary men, not spruce, but most of them could have got by in a crowd. Not a woman in the audience could have got by in any crowd other than the one she was in now. A woman without a pocketbook or a compact or a pair of gloves or a hat or even a handkerchief is a lost soul. Miss Hart had seen to it that her charges had stowed away their bags and boxes before coming to the theater and apparently the other nurses had taken the same precaution. The ladies had nothing to do with themselves. No hats to take off, no nice hair-dos to pat, no handkerchiefs to flutter. . . .

It was odd to be in a room with a thousand or more insane persons. The audience was far quieter than the usual audience of a thousand normal people.

When the room was darkened the picture began. Virginia did not bother to follow it. It must have been a comedy; the audience laughed frequently and sometimes there was applause. In case a nurse might be watching for her reaction Virginia laughed when the others laughed and she clapped when the others clapped. The faces on the screen were familiar but she could not think of the actors' names. Hardly an abnormal state for me, I never could remember their names.

Now and then someone would stand up and shout but otherwise there was no more audience disturbance than you would find in any theater of this size. Less, really. There was no popcorn eating and no cellophane rattling; there was no running back and forth to the rest rooms and no wandering about for better seats.

The picture was short. The lights were turned on and the nurses began to guide their charges out of the room. The show was over. The men remained seated while the ladies filed out.

The sun had set. It was night. Virginia breathed deeply. This was the first time she had been outside at night in many many months. She looked beyond the blackness of the buildings and saw that there were stars.

"Wasn't it a cute show?" said Miss Fredericks when they were back in the washroom. Miss Hart had vanished somewhere along the line and of course, even so, she had put in more time tonight than she was supposed to.

Ordinary nights she went off duty at seven, after the ladies were in bed. But tonight Miss Fredericks, the night head nurse, had to put them to bed. "Wasn't it a scream, ladies?"

And the stars had been shining for the first time since last February. You can go along for weeks maybe months without thinking about the stars. They are there, on clear nights, and you can look at them if you want to. Sometimes you may notice them and say there is the Big Dipper. You may, if you are not in a hurry, hunt for the Pleiades; but you do not think much about the stars. They are always there. Look at them when you have a moment.

Until you contracted an illness that caused you to be shut up like a criminal.

They took the night away from you then. They drugged you and put you to bed before dark. But inadvertently, in connection with giving you a movie, they had also given you a glimpse of genuine stars. For perhaps two minutes you walked under the star-pierced sky.

"And how did you like the show, Virginia?" asked Miss Fredericks. Ordinarily this nurse had very little truck with the ladies. She was the one who got them started of a morning, but of a morning she was not affable or willing to delay the routine for the sake of a little conversation.

"Fine, thank you."

"I thought it was terribly cute," said Miss Fredericks. "Medication, ladies!"

Virginia went with the other Medication Ladies and drank her share of the hypnotic that made them smell like badly tended lions and then she went to her dormitory. She was the only one of her dormitory who had been allowed to attend the movie. Her roommates lay sleeping on their cots.

She turned down the covers of her cot and got into bed. You can bury your aching throat in the flat pillow and you can stuff the rough sheet into your mouth. You can beat your fists on the hard mattress and none of this will disturb the paraldehyde sleepers. And even as you weep you know it will be only a few minutes before you will sink into the paraldehyde emptiness.

CHAPTER SIX

WHEN she saw Miss Hart coming, Virginia took the polisher from Gladys. Gladys was one of the three who thought Virginia the doctor; this had been useful in the matter of the polisher. "Certainly, Doctor," said Gladys.

Virginia was hard at work when Miss Hart reached her. "But not today," said Miss Hart. "Gladys, you take the polisher. Virginia, have you forgotten what day it is?"

Of course Virginia had forgotten. She had no idea what day of the week it was, what week of the month, what month of what year. She tried to explain this to the nurse. "It isn't so much a matter of forgetting as it is of not knowing. When your memory is all tied up and separated from the rest of you, you don't forget. In order to forget you have first to remember, don't you, even though briefly?"

"Don't give me the fancy talk," laughed Miss Hart. She took Virginia by the hand. "We better get ready now. I might not have the time later on."

Virginia understood how that could be. Time was different here; sometimes it was long and sometimes it was short and sometimes—this was disconcerting—it was not at all. In real life you had been able to count on time; you might feel you hadn't enough of it, but it was always there, nicely parceled out in seconds and minutes and hours. Each day had twenty-four hours and you were able to depend on tomorrow. As with the stars it was something you took for granted. But here, here in the world of Juniper Hill, a day might consist of weeks, of hours, of a minute, or, frighteningly, of not even a second.

The nurse led her to a door she had never seen before. Naturally. The door was not there before. Just as the washroom was at one end of the corridor one day and at the other end the next day. Entirely new doors were created in order to insure perpetual confusion. You fancied them saying, Look, the ladies are getting on to the Ward; last night Virginia found the washroom without half trying; time for change, gentlemen.

Miss Hart unlocked the new door—they were careful always to have the same lock. The new door opened into a small room that was lined with dresses and cupboards. In the center of the room was an ironing board. I can never iron all those dresses. I simply cannot do it. I am going to have to explain to this woman what a favor is. Ironing is not a favor, I'll say. At least not for me, nurse.

"What do you want to wear today?" asked Miss Hart.

Virginia stared at the racks. She recognized several of the garments. Of course they were not really her own clothes; the hospital had made duplicates to fool her. "It doesn't make any difference," she said. Would all this be reported in the chart? Watch what you say.

"It's cooler today." The nurse made her mouth look profound. "I think the gray suit."

"It's awfully tight," said Virginia. "A friend gave it to me and she's only a twelve. I always meant to have it altered."

Miss Hart had taken the suit from its hanger. As in the real world, the person offering the choice had already made the decision. Virginia took off her dress and the nurse put the skirt on her and zipped it up so quickly that it closed all the way. Virginia had never been able to do this. What strength the nurse had!

The white-silk blouse, also a gift, was too large now and the jacket—you could have been pregnant in it.

"There," said Miss Hart. "That's just dandy. Now hand me your comb."

This reminded Virginia that the black bag must be discarded. She told Miss Hart about the ladies who were accusing her of being a doctor and Miss Hart shook her head and said what next. "Never a dull moment," she said. She must have had a peculiar life before coming to Juniper where all moments were insufferably dull. "You might put the things you have to have every day in that candy box you wouldn't let me throw out. No sense in lugging that bag around anyhow. Good thing you made me save the box."

"Yes," said Virginia, although she remembered nothing about a candy box. "I thought it might come in handy."

When the nurse was shuffling around in the bag for the essentials for the candy box, she came upon Robert's letters. Virginia failed to restrain a cry, but the nurse said gently, really gently, that the letters would be safe in the bag. "Anyhow, it's better to see him than the letters, isn't it?"

It was an unnecessary jab for which the gentleness had not prepared you. Virginia turned her head to hide her tears. To keep from going to pieces she thought of names to call the nurse.

"There," said Miss Hart, the pig of a dog. "Where is the rouge? A little rouge and then . . ." She rubbed the small puff on Virginia's cheeks and then stepped off a way to inspect her creation. "You look swell," she said. "Just swell."

Then she told Virginia to go back to the dayroom and that seemed to be that. Virginia sat in the dayroom and waited for something to happen and after a while Miss Hart called Dinner Ladies. Virginia wondered if she was supposed to go to the dining room with the others. Except that she lacked hat and bag and gloves, she was dressed for the street.

"Come on, Virginia. Don't keep the ladies waiting."

All dressed up and nowhere to go. As they passed the gold-lettered door she thought perhaps that was where she was going, but Miss Hart gave her a little push toward the dining room.

The Champion immediately noticed the change in costume. She broke into her series of hellos. "Well, where do you think you are going?" she asked. She had bright eyes and appeared to be a little too alert.

"I don't know," said Virginia. Nothing too alert about me. No little bright eyes here.

The Champion nodded. "Staff," she said. "They always fix you up for Staff. They had me wear my good green dress that I paid nineteen dollars for reduced from forty-seven fifty, but it didn't do any good."

"This suit cost a lot," said Virginia. "A rich friend of mine bought it and then decided it didn't become her."

"You had that suit on the day Bobby caught the rabbit," said Margaret. "I remember it like it was yesterday."

"No talking, ladies," bawled Miss Hart.

Perhaps it was the suit. The Nose, although she stirred her plate of food as usual, changed her routine. When she had finished blending the mixture she threw it on the floor.

Miss Hart came running. "Oh, you bad girl, Hazel," she said, "you bad, bad girl. Just for that you can't have any dessert."

The Nose began to sob bitterly.

When dessert came Virginia clung to her little pan and the Champion could not get it away from her. "No, not today," said Virginia. Then she slid the pan over to the Nose. "There. Stop crying."

The Nose stopped the ghastly racket. She picked up the pan and threw it on the floor. At once several ladies, including the devoted Margaret, announced that Virginia was responsible.

Again Miss Hart came running. "A dozen times, Virginia, I've told you not to have anything to do with Hazel."

"I'll clean it up," said Virginia. "I'm so sorry."

"You'll do nothing of the sort. Hazel, any more tricks out of you and you'll go back to pack as sure as you're born."

While the nurse wiped up the mess there was angelic silence, but as soon as Miss Hart had gone to another part of the room the Nose whirled around and slapped Virginia's face.

This was too much for Margaret. She leapt from her chair and came round the table to defend her temporary sister. Food, ladies and chairs flashed helter-skelter past Virginia, but after a few moments Miss Hart and her assistant quelled the riot. The ladies, said Miss Hart, would all be sent to pack if they did not watch out.

Virginia realized by now that this frequently used expression was an idiom. It did not mean that you would be sent to pack your suitcase; it meant you would be sent

97

packing. I must make a note of this so that if I sometime have occasion for an Eastern person to tell someone off I will get the idiom right. Sir, if you do not cease to pay your disgusting attentions to my daughter, I shall find it necessary to send you to pack. For books issued in the Middle West you would almost have to make a note: Algy was not staying at the Sherwoods' residence. The old man meant he would be sent packing. . . . How would the old man manage this? Call in the police? How would Miss Hart manage to send fifty ladies packing? Did she mean she would chase them through the hall with a whip? But we use these idiomatic phrases carelessly. She doesn't know what she means, except that she is angry.

Back in the dayroom Virginia decided that her change of clothing represented Dressing Therapy. D.T. Today was my turn for D.T. This would have been rather amusing if you had had a good stiff drink. Of paraldehyde. The Juniper Cocktail, as we call it, we gay ladies of Juniper Hill. A martini, please, we more sophisticated ones say. And where, nurse, is the olive?

She went to one of the windows and looked out. The view from this side was pleasant, so very pleasant that she fancied she saw Robert below on the sidewalk. Better look out of the other side or you will start imagining all sorts of things and that is bad for a crazy woman. . . .

"Virginia," called Miss Hart. "He's here."

"Is he?" The nurse had said you would see the doctor next week and although you had thought this was still this week you were, as usual, mistaken. She went to the nurse and the door was unlocked and the nurse pushed it open and there was Robert. Of course it was not Robert, but they had managed to make it look very much like him.

"Hello," said the man.

"Hello," said Virginia.

"Right on the dot, as usual," said Miss Hart. "But we've been ready a long time, haven't we, Virginia?"

"Oh, yes," said Virginia. She smiled to think they expected to fool her with so crude a joke.

"Well, go along, you two," said Miss Hart. "Don't you eat so much that you won't touch your supper, like last time. . . ."

Time. Is it more sensible to alter time to suit your convenience than to alter your convenience to suit time? Why don't people on the outside discover that time is a slave to be shortened or lengthened, to be banished or borne, to be known or ignored, like last time?

"Mr. Cunningham, don't let her stuff herself."

"I won't," said the man. He sounded like Robert, too. They were fiendishly thorough.

She found herself looking at the man with admiration. The creation demanded certain tribute.

"You have your glasses," he said. "That's good."

He led her to a small alcove that had been set into the hall since dinner time. In the alcove were a few chairs, a settee and a replica of the Cunninghams' picnic hamper. On the hamper was a fair copy of the steamer rug Robert had bought in Scotland.

"Do you want to sit down a minute?" the man asked.

"All right," she said. Her knees were shaking.

They sat on the settee and she was careful not to get too close to him.

He nodded toward the gold-lettered door. "I just now saw Kik for a few minutes," he said.

"Yes?" she said politely.

"He says you are so much better."

"Does he?"

"He says it won't be much longer. . . . I hope you didn't eat much lunch because I brought another picnic along."

The hamper was very attractive. She could not help being interested and anyway it could do no harm to talk to the man. "What did you bring?" she asked.

"You'll see. Do you feel like going now? You aren't shaky?"

"Of course not," she said.

"I'm glad you are wearing your suit," he said. "It's cooler today."

"It's not mine," she said.

"You look better in it than Alice ever did," he said. How carefully they had coached him!

"Thank you," she said. "They have made it larger in some way. It's much too large for me."

"Well . . ." He cleared his throat. "Well, we better be getting along. The days are shorter now and the sun isn't very warm after three o'clock." There was something the matter with his throat. He coughed.

"Do you have a key?" she asked when they turned toward the outer door.

"This door isn't locked."

"That's funny. It usually is. They are very careful about doors."

"Did you enjoy the movie?"

"How did you know?"

"Dr. Kik told me," he said. At least he was frank about the source of his information.

"Kik?" Could all of those letters shrink into one ridiculous little syllable? "I didn't see him there."

They walked along and when they came to the turn for

the gymnasium they went the other way. "Is it all right to do this?" she asked.

"Absolutely," he said. "We're just going to the same place."

"Oh," she said. She was beginning to think maybe he was Robert. Surely an actor, even a fine actor, wouldn't have been able to make his throat go bad on account of the too-large suit. She did not understand why Robert would become emotional over an ill-fitting suit and yet the clouded voice had somehow shaken her belief in the impostor.

"The stars were wonderful last night," she said.

"It rained in town," he said.

"It did? It was clear as a bell here. I looked at the stars on the way home from the movie."

"The movie was night before last, darling."

"Was it?"

"Yes. I noticed the stars night before last."

"Then I have lost another day," she said. "I don't suppose I'll ever find it."

He was holding her hand the way he had always done, her fingers laced through his. "It doesn't make any difference," he said. "In a hospital all days are alike and the less you think about them the better. This afternoon is all we care about now."

"Are you really Robert?" she said. "I have to be sure, you know."

He squeezed her fingers until they ached. It was odd that he did not answer her question and even odder that his not answering banished her last doubt.

"Don't mind me," she said. "I say things without meaning anything."

"Who doesn't?" he said. He had brought her to a tiny

park that was screened from the hospital buildings by tall thick hedges that were yellow and red with fall. "Well, here we are. And no one else. That's the advantage of my coming on a week day. On a Sunday this place would be jammed."

There were three brick fireplaces, some refuse baskets and several benches. Robert spread the steamer rug on the ground. He opened the hamper and took out a beautiful little roast chicken. "Bigger than last time," he said.

It was one of those glazed birds you see in delicatessens. They never look real and so are suitable for an unreal time. Robert is real, but I and the time are dreams.

"Tomatoes," he was saying, "for vitamins. Apple pie and a thermos of coffee. I remembered the salt this time."

It was a feast. It was like long ago. But we never took bought roast chicken on those picnics of long ago. "You shouldn't have spent so much money, Robert."

"I've got plenty."

"How much does it cost to keep me here?"

"Not much," he said. He looked away from her.

"How much?" Why did he always think he could avoid telling her how much?

"It's based on my salary and so it can't be much," he said. "Don't give it a second thought."

I shall give it a second and a third thought later on but now . . . "There is nothing like a good meal," she said. "I don't mean that the food here isn't all right," she added when she noticed the distress in his eyes, "but it's different without you."

"Don't," he said. He stood up. "I think we had better sit on a bench now. I'll put the rug around you. You mustn't catch a cold."

"I wouldn't mind having a cold, double pneumonia

or something I could understand. You talk about second thoughts. I have no first thoughts. What's the matter with me? Is it a brain tumor?"

"God, no," he said. "Whatever made you think of that?"

"I don't know," she said. "I just now thought of it."

"It's a nervous breakdown," he said.

"That doesn't sound bad, does it?"

"It takes time, that's all."

"What do they do for it besides take time?"

"Well, there are those shock treatments. The electrical ones are rather new, you know. Charles writes that he has had several of his patients take them, people who aren't sick enough to be hospitalized. He thinks it's the answer."

"Charles and his thinking. He's always thinking. I wish he would take a shock treatment himself. That would stop him for a while. . . . How many have I had?"

"I don't know exactly. A dozen or so, I think."

"Are they going to give me more?"

"Kik says he will see."

"Is that really the way to pronounce his name?"

"It's the nearest I can come to it," said Robert. "He sort of spits and gargles around but it boils down to being something like Kik."

"How much longer is it going to be?"

"He can't say. We have to be very patient, darling. It isn't the sort of thing that can be hurried."

"I want to hurry it. I want to leave now, this afternoon. I'll get well right away if I can leave now."

"Darling," he said, "we have to do what the doctors say. But it won't be long. You just don't think about it. You just sort of vegetate and take things easy."

Thinking about the hours she spent laboriously pulling and shoving the polisher she looked down at the fringe of the steamer rug. "Have you ever been in our dayroom?" she asked.

"No," he said. "They don't let visitors in there. Why?"

She smiled. "Oh, nothing," she said. "I was just wondering."

ii

Did I imagine the picnic with him? I remember it clearly but sometimes you remember a dream clearly. I remember what we had to eat and how good everything tasted. If it was a dream it was the first dream in which I ever ate and got full. I remember how he tucked the rug around me, how he held my hand. . . . But I no longer can be sure of things.

This made her wonder if she actually was at Juniper Hill. Perhaps she was somewhere else; perhaps she was at home in bed and having a long nightmare. They say these long involved dreams take only a few minutes; perhaps the months at Juniper Hill are minutes in a night. Look at the years it took to write down what Earwicker dreamed in one night. But could you dream something entirely foreign to your experience? I have read twelve books about mental hospitals but Juniper Hill, real or dreamed, never appeared in those works. Juniper Hill, one of the best in the country if not *the* best. Preserve me from the worst.

People used to say I had an imagination. Oh, Gin, what an imagination you have. They didn't say this so much after they read my writing. Why write about the sordid, they said. What they meant was why not write about them as they imagine themselves. Well, I shall try to remember Juniper Hill for a book and then they will say what an imagination you have, my dear. Don't you know that modern mental hospitals aren't at all like your trumped-up Juniper Hill? Why, the patients are all so happy and, my dear, they do the darnedest things. Of course it's pathetic in a way but it really is a scream, what they say and do, thinking themselves Napoleon and all. They have a good roof over their heads and they don't have to worry about where the next meal is coming from or who's going to pay the gas bill. I'd say it is an ideal existence and here you've gone and made it sound perfectly icky. Why, I've always said if anything ever happened to one of my family (it is interesting that they always have it happening to one of the family or to a friend, never to themselves) I would put him into an institution right off the bat and my heavens if I believed your book I'd hesitate. Everyone knows we don't treat our insane like cattle. They are so much happier with their own kind and they just play around like happy little children all day long.

Could I have dreamed the taste of paraldehyde?

While the nurse was fussing around about putting the gray suit away she forgot about Virginia's medication and Virginia did not remind her. So now she lay awake. Or, in her dream, she thought herself awake. A simple test is to go to the bathroom. I won't think about where it is. If I am at home it will be the adjoining room.

Chancing a genuine or an imaginary case of athlete's foot she padded barefoot down the hall. The corridors were never without some light but after the ladies had retired the lights were dimmed. Near the office door Miss Fredericks and another night nurse stood talking. They did not see Virginia. She went into the washroom and got a drink of water. There was a fountain in the hall but near the nurses. She drank from cupped hands and then went back to the dormitory. She had counted the doorways and so knew that her dormitory was the fourth from the washroom.

Before long Miss Hart was saying Good Morning Ladies. It was a chilly morning. If I am dreaming I wish I would wake up enough to get another cover.

iii

It might have been the next day or the same day or the next week or the week after that; she might have had another picnic with Robert in the interval. You never knew afterwards. But one day was a special day. It was not Thursday or yesterday or tomorrow or anything like that; it was a special day, as if you were crossing the Equator. At first when Miss Hart started going on about what day it was Virginia thought Robert was coming.

"Well, Virginia," said Miss Hart, "this is your Red-Letter Day."

A red-letter day is a holiday and maybe Robert can come an extra time on a holiday. "Am I going to wear my gray suit?"

"Well," said Miss Hart. "No, I don't think so. You won't be out of the building. Of course you can't wear that old blue thing. They dress so much better there."

"Do they?" Virginia asked this for the sake of conversation, not because she doubted that they would not dress better anywhere.

"Yes. They are quite classy in One. Quite the finishing school." The nurse gave a laugh that sounded malicious.

"One? You mean Ward One?"

"Why, yes. Didn't Miss Fredericks tell you? You're being transferred to One."

Virginia began to tremble. "Oh," she said. "Does my husband know? Will he be able to find me?"

"Sure. Dr. Kik told him. We're all so happy for you, Virginia."

"It's a promotion then."

"I'll say. We don't often have anyone skip Two, but Dr. Kik gave the order. You're lucky to have a doctor who takes such a personal interest in you. He's really made quite a special case of you, you know."

"He has?" If so, why doesn't he come and see me? Do they have a rule for doctors, as for husbands? "I wonder what happens to the ones he isn't especially interested in."

Miss Hart looked at her. She seemed about to say something out of character. But then she put on her R.N. look and said they must get ready. "There is no cut-and-dried rule about patients having to go to One before they are released . . . uh, I mean, before they go home. I mean, you can go from any of the wards. But they usually go from One. It's like a convalescent home."

"I'm not ready for it," Virginia heard herself say. "And you know it, Miss Hart." They were in the cupboard room now. "I could go home, but I am not well enough for One."

The nurse stopped packing Virginia's things for a moment but then she patted a dress down into the large box. "Nonsense," she said. "I suppose you've heard some of the ladies talking. . . ."

"Yes." I can't remember what they said but there is something terrible about Ward One.

"You know better than to pay any attention to them. They're sick. Only one or two of them have ever been inside of Ward One."

"You mean some of them go there and then come back?"

"Practically everyone goes home from Ward One," said Miss Hart as if reading from a book. "You are not sent to Ward One unless you are practically ready to go home. That is understood." She was using the loud firm voice you always use when you are not sure of what you are saying.

"That's good," said Virginia.

"I tell you what," said Miss Hart when they were crossing the dayroom. "You do everything Miss Davis says. Don't think about it, just do it. You'll get along all right."

As soon as she heard the name Virginia knew what was terrible about Ward One. Miss Davis. "Is she the head nurse?"

"And how," muttered Miss Hart. And then she raised her voice. The nurses had a way of acting as if the patients were unable to hear anything that was not shouted. Frequently they said things in normal voices that the ladies were not supposed to hear; if they had not been nurses you would have said they frequently talked to themselves. "A most competent and efficient person, Miss Davis," announced Miss Hart. "One of the finest nurses in the country, if not *the* finest."

Virginia and a student nurse, a very young person in blue-and-white stripes and a white apron without a bib, went down the hall. They went past the dining-room door, past the doctor's door, past Robert's door. They turned corners and finally the student unlocked a door that said, in black letters, Ward One. The corridor inside of the door was just like the corridor of Ward Three.

They went to the office where an all white nurse, a very handsome woman who was around thirty, was sitting at a desk. The woman looked at the student and frowned, as if it made her ill to see the student; she then looked at Virginia and scowled. "V. Cunningham from Three?"

"Yes, Miss Davis," said the student.

Miss Davis lifted her head even higher. "Miss Gold!" she shouted.

There was the sound of a nurse coming fast. This was one sound Juniper Hill had in common with an ordinary hospital. A nurse coming fast always sounds the same. It was a sound Virginia connected with Gordon. Once in a sailboat a sudden change in the wind brought that sound and she thought she smelled disinfectant.

"Miss Gold," said Miss Davis to the nurse who had just come into the office, "this is the new patient from Three. Dr. Kik's patient."

Virginia looked at Miss Gold. Then she looked at the student nurse. The student seemed terrified. I don't know why she should be scared. I'm the one.

"Show her to her room, Miss Gold. That will be all. You will wait in your room until I come." The head nurse shot this last at V. Cunningham and then she turned on the student. "Were you waiting for something?"

"Oh, no, ma'am. Will that be all, ma'am?"

"Get back to your duties, please."

Clumsily Virginia and the student pushed through the doorway together.

"This way," said Miss Gold.

They passed a dozen cubicles. These doorless alcoves were called rooms. Each room had a cot and a table or a chest or some sort of washstand. A few of the rooms had what you might, in so barren a land, call homelike touches. Here was a photograph and there a crucifix.

"This is your room," said Miss Gold when they came to the end of the hall.

There was no linoleum on the floor. The floor was cement that was gritty to walk upon. There was a cot and there was a table. The cot was the sort they had in Three, an iron army cot, but it was made up with far more arithmetical exactness than they had managed in Three. There was no wrinkle or lump in the gray blanket that served as counterpane.

The room was large enough to turn around in. You wouldn't have thought so, but Miss Gold turned around. "You just wait here until Miss Davis comes," she said.

"Shall I sit on the bed?"

"I don't think I would," said Miss Gold. "You can put your box down on the table, though."

Virginia put the candy box on the table. After Miss Gold went away she stepped to the window and looked out. The view wasn't very good. Several yards from the window was a blank red-brick wall.

After a while she sat down on the floor; after more of a while she lay down. When she awoke, Miss Davis was standing in the doorway and saying to get up. "In Ward One," said Miss Davis, "we do not lie on the floors."

"I was afraid I would muss the bed," said Virginia.

"There is a rest period every afternoon after dinner," said Miss Davis. "There is ample time for rest. Ward One has rules that are quite different from the other wards. We take care of our own rooms, of course, and make our own beds. . . ."

Virginia looked at the bed and sighed.

". . . and keep things picked up. You will co-operate, of course."

"I can never make a bed look that way."

Miss Davis frowned. "You will find the ladies in One very serious and co-operative. I'll take you to the dayroom now. You may leave your box. Personal belongings are quite safe in One."

"There are some things I may need," said Virginia. She picked the box up. For a moment she thought the nurse would take it from her. This woman is a hired person. I pay her. If Robert did not pay my way here we would still be paying her through taxes. As a public servant she has no right to treat me this way and I am foolish to be afraid.

Evidently Miss Davis sensed rebellion. "I trust you will be co-operative," she said. "Ladies who are co-operative find Ward One very pleasant."

"I'll do my best."

"Our ladies do not eat between meals. If you are afraid to leave your candy here you may give it to me and I'll put it in the cupboard. You will have access to the cupboards just before and just after meals."

"This," said Virginia, "is my pocketbook." She smiled. "My overnight bag. The candy is quite gone, unfortunately."

The smile had been a mistake. The nurse's expression curdled. Had you come upon Miss Davis outside you would have said to yourself there is a woman who is not all there, not entirely normal. Look at those eyes. Miss Davis' eyes had a look you do not mind seeing in the eyes of your cat.

CHAPTER SEVEN

AFTER so long a time of dark brown Virginia was thrilled by the zinnia colors of One's dayroom. The bright cretonne curtains and cushions might have been hideous in real life but they were beautiful here. Of course once you stopped looking at the gay colors you saw the brown furniture and the brown linoleum; you saw that the essentials were the same as they were in Three. Though what is essential?

There was one other person in the large room. The scarcity of business in One was encouraging. The others must have gone home. Just think, they come and go so fast that when I arrived at One there was only one other patient. The thought was bracing.

"I am Virginia Cunningham," she said to the other patient. "I've just come."

The woman was perhaps forty but neither fair nor fat. She was the kind you would not know a second time. Her hair and face were about the same color and this neutral shade was repeated in her dress. She looked at Virginia, at first without interest, but then her eyes took on warmth. "I see you have a box of candy," she said graciously.

"I'm sorry," said Virginia, "but it's empty. I mean, there is no candy. I carry my powder and things in it."

The warmth changed to suspicion. "Where did you come from?"

Out of the nowhere into the here. "Three."

"No," said the dun-colored woman, "one does not come from Three. I myself was in Two less than a week but of course I have money."

"That must be convenient," said Virginia. She looked around the room and saw that there was a piano. "I didn't notice the piano before. How nice."

"It is not played without permission. At present there are no pianists in the ward."

"Oh. Well, I play a little."

"Enough to call yourself a pianist?"

"No."

"Then you will not get permission. There is no use to ask. The standards in One are very high. I wouldn't be here this morning if I didn't have a slight cold. As a rule I am working."

"Of course."

"It's menial work. They don't seem to understand that I'm not the type they usually get. My husband, Mr. Grier, is very wealthy. I was in a number of exclusive hospitals before I came here. All restricted, of course. I came here at the insistence of a very expensive doctor. My husband, Mr. Grier, is very wealthy. I have more jewels than I can possibly wear."

"How annoying," said Virginia.

"You, of course, are a charity patient."

"No. It so happens that my husband, Mr. Cunningham, is very wealthy." What the hell. If you have to be here why not try to get a kick out of it? "I too have many jewels. The diamonds simply weigh me down."

"I have the Hope diamond."

113

"I have the Hopeless Emerald. It carries the Cunningham Curse. You've probably read of it."

"Mr. Grier, my husband, considered buying it, but it has a flaw. You cannot put an imperfect stone on the most beautiful hands in the world." Mrs. Grier held up her hands. They were not bad hands; each had four fingers and a thumb. "It is a responsibility. Often I wish I had just ordinary hands, like yours."

This wasn't much fun, really. "When you said you aren't here as a rule did you mean there are other patients in the ward?"

"Thousands," said Mrs. Grier, "and all of the lower classes. Mr. Grier . . ."

"Your husband."

"Mr. Grier, my husband, was saying the last time he was here that he has never seen so many of the lower classes."

"If you look at it from a certain viewpoint you might find it very interesting."

"I would not."

"I mean the *you* one substitutes for *one,* the general you."

"General who?"

"Oh—Pershing."

"A cousin of mine," said Mrs. Grier. "One of the minor branches of the family."

This went on for some time. Virginia suspected that Mrs. Grier knew she was talking nonsense, but there was no sense to discuss. They had been comparing jewels and relatives for about an hour when the other ladies came. There were dozens. Fifty or sixty. Virginia studied them as they entered the dayroom. Taken as a group they appeared to be normal women.

Most of the newcomers were under middle age and although Virginia tried to be critical when she scrutinized them they seemed distressingly well. It struck her that she and Mrs. Grier were the only stupid ladies of Ward One. And it had been evident that Mrs. Grier was reluctant to accept her. Yes, I don't look as well as she does. I need a permanent, a manicure and a good hot bath.

The ladies gathered into little groups and talked. None of them paid any attention to Virginia and Mrs. Grier. So Virginia got up and went away from Mrs. Grier. She might have been invisible, except that one or two ladies eyed her candy box.

Miss Gold came to the door. "Dinner, ladies," she said.

The ladies strolled out of the dayroom and down the hall; there was no forming in line, no waiting for silence. In the dining room Virginia asked Miss Gold where she should sit and Miss Gold said anywhere. But it was some time before the new patient could discover a place that was not reserved and eventually she ended up beside Mrs. Grier.

The food was somewhat reminiscent of real food. You had meat that required cutting and you were provided with a knife. There was a salad. The plates were not metal and you could have your coffee black. Four of the women at Virginia's table carried on a sprightly conversation about their morning's work.

"I beg your pardon," said Virginia when there was a pause, "but did you happen to know a girl named Grace? I don't know her last name. She was fair and quite pretty and she was a newspaperwoman."

"Grace?" said one of the ladies. "I don't remember any Grace."

"There was Grace Jenks," said another.

"She said pretty."

"Pardon me."

"Anyhow Grace Jenks wasn't a newspaperwoman."

There was laughter.

"Just what was Grace Jenks?"

"My dear, you're asking?"

It might have been at your club back home. If Mrs. Grier had just kept her face shut you might have forgotten where you were.

ii

After dinner the ladies went to the washroom and those who wished to smoke and had cigarettes, smoked. Virginia had a full pack of cigarettes and was quite popular until they were gone. She was disappointed to see that the lighting system was like Three's. She knew that Mrs. Grier shouldn't be allowed to have matches, but surely the others could be trusted.

The toilet-paper system was the same here, too. The washroom was exactly like Three's, but you hoped the shower stalls were used more frequently. The ladies looked as if they bathed often.

After Washroom came Rest. You could write letters, if you had paper and pencil; you could take a nap. You could do anything as long as you did it in your room and broke no rules. Virginia sat on the edge of her bed and prayed she would not wrinkle the blanket.

Later in the dayroom she became acquainted with Lola. Lola was married and had dark hair and two very important teeth out and a sweetheart, not the husband of course, and two children. She said she was going to stay at Juniper Hill until her husband agreed to let her have a divorce and the children. Virginia said she hoped it would work out. She said this several times. Lola was a talker. She talked until Miss Gold announced supper and this was a long time after the Oatey Ladies returned. Virginia wanted to ask Lola what the Oatey Ladies were but Lola was engrossed in talking about her sweetheart. Lola arranged for them to sit together at supper and the saga of the sweetheart was continued. Virginia said she hoped it would work out.

But Lola was generous. At Washroom Time she gave Virginia one of the six cigarettes she had taken from Virginia's pack at noon. But Lola really was generous; she had forgotten that the cigarettes had once been Virginia's.

There was no medication in Ward One; there was no bad smell at all. The ladies washed carefully before they retired and there was a good deal of stocking washing. The nightgowns were the same old nightgowns, though, and the cot was as hard as the one you had in Three. Scratch the surface and you found Juniper Hill.

But remember, this is the ward you go home from. This is the springboard. Forget that Lola said she has been here nine months. Nine months in One, almost two years in Juniper's other wards. But Lola is not sick; she is simply waiting for the husband to give in.

iii

That first day was an unreliable sample. During the first day Virginia scarcely saw Miss Davis; during subsequent days she scarcely did not see Miss Davis. It developed that Ward One had harder and faster rules than any you had ever encountered. And the presiding officer had no intention of relaxing.

The head nurse made it obvious that she thought Dr. Kik had overstepped when he put V. Cunningham in One. It seemed that she set out deliberately to prove the doctor a fool. Of course Virginia may have had a persecution complex, but she was convinced that Miss Davis went far out of her way to make the wet and dry mop business confusing.

Virginia's chore, of a morning, had to do with wet and dry mops and a series of unbelievably heavy buckets with wringer attachments. It was forbidden to shove the buckets and next to impossible to lift them. You were supposed to dip a wet mop into a bucket, through the wringer thing; then you were to wring it; then you were to mop. Then you were to finish off with a dry mop. The wet and dry mops were different mops. A wet mop was a wet mop even when it was dry. A dry mop was the mop Virginia mistook for a wet mop. Whenever Miss Davis approached, the mop Virginia held turned into being the wrong one. Miss Davis said the mops were unmistakable, but Virginia mistook them easily.

But before you began to mop you had to find the equipment. The equipment was kept in a utility room and this room was in a different place each morning. Virginia would follow the other ladies and hope they were headed for the utility room. Sometimes they were. Some of the ladies were kind about helping her. Lola was especially helpful. Of course when you asked Lola for help you had to listen to a good deal about her sweetheart but eventually she told you where the utility room had got to and which mop was which.

Virginia shoved the buckets along and when she did this Miss Davis appeared and said was she trying to ruin the linoleum. Virginia asked if that was how her room

118

had lost its linoleum and Miss Davis told her to attend to her own business.

Occasionally Lola had a job off the ward but Virginia stayed on the ward all the time; she was the only lady who stayed on the ward all the time; even Mrs. Grier sometimes went off to a job. In addition to her general work on the ward Virginia had to take care of her room. Miss Davis said her room always looked like a hogpen. No matter how hard you scrubbed the rough cement it looked as if it needed a good scrubbing. Miss Davis said Virginia's room was a disgrace to the ward and that she had never had so many dry mops ruined and that Virginia never put anything back. Miss Davis said she not only left mops and buckets all over the place but that she also took other people's mops and buckets and hid them. If Virginia had known of a good hiding place she would have put herself there.

After a week or so Miss Davis and Miss Gold brought a typewriter to Virginia's room. "Your doctor," said Miss Davis, "says you may write for an hour each day. Put it on the table, Miss Gold."

Miss Gold put the typewriter on the table.

"I'll have to have a chair," said Virginia.

"Naturally."

"And some paper."

"I am fully aware of what is necessary. You will use the machine only during Rest Hour. I suppose you'll make a great racket."

"I don't want to bother anyone," said Virginia. "I don't have to write."

"Dr. Kik says you are to write," said Miss Davis. "There will be no argument, please."

And so Virginia wrote. She wrote that now was the

time for all good men to come to the aid of V. Cunningham. She wrote that Virginia lay sleeping in the moonlight, and longed to be on Wolfe's thundering train. She wrote a story about the short happy life and changed it around and had him shoot his wife and she called this story The Short Happy Life of Mrs. Francis McComber. She wrote about the cops rushing in. She could not remember why they had rushed and so she wrote that J. Moncure March wrote a poem and then the cops rushed in.

It was awful to think of things to write. If she paused more than a minute Miss Davis would come to the doorway and ask what the matter was. When she heard the nurse's skirts flapping Virginia would hurry to write that a rose was a rose was a rose alas.

After Rest Hour she would tear her manuscript into small pieces and put them down the toilet. Miss Davis never caught her at this but she was terrified that some day the nurse would discover her in the act and that from then on all drainage difficulties would be the fault of V. Cunningham. It was imperative, however, to destroy the plagiarized and absurd writing.

One afternoon Miss Davis asked her what she was writing. Virginia leaned over the typewriter to hide the story. Today she was doing a piece about a woman who sold her hair and a man who sold his watch. It was difficult for a person who had never considered fob chains or hair combs especially desirable to put any pathos into the sacrifices of Jim and Della. "A book," she said to the nurse.

"What kind of a book?"

"A novel."

"Oh," said Miss Davis. "I understand from Dr. Kik that you've had something published."

"A couple of novels."

"I should think you would be interested in serious writing."

"Some people think fiction can be serious."

"There is far too much to be done in the world without storytelling," said Miss Davis. "From my own experience I can assure you that you will get well sooner if you face reality."

Virginia said nothing. It had been years since she had let herself get hot under the collar about fiction. The last time had been when Florence Young had said she only read fiction in the summer time. "Not that I let myself lie around fallow all summer," said Florence, "but I mean that there are times in the summer when one simply can't face the thought of anything important." Virginia had got very hot under the collar then. But suddenly she had cooled off and started laughing and since then she hadn't bothered about the people who said fiction was inevitably silly.

"I notice you do not use the touch system," said Miss Davis.

"No, I never learned it."

"Why not?"

"It wasn't given in the pre-college course that I took. It was available only for those who were not going to college."

"How impractical."

"Yes. They have changed it now."

"You could have learned later on."

"I can go rather fast."

"But it's not efficient."

"I've always done all my own typing. I like to do it, even though I'm not efficient."

"You know, Virginia," said Miss Davis, "I say this only

for your own good, but when you get a more co-operative attitude you'll be better off. I think if you would forget that you have had a little something published. . . . After all, it's nothing to be so excited about, is it? It doesn't set you above the other ladies."

Virginia got up. "Miss Davis," she said, "do I tell you how to be a nurse?"

The nurse smiled; she had drawn blood, "As I said, my dear, you lack the spirit of co-operation. You really must get rid of your exalted idea of your importance. . . . That is, if you want to get well."

She turned away and the starched skirt flapped briskly down the hall.

In a way, the nurse had paid you a compliment. A nurse, provided she was sane, would not permit herself to talk that way to an ill person. Professional dignity would not permit one of the best nurses in the country, if not *the* best, to enter into an argument with a mental case. Virginia clung to the windowsill and looked at the vista of red brick. It can't be that she hates me personally; she hated me before I came; it has to be something that lies between her and Dr. Kik. But I refuse to be their football. I've got to get out of One.

It isn't that I'm afraid she will do me any bodily injury, but I know I can't take much more and she is very very much more.

For a while we thought he was going to recover, but then—well, he got worse. . . .

Don, was there a time when you saw, as if at the end of a dark hallway, the light of the outside, a time when you knew you hung at a balance and that such a little push, one way or another, would determine your life? Did you, at this wavering instant, come up against a Miss

Davis who laughed you, sneered you, chilled you back into the dark?

The delicacy of one's intellect, one's sanity, when it is laid open to the specialists. The tissue quivers as under a knife and you, only partly anesthetized, see the light of recovery and the dark of death that is called living, the happy life, the long happy life of the idiot.

She heard a scream. That was I who screamed? A *voice*? I? An insane neighbor? For a minute the balance was lost. "Robert," she said softly. "Robert Cunningham." It was one woman's way of praying.

iv

When he came to visit she did not tell him about her difficulties; she was ashamed to tell him she could not tell the difference between a dry wet mop and a wet dry mop.

He spent most of the visit talking about what they would do as soon as she left Juniper Hill. He said it would be very soon and while he was there she believed it would be very soon. He quoted Dr. Kik. He had written home to say they would be there for Thanksgiving.

When Virginia was called to the Ward door Robert was there talking to the head nurse. "Who was that old hen?" he asked when they had sat down in the visitors' room.

"That is Miss Davis," said Virginia. "She is very efficient. And she's rather beautiful, don't you think?"

"God, no," said Robert. "She looks like a hard proposition to me. I don't like her."

Lola was entertaining today, too. You wished she could have had her plate, but you imagined she wasn't very pretty even with her teeth. The man she was entertaining was startlingly handsome. It was strange that such a good-looking man, obviously years younger than Lola, would fall in love with an unattractive woman who was married.

"That dark-haired one over there is my friend Lola," Virginia whispered to Robert. "That's her beau. She has a husband, too."

Robert grunted. He was not interested in Lola. "The hell with Lola," he said. "Listen, darling, Kik said . . ."

When visiting time was over Miss Davis came to the door. She called Lola and then she called Virginia. Her voice indicated that Lola and Virginia had been up to no good.

Robert got up and went over to the nurse. "Did you call Mrs. Cunningham?" he asked.

It was a small thing and yet Virginia was sure that Miss Davis was harder on her from then on. And perhaps she imagined that her lot was made harder by Miss Gold saying, in Miss Davis' presence, that Mr. Cunningham was a keen-looking fella. Imagination, of course. But the shaking Miss Davis gave you the next morning over a mop mix-up was not imaginary. You were not injured but you were upset to the point of forgetting. Before you had time to think you said for the nurse to kindly take her hands off.

It seemed unlikely that you could graduate from One. Clearly Miss Davis was eager to get rid of such a cotton-head, but you knew she planned to speed you through the back door. So you began on a plot of your own.

One morning V. Cunningham mentioned to Miss Gold that she had a pain in her side. Having had appendicitis she knew just where to point.

Miss Gold was immediately roused. Was it a sharp pain?

124

Oh, no, said Virginia, nothing very bad. She could stand it. "Just a little indigestion. I wouldn't have mentioned it, but I thought you might give me a laxative." Ah, innocence.

Miss Gold gasped. That might be the very worst thing. She touched Virginia's appendectomy scar and Virginia said ooh. "Sorry, but it's a little tender there. You didn't really hurt me."

In less than a half hour Virginia was sitting in Dr. Kik's office.

"So you have decided to grow another appendix, Jeannie," he said.

"I had to see you," she said. "It was the only way I could think of."

"Oh, you are thinking up a book plot."

"No, you know Miss Davis wouldn't have let me come just for the asking. I had to have a reason and she never would have accepted the real reason."

"And that is?"

"Dr. Kik, I can't stay in One. I just can't."

The doctor raised his eyebrows. She could not remember ever having seen him before and yet she felt as if she knew him intimately. His eyebrows went up exactly as she had known they would.

"Cannot, Jeannie?"

"I am not up to it," she said. "I can't remember where things are. I get the mops mixed up."

"You are writing."

She shrugged. "I can't write away from home."

"But you are."

"I'm typing. She comes and asks me what's wrong if I stop. It is true, isn't it, that you can go home from any ward?"

"Yes," he said, "it is true."

"Then I want to be transferred."

"What about the ladies in One? Do you become friends with them, yes?"

"Yes. They are kind to me. But it's so hard to become friends, really friends, here. I'm always thinking about going home, you know. It's like making friends in a depot."

"And what does Mr. Cunningham say about the transfer?" He had leaned back and now he sat with his fingertips pressed together. Probably he thought he was looking old. He's no older than I am, maybe younger.

"Robert doesn't know. You see, he's so pleased about my being there. I haven't told him how hard it is. All those women know so much more than I do. They never get the mops mixed up and they always know where the utility room is. I never was good at making beds and I simply can't make one to suit. I don't fit in, Doctor." There at last was the truth. It wasn't Miss Davis, it was that you were not well enough for Ward One. "I am not well enough."

"You do not consider yourself well enough for Ward One?"

"I know I'm not well enough. I forget what I'm supposed to do. I forget where my room is. It isn't that I don't try. I do. I really do."

"Well," he said, "we shall attend to this."

She got up. "Thank you so much."

He smiled. "You no longer have the pain in the side?"

"Only in the head," she said. "And in the neck."

He burst out laughing; for a foreigner he was very quick. "Jeannie," he said, "you must learn discretion."

"I know. I don't mean it. Oh, I do mean it but the chief

thing is that I know I'm not well enough. She's only a small part of it."

"Thank you for coming to me. It was brave of you." He held out his hand.

When she left the student nurse who had acted as her guide, she passed the office of Ward One. Miss Davis looked up from the desk. Virginia nodded a formal acknowledgment and went on to the dayroom. Lola was there. Lola was very excited. Her sweetheart was coming to visit. The husband had been forced to give up his visiting day to the rival. It was arranged.

"But I thought your sweetheart was here last visiting day," said Virginia. She had been beginning to realize that Lola was still quite sick.

"That?" Lola gave a scornful laugh. "That was my husband."

Yes, still quite sick.

CHAPTER EIGHT

"I can't understand it," said Miss Gold. "I wish I'd never made that appointment for you to see him. But I'm afraid of appendicitis. I had a girl friend to die of it."

"You did right," said Virginia. "You can't take chances with a thing like that."

"But he said it's nothing to worry about?"

"Yes. It was just one of those things. I probably imagined it."

"Well, I certainly hate to see you leave One. You're so nearly well and writing every day and all. . . . But don't pay any attention to me. I talk too much. I'm sure you'll be back with us very soon."

"Um," said Virginia. "I understand you can go home from any ward, though."

"Oh, sure, sure. And I know you'll like Mrs. Fledderson. I took my training under her. She's so, well, not easy, I guess, but she makes it seem easy." Miss Gold closed the box that held Virginia's things. "Well, we can go now. I got permission to take you. I don't get to see Mrs. Fledderson often. Funny, with her right down the hall."

Miss Davis was not in the office when they went past it. "In the dayroom," said Miss Gold, as if Virginia had asked where the head nurse was.

"Nursing here must be awfully hard," said Virginia when they were outside of the ward. "I should think you'd rather be in a regular hospital."

"Well, you see I'm engaged to a man here, a patient, I mean. We were engaged before he got sick, I mean. This way I can kind of keep track of him."

"I'm sorry," said Virginia. "I hope he is getting better."

Miss Gold sighed. "It takes so long. I mean, for some cases. He's not like you. But he'll get well. I always knew he would and now even some of the doctors say so." She took her key chain in her free hand. "Here we are."

Ward Two. It looked like Ward Three; it looked like Ward One. Anyhow the hallway and the office. At the office desk was a small gray-haired nurse. She jumped up when she saw Miss Gold and Virginia. "Goldie," she said. "How'd you get away? You been fired?"

Miss Gold laughed. "And that's no joke," she said. "This is Mrs. Cunningham, Mrs. Fledderson."

Virginia started to hand over her candy box, but then she realized that Mrs. Fledderson's outstretched hand meant something else.

"I'm real glad to have you with us, Mrs. Cunningham. Dr. Kik has told me about you."

I would give a pretty to know what he said. Out in the world you would say, Nothing bad, I hope; and the other person would simper and say, Well, now, I'm not saying. But you keep your mouth shut here. Remember you can't trust yourself; you might say something and give yourself away.

"Goldie, you wait till I take her to the dayroom and then we can have a little visit. . . ."

"Gee, I can't, Fled. You know how it is."

"Honestly," said Mrs. Fledderson. She turned her eyes

up to the ceiling. "When I think about some things I about pass out."

She and Miss Gold exchanged glances. Virginia looked at the floor and pretended not to know what they were talking about.

"Just wait till I tell you the latest," said Miss Gold.

"Honestly, something ought to be done about it."

"I might get appendicitis," said Miss Gold. "I just now thought of that. It might be an idea. What do you think, Virginia?"

Virginia felt herself blushing. "I don't know what you mean," she said.

Miss Gold laughed. "Gee, was I dumb. I just now caught on to something. Fled, your new one is a schemer. . . . Kid, I hand it to you. It's been tried before, the general idea, I mean, but it's never worked before. Fleddie, keep an eye on her or she'll talk her way out of here before you know it."

"Fine," said Mrs. Fledderson.

After Miss Gold left them they went to the dayroom. "Of course it's nothing so grand as One," said Mrs. Fledderson, "but we get along. No one wants to be at Juniper Hill. I don't much want to be here myself. But if you've got to stay a while you might as well try to make the best of it and take it easy while you can. Dr. Kik says you write."

"Yes," said Virginia, "but I'd rather not do any here, if it's all right not to."

"Sure, it's all right not to. I don't see how you could do any here anyhow. Wait till you get home. Well, this is the parlor. We have a radio, you hear. Madge, will you turn that radio down a little? You want to split our eardrums?"

The ladies of Two were very friendly. They were not so well groomed and bright as the ladies in One, but they seemed more relaxed. Each morning there was a big to-do about mopping floors and making beds, but it was rather fun. People helped you and you helped them. Mrs. Fledderson's idea appeared to be to make the work as light a burden as possible. Her ward did not begin to look as neat as Miss Davis'. It is the sad truth that ladies anywhere will take advantage.

"Kids," the head nurse might say some morning, "I wish you'd give it the old business today. One of the big shots coming through and I don't want to lose my job."

And that morning the kids would go to town on the mopping and polishing and the next day Mrs. Fledderson would bring around a box of cookies or something.

"Everyone hates to leave Two," a lady told Virginia. "When one of us is sent to One it's like a funeral."

When Robert came he met Mrs. Fledderson and then he was reconciled to the change. He said Dr. Kik had explained it to him. "He thought it was wonderful of you," he said.

"I just couldn't bear that woman another day," said Virginia, "and I had to think up some way to skin a cat."

"He says you're almost well. He says you'll be going to Staff soon."

"Where's that?"

"It's just a group of doctors. They talk to you a little before you go home. That's all."

"It sounds terrible," she said.

"Why, it's just a matter of routine," said Robert. "Dr.

Kik will be there and he'll take care of everything. You promise me you won't worry."

Virginia smiled. She was having to use that smile a good deal. Two, for all its informal atmosphere, was confusing. There were things to remember; you were supposed to remember where your bed was and where the washroom was and things like that. The nurses didn't get mad if you forgot; but you could tell they were surprised. The ladies of Two were not as bright as buttons and yet, except for Virginia, they always knew where their beds were and where the washroom was. They remembered the general schedule of the day and they usually knew what day it was.

Virginia couldn't remember anything but her name. Often she wondered how she remembered that. She forgot what ward she was in; she forgot Mrs. Fledderson's name; she forgot the names of her new friends; she forgot Dr. Kik's name. Dr. Kik did not know this. She called him Doctor and he was satisfied. He said she was coming along beautifully beautifully.

She went with a group of Two ladies to Oatey. This was O.T., Occupational Therapy. The ladies sat in a circle and sewed and embroidered. The teacher gave Virginia a towel with a stamped pattern for cross-stitch. She told Virginia how to cross-stitch. Virginia knew how, or at any rate she had once known how. She didn't say so. You couldn't be sure that it was like riding a bicycle.

But when you started out the skill of your childhood returned and you cross-stitched every bit as well as you had done when you were seven, and the teacher praised you so highly that one of the ladies, Betsy, cried and cried.

And the next time Robert came he knew about that towel. When you thought about the things Dr. Kik noted down you didn't know whether to laugh or to be terrified. You thought about him trying to say cross-stitch, but you didn't dare laugh about Dr. Kik to Robert. Robert changed his voice when he said the doctor's name. Robert simply worshipped that doctor.

"Mrs. Fledderson says I can take you to the store for a soda," Robert said, after he had stopped talking about the famous towel.

"But I don't have any coat," said Virginia, "and you said it's cold outside."

But here came Mrs. Fledderson with the green coat and the green hat with the fur cuff. "You look like a million dollars in that outfit," the nurse said, after Robert had helped you into the coat.

A million dollars. I would rather look like an ordinary woman. I would rather have them say you look well, well in that outfit. "Why, it is cold. It must be winter."

"You ought to have your muff," said Robert anxiously.

"Oh no, it's too nice for here. I can put my hands in my pockets." She thrust her hands into the coat pockets and in each pocket was a glove; in one pocket was a crumpled handkerchief. "Look what's been in here all the time," she said. It was like getting into the pockets of a dead woman. The faint perfume of the handkerchief was like the scent from withered burial wreaths.

"Maybe I ought to bring your muff next time."

"No, I said it's too nice for here. Something might happen to it."

"You'll want it when you leave, though."

"You'll come after me, won't you?"

"What do you think?"

"You might bring the muff along that day. A signal."

133

"All right. It won't be long. Kik said today that you'll be going to Staff very soon."

Can I ever fake it? How long can reflex action carry you through?

The store was a little drug store with tables and wire-backed chairs and a soda fountain. She had always thought of Juniper's store as being just a storeroom, but it was a real store. Oh, maybe not entirely real. Some of the customers were not real. You could tell. You could tell when you were one of the unreal ones.

Robert seated her at a table and then he went to get the sodas. It was self-service, he explained. She sat there, trembling. Alone, alone, and some of the people around her were well people. Were they looking at her and thinking there is one of the sick ones, there is one of the people who live here? I won't let them scare me. I'll look at them.

She looked around the room and she saw Lola and Lola was sitting with a little old bald-headed man and grinning like a Cheshire. She waved at Virginia. Virginia waved but not vigorously. She had a feeling that Lola's athletic wave must look very strange to the real people who were here.

Robert said the sodas were good, but Virginia was too self-conscious to taste the drink. At the next table an old lady was trying to persuade a young man not to eat his sundae with his hands; she swiped at him now and then with a napkin. At another table two men were having coffee. I can't tell which is which; maybe they can't tell about me. She looked at Robert. No, no one would ever think he might be the one. Whereas I was always rather silly-looking. It isn't fair.

Robert talked about what was going on in town. He had been to see Helene; he told a funny story about one of Helene's radicals. When he laughed Virginia knew it had been a funny story and so she laughed too. "Oh, that Helene," she said. We are talking just like people.

He told her about a play he had been to. Afterwards he was invited to the apartment of one of the cast; he had met so many people, in these months, that she did not know. "It sounds like fun," she said.

"But nothing's fun," he said, "when you aren't along. But you'll be along very soon, darling."

He told her about their plans, how the family had arranged for them to stay at home with them until Virginia was well enough. ". . . well enough for a place of our own." He told about Mag and Ted and the baby. Virginia listened. No, she didn't listen. She put on the face that a listener wears. Reflex action. Slower, Robert, slower. I can't follow. I can't keep up. I'm not as well as you think.

And then Lola came over to the table and grinned that deplorable toothless grin. Only two teeth out but two very important teeth. "I've worried so much about you thinking my husband was him," she said. "I wanted to be sure you saw him today."

"I see him," said Virginia. The little old bald-head over by the door. "I hope everything is working out."

"It's going to be wonderful," said Lola. "My husband's going to let me have a divorce and the children. So as soon as I get out . . . But I mustn't keep my boy-friend waiting."

"I should have introduced you," said Virginia to Robert after Lola had rushed back to the boy-friend, "but I don't know her last name. And anyway, things seem different here."

"Yes," said Robert, "they do."

135

There was another way to look at it. You had always heard that crazy people think themselves sane. Does it follow then that if you think you are crazy, you are sane?

Dr. Kik, when she saw him, went on at great rate about how much better she was; like Robert, he talked too fast for her. He never seemed disturbed by her answers and so they must have fitted. How long could she continue the pretense? Or was she mistaken?

The nearest well ladies of Two treated her as if she was one of them. They told her about the few who were not so well. They talked a good deal about going to Staff, about going to One, about going home. Like people outside they talked a good deal about themselves. Virginia had been no slouch about talking. While the ladies talked she remembered that once she had been a talker, but now she sat silent and pretended to listen, pretended to understand. The few necessary responses made her feel as if she had been climbing mountains. "You are so sympathetic," said one lady. "I can tell you everything and you understand what I mean."

And Virginia wouldn't know if this lady was just starting on everything or just finishing; she would not know how long she had been sitting with the lady; it made no difference to the lady but it made a difference to V. Cunningham.

Wise people say I am almost ready to go home. If I am going to be this way the rest of my life I would rather be dead. But that is not the choice.

What you heard about Staff was not reassuring. All of the ladies were scared of Staff; quite a few of them had been there once or twice and they shuddered when they spoke of their experiences. Virginia tried to listen, to pick up pointers, but all she picked up was the terror.

As the days ran faster she moved in a thickening fog and Staff came closer.

Mrs. Fledderson rounded up the candidates and gave them a cheery send-off. She acted as if they were going to a party. She laid it on a little too thick and the ladies giggled nervously.

"You're my honor students," said Mrs. Fledderson. "Go in and pitch. You're the first team." A muscle in her face twitched and her smile might have been built by an undertaker.

An assistant nurse took them away. Silently they marched down the corridor to a little room where the nurse said they would wait. The ladies sat in a row on folding chairs. Now and then the nurse went out to the hall. She seemed uncertain about the procedure and her manner destroyed any remnant of confidence Virginia's reflex might have retained.

At last the nurse called out a name. There was a smothered laugh, or was it a sob, and then one lady got up and went out. After a long time she came back. "They don't tell you anything," she said. "I don't know. They don't tell you anything. They just write things. Every time you open your mouth they write something down."

"Now, now," said the nurse, "don't get the ladies upset."

Another lady was called.

This went on for a long time.

Finally Virginia was called. She got up. She had on her glasses but she couldn't see. She stumbled after the nurse. Going through the door she struck one of her shoulders against the door frame.

The nurse took her to a room where six or eight or

maybe six or seven people sat. They sat facing an empty chair. She looked for Dr. Kik but she could not see him.

Someone told her to sit down. The only vacant chair was the one facing the audience.

"Now, Mrs. Cunningham," said a voice that was all wrong, "just make yourself comfortable. We want to ask you a few questions." The man was standing near her now. It was not Dr. Kik. It was a short fat man with a harsh voice.

He asked her her name. He was holding a paper and she was sure her name was on that paper. "Virginia Stuart Cunningham," she said.

Her vision had cleared a little and she saw that the people in the audience had papers and pencils. When she spoke they used their pencils. Dr. Kik was not there. There were two women and the rest were men but none of them was Dr. Kik.

The man asked her where she had been born and when. Maybe I can get through it without my own doctor. Maybe I can.

"Where were you living when you became ill?"

"New York," she said.

"Where in New York?"

"New York City."

"I mean, where in New York City?"

"Manhattan," she said.

"Yes?"

"Yes."

"Mrs. Cunningham, what was your address in New York?"

I knew all the time that was what you meant. "I don't know."

The audience wrote intently.

138

"Come now, you know your own address. Just think a moment."

"I've forgotten it," she said. "I never could remember figures."

"What street did you live on?"

"I can't remember. We lived on Waverly and we lived on Ninth and on Tenth and I think there was another one, not Bleecker, but another one. Maybe Christopher." No, that's Helene.

"Is your husband still occupying your apartment?"

"Of course."

"You are sure of this?"

"No, but I think he would have said something if he had moved."

The audience wrote on the papers.

"Your husband has been here to see you?" asked the little man.

"Yes."

"How often does he come?"

"As often as the rule allows."

"How often is that?"

She looked at him in surprise. "Why, don't you know?"

There was a sound from the audience; the little man turned around for a moment. "Mrs. Cunningham," he said crossly, as if irritated by her getting a laugh he should have had, "I know. I know all about it. I am simply trying to find out if you know."

"I can't see what difference it makes. Would you change the rule?"

"How often are you allowed to have visitors, Mrs. Cunningham? Will you please answer the questions? It will make it easier for all of us."

"Once every two weeks, that is, my husband is allowed

to come once every two weeks. I wouldn't know about other visitors."

"What is your husband's occupation?"

"He's an auditor."

"Yes?"

"Yes."

"I mean, go on."

Why don't you say what you mean, you old fool? "Go on about what?"

"Please pay attention. Tell me about your husband's occupation."

"I couldn't possibly. I don't understand it at all."

The little man's face was getting red. Was he too warm? The room didn't seem warm to Virginia.

"By whom is he employed?"

"The Alden Hotels."

"*Alden* Hotels?"

"Yes."

"Are you sure?"

"Why, yes," she said. "The Alden Hotels. Maybe you've never heard of them. It's a rather small chain. He audits for their New York hotels."

"Are you sure your husband does not work for the Kraft Hotels?"

"He works for the Alden Hotels."

The audience rustled its papers.

"Mrs. Cunningham, would you recognize your husband's handwriting?"

"Of course."

"Will you look at this?" He held his paper out for her to look. He pointed to a line written in Robert's hand. "What do you see?"

"I see that he has written that his employer is the Kraft Hotels, Incorporated."

"And you still insist that he is employed by a chain called Alden?"

"Of course not. If he says Kraft, it is Kraft. Obviously I was mistaken. I'm sorry."

She knew she had not been mistaken. Somehow they had got Robert to write the wrong name. She felt very ill. She thought she was going to faint. The little man was waggling a finger close to her nose.

"I understand you were distressed to be without your glasses," he said.

"I am very nearsighted."

"Yes?"

This meant give further information. "Minus five point seven five minus point twenty-five . . . five. That's the right. Minus five point. . . ."

"What are you talking about?"

"I thought you wanted my prescription."

"That will not be necessary. Have you had your lenses changed recently?"

"Not for several years."

"How do you explain the fact that you remember a rather involved and lengthy prescription when you can't remember your home address?"

She hated this man. "There is nothing mysterious about it," she said. "You don't expect to forget your address and so you make no effort to memorize it."

"And you made an effort to memorize your prescription?"

"Yes. I've always had a horror of losing my glasses away from home, where I can get a duplicate pair."

"Doesn't your address seem important to you?"

141

"I don't suppose I'll have to find my way back there alone."

One of the women in the audience nudged the man who was sitting next to her. The session might be going well for the audience but it was going very badly for the patient and for the examiner. His face was nearing purple now. "Mrs. Cunningham," he said, "a friendly attitude will get us along more rapidly. Now, to get back to Mr. Cunningham, who is employed by Kraft Hotels, Incorporated. You are certain that he is residing in your former apartment?"

"I was," she said. "Of course now you have made it obvious that he isn't."

The little man shook his finger again. He was shaking it so close to her face that in a moment he would be striking her.

CHAPTER NINE

"Do you know Mrs. Fledderson?" Virginia asked the woman who was standing next to her.

"Sure," said the woman. "Say, what do you take me for?"

Virginia looked around the dayroom. Perhaps this was Two. It didn't look the same, though. They were always changing things at Juniper but now they seemed to have changed the ladies.

I was in Two. I and several other patients started out to go to Staff but something happened and I never got there.

A strange nurse came into the dayroom and Virginia got up. "Not now," said the nurse. "Wait till I call the Sorting Ladies."

"Could I speak to Mrs. Fledderson?"

"I'm afraid not. She's in Two, you know."

Virginia sat down again.

Later the nurse came back. "Sorting Ladies," she called.

A half dozen women went over to her. Virginia watched them and wondered what Sorting Ladies were. The nurse looked at them and then she looked over at Virginia. "Virginia!" she said.

Virginia got up and went over to her.

"You are taking Virginia with you this morning," said the nurse. "Valerie, you introduce her to Miss Rowe."

"Yes, Miss Torrel," said one of the ladies.

"Virginia, you do what Miss Rowe tells you."

"Yes, Miss Torrel," said Virginia. I used to know a boy named that. I wonder if she's any relation. He wasn't very cute either.

"All right, ladies. Here is Miss Jenkins."

Miss Jenkins was a student nurse. She didn't have her cap yet and so Virginia paid very little attention to her.

"All right, ladies," said Miss Jenkins.

They went out into the hall. Virginia looked back and saw that the door said Ward Five. What had happened to Two? It had to be somewhere; Miss Torrel had said Mrs. Fledderson was there. "I don't belong here. I'm in the wrong place."

"You mustn't talk," said the lady who was Valerie. "We're going to the sorting room. You have to be good or you won't get to go again."

"What happened to Two?"

"Ladies," said Miss Jenkins uncertainly, "you shouldn't ought to talk in the halls."

They went down several flights of stairs. The stairs seemed familiar but then all very plain things are alike. It was just a concrete and steel stairway. Very fireproof. When they passed a window Virginia went as slowly as she dared. She looked out and saw that it was a dull gray day.

They went down into the basement and then through another hall. There were lights in the hall but there were deep shadows. Valerie walked along as if nothing could leap out from the shadows.

They went into a room that had long tables stacked with white stuff.

"Good morning, Miss Rowe," said Miss Jenkins.

"Good morning, Miss Jenkins," said a large woman in a light-blue house dress. "Good morning, ladies."

"I have a new one for you this morning," said Miss Jenkins.

Valerie pulled Virginia forward. "This is Virginia," she said. "Miss Torrel said to tell you."

"Hello, Virginia," said Miss Rowe.

"How do you do," said Virginia.

"Connie," said Miss Rowe to the tall girl who stood beside her, "here is a new one for you."

"Christ," said Connie.

"No, Connie," said Miss Rowe. "The more hands, the lighter the work. . . . All right, ladies, let's get busy."

The ladies scattered around the tables and began to throw things. Connie looked at Virginia. "I hope you can count to ten," she said. She swept her hair out of her eyes. As soon as she took her hand away the pale-brown hair fell back. Virginia wondered if she had just washed it and was letting it dry. It was very long fine straight hair and it hung free from restraint other than the continual sweeping of the girl's hands. "We stack things into piles of ten. You have to get it right. Otherwise some wards would be without and some with too much."

"I see," said Virginia.

"You might as well start here," said Connie. She pushed her hair away and pointed to the nearest table. "There are nightgowns, pillowcases and sheets. You sort them into piles of ten. Ten nightgowns, ten pillowcases, ten sheets. . . . Do you get it?"

"Yes," said Virginia. "Three different piles."

"Four," said Connie. "Four, for God's sake."

"You said nightgowns and sheets and pillowcases. Are some of the sheets double and some single?"

"Nightgowns, slips, pillowcases and sheets."

"Would you show me which are pillowslips and which are pillowcases? I don't know the difference."

"Holy Mary," said Connie. "Slips. Underwear. Nightgowns without sleeves."

"I beg your pardon."

"When you've finished this table come and tell me. I'll come and check your work. I'm the checker."

"I see," said Virginia.

She stood at the table and sorted out the linen. Linen in a manner of speaking. When she finished she went to Connie and said she was through. Connie came back to the table with her and flipped through the stacks. The checker found that almost every pile was either one short or one long or perhaps two. "You can't make mistakes like this in a hospital," she said in the manner of an old doctor to a dumb intern.

Virginia counted the piles over and over but Connie could always find mistakes. Counting this stuff was difficult because it was already folded. It was almost impossible to tell the things apart; they were made from the same material. But if you unfolded something to try to discover what it was, Connie rushed over to you and said what the hell were you doing. "Do you think we fold this stuff up just for you to unfold?" she said. In a twinkling she straightened out the mess Virginia had got into. "It just takes a little concentration," she said as she swept her hair out of her eyes.

Connie looked to be around twenty. She was wearing a pretty dirndl of hand-blocked linen, real linen, and her blouse was of sheer batiste edged with Irish crochet. Virginia thought she had never seen such a beautiful costume.

When Miss Jenkins came back she rounded up the ladies

and took them back upstairs. They went to a washroom that was somewhere in back of the door that said Ward Five and then it was time to go to dinner. In the dining room Virginia sat beside Valerie and Valerie talked to her the way a professional person talks to a colleague. Valerie was very fond of her job in the sorting room. She said Miss Rowe was wonderful and that Connie was beautiful and didn't she have the most beautiful clothes.

"Who is she?" asked Virginia. "Is she a nurse?"

Valerie smiled. She had a front tooth out and one eye tooth out. She was a heavy set woman of about forty and there were streaks of gray in her untidy dark hair. "She fools you, doesn't she? She's no nurse. She's sick. She's awful sick. She's been in one hospital after another ever since she was a child. Her folks are rich. Her father teaches in a college."

"For goodness' sakes," said Virginia.

"She isn't ever going to get well," said Valerie, in the pleased tone that normal women use when discussing hopeless ailments. "She's got a drag, though. You aren't supposed to be in this building if you are that sick; you aren't supposed to be here unless you are for sure going to get well. She doesn't even live in a ward."

"She doesn't?"

"No. She and Miss Rowe have a room somewhere in the building. Miss Rowe isn't a nurse exactly, but she's a housekeeper or something. I don't know. But Connie is awfully sick. Gee, she sure can light into you if you make a mistake. But she sure can tell the dirty stories when she's feeling good. She'll start in again after you've been with us for a while. She never likes the new ones."

"That's something. I thought it was just me."

"She socked me a couple of times when I was new."

"How awful!"

"It's nothing," said Valerie. "I could kill her easy. But if she socks you, just remember not to sock her back. She's got a big drag. I socked her back the first time and there was an awful stink. I almost got sent back to tubs."

"Do some of the ladies have to do the washing?" asked Virginia. "Don't they have machines for all that heavy stuff?"

"Why, I suppose so," said Valerie. "Sure. Why?"

"You said something about tubs."

Valerie stared at her and then she laughed. "Say," she said, "you don't know much, do you?" She turned to the lady who was sitting on the other side of her. "Esther," she said, "here's a good one. Virginia thinks tubs means laundry."

Esther craned her neck and looked at Virginia. "She does?"

"I guess she hasn't had much experience," said Valerie. "Kid, I was in tubs for weeks and weeks."

"Me too," said Esther.

"She doesn't know what we're talking about," said Valerie. "Look at her."

Esther looked at her. "I guess she doesn't."

"Sure, she doesn't. She doesn't know anything. Do you, kid?"

"I guess not," said Virginia.

Valerie chuckled. "I bet you don't even know what shock is."

A shiver ran through Virginia. "Yes," she said. "I know what shock is."

"Honest?"

"Yes. It's a little room and there's a red glass eye and they put some paste on your head. . . ."

148

"She knows," said Esther. "Don't talk about it. It makes me sick to my stomach."

"Well, I can't understand it," said Valerie. "Knowing about shock and not knowing about tubs."

"Every case is different," said Esther profoundly.

"But shock before tubs, Esther. I don't get it. I had tubs and then I had shock."

"Me too," said Esther. She looked suspiciously at Virginia. "I bet she did too."

"I bet so too," said Valerie. "It stands to reason."

Dessert was finished. They had had a sort of bread pudding made of stale cake and a thin sweetish gray sauce. There were lumps of cornstarch in the sauce.

The ladies went back to the washroom. Some of the ladies smoked. Virginia looked in her box but she had no cigarettes. She didn't care one way or another.

They hung around in the dayroom for a half an hour and then Miss Torrel said Sorting Ladies. Along toward the end of the afternoon Connie told a dirty joke.

ii

Virginia was very lucky to get in with Valerie. For a time she did not realize this. In some ways she reacted to things the way she had reacted to reality. In life you got into the habit of taking good things for granted. You had always had friends. You had never known how it felt to be left out and so you would never have thought about your present good luck if Esther hadn't told you. "You're lucky to get in with Val," said Esther. "She doesn't take up with everyone. She's hardly sick at all."

"I know," said Virginia. "I would say she isn't a bit."

"It's sex," said Esther. "It's too bad they can't do something about it. My own trouble is nothing in that line, of course."

"Of course," said Virginia.

"She's over-sexed," said Esther, "but don't you ever tell her I said so. She's my best friend. We came in at the same time and we were in tubs together."

How could you be in tubs together?

"Of course she's in love now," said Esther, "and that makes it so much worse. She doesn't see that she hasn't got a chance with him. Not him." Esther put on a face that evidently was supposed to portray him. She arched her eyebrows and looked as if she smelled paraldehyde. "Personally, I don't see him at all, but don't tell her I said so. She really thinks she's going to get him. She read a book where it happened. I keep telling her that what you read in a book is all hooey but she keeps saying it can happen. Anyway he's too young for her and he's too high and mighty to have a mother complex. Not that I say she's old enough to be his mother, but he thinks he's so smart. I hate foreigners."

"Is he a foreigner?"

"Say, you ought to hear him. Worse than Charles Boyer."

"I always liked to hear Charles Boyer."

"Not me. I don't fall for that stuff. I hear he's bald-headed."

"I don't care," said Virginia. "I like to hear him talk."

"Not me. Me, I'll take an American any day," said Esther. "Cary Grant's the one for me."

"I thought he was an Englishman."

Esther snorted. "Well, since when is an Englishman a foreigner?"

"Since the Revolutionary War," said Virginia primly. She can't beat me. I know.

"Gee, you sound like Colonel McCormick," said Esther. "Why, are you from Chicago?"

"Sure, I'm from Chicago," said Esther belligerently. "Is there anything wrong with being from Chicago?"

"I'm from Evanston," said Virginia.

Esther looked at her for a minute. "Yeah," she said. "Yeah, you would be." She called over to Valerie who was washing out some stockings. "Val, what do you know? Virginia here's from Evanston."

"Where's that?" asked Valerie.

"You see," said Esther to Virginia. She laughed. "I feel better. Evanston. Where's that?" She raised her voice again. "It's the Athens of the Middle West, Val."

"No kid!" said Val. She rinsed her stockings and took them over to her hanger. "You better get undressed, you two. She'll be back in a minute."

Virginia began to undress. She noticed that several of the ladies were looking enviously at her and Esther and Valerie. We are the Upper Crust of Ward Five. And Val's the Ring Leader.

Valerie deserved to be Ring Leader. She was the only Ward Five lady who smiled regularly. The nurses depended on her and gave her little responsibilities. When a nurse went out of the room she left Valerie in charge. The ladies always did what Valerie said. One lady explained to Virginia that Valerie really was a nurse just fixed to look like a patient. Virginia gave this possibility serious consideration. It might be. Valerie might be a sort of spy. It didn't seem possible, but you knew a boy back home who gave the impression of being the sweetest boy alive and he was a labor spy. His family bragged about how he dressed up like a laborer and mixed with the common people. They thought him a regular Mr. Mata Hari saving the world from the CIO.

So Valerie might be a spy. So Virginia always tried to put her best foot forward when she was with Valerie. She did wonder, though, if a spy wouldn't have pretended a little illness. There simply was nothing wrong with Valerie. Esther, the next nearest well patient in Five, had periods of being very queer. There were times when Esther was ready to slaughter anyone who looked at her. Virginia wished they would take the woman away when she had one of her spells, but Valerie never minded. "Just keep clear of Esther today," she would say nonchalantly. "She's not feeling so good."

And Valerie was a great help to Virginia in the sorting room. When Mrs. Rowe and Connie were occupied elsewhere, Valerie would come over and straighten out Virginia's tangle. Then Mrs. Rowe and Connie would say, "See, you can do it." Virginia never once got the sorting done properly by herself, not even once.

"You'll get onto it," Valerie would say. "Some people just haven't got that kind of mind, I guess. Take me. I was always a whiz at housework. That's why I got so sick of teaching school. I always wanted to keep house."

"I didn't know you were a teacher."

"Yeah. Primary. I didn't mind the kids, but the mothers got me down. Always this and that, this and that. I keep telling Dr. Kik I liked the kids and that the mothers were the ones . . ."

"Is Dr. Kik your doctor?" Virginia hadn't thought about him being anyone else's doctor, but of course you couldn't be his only patient. "He's mine, too."

"I don't believe it," said Valerie.

"Well, he is."

"You never said so."

"You never asked me."

"What does your doctor look like?"

"Like Dr. Kik."

"Describe him."

How different Valerie was looking; you were almost afraid of her. "Well," said Virginia, "he's got light hair. I think his eyes are blue. I don't know for sure. I suppose they are."

"Suppose!" said Valerie. "They're as blue as blue."

"Yes, he would look funny with brown."

"Go on."

"Val, you know what he looks like. If he's your doctor . . ."

"So you think he isn't my doctor?"

Virginia moved a little away from her friend. There was no nurse in the washroom just now. "Of course I think he's your doctor. Why shouldn't I? Goodness, you don't suppose I think I'm the only patient he has, do you?"

"I bet you think you're his favorite."

"Don't be silly."

"I know," said Valerie. "Just because I've only been to Normal you think he's more interested in you."

"No, Valerie. I don't. I hardly ever see him."

"Huh," said Valerie, "I bet you're in love with him."

Virginia had to laugh at this. "Why, Val, what a thing to say. What would my husband think?"

"Some women aren't satisfied with one man," said Valerie. "Red-haired women," she added darkly.

"Look," said Virginia. "I'm in love with my husband. It's a bit thick for you to start talking this way just because my hair happens to be slightly auburn."

153

"Slightly!" said Valerie.

"I've seen redder," said Virginia.

"Where?" said Valerie. "Just tell me where."

This happened shortly after dinner. That afternoon Valerie didn't come to sort the stacks for Virginia and that evening at supper she sat on the other side of Esther. In the washroom Esther told Virginia she never should have let Valerie know she had a crush on Dr. Kik. "It was mean of you to let her know," she said.

"I haven't got any crush on any doctor," said Virginia.

"You better lay off Kik if you don't want to get into trouble with Val," said Esther. "Don't say I didn't warn you. I don't think it was very nice of you to get her so upset. She's been fine for weeks and then you come along and talk about taking her man away from her."

"I won't bother to get mad about this," said Virginia. "It's too silly."

"If they take Val back to tubs you'll know whose fault it is," said Esther. "I suppose you'll be glad."

And now Valerie came charging over to them. "Talking behind my back," she screamed at Virginia. "I'll report you, you little two-timer. I'll tell him and then you'll be sorry."

"Watch out," said Esther. "Miss Torrel's just outside in the hall."

"I'll tell her too. You just see. You can't get away with that stuff, Virginia Cunningham Bitch."

"Valerie," begged Esther. She caught hold of the distraught woman's shoulders. Esther wasn't so large a woman as Valerie, but she was younger; it looked as if it would be a fair match.

The ladies in the washroom stood at a safe distance and watched.

Virginia had already prepared herself for the night and so she slipped out of the washroom. In the hall she met Miss Torrel.

"What's going on in there?" asked the nurse.

"An argument, I guess," said Virginia.

The nurse rushed into the washroom and Virginia, no longer being a medication lady, went quietly to bed.

The next morning Esther appeared with a bruised eye, and a long scratch on one cheek. The scratch had been treated with iodine and looked pretty bad. "I guess they took Val away to tubs," she said to Virginia. "Serves her right. Scratching me like that. Last time she put on her act they took her away for a couple of days but this time I hope they'll keep her till I go home. She just puts it on to get more attention from that man. She's no more sick than I am. She just puts it on so he'll palaver over her. Baloney."

Virginia was glad Esther didn't blame her for Valerie's relapse, but all the same she was blue about it. Without Val the sorting was impossible. Miss Rowe and Connie were very cross. They said with two new ones, Virginia and the one who was replacing Valerie, they didn't know how they would ever get anything done.

Connie, who for days had been telling dirty jokes, never opened her mouth except to scold a worker. Miss Rowe said maybe Virginia would do better in the sewing room and when Robert came Virginia had to tell him that she had flunked out of sorting.

iii

But before he came a strange thing happened. It happened the afternoon before his visiting day. Virginia had been relieved of her work in the sorting room and she was spending a day on the ward. Miss Torrel had said there was no point in starting in the sewing room until after visiting day. And so Virginia was sitting in the day-room and thinking about nothing much when all of a sudden there was a man standing in front of her. He had not come into the room. "Mrs. Cunningham," he said. He was a short fat man.

She looked for Miss Torrel, but there was no nurse in the dayroom. The other patients were way off at the other end. "Yes?" she said. How had he escaped from his own quarters? He must have come in through one of the windows. I was looking right at the door and I never saw him come in. But he's too fat to get through the window. Why don't those fool women do something? Call a nurse!

"Mrs. Cunningham," said the little man, "just why did you bite me?"

"Bite you—why—I wouldn't bite you."

"You bit me," he said.

How tired I am of this place. First they accuse me of being in love with someone who isn't Robert and then they come around and say I bite them. "No one would want to bite you," she said. "You are a very nice person, I'm sure." Get his mind off of violence. "If you would just lose a little weight . . ." That should do it. Fat people like to talk about how they eat practically nothing.

The little man looked hard at her. I never should have said that. He's touchy on the subject. "I didn't mean it critically," she explained. "Personally, I think a little extra weight is very becoming. But they do say that when a person gets older . . ."

He turned from her and went to the other end of the room. He began to talk to some of the other ladies. Virginia got out of her chair and crouched behind it. If she saw someone being hurt she would go help them, but in the meantime it was just as well to have the chair in front of you. I can hold him off quite a long time. Like an animal trainer.

It wasn't long before Miss Torrel came and took the little man away. Until now Virginia hadn't given the woman credit for being much but now when Miss Torrel led the little man away quietly Virginia knew the nurse was all right.

She sat down in the chair. Her knees were weak and her hands were covered with perspiration. I won't tell Robert about this. He has enough on his mind without having to worry about the way they let their dangerous male patients get into the women's building. I'll tell him about the sorting-room fiasco. I'll have to because Kik already will have told him anyhow. I hope Dr. Kik knows how much nightgowns and slips and pillowcases and sheets look alike when they are all made from the same goods and all folded up.

"And you see, Robert, by the time you've decided what one thing is you forget what your count was for that pile."

"Darling," said Robert, "don't think about it. It wasn't important."

"But it was. They were furious."

"No," said Robert. "No, they weren't. It's just occupational therapy, something to make the time pass. You mustn't get the idea it's anything serious."

"Well," said Virginia, "it is interesting to me that most of their occupational therapy gets work done that they would have to hire out otherwise."

Robert laughed. "Cynical, aren't you?"

They were sitting in the visitors' room. Only one other Ward Five lady was entertaining today; it was almost like being alone together. Robert had brought a box of candy and some fruit and they could smoke in here. When he started to light a cigarette for her Virginia asked if he minded letting her do it. "Let me have the matches," she said.

He handed her the folder.

"First time I've done this in a long time," she said. After she had lighted her cigarette she considered asking him to let her keep the matches. But it wouldn't do any good. He wouldn't let me keep them.

Robert was different today. He was acting as if she had just had a serious operation that hadn't been quite successful. He was so gentle that she felt as if she was dying. Maybe he's lost his job. I wouldn't expect that to worry him much, though.

After a while he asked if she would like to take a little walk. It was a bad day out, he said, cold and raw, but they might go to the store for a cup of coffee; it wasn't far.

They were going toward the store when Virginia saw the fat little man. He was approaching them. He was walking rapidly. "Oh, Robert," she said. There was no time for further warning.

"Good afternoon, Doctor," said Robert.

The little man grunted. He tipped his hat. He passed them as if in a great hurry.

"I went to see him after that staff meeting," said Robert. "After Kik told me what happened."

"What did you say, dear? I was thinking about that terrible little man. I wasn't going to tell you but he . . ."

"Kik told me. Darling, we all owe you an apology. It's

my fault, really, but I didn't think to tell you. I didn't want to worry you and anyhow I didn't see that it made any difference. The damn fool. Making such an issue of it. If Kik had been there . . ."

Of course when you are ill you don't expect to understand what well people say. Virginia walked along and wondered what Robert was talking about. She kept thinking how funny it was that he had called that little man Doctor. Of course he assumed that any man loose around here was a doctor.

They went into the store. Robert seated her and then went to the fountain to give their orders. When he came back she said it was terrible the way she was always starving when he was visiting her. "I act as if I can't think about anything but food."

"It would have been different if Kik had been there," said Robert. "He had to go out of town. If I'd known it I would have done something. I don't know why he didn't have you wait. Sometimes I . . . No, he's a wonderful doctor. Everyone says so. And he was really sick about it. Not that that helps matters so much. The fat was in the fire. Of course he explained everything to Curtis and Curtis was decent about it. I mean, he said he was sorry he hadn't known I hadn't told you about going with Kraft. It was while you were in the other hospital. Kraft bought out the Alden chain."

"Other hospital?"

"The one in town. I never knew they'd be asking you things like that. Well, Curtis apologized."

"Curtis?"

"He's head of Women's Reception," said Robert. "That little guy we just now passed."

Carefully Virginia set her coffee down. No matter how

startled I am, I do not spill things. "I thought he was a patient."

Robert laughed. "I'd like to tell him that. The numskull. And I told him I hadn't said anything to you about giving up the apartment. I don't know why he had to go into that. I didn't want you to think about it. I hope it hasn't worried you."

"No, it hasn't," she said. "All I've been worrying about is counting to ten."

"You take things too seriously."

"Well, I'll tell you one thing, Robert. That Dr. Curtis may be a doctor and all that, but he's definitely queer. He came into our ward yesterday and asked me why I bit him. What do you think of that? I think they better put him in those tubs they are always talking about."

Robert put sugar into his coffee. He had already put a sickening amount into it. When he wasn't sure if he had sugared it he didn't try it to see; he put in more.

Her joke fell flat. "I suppose they can't help it," she said. Yes, the joke was in poor taste. "Being around sick people all the time. Just the same I think he's too fat."

"Kik smoothed it over all right," said Robert. "He said it didn't have anything to do with them deciding you should stay a little longer."

"I knew I hadn't passed," she said. She looked across the room and saw a girl she recognized. She did not remember where she had seen the girl, but she had known her somewhere here in the hospital. The girl was rouging her nose. It could happen to anyone in an absent-minded mood, anyone with a double compact. Virginia shook her head and pointed to her nose, but the girl continued to use the rouge. Then she put the compact away and she and the man she was with got up and left the store.

"Why didn't that man tell her?"

160

"Tell her what?"

"Tell that girl she had rouged her nose. Didn't you notice?"

"Yes," said Robert. "But, look, honey, I was just thinking . . . It might be a good idea to be nice to Curtis if you ever see him again. I think he's kind of a grouch."

"I tell you he's nuts," she said. "Saying I bit him!" She looked at Robert, but he was avoiding her eyes. "Robert! I didn't, did I?"

He stirred his coffee. If he put more sugar in it! "Well," he said, "I guess you did. Anyhow, that's the story."

"But when?"

"When he was asking questions, I guess."

She sat back and thought. I remember a little. "I remember that he was always wagging his finger in front of my face."

"He had no business asking you those things. Heckling you. The old fool. Kik as much as came right out and said he's an old fool."

"Did I bite his finger?"

"It's over now. It doesn't make any difference."

"I can't help laughing," she said. "Excuse me. What did Dr. Kik say?"

"Well, he said he'd often wanted to do more than bite the old buzzard. . . . But look, Virginia, Curtis is over Kik. Remember that. Next time you want to bite someone, darling, don't make it such a big shot."

She stopped laughing. "I know it isn't funny," she said. "It isn't like me to go around biting people."

"Forget it."

"I wish I could remember it," she said. She ate the last of her sandwich and Robert said they had better be getting back. He had returned her to the ward and gone away before she remembered that she had not asked him where he was living. It was odd not to know where your husband was living.

I must have him write the address down for me. I'll take a pony along the next time I go to Staff. I'll hide it in my handkerchief. . . .

The next morning she asked Esther about Dr. Curtis and Esther said he was a swell guy. "He gave me a candy bar once," she said. "Say, Miss Torrel says you're going to sewing with us today."

"Yes," said Virginia.

"Swell."

"Have you heard anything about Valerie?"

"Don't mention that woman to me," said Esther. "I hope she's in pack."

"Your scratch is almost gone."

"It's no fault of hers. She tried to kill me. I hope she's in pack. There's two things I don't like about this place and one is that Valerie and the other is that Valerie." Esther threw back her head and laughed.

In the washroom a lady named Rosabelle came up and whispered to Virginia to watch out for Esther. "I heard her laughing in the dining room," said Rosabelle, "and I thought I better warn you. When she laughs that way it means she's going to have one of her bad spells."

"Thank you," said Virginia. "I'll be careful."

"I'll read your palm," said Rosabelle. "Sometime I'll read your palm and tell you the rest."

iv

When she was asked if she had ever used a sewing machine Virginia made the mistake of saying yes. "But not for a long time," she said.

162

The woman who was in charge said that didn't matter. Virginia waited for her to say it was like riding a bicycle. The woman said it. She added that the sewing was simple. She gave Virginia a stack of bathrobes and a lot of little white squares of cotton material. "Labels," she said. "All you do is turn the edges under. No basting. Just sew them on the robes. Nothing to it."

Some sewing machines start forward; some start backward. The machine Virginia was assigned started forward when you pushed backward and backward when you pushed forward. It was one of the bobbin-eating type. The bobbin was always empty. It took you ages to refill the bobbin and then you couldn't make it stay in the machine.

Virginia's first day, also her last day, in the sewing room was very difficult.

After that she stayed on the ward. She helped out with the ward chores and then sat around and talked with the other ward-bound ladies. Or just sat around. Except for Florence, none of these ladies was very interesting. Florence was the one who had charge of the radio. She would not permit anyone else to go near it. She had made a rule that only classical music could be played in Ward Five. Virginia would have liked to discuss music with Florence but Florence was friendly only with the Great Masters. She stood on guard at the radio and tapped her foot. She stood with her arms folded until someone came near and then she turned into an effective windmill.

The routine of Ward Five was similar to what you had known in other wards. You bathed, that is, you were permitted to share a shower twice a week. Once a week you were fine-combed and once a week you could put in a store order. If you had credit at the store. You had three meals a day. At breakfast there always was a bowl of glutinous cereal. At dinner there was a bowl of pale-brown stew, also sticky. At supper there was another sort of stew, but without the shreds of meat sometimes found in the noon mixture. The desserts were cottage puddings and custards and sometimes jello; on Sunday there was ice cream.

You assumed that the food was nutritious; there could be no other reason for serving it.

You were weighed once a week. After dinner. If you forgot what day was weighing day you could tell by the meal. Weighing-day dinner was always the biggest of the week. Virginia ate more bread and drank more water on that day. Dr. Kik and Robert had said she must gain weight.

One weighing day Esther, who had recovered from her bad spell, assisted greatly by putting one of her feet on the scales. Virginia weighed five more pounds that day and the nurse was delighted. It was bad the next week, though, when Esther was beginning on another tantrum and you had no help.

Miss Torrel took store orders for the stay-at-home ladies in the afternoon when the other patients were still off at work. Virginia went to the office to give her order late one afternoon and just as she started to say what she wanted, Miss Torrel was called away. "Just a minute," she said to Virginia. "I'll be right back."

After waiting at the desk a while Virginia began to walk around. The office had a door she had not noticed before. She tried the knob, as a matter of routine, and was delighted to find that the door was not locked. There could be no harm in peeking. Probably just a coat closet.

She pushed the door open. It was a little toilet or, as

they would say in Evanston and other centers of culture, a powder room. The porcelain was plain white, however, and there were no fishes painted on the walls. Virginia stepped in to look more closely. Near the toilet was a roll of paper on a chromium fixture and there were a half dozen towels on the rack beside the washbowl. A very clean piece of soap lay in the soap indentation. The soap had a pleasant woodsy scent.

She had put the soap back when she heard someone enter the office and so she quietly pulled the toilet door shut. A moment later someone said her name. She pushed the bolt cautiously. The door locked easily.

It had been a long time since she had been alone. She lowered the toilet lid and sat down. The toilet lid had no muff of cotton fur, but when you had not seen a frame or a lid in so many months you did not ask for the muff. I'll sit here a few minutes and enjoy being alone. When Miss Torrel leaves the office I'll go back to the dayroom.

"She was here a minute ago," she heard Miss Torrel say.

"Well," said another voice, "she's not in the dayroom."

"Look in the dorms, will you? Under the beds."

As if I would get under a bed! What do they take me for?

The office was quiet for some minutes and then Miss Anderson came back and said she had looked high and low. "She isn't anywhere on the ward, Miss Torrel."

"Nonsense," said Miss Torrel. "Of course she is. Go find her."

Virginia leaned on the washbowl. It wasn't very comfortable. She took the towels from the rack and folded them into a pillow and then she lay down on the floor. She was used to lying or sitting on a floor. None of the dayrooms she had been in so far had had enough chairs to go around and so the ladies had used the floor a good deal. Except in that hoity-toity One.

She was awakened by Miss Torrel's voice. ". . . in here and when I came back she was gone. She can't have got out of the ward, Miss Anderson. You know that."

"Well, I can't find her. I give up."

"I'll find her," said Miss Torrel. "I know all their tricks."

There was silence again and Virginia went back to sleep.

She was awakened by someone trying the door. She got up. She picked up the towels and hung them on the rack.

"Sorry," said Miss Torrel. "No hurry."

So Virginia rearranged the towels and then sat down.

"I hope you don't think it's my fault," came Miss Anderson's voice.

"Of course not," said Miss Torrel. "I was with her last. I assume you wouldn't have let her get past you and into Six."

"That door was locked. Ever since it's been unlocked Miss Thomas has been standing there. I had her take over before I started to search the dorms."

"She couldn't possibly have got away," said Miss Torrel. "Say, did you just now come into the office?"

"Why, yes. I just now came in. You saw me."

"How did you get past me and into the hall? Really, this place is getting on my nerves!"

"But I already was in the hall. I was talking to Miss Thomas and asking her to check in her dayroom and then I . . ."

"My dear, when I tried the toilet door . . ."

Suddenly Virginia couldn't hear what they were saying. They were whispering. Then Miss Torrel spoke up. "Virginia," she said. "We know you are in there. Unlock that door and come out at once."

Virginia's hand was on the bolt. She was ready to leave the little toilet, but there was something about Miss Torrel's voice that she did not like. She dropped her hand to her side.

"Virginia!"

She looked out of the window. She could never squeeze through that narrow opening, but neither could they.

"Virginia, you don't want to stay in that stuffy place. Come on, dear." This was Miss Anderson, and psychology.

Virginia smiled. "I'm not coming out until Robert comes," she said. Inspiration. "I won't come out until you send for my husband." I knew that eventually I would find a way to get out of Juniper Hill. I knew it. I knew it. I've finally got them. He will come and he will take me away.

It worked. The nurses argued a little but then they went from the office. They had gone for Robert. They had said so.

In a surprisingly short time they were back. They said he was here. He must have been on the way. Perhaps they notified him as soon as I was missing. Yes, it has been at least an hour. He could have got here by now.

She unbolted the door. Where was he? Rules. Rules. Couldn't they let him come into the office, just once? She shot past the nurses so quickly that she did not hear what they said. She was hunting Robert. He was here. They had said so.

She ran into the dayroom.

Ward Five's dayroom connected with Ward Six's. Sometimes the door between the two dayrooms was opened. This was not done to let the Five and Six ladies stare at each other, but to permit one nurse to oversee both rooms. There was a nursing shortage. Now, with Miss Torrel and Miss Anderson occupied in rounding up a patient, one of Six's nurses was doing the honors for both wards.

"Robert," called Virginia. He had to be somewhere.

She dashed past the Ward Six nurse and into the strange dayroom.

They caught her, of course. Someone tripped her and she fell. Instantly her head was encased in a sack and someone was sitting on her legs. The sack was bound tightly around her chest and she could not breathe.

There was no time for suitable thoughts. You would think smothering to death would feel very different. You felt as if you were being blown up with a tire pump and yet what was being forced into your chest was vacuum. I am going to burst I am going to burst I am . . .

CHAPTER TEN

THE sea slashed at the rocky coast and sometimes a wave
—it would be the seventh—would strike against the walls
of the prison. High tide. High tide.

The cell's only piece of furniture was the narrow bed
on which she lay, and the walls were bare and plain save
for the window. She had never seen the exterior of the
building, but the slotlike opening told her what the tower
was like. A small high building of stone. She was bound
but she saw the building with its turret top. And the
island. Now at high tide not much larger than the building, a handful of stones dropped by a giant. No grass, no
weeds, no bushes or trees. The gulls circled and then
swooped away. Sometimes a large boat passed at a safe
distance and passengers who knew no better said there is
a lighthouse.

She could wriggle her toes and her fingers, but otherwise she was tied down tightly in cold wet cloths. It was
winter and the cloths would have frozen had they not
been drenched with salt water. It was night.

Far on the fog-hidden shore Robert was finishing his
share of the plot. The boatman would have been engaged
days ago. The old one, the knowing one, the one who
had done it before. Now he and Robert would be setting

out on the dangerous journey. Careful, careful, not too close to the island. Robert would not know how the stones sucked heedless boats close, to dash them to bits. But the fisherman would know. He would not allow amateur anxiety to urge him beyond the sea-edge of the great waves. Again he would explain how he had rescued the other one and Robert, remembering the book, would become less strained. He would touch the waterproof package of blankets and think how before long she would be in the boat and wrapped in the blankets. He would touch the knife brought to cut through the heavy canvas and he would feel for the flask of whisky. Again and again he would go over his list to reassure himself. The boat, the trustworthy and experienced boatman, the car waiting near the dock, and at home the fire laid and hot-water bottles warming the blue percale sheets.

He would ask the boatman if he could be sure they would reach her before she drowned, and the boatman would repeat the story of his famous rescue and Robert would wonder if the old man remembered it as it had happened or as he had read about it afterwards.

There were so many unattractive aspects in the plan. Though I am cold and wet already. . . . Nevertheless the raging of the waves terrified her and she wished they would hurry hurry, Robert and the boatman. Her share of the plan was to die. The boatman, for all his bragging, hadn't had this sort of case; Edmund hadn't had to do his own dying. He had a friend to do it for him, but I have no friend here.

She began on the dying. She let herself get colder and colder. She had been doing this some minutes when a man came into the room. Perhaps the boatman had arranged for a friend, after all. The old man's lighter than I thought, the jailers would say in this case as they threw the sack into the sea.

But the man leaning over her was neither old nor ill. He spoke to her, but she did not understand his language. He put a hand on her forehead and then she knew he was one of the jailers. She closed her eyes and resumed her role. In a moment this jailer, this man with the deceptively solicitous voice, would rush into the hall. Well, he would say, she's gone. The redhead, he would say, she's dead.

The other jailer, the older one, would groan and say what a nuisance on such a bad night. We'll get good and soaked, he would say.

Let it go till morning when the sea's down a bit, the young one would say.

But the older one would shake his head and say a rule is a rule.

They would come with the canvas sack and put her into it and they would carry her up to the turret and one—two—heave. They must throw wide of the rocks. They will. They would not want the mess. One—two—through the air. Deep into the cold water. For a terrifying moment the weight of the ocean would clamp her to the bottom, but then slowly she would begin to rise. Robert and the boatman would catch the canvas with their grappling hooks and the ascent would become rapid and then they would hoist her into the boat and quickly slit the dripping shroud.

I thought I saw a boat, the old jailer would say.

Who'd be out on a night like this? the young one would say.

It was such a night he escaped. Him that I've told you about. Before your time, lad.

You've let that become an obsession, dad, the young one would say. Anyhow, boat or no boat, she was deader than a cod and twice as cold.

Colder now. The old one would shiver. Bad night, he would say.

The young jailer's hand left her head. He said something. It was a question; she knew from the lift in his voice. She did not open her eyes. She heard him move from the bed but she was careful to keep her eyes shut. He might look around quickly to test her.

Now it was a matter of waiting until he found the older man and then the two of them would go for the canvas coffin. The younger man might complain, as they went for the shroud, that too many of the prisoners died. You don't give them enough covers, he might say, and what they've got is cold and wet from the sea splashing in at the windows.

But the older man would shrug and say he did his job. You look out for your job, young man, he would say. They've no use for modrun notions with featherbeds and la-de-da.

She was young, the young jailer would say—the young always touched by the death of the young.

Better for her dead then, the old man would say.

But she might have escaped—some time.

This would make the old man stop short. Might have, might she? You and Dumas, boy. I know it happened the once but anything can happen the once. It hasn't never happened since.

. . . breathing shallow breaths so your chest will not rise. Now they will be coming back down the hall with the canvas. Now is the time. Now.

Under her closed lids she rolled her eyes high.

So smooth a road was an irresistible temptation for some drivers. Not for Virginia. She was a slow one; she was more interested in seeing where she was going than in the going. But she was not driving and the car raced the scenery into a solid brown mass.

They were in the mountains and the barren hills rose up like walls from the narrow road. Where are the warning signs and the white-topped posts? Dare I ask to stop a little to look at the view?

It was a new sort of automobile; she was alone in the front seat, but she was not the driver. She never would have driven at this rate. Sixty miles an hour. Eighty miles an hour, maybe a hundred. She felt for the pedals but her feet were swathed in blankets. No, I absolutely am not the driver, I have no wheel or anything. It is a back-seat-driven machine. Invented at first as a joke and then found to be practical. Anyway speedy. Watch out!

Straight ahead was a mountain that rose at right angles from the road. The driver would have to see it. It rose as high as the sky and was only a few yards ahead. Virginia pushed hard on the floor of the car as if she had had brakes. She leaned forward, prepared to leap. The blankets were a disastrous impediment.

The car swerved and the smash was avoided by a hair. Holy Mother of Jesus.

The car stopped. The driver, undoubtedly shaken and ashamed, came around front. It was a woman.

"A close call," said Virginia. She tried to laugh a little. No use to heckle now that it was over.

The driver unwound the blankets. "All right," she said.

Virginia tried to rise, but the floor went around. "I must be dizzy," she said.

The chauffeur pulled her up. "Lean on me and you can walk."

"Of course," said Virginia. "It was just that last turn."

They went toward the sound of water and they came presently to a steamy place. It was a sort of hot springs. It must be a cure. Yes, there was a nurse. You'll have to pay extra for this. And going up the mountains in a private car with a chauffeur. Have I sold a book to the movies? Hail Mary, Mother of Jesus.

"Good morning, Society Lady," said the nurse.

Society lady? The chauffeur?

"How's it going?" asked the chauffeur.

"Can't complain," said the nurse. "How'd your party go?"

"Ouch," said the chauffeur. "Don't mention it. The head I've got."

"Well," said the nurse, "it's fine if you have the water-works for it. All right, Society Lady, take my arm." She held out her arm to Virginia.

"Watch it," said the chauffeur. "Had a little oubletray this morning. It ickskay and itesbay."

"Oh, hell," said the nurse, "I and the Society Lady get along like a house afire. Trouble with you, Kate, you don't butter them up."

"I'm sick of it," said the chauffeur. "I got my name in the register now. Believe me, when I shake the dust of Juniper Hill from my feet . . ."

Juniper Hill. That is the Death Mountain. "Me too," said Virginia.

"You see what I mean," said the chauffeur. "One minute completely utsnay and the next . . ."

174

"Tie a can to it," said the nurse sharply. "Come on, Society Lady, it's getting late."

The nurse took Virginia into a cubicle where there was a tub. "Not a bad idea," said Virginia. The perspiration was still running down the backs of her legs.

She stepped into the tub. She was not able to get all the way down into it, though. "There's something in it," she said to the nurse. "Cloth or something."

"Never mind the gags, Society Lady. Just lay down."

Virginia lay back in the canvas hammock that was swung in the tub. There was a pillow, a very hard pillow, for your head. The tub was filled with water but the tap was still running. "I'd like it a little warmer, please."

"I never saw one for being so cold," said the nurse. She pulled a wooden gadget out of the tub and looked at it. Then she dropped it back into the water. "Right on the nose. Body temperature, Society Lady."

"My body is cold. More hot water, please."

"You lay back and relax." The nurse threw a sheet over the top of the tub, as if it was a bed, as if the sheet would warm the wretchedly tepid water. "There now, take a little shut-eye."

"Sleep in a tub? That's a very dangerous thing to do. Don't you know that more accidents happen in the bathroom? Not that this is a bathroom but . . ."

"I'll keep an eye on you. Just you relax, Society Lady."

"What society?"

"Hm? Oh, Ultra. Very Ultra. Look, I can't hang around and chin. I got my work. But I'm keeping an eye on you, so don't you worry none."

"The person whose blood they measured to find out how much to warm this water," said Virginia, "was a fish. A dead cod." This was philosophy; the one who said this

175

was not utsnay. I don't like that chauffeur, calling people utsnay when she can't drive any better.

"That's telling them," said the nurse cheerfully.

She could afford to be cheerful. She had a sweater on over her uniform. She folded Virginia's robe, looked at that wooden thermometer thing again and then went away.

She had forgotten to turn off the water. At first Virginia thought she was going to be drowned. She was tied into the tub in some way and could not get out. Then she realized that her head was higher than the tub and that the whole room would have to start filling up first. And the little room was only a part of a long hall that had lots of little nooks like this and they would all have to fill up first. You could not figure all this out if you were utsnay.

She heard water running elsewhere and she heard voices. If the water filled the whole spa then it would run down Juniper Hill and into the sea, the cold water, the wet always and the skin sloughing from the palms of my hands. I am very tired of the water cure.

When she opened her eyes the nurse was back and saying it was time to move. With the assistance of the nurse she got out of the tub. She hoped the trip down the hill wouldn't be so swift. I do not like the chauffeur. No wonder people ickkay and itebay her. If I were you, auffeurchay, I would watch out.

Wrapped in the robe she was led into another cubicle and the nurse said to get into the tub.

"Is it different water?"

"Yep."

"It looks the same. I thought medicinal waters were colored." She got into the tub. She did not want to. If

176

my hands keep on peeling I will have no more hands. But anything to avoid the ride. "I didn't wash before," she said. "Could I have some soap?"

"You're clean as a newborn babe."

"Are they clean?"

"Don't go technical on me, Society Lady."

"I think I would like to go to the bathroom."

"Well, go ahead. Don't mind me." The nurse spread a sheet over the tub.

"I have to go to the toilet, nurse."

"Go ahead."

"You'll have to help me out."

"Look, Society Lady, if you gotta go, go."

"In the tub!"

"The water's changing all the time."

"I think that's perfectly disgusting."

"Don't give me that, Society Lady."

"What's the point of changing tubs?"

"It's the law," said the nurse. "We are getting around the law, but don't you worry about that."

"I am tired of being in a tub."

"Relax." The nurse inspected the thermometer and then readjusted the taps. "A degree over," she said. "Maybe you did that, eh, hot baby?"

"Remember to turn off the tap before you leave," said Virginia. "You might have drowned me the last time."

"It runs out as fast as it runs in. Nothing to worry about."

The nurse went away. The next time she came she had a tray. "Here is your lunch, Society Lady," she said.

"My name is Cunningham," said Virginia. "Mrs. Cunningham."

"I know. Mrs. Cunningham."

"I don't know your name."

"Johnson."

"Miss?"

"Don't need to rub it in. Here. A lovely lunch. Make you feel like a million. Tomato juice cocktail."

"Thank you," said Virginia, "but I do not care for any lunch."

"Come on now." The nurse shoved the cup at her.

Virginia closed her mouth and turned her head. For a long time Miss Johnson tried to shove food into her mouth. Once she caught Virginia off guard but Virginia spat the bit of potato out onto the sheet.

The nurse went away and after a while she came back. She was talking to someone with her. "Of course you aren't supposed to be in here, Mr. Cunningham," she was saying, "but we thought . . . Virginia, your husband is here. He's going to give you your lunch now. Isn't that nice?"

The man sat on the low chair beside the tub. Virginia looked at him long enough to see that he resembled Robert very closely. Then she turned her head away. They had fooled her once, but they could never fool her again. They had put her head into a sack the last time. I remember. I remember very well that they fooled me about him coming and then they put my head into a sack. I am not utsnay enough to fall for that trick again.

The man talked and talked. She would have told him what she thought of anyone who made a business of masquerading as other people's husbands, but she knew if she opened her mouth he would stick food into it. She was smart. She kept her mouth and her eyes shut tight and after a while he went away.

When she opened her eyes another man was there. It

178

may have been the same clever impersonator; it may have been himself as himself. This time he was not calling her darling as he had done before; he was calling her Jeannie now. But he was harping on the same subject. Food. She would throw up in his face.

They had let the water run out of the tub but the bedding was sopping wet. They had taken the tile walls away and enlarged the cubicle to make it look like a room. They had even put a window into it. Oh, the trouble they went to. They couldn't be satisfied with electrocuting you and choking you; they had to bundle you up in icy wrappings and then torture you with food. Say it again and I'll scream.

He said it again. "Jeannie, you must eat." His accent was heavier than Boyer's; it was almost as thick as Senja's. He thinks he is going to persuade me to take this poison. What a fool. Ya ga to hal. See, I can speak your wretched language.

His hands were on her shoulders. "Jeannie, come now, you must eat."

Robert will have the satisfaction of knowing I fought for my life. This man will win. He always has won. But not easily. Ah, no, I have caused him trouble before and I shall cause him plenty now. Come now, indeed.

Come into the deep hole. It was not like falling. First you were not there and then you were there, deep in the dark. She wanted to tell the man where she was. I have always told him everything. He means well. Yes, I must remember that he means well. Robert said so and Robert knows. But how can you speak from the bottom of a deep hole? I'm too tired to shout. And the quicksand is seeping into my nostrils.

She opened her eyes to blinding light. She was out of

the hole, but the quicksand continued to flow into her nose. She tried to speak, to ask him what in God's name he was doing, shoving a tube into her nose and forcing mush into it.

She strangled and started to cough, but the mush continued to pass through the tube. She could see his hands. Delicate hands for a man. Thin and rather bony and with traces of very fair hair. He was holding the tube. In the brilliant round of light was another pair of hands. These were fattish, womanish hands without hair.

Tottering on the edge she tried to keep her balance but again she sank into the hole. When she came up again the circle of intense light had merged into general paleness and the man was winding up the tube. "There, Jeannie. There, there," he said. "It is over."

Now she saw his face and she shrank close to the bed as she recognized him. It was the Young Jailer.

iii

Occasionally she was aware of being moved from a tub to a bed. From a wet hammock to a wet bed. During this long period there was no normal eating. The tube business happened again and again and eventually she understood that it was a way of feeding her. When she neared the top of the hole and found the tube in her nose she wanted to tell the Young Jailer she would gladly eat if he would give her an opportunity, but she was unable to speak. The quicksand of the hole pulled her down and stifled her attempts at speech.

Then gradually she began to come out of it; gradually the periods of being out of it lengthened and now she walked from bed to tub and from tub to bed. And the time came when she went to a small room that had a table and two long benches and there, along with several other robed creatures, she ate meals of gravy and gruel. She ate eagerly. The food was revolting looking and tasting stuff but she had learned that by eating it she avoided the tube feeding.

Sometimes the real Robert came to see her. She tried to talk to him, to tell him how cold she was, but all she could do was cry. She wept while Robert talked quietly to her. She liked to hear his voice, but she never knew what he was saying. It was terrible when he went away. He went away and the old routine of tub and bed and meals in the little room was resumed.

An icy draft blew in around the windows at the end of the tub room. In front of the windows a nurse sat at a desk and marked on papers. She wore a sweater and had a coat over the back of her chair. All of the nurses in the tub room wore sweaters but the patients went from tub to tub in sheets or in cotton robes. When the wind was blowing hard and cold the tub water, when you first got into it, felt good. It always cooled, though. The nurses said not, but by the time you had to move on to another tub the water seemed as cold as the winter wind.

Now came days when Virginia watched the women with whom she ate her meals. These women never talked to each other. Now and then one of them would speak, but she was not speaking to anyone in the room. Virginia decided that she would start talking but she could not think of anything to say and her throat was stiff and shy and so she watched.

There was one woman who had great energy. This one wound her sheet into a reasonable facsimile of an evening gown. She wrapped it tightly around her breasts and tucked it snugly around her waist and fixed the skirt so that it dragged. She went around the little room elegantly kicking the train out of her way. She spoke frequently, but not in English. She was a graceful and rather beautiful woman and Virginia admired her and wished she could understand her language.

There was another woman who spoke often. This one always sat, sat and mumbled. Whether her language was English was not to say; she had no visible teeth and her lisping might have been anything. Virginia watched this woman and the elegant one and remembered them. The others might have been different ones each time the little group met in the small dining room.

After the meal the nurse came and took them away. Usually two nurses called for Virginia. Great strapping women with large arms, they lifted her up to a bed as if she was a baby. They bounced her on the wet sheets and expertly wrapped her into the frigid cocoon.

"That's quite a trick," she said to them one night. "A dirty trick."

The nurses looked at each other. "Well," said one of them, "it's nice to know you can talk. You are always so quiet."

They spread a dry sheet over her. Why? No bit of the dry sheet touched her. It was not to be endured. Hurry and get out, you two, so I can hurry and get out.

She watched with a purpose this night but they worked too rapidly. She was unable to memorize the motions that created the cocoon. It was not, however, to be endured. So when the nurses left she began to get out of the mummy trappings.

It took a long time.

First she wriggled under the wide binder that was

tucked between the mattress and the springs. This took a very long time. For a while, when her head was under the binder, she thought she would never manage it; it was like crawling out of your own skin. Free of the binder she twisted her body until she could swing the lower part of it over the side of the bed. After sliding to the floor it was comparatively easy. Using her teeth, good strong teeth and none missing, she loosened the twists that went over her shoulders and then swayed from side to side until the sheets unwound.

She stook naked and free in air that felt comfortingly warm. She took the dry sheet to the radiator and made herself a tent. To be warm in winter. One of the very finest things in life.

When she became sleepy she went back to the bed. She shoved the wet sheets way down to the foot of the bed and, wrapped in her dry sheet, curled up on the rubber mattress. She would, she promised herself, wake up early enough to rewrap herself in the wet sheets but instantly a voice was screeching. "Virginia—how on earth! Who put you in pack last night?"

"I don't know," said Virginia.

"How did you get out?"

"I was cold." Why had morning to come so quickly?

"Well," said this morning nurse, "I'll attend to your pack myself tonight and that's for sure."

Yes, this one who thought she was so smart, this one attended to Virginia's pack that night and maybe it did take Virginia longer to get out of it. Maybe it did. But she got out and she had another comfortable sleep. And the next night they put a large canvas spread over her bed and they laced this spread under the springs in some way. The spread had one hole in it, for your head. It was most unsporting. No one could have got out of that pack. Virginia heard some of the nurses saying that no one had ever got out of an ordinary pack before. When the very smart nurse wasn't around, the not so smart ones called Virginia Mrs. Houdini. They seemed proud of her but at the same time they gave her no further opportunity. Although one night something very nice did happen.

After the evening meal a nurse left the dining room door open when she took one of the patients away, and Virginia lost no time taking herself away. She was wise enough not to run. Walk to the nearest exit, she said to herself firmly. But then she remembered the keys and so she started to search for a dry bed. She looked and looked and finally she found one. It was in a dark little cubby, but it was made up with dry sheets and two blankets. She got into the bed and when the wind rattled the window she made herself into a ball and she smiled.

She awakened before the Good Morning Ladies. Hearing sounds in the corridor she knew it was time to get up and so she got up and went to the little dining room and when the nurse came with the trays nothing was said. There was a crying need for nurses. Virginia had heard the nurses say this again and again; she had heard them arguing about what duties belonged to what nurse.

That night when she went again to find the dry bed someone was already in it. Clinging to shadows she scouted around for another bed and at last she came to a room as large as a dayroom. In it were mattresses, on the floor. A dozen or more beds were made up on the floor. Most of them were laid with wet sheets folded in the diabolically exact pattern. Better get out of here. . . .

"Oh, Virginia. Wait a minute."

It was too late. The nurse had seen her.

The nurse consulted her chart. "Dry bed," she said. "Well, you might as well take that one."

"Thank you," said Virginia. She got into the dry bed. The Juniper floors were no harder than the Juniper cots, and a dry bed, no matter where it is, is luxury. She had never been able to sleep well on her back and of course that was the wet-pack position. Flat on your back, feet and legs straight, arms and hands straight; fair enough in a coffin but cruel in a bed. Inevitably your nose would itch.

V. Cunningham never had to sleep in a wet bed again. It goes to show that you have to use a little initiative. Also it goes to show that when there are more wet-pack patients than there are nurses to make up the packs—you have a fair chance.

And not long after this the tub days came to an end. During the daytime Virginia stayed in the dayroom, the room which became the large dormitory at night. In the daytime the mattresses were piled up in a corner and several long benches were pulled out from the walls. The ladies who spent their days in this room wore long shirt-like garments or gray terrycloth robes with numbers stamped on the back.

The two women who had been with Virginia in the small dining room were now with her in the dayroom. The foreigner attempted to convert her robe into an evening gown and she walked around and around and seemed at times to be welcoming guests to a formal reception. The old toothless one sat on the floor and mumbled. There was another old one. This one had a white beard that would have been stunning on a diplomat, preferably a male diplomat. Sometimes Virginia wondered if the bearded person was a man.

But the days, in spite of the bearded lady and the

foreign belle, were extremely dull. Most of the ladies just sat and looked at nothing, at any rate at nothing Virginia could see.

Sometimes she thought. Thinking was very difficult. It was far more painful than the exercises you have to do after a major operation. I must start to think, she would tell herself, but then she would put it off for later in the day. One of the difficulties was not being able to hit upon anything to think about. She tried verbs: run, ran, run, amo, amas, amat and that sort of thing, but her supply was limited. Finally she asked a nurse if she might have something to read. "I shouldn't read without my glasses, I suppose," she said, "but if there is something . . . I don't care what. An old magazine or something."

"Something to read!" The nurse spoke as if the patient had asked for a shotgun.

"I haven't anything to do," said Virginia.

"I'll speak to Dr. Kik," said the nurse. "I think it's time for you to be transferred myself but I'll have to see what Dr. Kik says."

"You are awfully crowded, aren't you?" said Virginia.

"Dear me," said the nurse, "I wasn't thinking of that."

All the same it was this nurse who sounded off that night about not being able to locate enough mattresses. "I've got used to not having enough cots to go around," Virginia heard her saying to another nurse, "but when there aren't enough mattresses, I give up. They seem to think Ward Twelve can get along without anything— just because our ladies . . ."

"Did you say anything to my doctor?" Virginia asked this nurse when she came around with the paraldehyde.

"Yes. You are being transferred."

"Good," said Virginia. She tried to read the nurse's eyes. "Or is it?"

"I think it will stick this time," said the nurse. "I really don't think you'll be coming back to Twelve again. You're going to Eight. You've made great improvement. You're so much better than you were the other times you left us."

Other times? What other times? Now surely I would have remembered a place like Twelve. The nurse must have confused me with another patient. They couldn't remember everyone . . . Says I'm so much better and that it will stick this time. I doubt if I can think any better than many of the ladies in this combination dayroom and dormitory, but there is one thing that's in my favor. I know about bathrooms.

She hoped the patients in Eight would not be too bright, but at the same time she did hope they would be housebroken.

CHAPTER ELEVEN

SOME of the Ward Eight patients were employed off the ward. They were the Upper Classmen. Virginia prayed that she would be allowed to remain an Under Classman.

You wanted to get well. You never had a conscious moment in which you were not aware of being sick. You could no more, while conscious, forget your sickness than you could forget to breathe. Asked your greatest wish in life you would have replied at once—sanity. How remote was the world in which sanity was taken for granted. In the world outside, people longed desperately to be millionaires, movie actors, club presidents and even, tell me little gypsy what force creates this one, even novelists. True, a bad cold, a touch of heartburn, an allergy to a favorite dog's hair, could blot out for a time the desire for money, power or fame. During the period of the running nose, the stomach ache or the asthmatic wheeze physical well-being would stand alone in the spotlight of yearning. But nowhere, nowhere save in a madhouse, did mental health get its share of prayers.

At Juniper Hill there was one real god, one real goal, one real love. The patient who possessed the smallest seed of sanity cherished it tenderly. And yet V. Cunningham did not want to be sent off the ward to work. Though she wanted, above all, to be well, she cringed from the transition period and when the time approached when she might be considered intelligent enough to count to ten she became limp with fear.

The nurses in Eight rapidly fell into the habit of treating her as if she had more sense than she actually had. They were good nurses; they gave her her glasses almost every day and she was not required to drink paraldehyde. They complimented her upon the way she did her ward duties and seemed unconcerned when she dipped a dry mop into a bucket. Of the sicker ones they appeared to consider her their star. The time was coming near. She practiced counting to ten. She could quote long passages of Chaucer to herself but she could not always be certain that seven came after six.

When the promotion came she was somewhat relieved to discover that her work squad went out of the building. Led by a nurse they went to a street she had never seen. Facing each other were two rows of three-story houses. Had each of these red-brick houses been off to itself you would have thought it an ordinary dwelling, but here in the double row the houses were unmistakably institutional. "Staff houses," said Virginia's marching partner. "We do Number Nine."

Inside, Number Nine looked like a house, something like a house. From the hallway you could see a segment of a living room that was not at all a dayroom. Virginia hoped that some day she would get to enter this room but she never did. Her job was on the second floor.

Her job was to scrub the floor of a large washroom and to scour the fixtures and polish the mirrors. After that was finished she did private bathrooms. The large wash-

189

room was reminiscent of a ward washroom, except that it was fully equipped, but the private bathrooms reminded you of home. In the little bathrooms were bottles of perfume, bath salts, medicines, personal towels, bath mats, stockings and lingerie drying on racks. . . . She always did the washroom first, to get it over with. She didn't, at first, skimp her work in the large room, but she never lingered over it. It was a pleasure, however, to go into the private suites where there were carpets and pictures.

The buckets were heavy and the exasperating problem of the wet and dry mops was always with you; the water was hard and the soap cruelly strong and your hands, after the first day, were continually raw and chapped. But the work was so much better than you had anticipated and the housekeeper said you were a good girl. "You aren't built for it," she would say, "but you are doing fine. Sometimes the strong ones just throw things and splash water all over."

But a perpetual backache is annoying and sore hands are a nuisance and after having spent a morning at House Nine, Ward Eight was browner and more depressing than ever. And one morning something happened that made you nervous about House Nine.

One morning when Virginia was scrubbing in the large washroom a man came in. She tried to be nonchalant. She thought about postmen being invisible and she hoped scrubwomen were equally endowed. She went casually into the hall while the man was going, not so casually, to one of the booths. She had not known it was a men's bathroom. When, fifteen minutes later, a woman came into that room she was very confused and she asked the housekeeper about it. And the housekeeper said the room was for both sexes.

When Virginia raised her eyebrows the woman grinned and said, "Scientific people. They are above such things, you know."

After that Virginia was not painstaking with her work in the large washroom. She did not approve.

Most of the ladies in the House Nine Squad seemed to take their work in their stride and if their backs ached they did not complain. Of an afternoon Virginia would have given a great deal to lie down on a bed. You could stretch out on the floor any time but when your back hurt so terribly even one of the Juniper cots would have been welcome.

Ward Eight, after you had done your morning stint, was Liberty Hall. Oh, you couldn't go into the dormitories or private bedrooms, but you could do whatever you liked in the dayroom. Some of the ladies played bridge and Virginia was invited to join their club. They played a kind of bridge you had never encountered elsewhere. Perhaps you had encountered something like it but the people outside who played that way were never asked to play again. Here you could change trumps any time you felt like it and the game was one that could be played by any number of ladies. A trick might consist of five cards, seven, three, one, or none. However you felt. If you had good cards and wanted to save them to admire, all right. Or you could save them for a flourish at the end. No one ever bid and lost. That was the only rigid rule. You bid and then everyone else became your helpful partners. Sometimes Dummy played the hand for you. The dummy hand was seldom laid down, as that, thought the ladies, took the spice out of the game. They liked a game with spice. It was a good, friendly, though spicy game, and no one ever got mad. Everyone was given the bidder's score and so everyone came out even and everyone was happy.

One of the best players of the ward was going to have a baby, two babies, in Virginia's opinion, and very soon. When she was not playing bridge the expectant mother was weeping. She was so afraid that her baby would be born at Juniper Hill. "But you can always just tell it it was born at a hospital," Virginia would say. "You don't have to say what hospital."

But the girl was not to be consoled. She spoke continually of her husband with whom she was very much in love and who was always sending her nice presents. All the best ladies of the ward were very gentle with her and saw to it that she always had a place to sit. As there were at least four ladies to each chair this devotion required constant watchfulness.

In Ward Eight was a spirit of co-operation Virginia had never noticed elsewhere. She did remember that previously she had seen much give and take about cigarettes but as she had always been on the giving end she had not thought of this as being especially commendable. In Eight, though, you were also in on the take. When the ladies received packages from home they shared with everyone. When the store orders came through you divided with those who hadn't store credit. If you had wanted to be in Juniper Hill, Ward Eight would have been a good place to be. None of the ladies, however, wanted to be at the hospital. Whatever their troubles had been outside they were anxious to get back to them and with one exception they all knew where they were and approximately why. You would have supposed that the one who had no conception of her surroundings might have been happy, but Tamara was the most wretched of all.

She stood off by herself. The nurses warned the others repeatedly to stay away from her and as Tamara was tall and muscular and the owner of a glowering expression, the ladies obeyed.

Tamara had a fur coat which she wore to the dining room. The nurses tried again and again to persuade her not to wear it. The dining room was less than a hundred feet from the dayroom and the hallway was no colder than the dayroom, but Tamara would wear her coat. If they hid it from her she would not leave the dayroom. In an earlier period, the ladies whispered, Tamara had given them a tale about being a Russian countess. But one visiting day they had seen her sister in a maid's uniform. They laughed a little among themselves about Tamara's airs. Virginia said the fact that the sister was a maid did not disprove the countess tale, but the ladies said that fur coat was no countess' coat. It was very commonplace, simply dyed muskrat that would fool no one. Tamara had had five operations on her head, said the ladies, and was hopeless. They were very snobbish about hopeless cases and they blamed Tamara for being hopeless. Their attitude about hopeless insanity was very like the attitude outside. They hated Tamara for being insane.

Perhaps once a week Tamara spoke. She spoke to the nurses as if they were her slaves. "Get all of these people out of my house at once," she would say. The nurses said they couldn't understand why Tamara was saddled off onto Ward Eight where all of the other ladies were so nice.

But one time Virginia had a small experience with Tamara which made her wonder if perhaps there might be a chance for Tamara if someone were to bother to follow up an operation with a little post-operative care. There was a piano in Ward Eight and sometimes Virginia played it. Once when she was playing snatches of this and that by ear, Tamara came and sat on the bench with her. Virginia was so frightened that she thought she would fall off the bench, but she continued to play for a while. When she felt she could endure it no longer she said softly that now she must stop. And Tamara smiled at her and said, "Thank you so much, my friend."

And a nurse came flapping excitedly. "Virginia you know better than to get near Tamara."

"Sometimes a sick animal knows more about how another sick animal should be treated," said Virginia. But, to tell the truth, she was not unwilling to go away from the dangerous patient.

ii

It was days before she noticed the old lady. Oh, she knew the old lady's name was Jenny and that she had one of the dozen or so private bedrooms, the cubicles that were called bedrooms. But she had never really noticed the old woman until the afternoon that Jenny asked her to tea.

Jenny's room had a cot and a chair and it was so near the dayroom that the nurses allowed her to go there of an afternoon. Virginia supposed that the "to tea" was just a phrase and that Jenny simply wanted to show off her room. However, Jenny had a can of pineapple juice on her windowsill and that was to be the tea. Virginia asked if she should take the can to a nurse to be opened. The nurses were kind about opening things for you. But Jenny winked. She put a hand down into her dress and brought out a beer-can opener that was strung on a dirty string.

Virginia was horrified. There was a strict rule about things of this sort. One of the Eight ladies had been a professional manicurist and she kept the fingertips of the ward ladies, always with the exception of the dangerous Tamara, beautifully filed and lacquered. A nurse was never very far away when the manicurist was at work and the implements of the process were taken from her the instant she was through with them. And here sat old Jenny with a beer-can opener.

The juice was served in paper cups and accompanied by crackers. During the party Jenny told Virginia her personal history. All the time she talked she toyed with the opener. Virginia could not keep her eyes off the opener and she was glad when she could decently say it was time to leave. She and Jenny left together, of course. They went back to the dayroom.

The next day Jenny invited Virginia to tea again. And the day after that. She seemed to have an unlimited supply of pineapple juice and an inexhaustible personal history. While she talked she played with the beer-can opener. Virginia wanted to report the opener but how could you betray a fellow patient?

Of a morning you worked at House Nine; of an early afternoon you played bridge or took a nap on the floor; always of a late afternoon you had tea with Jenny. There was no way out of it.

It may have been partly Jenny's illness and it may have been partly her age; it may have been entirely Virginia's imagination, but the old lady seemed to have a very peculiar look in her eyes. When she glanced up from the can opener to Virginia there was a sort of contemplative expression in the old eyes. Before long Virginia was under the impression that Jenny was planning to kill her. She was marvelously polite to the old woman.

She never mentioned Jenny to Robert when he came

to visit. He was looking so tired and drawn these days that she could not bear to add to his worries. Although she was certain that he would be disturbed if he knew what she was fearing she also knew that he would not think her in any danger. He would think that on top of everything else she had got a worse persecution complex. Maybe I have. Maybe that is it.

But the sharpness of that can opener was not imagined. How easily it bit into a can. "Don't sit so far away," Jenny would say. "I'm a little deaf. I can't hear you when you are so far away. Come closer, my dear. Come a little closer."

And then one afternoon Virginia knew it was going to happen. Jenny opened the can, as usual, but then she set it back on the window ledge. She wiped the opener on her dress and looked at it a long time. Then she looked at Virginia. "A penny for your thoughts, dear," she said.

Virginia sprang from the cot. She ran out into the hall and to the office. A nurse, Miss Bixby, was at the desk. "Why, Virginia," said Miss Bixby, "what's the matter?"

Virginia tried to think. It had been urgent, she knew, to reach a nurse but now she could not remember why. Something awful was going to happen to her. "Get a doctor, please. Get my doctor, please," she said, as the floor began to soften and swirl.

"Take it easy," said Miss Bixby. "It's all right. Just hang on . . . Miss Jones! All right, Virginia . . . just hang on to me. Miss Jones, get . . ."

They were fighting their way through the deep varnish of the hall now. "Just hang on," said Miss Bixby.

"It's never happened this way before," gasped Virginia.

I never had such definite warning. I never had warning before that I knew was warning.

"Your doctor will be here in a minute. We'll go to meet him. We won't have any trouble at all. See, it's not far to the door."

Virginia bit her lips. "Take my glasses," she said. "I would hate to break them."

Miss Bixby took the glasses. "You are going to be all right," she said. "It may be just something you ate. You are just feeling faint."

She spoke without conviction, all the time urging Virginia forward. Wants to get me out of her ward before it happens, wants to get me to wherever it is more convenient for them, wants to get me into his hands, slender hands for a man but they are strong.

It was coming rapidly now. Could he come so fast?

Miss Bixby opened the door. "You see," she said, "there he is. He is coming as fast as he can."

Virginia could tell that he was running, but she knew he would not reach her in time.

CHAPTER TWELVE

THE sun is shining. It is summer again. Again? Perhaps still.

Now white flakes, like snow, began to dance in the sunshine. There may be a bonfire near by. I would like to see a bonfire. I would like to sit near it and get warm.

"It's snowing," said someone. "High time."

"I was wondering what time it was," said Virginia. High time. It must mean time for high tea. She frowned. She did not like to think about tea time. Why? I always used to like tea.

But then she remembered something. She had gone to a tea where an old woman had tried to knife her. She tried to kill me and I ran and ran and the Young Jailer came to my rescue. Because he is under the impression that he is the only one who is permitted to kill me. Jeannie is my special interest, my major project, he says. Each day I kill her once, each week day once and twice on Sundays. Do not weep, he says when he finishes, it is finished and you are no more hurt.

She looked at the woman who had announced the time. The woman was a stranger with a cropped head. She wore a heavy red delivery-boy sweater and her nose was dripping. "Do you have a cold?" said Virginia to suggest that a handkerchief was needed.

The woman snuffled and the drizzle vanished. "Freeze you to death if they can," she said. "What did you say your name was again?"

"Virginia Cunningham, though you can't say again until you've said once. What's yours?"

"Margie," said the woman. "You talk like a school teacher. You must have been a school teacher."

"Must have been and was are two different matters," said Virginia wisely. "What time did you say it was?"

"About time for dinner," said Margie, "but I don't suppose you'll be wanting any. Not after the feed they give you after shock. What did you have this morning?"

"Oh, the usual," said Virginia. She squinted at the dancing flakes. Shock. The little room with the egg-beater smell. The Young Jailer bending over you and saying what a joker you are, Jeannie. "You make such jokes," he said. Jeannie. He does not even know my real name.

She put her hands to the small of her back. Yes, the wedge was there this morning. And touching her temples she discovered a trace of the paste. . . . A very low percentage of mishaps—I like that word mishaps—in connection with electric-shock treatments. I read that once upon a time when I had no interest in the subject. His assistant has a silly voice and there is another nurse who comes in to hold your legs down. You wake up in a different room and are given an enormous breakfast. One thing, I said to him, you get a decent meal for a change. And he said I was his little joker. Talking without thinking what he was saying, his hands busy. If anything goes wrong I hope you get it too, I wanted to say to him. Maybe I did. Maybe he thought that also a great joke. But I figured out that if he gave me too much he would get it too. He would be touching me, would he not? It would serve him right. Or has he some special insulation? Yes, he must have. Otherwise he would not be so light-hearted. They would see to it that they are always safe. No mishaps for the operators.

"I read somewhere," she said cautiously to Margie, "that shock treatments impair the memory."

"Never repaired mine," said Margie. "I got the most wunnerful memry. I member everthin that ever happened. . . . And lots that never did. How many shocks you had?"

"I don't know for sure. Sixteen or eighteen, I think."

"My," said Margie, "you must be real sick."

"I hate to forget things."

"I'd like to. Plenty I'd like to fergit. But I'm a Republican and a nelefun never fergits." Margie laughed and a shower of mucus sprayed from her nose.

Virginia moved away from her. She went to another window to watch the snow. Even though it had a false, theatrical look and vanished as soon as it touched the ground it probably was snow. It might be piling up on the other side of the building, in the shade. She started to cross the room to see.

In the center of the room was a rug. It was a nine by twelve, a ridiculous pale-gray stamp on the large brown floor. They did not have this before. But maybe it is a different ward. Yes, I have not been in this dayroom before.

It was a poor rug but it felt good after so many months of linoleum.

Someone was shrieking. Virginia turned to see what the trouble was. Margie was shouting for Miss Green. "Virginia's on the rug again," she called.

A nurse came into the dayroom and now she began to yell. "You get off that rug, Virginia Cunningham," she shouted.

Virginia got off the rug. She did not walk toward Miss Green but Miss Green caught up with her.

"We do not walk on our rug," the nurse said. "We have told you a dozen times. We do not walk on our carpet."

"Why not?" asked Virginia.

"Because we don't," said the nurse. "Understand? You can't come to this ward and do as you please. I don't know how you got along in your other wards but here we have rules and we stick to them. We do not walk on our rug. We are the only ward that has a rug."

Virginia looked at the rug. It seemed very ordinary. Twenty-nine seventy-five, you would guess. Maybe it covers a dangerous sink-hole. Maybe I barely escaped with my life. I was deep in a hole for a while and maybe that was the hole.

"And we mean to keep it looking like new," Miss Green was saying. "See that you don't go tramping all over it."

"You might hang it on the wall," suggested Virginia.

"Your wisecracks may have been appreciated in some wards," said the nurse, "but definitely in Fourteen they do not go over. That rug is strictly safe right where it is if you will keep your big feet off of it."

Virginia studied Miss Green's feet. About size nine. What's she mean calling a five and a half big?

"You've walked on it every day since you've been here," said Miss Green. "I am getting good and tired of it. I have my work to do. I can't come in here every few minutes to chase you off. It isn't as if you didn't know better."

"How long have I been here?"

"Too long," said Miss Green.

This was a new type of nurse. It is true that Virginia

had annoyed nurses before, but she had never seen one quite like Miss Green. Miss Green appeared to be hysterical. "I'm sorry," said Virginia. "I wish you could understand that I can't remember anything."

"Excuses all the time," said the nurse. "I never in all my . . ."

"Miss Green," screamed Margie, "Emma's on the rug."

A fat middle-aged woman was in the center of the rug and doing a rather good Charleston. She began to sing. Sweet Georgie Brown. "Oh, do let her finish," begged Virginia. "She's good."

But the nurse was now putting her own big feet on the rug

ii

Miss Green, though she acted as if she was the whole cheese, was not the head of Ward Fourteen. The head nurse was all right.

When Robert came to visit, Virginia told him about the rug and he laughed and said she had invented the story. He never would have said that if he had not thought her much better. It was most encouraging.

On Christmas Day, when he was allowed to pay an extra visit, he and the other visitors were permitted to come into the dayroom and Virginia was able to show him how vigilantly the patients were trying to keep the guests off the rug.

It was a sad Christmas in spite of the joke about the rug. In the morning the ladies were taken to the great hall where you had once seen a movie. There was no movie this time. A man stood on the stage beside a Christmas tree and led the patients in carol singing. Among the carols they sang that morning was Yankee Doodle.

When Robert came, in the early afternoon, he brought a large box. He brought Virginia two woolen nightgowns, some woolen underthings and a sort of hood that he claimed women on the outside were wearing. It was an absurdly childish cap but it was warm and anyhow things made no difference here. He had also brought a box from Margaret and Mother. It was an assortment of interesting food. She was not, said Robert, to pass this around as she had done with everything else. She was to give it to the nurse and just take one thing at a time. There were lovely cookies and all sorts of canape pastes.

"I should have done something about Christmas," said Virginia. "But it slipped up on me. I could have got you a little something at the store."

But Robert said her being so well was the only present he wanted. "You really are getting well now," he said. "There won't be any more set-backs."

"This is Ward Fourteen," she said. "Will I have to work my way back to One?"

"Absolutely not," he said. "You know, Kik told me he would hate to be stuck in One."

Virginia laughed at that. She remembered now how Miss Davis had disliked Dr. Kik. "She'd make it hard for him, all right. And I bet he wouldn't know the mops apart, either."

They took a little walk to try out the new hood. Robert pretended that she looked enchanting and maybe he actually thought this. In some ways he was a very stupid man. Often she had thought what a help it would be to have a critical husband who would tell you when your makeup wasn't right. Robert was no help. He always said everything was charming.

On their way out of the ward she called his attention

203

to the bedspreads. "I never saw them before," she said. "They were got out on account of company coming into the ward. So you see we have spreads as well as a rug."

Robert said it was all very swanky. He especially enjoyed the rug. "My God," he said, "if I had had any idea of what it was going to be . . . But it won't be long now."

It would have been cruel to remind him that he had been saying this for months.

During their walk he told her about his most recent interview with Dr. Kik. The doctor, he said, had been favorably impressed by her insisting upon going to a ward where there was no racial discrimination. Virginia had no recollection of any such insistence, but since the doctor had been favorably impressed she decided not to question it.

After the visitors had left, the ladies handed in their Christmas presents and the nurses locked the things up in the cupboards. Then the spreads were taken from the cots and locked away. The ladies went to the dayroom and waited for the call to supper.

Recalling Robert's odd story about racial discrimination, Virginia looked around the room and noticed, for the first time, that some of the patients were colored. One of the nurses was colored. Not Miss Green. Miss Green never would have tolerated that.

One of the colored patients seemed to be a special friend of Virginia. She brought her a candy bar. Virginia hated to take it; she was afraid that the girl had only the one bar, but the girl insisted. "You are always giving me things," she said.

The next day this girl and several other Fourteen ladies were invited to a dance which was to be held in the large theater. When the dancing party lined up Virginia saw that her friend had no hat. It was snowing heavily and so Virginia went to the closet, which was still unlocked for the benefit of the dancers, and got her new hood. She took this to the colored girl and after some argument the girl put the cap on. She looked very cute in it. She was young and pretty and the bright colors became her. "I won't take it off," she said. "Someone might steal it."

Just then Miss Green came around the corner. "What are you doing with Virginia's hood?" she said to the colored girl.

"I said she could wear it," said Virginia.

"Your poor husband," said Miss Green. "He tries so hard. Don't you know that cap came from Saks Fifth Avenue? And then you let a . . ."

"He would want her to wear it," said Virginia hastily.

The colored girl had shrunk back against the wall. Her round black eyes were full of tears. "I don't want to cause any trouble," she whispered. The hood was in her brown hands and she was holding it out to Virginia. "Please, I don't want to cause any trouble."

"You see, Virginia," said Miss Green. "It's people like you that stir up all this racial business. All right, Party Ladies! Form a neat line, if you please. Ladies! No talking! Ladies who do not form a neat line and who keep on whispering will definitely not be allowed to go to the party."

iii

One morning Miss Green brought a pile of coats into the dayroom and threw them on the floor. Then she read off a list of names and said for those ladies to put on the coats. Virginia rushed to the pile. Daring to throw my good coat on the floor!

After some shoving she was able to get to the pile. Her

205

coat was not there. Her name had been called but her coat was not there. It was a chance to trip the comically and pathetically important Miss Green.

"Take any one," said Miss Green. "It doesn't make any difference. Your own things have gone. Hurry up."

"Gone where?"

"Hurry up. The car's waiting."

So we are going out for a ride. Good. There was one coat left now and Virginia took that. It was very heavy. It was dark blue, a man's coat. The sleeves hung down beyond her hands and the skirt reached her heels. When she started to button the coat she noticed that the front was covered with some sort of dried paste, not, she hoped, gravy that had been eaten and regurgitated, exactly what it looked like.

The coated ones lined up near the hall door and then the head nurse came and said their names. "Well, ladies," she said, "be good girls and do what the nurses say. Good-bye."

The ladies said good-bye. Virginia glanced back to the part of the room where some of her friends were sitting. None of the ones she had been friendly with was in the coated group. The coated ones, strangely, were those she had always avoided, those she had considered too sick to be socially possible. But she waved to her friends. When you've not had a ride in about a year you can't be too particular. Her friends did not wave back to her. They were looking very unhappy. Several of them were weeping. Dear me, I wouldn't show my jealousy so plainly if any of them had got to go out riding.

Outside a car was waiting for them. "I don't know how we'll see anything," said Virginia as she got into the car. The seats were along the sides, as in a station wagon or, perhaps, a police wagon. When the rear door was closed the ladies sat in twilight. "I would about as soon have stayed behind," grumbled Virginia. "Where are we going?"

"No talking," said Miss Green.

The ride was very short. "Hardly worth the effort," commented Virginia. She was reminded of the time she and two friends went to the opera. It was during their freshman year at college and at the last possible moment someone had given them tickets for the opera. None of them had ever been to a real opera. They drove in town and parked where someone had told them to. It was a miserable snowy night and they all had on their dancing slippers. They huddled close to a building until they attracted a cab. "To the Opera," they ordered recklessly. Between them, they had decided, they would surely have enough to pay for it. The driver was very fresh. "No kidding?" he said. Then I said we were in a hurry and would he please drive us to the Opera at once. And he drove to the other side of the street. "Presto chango," he said, "here you are."

Well, here we are, back in a flash. The weather would not have injured today's chic costume, driver.

But they were not back. Though they went through a cage porch that was familiar they then went into a day-room that was different. Very different. There was no regular furniture. There was no carpet. As the coated ladies walked through this room the creatures who had already been in it gathered into an audience. They were queer-looking women. They were dressed in gray-blue denim butterfly garments cut from the Juniper Hill night-gown pattern. They had very short hair. They stared at the newcomers as if this was a parade especially arranged for their entertainment. Miss Green spoke to a nurse who apparently was attached to the place and then she turned to her group and said to come along.

They marched on through the dayroom to a cemented corridor and a staircase. At the first stop some of them were turned over to another nurse. At the next stop Miss Green counted them. "Here they are," she said to the nurse who had appeared. Then she said good-bye to this nurse; she did not say good-bye to the ladies.

"I am Miss Vance," said the new nurse. "Come into the dayroom. You can put your coats on one of the benches."

The dayroom was very like the one downstairs. There were four or five long wooden benches. Some of the patients were sitting on the benches; some were sitting on the brown linoleum; some were walking around. In the center of the room an obese woman with a great deal of rouge on her face was singing. You could tell she had had voice training; you could tell this more from her professional stance than from her voice. She stood with her hands clasped over her bay window and she had the self-assurance you do not find in amateurs. Her hair was black and cut into a Dutch bob and at her neck was a large bow of red-tissue paper. Her dress was one of the gray-blue habits.

When the prima donna had finished her song someone clapped. Virginia clapped too. The singer bowed. It was an experienced bow. She held up a hand to quell the applause that had died almost at birth and smiled and shook her head. Then she retired from the center of the room and the concert was finished.

Well, said Virginia to herself, this is it.

She sat down on one of the benches. In one corner a woman was dancing. By studying the woman's feet Virginia discovered that she was doing accurate formal ball-room dancing. She did the sort of tango your parents did when you were a little girl. Then a one-step, the kind you learned in dancing school. She danced beautifully. It was too bad she looked so much like a man. Her iron-gray hair was cut exactly like a man's and of course the shape-less dress did nothing for her.

"She was a school teacher," said a lady who was sitting beside Virginia.

"She knows the old dances," said Virginia. "That is the original fox-trot."

"She was a school teacher. What's your name?"

"Virginia."

"I'm Ruth."

"Is this the same building I was in before?" asked Virginia.

"Where were you before?" asked Ruth.

A very sick woman. "I think they called it Receiving."

"Reception," said Ruth. "No, this is different. I used to be in Reception."

"What do they call this building?"

"Five."

"Just Five?"

"Well, Building Five."

"Why did they change me?"

Ruth grinned at her. "Don't you know?" Virginia did not like her somehow.

"They just said we were going for a ride. They'll be coming to take us back soon, I expect."

Ruth laughed. "They brought me over, just for the ride, three years ago."

"But why didn't they keep me in Receiving?"

"Reception. You stay there till you go home, if you

go home before a year. Otherwise you have to go to one of the other buildings. You can't stay in Reception more than a year."

"I hadn't been there a year."

Ruth shrugged. "Sometimes they know sooner, I guess." She had a string which she was winding in and out of her fingers.

"What's that you're doing?" asked Virginia irritably.

"Cat's cradle."

"What?"

"Cat's cradle. You want to do it?" She handed Virginia the string.

"I don't know how."

"She doesn't know how to do a cat's cradle," said Ruth to another lady who had come up to them.

The new lady also had a string which she was winding. She looked hard at Virginia. "I never saw anyone who couldn't do a cat's cradle," she said.

"Look," said Ruth, "I'll show you. Give me the string." She took the string and in a twinkling made it into a complicated pattern. She said for Virginia to do it. She gave Virginia several chances but Virginia could not do it. "She's in a bad way," said Ruth to her colleague.

Another lady came up to show Virginia a doll. It was made of rags. "You see," said this lady. She pulled one of the arms and the other arm shortened. "Cute?"

"Very cute," said Virginia.

"I make them all the time," said the lady. She spoke jerkily and now and then raised her right hand into the air as if to catch something.

"Why do you do that with your arm?" asked Virginia.

"Do what?"

"Raise it up that way."

210

"I do not raise it up that way," said the lady. She raised it up that way. "I'm not nervous," she said. "You seem to be nervous. You can keep the doll."

"No, it's yours."

"That's all right. I'll let you keep it. I make them all the time. The others can make dolls but not with arms that pull." She pulled the doll's arms to demonstrate and then she went away from Ruth and Virginia.

"She's very sick," said Ruth.

Virginia got up and went toward a window. Most of the ladies in this ward, she noticed with revulsion, had horrible skin. They had great red sores on their faces. Syphilis. I must be very careful in the washroom.

Remember Senja. One morning Senja met me at the door of her apartment. Oh, Jeannie, she cried. . . . Someone else calls me Jeannie. . . . Senja couldn't say Ginny. Jeannie, she said, I haf syphil-lous. Yatzterday whan I was in store I haf to go my Gott how I haf an I dint put paper on the sit and now I haf the syphil-lous. . . . She was always having diseases. She read about them in the newspaper. Cancer of the brats was her favorite. She really was cracked. . . . Says you?

"Supper, ladies," shouted Miss Vance. She was an amazon of a woman. There was a nurse, a long time ago, that I thought was large; I hadn't seen anything.

The ladies scrambled over to Miss Vance. Virginia tried to keep a little air between herself and the others. However, such foul-smelling air was undoubtedly as thick with germs as were the ladies.

"I don't know yet," the nurse was saying. "Wait a sec." She cocked her head in the direction of the hall and then she bellowed, "Tunnel!"

She unlocked the door and the ladies sped down the

stairs. Virginia had a hard time keeping up with them. They raced into a basement and then into a tunnel.

The tunnel was something for a horror story. There were lights but the pale glow they gave off was swallowed in the midnight pools between the lights. The walls were cement patterned with cracks. Water seeped slowly from some of the wider cracks and on the uneven floor were puddles of dark water.

The tunnel was divided into two lanes. The dividing wall was of some sort of heavy chicken wire and on the other side of it ladies scurried along like gray-blue rats. Now and then there was a lady in a canvas jacket laced up the back. Virginia saw her breath in the pale light as she panted to catch up with her crowd.

They came to a staircase. This also was divided into two parts but the dividing agent in this case was merely a railing made of two iron bars. A very fat old lady crawled between the bars and went up the other side. It made no difference. You all came out on the same landing.

At the door was a nurse, oh, such a large nurse. She unlocked the door, but she held an arm across the opening and the ladies shoved against her. When she dropped her arm the ladies spilled into an enormous room and rushed for a line that was forming on one side.

There were tables and chairs in the room. There must have been forty tables. The line, more of a crack-the-whip, advanced rapidly toward a chromium counter. Ladies carrying trays were going to the tables now.

When Virginia came to the pile of trays she took one. A bowl of food was put on her tray and then another counter attendant slapped a sandwich onto it. The woman behind Virginia grabbed the sandwich, but the counter attendant gave Virginia another one.

She was handed a dessert. It was a custard in a small round pan. Then she picked up a mug of coffee. It had milk in it, of course, and she was quite sure it would also have sugar, but she hadn't the courage to ask for black unsweetened coffee. At the end of the steam table was a tray of forks and spoons. There were no knives.

She took her tray and went to a table where there were several empty places. She asked if it would be all right for her to sit there. Nobody looked up and so she sat down. She had eaten most of what was in the bowl when the meal was suddenly over. The ladies snatched up their trays and rushed to the front of the room where they slid the trays through a window. Everything was done as if a train had to be caught. They ran back to the door and down into the tunnel. They rushed through the tunnel and raced up the stairs. When Virginia started to turn in at one of the doors off the stair hall a nurse shook her head. "You don't belong here," she said.

Where had your own ladies got to? She hurried up another flight and there was Miss Vance. She went into the dayroom but none of the ladies was there. She could hear them, though, and she followed the noise and came to the washroom. The washroom was jammed.

The ladies milled about restlessly. Some of them were smoking. There was no standing in line for a booth. You elbowed your way. No matter how long you stood you still had to elbow your way. You had also to do some pushing while you remained sitting or else you did not remain.

A pasty-faced woman came to Virginia. She had a notebook and a pencil. "You are Mrs. Cunningham?" she asked.

"Yes," said Virginia. The woman was not wearing one of the denim sacks. She had on the kind of sweater the girls were making when you were in high school. You threw your thread around the needle twice to get that balloon effect. The woman's blue-serge skirt was very long and she had her hair done into puffs over her ears. Cootie garages.

"Have you had a bowel movement today, Mrs. Cunningham?" asked this relic.

"Well, really!" said Virginia.

"I keep the record. I'm Miss Sommerville."

"Oh."

"Have you?" Miss Sommerville looked at Virginia anxiously.

"Yes," said Virginia. She could not remember, but Miss Sommerville seemed pleased with the answer. She made a check in her notebook and went off to another lady.

Presently the rack of nightgowns was pushed in, but the nurse gave Virginia one of the Christmas gowns. Just inside of the neck, at the back, was one of the small labels which were so easy to sew on and which you had been unable to manage. A new number had been added to your label. The 14 was crossed off and now there was a 33. How swiftly I fly backward.

She was assigned to a dormitory that had seven beds. Along each of the side walls were three cots and one was in the center, just in front of the windows. That was Virginia's. She got into the cot. Having had to turn her glasses in she could not see what her roommates looked like. She could hear them, though. One of them was telling a story about the time she and Peter went to a Catholic church and Peter nudged her and said, Get up, old woman, they're all getting up. "And my knees were so stiff I couldn't, and I said to him, Peter, I said, I'm on my knees for life. I'll always have to be a Catholic."

Virginia thought it was a rather funny story and said so, but the narrator told her to mind her own business.

"You're the new one, aren't you?" said another voice. "Don't mind Molly. I'm Louise."

"My name is Virginia."

"How long have you been at Juniper Hill?"

"Since last February," said Virginia. "I was in Mendelin Hospital in the city for a little while before."

"I was there too," said Louise. "I liked it better than here, didn't you?"

"I don't remember it at all."

"I liked it," said Louise. "The halls were wider. It was sort of friendly."

"I got folks," said another voice. "I ain't like some. I got a place to go to and the doctor he knows it. You got a tempreture of nothin, Eva, he says. Eva, he says, you is got a tempreture of nothin and you can go home. He says this to me and I'm goin home. I got a place to go. I got folks that want me."

"I haven't," said Louise. "But I've made my way before and I can do it again. I just wish they'd say here's five dollars, Louise, get out. We never want to see you again. I'd get, all right. They wouldn't need to worry about that."

"What sort of job would you look for?" asked Virginia. It was getting dark now. She had figured out which bed Louise occupied, but she had no idea what she looked like. Eva, she gathered from the quality of the voice, was a colored woman. The woman who had gone to church with Peter sounded old.

"I was a telephone supervisor once," said Louise. "That was before Mr. Hawes, but I could do it again. Mr. Hawes

215

wanted to marry me but I said once was enough. I was married once, but he died."

"I'm sorry."

"It was a long time ago. I can hardly remember what he looked like. I never got over Lou, though. She was only six when she died. She looked so pretty in her coffin, just like she was asleep. I wish you could have seen her."

A nurse came into the dormitory and turned off the radiator and opened the windows. "It's a cold night, ladies," she said. "Good night."

"Good night," said Virginia.

"I got a tempreture of nothin," said Eva. "The doctor says so."

"You go to sleep, Eva," said the nurse. "Don't you go keeping the other ladies awake."

"I got folks to go to," said Eva.

"Peter," said the old woman, "turn over and stop snoring."

Virginia pulled her warm nightgown over her feet. She should have, she knew, been frightened and depressed by the newest transfer. She was in a much worse building now and none of the patients she had seen so far struck her as being good risks. And yet the hopelessness that had been hounding her had lessened and for the first time she dared to believe that she might get well. Perhaps her foundation for this beginning of optimism was childish or, terrifying thought, perhaps it was the start of delusions. However, when you realize you aren't the sickest in your ward, it does something for you. I'm not so ill as the old woman; I don't think Robert's here. I know where I am and I know I am sick—yes, still foggy, still stupid, still a woman who is not sane.

Shock treatments. Why bother with insulin, metrazol

216

or electricity? Long ago they lowered insane persons into snake pits; they thought that an experience that might drive a sane person out of his wits might send an insane person back into sanity. By design or by accident, she couldn't know, a more modern "they" had given V. Cunningham a far more drastic shock treatment now than Dr. Kik had been able to manage with his clamps and wedges and assistants. They had thrown her into a snake pit and she had been shocked into knowing that she would get well.

CHAPTER THIRTEEN

FOR a week it appeared that the only diversions offered the ladies in Thirty-three were the races to the cafeteria. Sometimes, when the weather was milder, they went outside to the cafeteria. It was quicker that way. When word came that the overland route was to be taken a nurse piled coats on one of the benches and several times Virginia got her old friend, Dried Gravy. Coats were not provided for the tunnel trips, although the tunnel was far colder than the out-of-doors.

All of the cafeteria meals were similar to the first one Virginia had had there. Of a morning there was cereal instead of stew and sometimes, gala occasions, there were hard-boiled eggs. There was always trouble on egg mornings. Invariably a few ladies would throw their eggs. Virginia was tempted to join in this game, but she forced herself to eat. The eggs smelled bad but then any eggs that have been cooked hard and long take on a peculiar sulphur smell. They were not necessarily spoiled eggs. The only really good part of each meal was the bread. The bread sandwiches were stuck together with a thin smear of butter.

There was no time to look around. You ate as fast as you could. Virginia choked down what she had time for, not because she was hungry but because she knew it was imperative to gain weight. The maddening pace set by the diners was never relaxed and she was never able to finish a meal. She considered copying a lady who stuffed bread into the front of her dress.

On Robert's visiting day there was real food and time to eat. He always brought a treat along and then took her to the store. She could have her coffee black at the store and this was nice; she had never been able to enjoy the smell of canned milk. On visiting day she wore her own coat and the nurses were very complimentary and they would not permit the other ladies to rub up against her.

Although there was a polisher in the dayroom there was no intense feeling about it. You shoved it around if you wanted to. The nurses were not very particular in Thirty-three. You had a feeling they knew when they were beaten. They seldom raised their voices, except to announce meals or to stop the occasional drifts toward violence. On the whole the ladies were well behaved. The singer sang. Sometimes she had a paper bow on her head; once she had a lavish sash of toilet paper around her abdomen. Virginia wondered where she kept her private stock. What the nurses doled out was not from rolls. It might be well to make up to the singer. There had been days when the nurse had said she was sorry, but there was no toilet paper. *She* was sorry.

The ladies who belonged to the cat's-cradle society worked at their strings by the hour. Virginia was never able to master the art. The lady who made dolls made dolls all day long. If she hadn't been interrupted so often by the need to clutch the air she would have filled the ward with arm-pulling dolls. And the dancer danced all day long.

There were ladies who talked. They fixed their eyes on things unseen by others and they spoke in animated voices. Some of them seemed to enjoy their conversations; they would pause, as if listening to the unseen and then they would chatter on. Virginia came to think of these women as not being especially crazy; it was a way to pass the time and possibly a better way than the cat's cradling.

There was a girl who would have been pretty had she not been disfigured by the Juniper Hill skin disease. This girl always carried a Bible and she preached sermons about vegetarianism. She had an effective voice but her sermons boiled down to a repetition of If you saw their eyes as they go to the slaughter house you would not eat their flesh. She always, somehow, made Virginia very hungry. "It says right here in the Holy Bible," the preacher would say, and she would slap her Bible and then go into the eye patter. Virginia sometimes wondered if the hospital had hired her to go around with this sermon. Certainly the commissary department did not believe in serving much, if any, meat.

There was another young woman who had a religious turn of mind. This one had given birth to Jesus some days. Virginia tried to talk the girl out of this obsession, but the girl smiled sweetly and said she was Mary, Mother of Our Lord. Some days she was not Mary. Then she was Hester, a twenty-year-old girl from Brooklyn. Until she got sick she was a star student in journalism. When she was not being the Mother of Our Lord she was talking about wanting to be a newspaperwoman. Virginia always regretted she had not met Hester earlier. Earlier she might have fallen in with the Mary idea and learned something about the Old Days, but now she was far too well.

"I had a friend here a long time ago," she said one day

to Hester—this was a day when Mary was not present. "It was back in Reception. She was a newspaperwoman and she was almost well. She's back at her job now, I imagine."

"Maybe she could help me," said Hester.

"Her name was Grace," said Virginia. "I wish I knew her last name."

"Never mind," said Hester. "I can find her. I think we'll always know each other, don't you?"

It was a rather terrible thought. "Just so everyone isn't able to spot us," said Virginia. "Could it leave a permanent scar, do you think?"

But Hester was too young for this sort of talk. On days when she was Mary, Virginia would remind the girl of the newspaper ambition but Hester would shake her head. "You speak of things I know nothing about," she would say. "I am the Mother of Our Lord. I gave birth to Jesus." It might have been interesting for a very well person or for a very sick person; for an in-between it was a great bore.

And in general the life in the ward was a great bore. Eccentricity that captured your attention at first became deadly monotonous. The dancer never stopped dancing; the talkers never stopped talking. Louise was one of the talkers. At night in the dormitory Louise was a perfectly normal woman, but in the daytime she was unable to see flesh and blood. Also she was one of the ladies who did not wear shoes.

One night Virginia asked her about this. "I'm sure they would give you a pair of shoes, Louise," she said.

"Yes, they would," said Louise. "They have. You should see the shoes they tried to make me wear. I've always been very careful with my feet. I wear a quad and I never in my life paid less than fifteen dollars."

"I know, but the sidewalk is so cold. And there's water in the tunnel."

"I won't wear what they give me. I have more respect for my feet."

Louise, however, would wear stockings, the long black cotton stockings issued to the patients who had no supplies of their own. Several of the Thirty-three ladies went barefoot. Sometimes there was snow on the sidewalk when the ladies went to the cafeteria but the barefooted ones padded along as if they did not mind.

ii

The dreary life seemed to go on indefinitely and then one day Miss Vance said Dr. Terry wanted to see Virginia. Virginia had never heard of any Dr. Terry and she said so. "He's your doctor," said Miss Vance, and Virginia said oh no, he was not, that Dr. Kik was her doctor. "Well," said the nurse, "you have a new one now. Dr. Terry."

She took Virginia downstairs to an office whose door said Dr. Terry and when Virginia went in she saw a young man in a white coat, a very young fellow who could not have been more than an intern. She was disgusted.

"How do you do, Mrs. Cunningham," said this young squirt. "Won't you sit down?"

She sat near the desk. Behind that desk he looked like a child. He squirmed around in the swivel chair and seemed desperate for something to say. Then suddenly he shot a question at her. "Just what is there about the hospital that you don't like?"

Was he serious? It would be more sensible to ask if

there is anything one does like. "I hate the smell of that formaldehyde," she said.

"Paraldehyde," he said.

"Yes. I confuse the words. And it tastes the way I imagine formaldehyde does."

His smile was the sort you use when you wish to let the other person know you understand he was trying for humor. "But you don't take it now."

"I know, but the others in my ward seem to."

"We admit that paraldehyde is a trifle—pungent," he said. "What else?"

"What else don't I like? For one thing, I'm so afraid I'll catch one of those dreadful diseases that make your skin break out. I can't think of the words. Oh, yes, syphilis and the other one. The washroom and all those women with the terrible sores . . ."

"Everyone has been examined," he said. "There is no one in this building who has either syphilis or gonorrhea."

"Are you sure?"

"Quite sure, Mrs. Cunningham," he said with the dignity that only very recent medical-school graduates can achieve.

"But why do they have the sores? Is it something about the diet?"

How his face stiffened! "Are you interested in the study of medicine, Mrs. Cunningham?"

Oh, dear, I shouldn't even imply that there could be something wrong with his dear Juniper. "I simply don't want to catch whatever it is," she said.

"You have no cause for alarm," he said.

And curiosity killed a cat? I'd very much like to know what makes those sores but I'll have to be satisfied with assuming it's dietary. If it had nothing to do with improper diet, wouldn't you have said so, smarty? And I've no interest in the study of medicine, thank you, but I am interested in people. My interest in one Dr. Terry is very slight, however, and so you can relax and stop waving the flag for Juniper Hill. "Where's Dr. Kik?"

"Dr. Kik? He is in Reception."

"I know, but I'm his patient. I want to see him."

The young man looked down at the enormous desk which undoubtedly made him feel important but which unfortunately made him look insignificant. "As a matter of fact," he said, "Dr. Kik's been ill."

Kik, the executioner, the Young Jailer—if he dies I am lost. He's a queer man who hides behind you and asks impertinent and impossible questions, but he came running when I needed him to come running and when he said, "It's all right now, Jeannie," I knew I was safe.

"Nothing to be alarmed about," said the alarmist of a doctor who adored the word "alarm." "Just a cold, as a matter of fact."

What a fool he is, scaring me half to death and then saying it is just a cold.

"Was that all you wanted to say to me?"

"I didn't ask to see you, Dr. Terry," she said.

On the way back to the ward she asked Miss Vance if Dr. Terry was an intern and the nurse said no, he was a full-fledged doctor. "I can hardly believe it," said Virginia. "He's so jittery and so pompous."

"Maybe it was you, kid," sniggered the nurse. She probably fancied herself a pile of monkeys.

"I won't have him for my doctor."

"Sure, sure," said Miss Vance. "But he's a nice kid, Virginia."

"I'd rather have a good doctor."

224

"He's no slouch at doctoring."

"I don't care. Dr. Kik's my doctor," said Virginia, "and I'm not interested in making a change."

But evidently Dr. Terry was meddling in her case. That afternoon she was invited to a popcorn party. Miss Vance thought that was just too super for words. When the Pop-corn Ladies were summoned, Virginia stumped over to the door to join the group. If you were going to get out of this prison it looked as if you'd have to do what they said, even to the extent of going to a damn popcorn party. I don't like popcorn and I don't feel like going to any kind of party, but has that anything to do with it? Believe me, when they throw a party here they can be very sure of their number, though come to think of it, perhaps some-times a patient goes off into the deep end of illness just at the very thought of a Juniper party.

They gave the party in an alcove just outside of Ward Thirty-three. Four card tables were set up. On a smaller table was an electric popper, and a nurse was turning the handle around and around.

Two women in civilian dress assisted at the party. Vir-ginia had a sickening conviction that they were church or club women earning merit badges and the privilege of telling their acquaintances over teacups about exotic and dangerous adventures among the insane. In loud saccharine voices these amateur social workers explained that there was to be a very gay game with prizes. Virginia was unable to concentrate on anything but the bitter difference be-tween her clothes and the costumes of the hostesses, but the other patients got through the game of lotto without effort or enthusiasm. They played it as if it was a chore to be got out of the way. When a lady filled a row she announced it and she took her prize, a candy bar, and divided it among the other players at her table. The hostesses were upset about this dividing and would try to explain that when you won you were entitled to keep the prize for yourself. The sick ladies looked at the well ladies and did not understand; they had quite forgotten the ways of the world.

It took about a half hour to get rid of the candy bars. By that time the hostesses were not looking so pleased and sleek and they were eager to state that the party was over. The nurse who was presiding at the popcorn table gave each guest a scoop of popcorn in a paper napkin.

"My, I bet you had fun," said Miss Vance.

"Yes," said Virginia. "Gambling and everything."

"Oh, boy," said Miss Vance. "Hot dog, eh?"

She accepted a few grains of popcorn. "I'm wasting away to a shadow," she mourned. "Down to two forty."

The night nurses were smaller than the day nurses. But at night the active ladies were given paraldehyde and so it was not necessary for the night nurses to be so large.

iii

Virginia had got into the habit of sitting or lying on the floor. It was simpler. If you sat on a bench you were likely to be shoved off very quickly and so why not start out on the floor? She had a favorite place, near a door. There was a crack under the door and the air that blew through that crack did not smell of paraldehyde. It was very refreshing, but after a few days she had a bad case of sniffles.

She asked Miss Vance for some kleenex, but the nurse said there was none. She gave her a rag, however. Virginia tore the rag into two pieces; the larger piece was for daytime use and the smaller piece for night. In the evening she washed the daytime handkerchief and hung it on the radiator behind her cot. In the morning she washed her night rag and hung it at her belt to dry. She had to guard her rags carefully because of the doll lady. One morning the doll-maker managed a brilliant coup and captured both of the rags and for two days Virginia had to use her skirt. She would have used her slip but by now her nose was far too tender for the coarse material. She tried to hold her skirt so that the used places would not show and whenever she was in the washroom she washed the soiled spots. It was a relief to find one of the rag dolls. She took the doll apart and so again she had handkerchiefs. By this time the doll-maker had got hold of other materials and so had no interest in Virginia's supplies.

The last time that Robert had visited he had left her two packs of cigarettes. Virginia was careful when she opened her candy box. Robert had said she was to keep the cigarettes for herself but of course she had to give a few away now and then. There was a colored woman who was always hounding her. She never once saw that colored woman smoke a whole cigarette. She put the whole ones down her neck and smoked the butts she was able to tease from the other ladies. Once Virginia asked her what she did with her whole cigarettes and the woman sneered at her. "I only smokes butts," she said.

After Virginia and Louise became such good friends in the dormitory Virginia fully expected they would be friends in the dayroom. Often she went to Louise in the hope of continuing a subject they had been discussing the night before but Louise would never talk to her in the daytime. She talked. She talked continually but to someone Virginia could not see. Virginia found herself

227

becoming very jealous of the unseen entertainers of Thirty-three. She was so terribly lonesome and she had no invisible companion.

One afternoon she was told she could go to O.T. She and five other ladies went down the hall to the alcove where the popcorn party had been held and there a young foreign woman was trying to teach the ladies to sew and knit. She tried to teach Virginia a complicated knitting stitch. "It's no use," said Virginia. "I can't concentrate. I would like to read."

"Ah," said the teacher, "you enjoy to read, yes?" You enjoy the choo-choo, yes? "Yes."

"Perhaps one day you will write, yes?"

"I've written for many years," said Virginia. God, how I hate to be spoken to as if I was a puppy.

"How interesting," said the teacher. "What is it that you write for many years?"

"Novels," said Virginia. "A couple of them have been published."

"So?" The teacher was giving her a queer look.

"*Afternoon of a Faun* and *A Little Night Music*," said Virginia. "Not that you would ever have heard of them."

"So you write music also," commented the teacher. She had a face that would have been tragic in an American, but for a foreign woman it was rather effective.

"No, those were the titles of my novels." It was obvious that the teacher thought she was making all this up. Why didn't you claim *Ulysses*? But for a minute I thought she was accepting me.

"Next time I shall bring you the *Times*' book section," said the teacher. "You are interested in books. You would like that part of the New York *Times* newspaper. It is about books."

"Yes," said Virginia.

But the next time she went to O.T. there was no mention of literature. This time the teacher insisted that Virginia work on a baby quilt. Virginia sat at the quilting frame and did almost no work. While she was sitting there a man came by and said how lovely the spread was and when he had gone one of the quilters said proudly that he was her doctor.

"Dr. Kik is my doctor," said Virginia.

"Kik," said the teacher. "I have never heard of any Dr. Kik."

"He's in Reception," said one of the ladies.

"He's my doctor just the same," said Virginia. "He's sick just now. He has a bad cold." There, that proves it.

And the very next day Miss Vance said Dr. Kik had sent word. He wanted to see Virginia. He would be in Dr. Terry's office. Oh, Virginia was excited. She smoothed out her largest rag and folded it to make it look like a real handkerchief. She asked if she might wear a different dress, but Miss Vance said her dress was all right. It was that same old blue dress. Virginia dampened the almost obliterated marks of the pleats and tried to set them with her fingers. This was not very successful. She was able, however, to sneak a piece of string from one of the cat's cradle ladies and she tied the string around the waist of her slip. Evidently it had been easier for the nurse to provide her with a hospital slip rather than to hunt up one of her own. The hospital slips were just like the nightgowns, except for sleeves. The slip Virginia was given hung four inches below the hem of her dress, but with the string tightly tied around her middle she could blouse up the voluminous garment.

Miss Vance accompanied her to Dr. Terry's office and

knocked on the door. The voice that said to come in was *his*.

"Ah, Jeannie," he said. "How are you?"

"I'm fine," she said, "except for a sniffle." She glanced at the rag she had folded so carefully. What a wad it looked. "But you, Doctor, how are you? I heard you had a cold."

He shrugged and then sat down in the swivel chair behind the desk. He looked as if he belonged behind an executive's desk; he was no squirt. "It was nothing. Tell me, how is it with you?"

"Well," she said, "it's rather dull."

"You have been to O.T. twice."

"And to a popcorn party," she said. "Even so, the days are very long. I wish I had something to read. But I suppose it would be almost impossible to read in that day-room."

"Yes," he said. "Yes, I am afraid so. Tell me, what is it you want?"

"Robert," she said.

He looked at her and then he got up and went over to the windows. "But what else?"

"I don't care," she said.

"When was he last here?" he asked.

"Wednesday," she said. "It's terrible to see him just one afternoon every two weeks."

"You will see him again this Wednesday."

"But he was here last Wednesday."

The doctor came back to his chair. "He will come this week also. I promise you."

"Oh, thank you. You have been so kind. This is Tuesday, isn't it?"

"Yes."

"Thank you so much."

There was a miniature rubber tire ash tray on the desk. Dr. Kik picked this up and looked at it as if trying to figure it out. She had the feeling that he was waiting for her to speak.

"There is something that bothers me a good deal," she said. "Seeing you I know I have seen you before. Many times. I mean, I know that I know you well, but I don't remember. Sometimes in the dining hall or on the walks or in the store I see people I know, that is, their faces are familiar, but I don't know why. I know I have been here almost a year and yet I remember nothing before last summer. And only patches since then."

"Oh, come," he said to the ash tray.

"I know, Robert told me, that first I was in another hospital. I remember nothing of that. I don't remember being brought to Juniper Hill."

"Come," he said. "Of course you remember. You and I had many conversations. You remember."

She shook her head. "No," she said. "I've read that shock treatments sometimes do that, but I want to know if it's temporary amnesia."

"You are becoming a doctor," he said. He put the ash tray down. "You interest yourself in psychiatry." His voice was still very beautiful. No change of mood could coarsen so lovely a voice, but she sensed that he was displeased. "You dramatize," he said. "You recall something you have read and you attempt to fit the facts into that pattern. You remember everything, of course."

"I'm sorry," she said, "but I don't. You are mistaken."

He shoved the ash tray from him. She understood that he wished her to leave. She understood also that he was no longer her doctor and that he did not wish to be

231

bothered by her. This interview, she realized, was un-official and for some reason it had gone badly. He was no longer interested in her as a case or as a person. I know this as a child knows how a magician does his tricks. The mentally ill woman reads the mind of the doctor. He does not like to be told he is mistaken.

Suddenly she was acutely conscious of her appearance. Her slip, she knew, was inching down from under the string. Her stockings were darned with various colors of thread, anything she had been able to beg from the nurses. Her hair was untidy and she had on no makeup. She believed this was the first time she had seen Dr. Kik out of his professional white jacket. Today he was wearing a handsome plaid coat and gray flannel trousers. He had a maroon tie and a matching breast-pocket handkerchief. She got up. "Good-bye," she said. She wanted to run from this elegant man.

He stood up. "Good-bye, Mrs. Cunningham," he said politely.

It was nearly supper time before she remembered he had promised that Robert would come the next day. She forgot her sorrow about losing Dr. Kik and went racing to the cafeteria with the other ladies.

Miss Vance had finally listened to her appeals and now she had her leather jacket every day. She wore it to meals whether they went by Tunnel Ladies or by Outside Ladies. Tonight as she hurried along through the tunnel a woman who was just ahead of her whirled around and grabbed the leather jacket by the lapels. She gave a brisk jerk and the three buttons popped off and went rolling.

"Now," said the woman, "you can stay with us." She gave Virginia a smile that was all golden teeth.

Virginia hunted the buttons and at last found them.

She put them into her candy box and rushed to catch up. There were people to avoid. The gold-toothed woman was to be added to the list. There was no point in getting excited; you simply remembered to avoid her the next time. It was the same with the husky young one who, without warning, lashed out and punched you hard on the nose; there was the doll woman who stole your rags; there was Ruth who might be an informer; there was Miss Sommerville—no one called this one by first name— who was always wanting information about bowel movements; there was the little colored woman who begged cigarettes and never smoked them; there was the one who got apples from home and insisted on giving you the cores—she stood by to watch you eat them. There were quite a few to avoid.

Virginia was thinking this as she went back through the tunnel. She was not able to think and to hurry at the same time and so now she fell behind the crowd that was running back to the ward. She was pretty much alone when she saw Grace.

Grace, the fair girl who had worn a hoover apron, the girl who had been almost well enough to go back to her job on the newspaper. "Oh, Grace," wailed Virginia.

The girl on the other side of the wire partition stopped when Virginia called her name. She stood very still and looked through the fence.

"But I thought you'd gone home," said Virginia. "Months and months ago."

Grace stared at her.

"I'm Virginia. You remember me. We were good friends. We used to sit in the sun and talk. Remember? It was in Ward Three, Grace. You used to tell me where my bed was and what number my hanger was and things like that. I was always forgetting everything but you always knew."

Grace's eyes were nearly black in the dim light of the tunnel. They were fixed on Virginia but they seemed not to see.

"They have cut your pretty hair so short," said Virginia. She put her hands up to her face to brush her tears away. "I'm sorry. I'm really glad to see you. Of course I'm not. You know what I mean. I'd thought you were back home."

Grace said absolutely nothing.

And then Virginia noticed that her friend was wearing one of the canvas jackets. She had seen many of these jackets since coming to Building Five and she supposed they were what are called strait jackets. Previously she had thought a strait jacket was something that covered all of you but perhaps the kind she was seeing here was semi-formal. They looked like lumberjacks. The armlike appendages were crossed and fastened in the back. The whole contraption was laced up the back. It looked as if there might be straps or something for the patient to rest her arms in, at any rate the arms did not dangle. The ladies who wore these jackets went directly to seats in the dining room and nurses took them trays and fed them. Just yesterday Virginia had sat next to a lady who was being fed. Between bites she told the nurse about a trip she had had in Europe some years back. She was an aristocratic-looking woman with a Best Bostonian way of speaking. The nurse appeared to be listening to her with interest and respect. Both of them gave the impression of being too well bred to notice that one was being fed by the other. Virginia had seen this Boston woman many times and always the woman was wearing a canvas jacket. You were tortured by curiosity. It was impossible to imagine that so dignified a person needed to be tied up.

Grace started to move away from the barrier. "Don't go," said Virginia. "Come back, Grace. Turn around and maybe I can reach through and unfasten that thing. It is ridiculous for them to . . . I never knew a kinder person, a more gentle person. As if you would . . ."

Grace paused long enough to give Virginia a look which made her grateful for the jacket and the fence. Yes, it was as if she would. Even the thought of Robert's coming visit failed to remove the memory of Grace's parting glare.

Louise tried to strike up the usual dormitory conversation, but Virginia was unresponsive this night. Off in her corner Eva rustled papers and spoke of her nonexistent temperature. Louise surmised that Eva had a quantity of candy bars hidden away and that she ate candy each night in bed. "My great ambition," said Louise, "is to have a candy bar in bed. A candy bar any place, any time. My, how I would like a piece of candy. Someone gave me a piece when I was in the other hospital. That was a nice place. So sort of friendly."

"I ain't like some," said Eva. "I got a tempreture of nothin and folks to go to. The doctor says so."

And the old one spoke sharply to Peter. Virginia knew now which old one Molly was. She was the one whose head was done up in adhesive. There was an adhesive strap under her chin and it gave her a rakish, sporting look.

"My husband's coming tomorrow," said Virginia, "and I want to get some sleep."

But before she went to sleep she thought a long time about Grace. Grace also had been so certain of recovery.

The next day she did not try to eat much at dinner. Robert was coming. After dinner she waited patiently in the dayroom and every time Miss Vance came into the room she expected her to say he had come.

At last she went to the nurse and asked why he was so late. "But he was here last week," said Miss Vance.

"I know, but Dr. Kik said yesterday that he would come today."

"Oh," said the nurse. "Well—he's flying." She winked at Virginia and rushed off.

Flying? Is it far enough from town? I wish he wouldn't. It only takes an hour by bus and so why is he later? It could not take more than a half hour by air.

It was supper time before she gave up hope. During the long afternoon she had imagined many gruesome things. She also decided that she had misunderstood Miss Vance, that the nurse had said "lying" instead of "flying" and had meant Dr. Kik. Apparently the doctor had not been telling the truth but you did not expect a nurse to be so blunt about a doctor. You knew that the nurses sometimes amused themselves by saying odd things to the patients and you supposed they thought it made no difference.

"Did your husband come?" asked Louise when they were in bed. She and Virginia had sat side by side most of the afternoon but of course Louise did not know that. She had spent most of the day with a hallucination brother and they had had a terrific fight. Virginia, listening now and then, had almost seen the brother. The fight was about Mama's will and involved sharp remarks about death-bed influence and who had paid most of the mortgage.

"No," said Virginia. "I suppose the doctor just said it to make me feel good at the time. I suppose he thought I would forget it right away. He won't believe me when I say I've forgotten him, though. I don't know. They talk to us as if we were children."

This reminded Louise of her daughter. She told a bright saying or two.

"I'm sick," said Virginia. "I know that all right. But damn if I'm that sick."

"What did you say?"

"Nothing. I guess I was talking to myself."

"Mercy," said Louise, "don't get started on that. The way some of the women in this ward talk to themselves . . ."

"I got a tempreture of nothin," said Eva. "I ain't like some."

CHAPTER FOURTEEN

NEXT day Virginia found something to read. It was a small piece of newspaper. It had been almost a year since she had seen any part of a newspaper. Fortunately the piece had been torn from the amusement advertisements and so gave more material for thought than you could have got from a torn-off news story. She studied the ads and felt less isolated. *Life with Father* was still running.

And here is the announcement of the Wagner cycle. We went last year. Just last year? What a long time Melchior and Flagstad stood and sang and sang that wonderful music and when we went out we felt as if we had been battered and squeezed and drained dry. But where is her name? What has happened to her?

The scrap of paper gave you something to think about for hours. It was not easy to hit upon things to think about and once you had assigned yourself a topic it was difficult to think. She had invented a private therapy. Thinking Therapy, she called it. T.T. All Right T.T. Lady, she would say to herself and then she would have her class in thinking. A one-pupil class. It was hard but she felt it was important to learn again how to think. It seemed queer to her that the hospital had no interest in teaching its patients to think. Juniper Hill's goal was to Keep Them Quiet.

Perhaps a group of thinking patients would have disturbed the peace. Let people think and at once they are drawing up petitions and demanding Rights. There simply were not enough nurses to handle thinkers.

One of Virginia's T.T. assignments was The History of the Modern American Novel. She had read a good deal on this subject and could remember enough to occupy herself for quite some time. She also thought, in a lighter mood, about Famous Writers I Have Heard Speak. She had heard many famous writers but none she could recall who should have accepted the invitation. It was, of course, rewarding to be able to say you had seen Sinclair Lewis and Theodore Dreiser, Sherwood Anderson and Zona Gale and so on. It was too bad not to be able to say what they had said, but of course no one cared. What people cared about was what the writers looked like and, to tell the truth, they did not care a great deal about this.

But what had happened to Flagstad? Virginia stopped in the tunnel to ask the nurse who stood at the fork to direct traffic. The nurse shook her head and motioned for Virginia to go on to the cafeteria. For a moment Virginia saw the tunnel as the nurse must have seen it. There the sane woman stood alone at the dark crossroad, alone except for several hundred crazy ladies who stampeded through the gloom. Virginia could sympathize with the nurse, but she did want to know what had happened to the world's greatest soprano. "Kirsten Flagstad," she said. "Why isn't she in the Wagner cycle this year?"

"Maybe she's in another building," said the nurse. "I don't know all the ladies' names. Go to the cafeteria, please."

Virginia ran to catch up with her ladies. She reached

the stairs in time to see the very fat one crawl through the iron bars. "That's the way she measures herself," said Virginia to anyone who might care to learn the answer. "When she can't get between the bars any more she will start to diet." She laughed.

In the dining room she ate her dessert first and in this way was certain of getting the most fattening part of the meal. She had developed speed and had almost finished her bowl of stew before the Big Run Back began.

Sometimes she wondered what the cafeteria workers thought about their customers. The women who served in back of the steam counters were not nurses and yet Virginia had seen one or two of them around Ward Thirty-three now and again. She supposed they were hired for a few ward duties as well as for their cafeteria work. There were men in the kitchen too. When you slid your tray through the dirty dish window you could see a young man working furiously at a gigantic dish-washing machine. He worked in an undershirt and you could see the red sores on his arms and shoulders. Imagine taking a job in a place where you caught the institution disease. Times must be hard outside. . . .

When she could not think of anything else for T.T. she thought about her life. She was not able to bring The Life up to date. She could think about what happened today, about the woman who had given her a cookie, about the one who had given her an orange and later cried out to the nurse that someone had stolen it. She could think about what happened yesterday and perhaps the day before. She could remember Robert's last visit and know for sure that she was thinking of the most recent one.

She also could go very far back. She did beautifully when she leaped a year, but no matter what Dr. Kik had said she could not remember the time just before the hospital in town or the early part of Juniper Hill. There should be a rule that all Juniper doctors must have been ill themselves at some time or another. Then they would know what you were talking about. But I would not want a doctor who had been sick. How could you be sure he had got over it? Will people be that way about me? Never quite sure?

The chief thing is not to look it. Silly Mary at home looks it. She looks goofy and yet the doctors say she is normal. You can't depend on looks.

For example, Robert. He looks practical. He has a conservative face and he dresses conservatively; you wouldn't catch him dead in that flashy outfit of Kik's. And, in keeping with his appearance, Robert graduated from a School of Commerce where he belonged to a good old fraternity limited to boys from good old families. The Cunninghams were solid people who had money. Had it is right; they did not spend it. They lived in the same house and did not worry about making it over. Virginia's people, once they settled down, began to take out partitions. The Stuarts could not enter a house without getting an if-you-moved-that-partition gleam in their eyes.

When Virginia and Robert were married everyone said she had done very well. They had been equally surprised about her and Gordon getting engaged, but Gordon's death had fixed that. She could tell they felt his death was in keeping with her character. Afterwards they waited expectantly for her to become a Fallen Woman or

241

something becomingly tragic. They were astounded when Robert married her. They were let down. They had counted on Virginia to give them something to talk about.

She and Robert started out the way you would expect young Cunninghams to start out. She thought it was a wonderful life but, to be consistent with what was expected of her, she did talk about kicking over the traces. She talked about how she and Robert would run off to Paris for a year. She was just talking. The Stuarts were great on just talking.

She had a sinking feeling when she and Robert got on the train for New York. They had been to New York a number of times for short vacations but now they had stored their furniture and Mother was saying she could not look Mrs. Cunningham in the face. "What is going to happen to you?" she had said over and over.

Virginia did not know. She wondered too. Robert was very bland. He said they would have a marvelous time. He said they would go to the theater every week. They would live on a funny street in the Village and ride on the ferry boats.

They did all of this and they had a marvelous time. Often it would be days before Virginia would remember that no money was coming in.

After a year Robert announced it was time to Face Facts. Virginia supposed this meant he was going to swallow the Bitter Pill of returning to Evanston, but he had no intention of going back home. He got himself a job in New York. He earned less money at this job than he had earned since his school-day vacation jobs, but that did not bother him. In order to live they had to keep dipping into the dwindling savings but that did not bother

242

Robert. He could not imagine what Virginia was worried about.

Robert, I think there is something the matter with my head.

ii

"You are to go with the Cafeteria Ladies this morning, Virginia," said Miss Vance.

Three times a day for many many days Virginia had been going with the cafeteria ladies. Or so she thought. However, this morning when the nurse called, "Cafeteria, ladies," she remembered that the usual shout was "Breakfast, ladies." Only a half dozen women responded to the cafeteria cry.

Among the half dozen were two whom Virginia had noticed in the cafeteria kitchen. Gracious, they have to report for work early and how silly to have to come here first. You'd like to have a crack at organizing Juniper Hill. But remember you are a patient; remember you are utsnay, dear.

She went with the Cafeteria Ladies. They went without a nurse, just the half dozen of them, through the tunnel. The nurse who guarded the fork had not come on duty yet. It was almost like being given a pass key. You couldn't help hesitating at that crossroad. Suppose you made a dash for it. Trouble was, you didn't know what *it* was. Trouble also, you were too well, far too well to think you could escape.

The Cafeteria Ladies paid no attention to her. One of them was around fifty and very heavy and tired-looking. She was the one who always dished out the main course at the counter. Two of the workers were very young, probably under twenty. They were cheerful and talked together as they walked along. Then there was a slightly

243

older one who had nice legs done up in amazingly sheer stockings. Another worker, around the vintage of Legs, looked Italian and had fine black eyes and beautiful skin.

The walk was leisurely and when they came to the dining room they went through it to the kitchen. The oldest woman told Virginia to hang her jacket on a hook near a locker. "And now you come with us and have your breakfast," she said.

They went through the kitchen and there, on the other side, was another dining room. Like going through the looking glass, Alice. This dining room was smaller than the other one and had a less institutional appearance. A tall colored woman behind the counter struck a glass with a fork. "Breakfast is served," she said in a glorious voice.

Breakfast also was glorious. You went past the steam counter and took whatever you wanted. There were eggs galore. There were several kinds of cereal. You could have coffee black; you could have cocoa and milk; you could take something of everything. You could have a knife. Virginia had been thirsty for weeks. Perhaps there was a fountain in Thirty-three, but she had never discovered it. This morning she took milk and coffee. She hadn't quite got the courage to take cocoa too, although she noticed that the fattest ones of her group took all three beverages.

One member of the group did not sit with them at breakfast. She was a tall thin one and she sat off at a table alone. She had snowy hair that hung in a long bob, a most unusual coiffure at Juniper Hill. "That's Treva," said the oldest woman when she saw that Virginia was looking at the tall one. "She's very sick. She never eats with us."

"Oh," said Virginia. She did not understand.

"I'm May," said the oldest woman.

"I'm Virginia."

"Yes, I know. This is Rachel." May pointed to one of the younger ones. "And that's Flo."

Rachel giggled. Flo turned wide eyes toward Virginia; queer eyes that seemed not to focus. That one is not well, that Flo. She can't be a regular worker. She is a visitor, like Treva, like me.

The one with the nice legs was Julia and Bianca was the Italian.

The ladies, having acknowledged the introductions, turned to their whopping big breakfasts. The bread on this side of the cafeteria was served unbuttered. You took butter from a bowl of cracked ice. Neat little squares. Bianca and Flo each had five pats.

"Time, girls," said May after a while.

The girls picked up their trays and took them to the dish window. This side of the cafeteria had its own dishwashing machine, its own coffee urns, its own staff of workers. This was the right side of the tracks. In addition to knives there were breakable plates and cups.

Virginia and her squad went to the other side and started to work. She was told to help make the sandwiches. The woman who worked with her would take three pieces of bread at a time and somehow butter the proper sides and slap the finished sandwiches into tall even piles. Virginia was very slow. May said she would get on to it.

You could smell your guests before you saw them. Way off at the far end of the dining room the nurse opened the door and the smell swept in. Then the ladies came. When you were with the breakfast crowd you did not realize what a din it made. The building seemed to quiver this morning and you stared across the counter and wondered if those really were people, those creatures in the sacking dresses. During the brief meal Virginia stood at the dirty dish chute and shoved trays on to the dish washer. The dirty trays started coming before the last lady was served.

When the dirty dishes were gathered in, Virginia helped the dish washer to put them into wooden crates which he shot on through the machine. He was a patient young man whose name was Joe. He told her again and again how to stack the plates and he said she reminded him of his sister. May whispered to Virginia to watch out for Joe. "He's very sick," she said. "Always keep the rail between you and him."

May was a great one for saying everyone was very sick. It was surprising to discover that all of the cafeteria workers, including May, were inmates. Sometimes there were no nurses around and at these times you had a funny feeling in your stomach. The kitchen was large and there were many workers.

In reality it was not a kitchen; it was a serving pantry on a gigantic scale. The food was wheeled in on carts. The sandwiches and the coffee were the only foods created here. The workers stayed here all day long. When they were not working at the preparing and serving of a meal they scoured and scrubbed the equipment. Oh, now and then you had a few minutes. There was a toilet you could go to whenever you liked; you did not have to ask permission. And as some thoughtful person had supplied the toilet with torn newspapers you were saved the embarrassment of asking the nurse.

The nurses who were in and out of the cafeteria were

sociable but unfortunately too energetic; they had a great passion for scouring the aluminum. Whenever Virginia thought she might have a moment to rest a nurse invariably would ask her if she wouldn't like to help with the scouring. The manner of asking was reminiscent of Miss Hart, back in the polishing days. You simply could not refuse so gracious an invitation. But all in all, it was a treat to get to spend an entire day away from the day-room. You had plenty to eat and plenty of time in which to eat.

And one day May gave you three pecans. What a treat. Virginia cracked one and ate it before she remembered Louise. How ashamed of herself she was then. Here she was in a position to have all the butter and coffee she wanted and like a pig she had gobbled up a rare delicacy. She cracked the other two nuts and tied the meats into a rag she had found and that night she gave them to Louise in the washroom.

The gift brought Louise into reality. She recognized Virginia and spoke to her gratefully. She exhibited the nuts to the ladies who crowded around her and she told them to help themselves. The generosity of the Juniper Hill paupers was something that never failed to make Virginia weep and now she had to pinch herself to keep from bawling. Louise held out her hand and offered the nuts as if she owned a forest of pecan trees. "Don't give them away," said Virginia. "There isn't enough. Eat it yourself."

Louise smiled. "I know what I'm doing, Virginia," she said. "Help yourself, girls."

The ladies helped themselves daintily. They broke the small pieces into smaller pieces and were careful to leave

Louise a crumb. Louise nibbled that crumb and said it was delicious.

The next day Virginia gave Treva two cigarettes. She had become extremely nervous about Treva's smoking. The tall white-haired woman usually smoked rolled up newspaper. Virginia never discovered where she got her lights but all day long Treva smoked something. She accepted the cigarettes from Virginia without comment but later on she came over to her. "You did not give me any cigarettes," she said. She sounded furious and Virginia shrank from her.

"I told you to keep away from Treva," hissed May. "You watch out. She's dangerous."

But the next day Virginia saw Treva put a lighted cigarette end into her mouth and it was impossible not to do something. She quickly filled a cup of water and hurried over to Treva and handed it to her. They were busy in the kitchen just then and no one was noticing Treva or Virginia. Treva took the cup and dashed the water into Virginia's face.

Virginia went back to her work and the next time she saw Treva eating fire she just let her eat it. After all, I am a patient in this place, not a nurse. But I am nearing non-patient status. The softness is leaving. The sympathy. Yes, and the generosity . . . I no longer distribute cigarettes the way I used to. It is a queer way to judge your sanity. I shall feel better about this return of selfishness if I consider it a return of antlike wisdom. I am able now to take heed of the day to come. I have three cigarettes and if I look ahead I'll see that I cannot order more until the day after tomorrow. Therefore I shall not share my supply but I shall hoard it so that each day I can be sure of having one smoke. That, dear lady, is sanity. An insane woman would give all three cigarettes away and then wonder why she hadn't any for herself. And sit off in a corner with a roll of newspaper . . .

There was much talk in the cafeteria about the coming dance. There was to be a dance Saturday afternoon. May was not going. Her dancing days, she said, were over. Virginia did not wish to do any dancing at Juniper Hill, but she decided to go along to watch. She might some day wish to write about a dance in an insane asylum. For some weeks now she had been unable to think of herself as a part of Juniper Hill. The Observer had come back and a novel was being formed.

On Saturday, all of the workers, except for May and the Observer, were somewhat slicked up. Treva had a paper flower in her hair and she was carrying a half-smoked cigar. Treva seldom gave assistance in the work but today she stuck her cigar through her belt and helped push dirty dishes along the chute. Joe muttered to Virginia that Treva had a guilty conscience on account of the dance. Joe was not going. He was religious. He was sad when he learned that Virginia planned to attend the party but his depression was lightened a little when she said she did not intend to dance. Joe did not fraternize with the workers. When he had a moment from his chores he opened a badly damaged copy of *The Vicar of Wakefield* and frowned steadily at whatever page he turned to. He did not read the book but he was very proud of it. It was his, his only possession. On the days when Virginia had her glasses she asked him if she might look at his book and he would hold it out for her to look. He would never let go of it.

Jack, who took care of the coffee urns, was more sociable. He never spoke, but he rolled cigarettes for the ladies and nodded politely when they thanked him. Virginia couldn't help being a trifle afraid of Jack; he looked dangerous and she especially avoided him when he was carrying buckets of boiling water. However, May insisted that Jack was fairly safe and that Joe was the one who might cut up rough. The only time Virginia saw Joe in action was when two of the kitchen workers got into an argument about which rows of tables in the dining room belonged to which one of them. When the argument became noisy Joe leapt over his railing and ran into the dining room and it took two nurses and the co-operation of the two irate workers to persuade him to go back to his machine. It was lucky for Joe, said May, that the nurses were not some others she could think of. "Most of them," she said, "would have had him put in pack for that. And don't you believe him when he tells you he isn't going to the dance on account of religion. They wouldn't let him go. Not him. Why, he'd as soon kill a woman as look at her."

The workers who were going to the dance went unattended. They were Special People. Bianca was more or less in charge of the group, at any rate she was the one who kept an eye on the undependable Treva. But Treva behaved nicely and although she would not walk on the sidewalk she stayed close enough to her contingent.

This Saturday afternoon the great hall was set up differently. The chairs were in rows along the sides. After the ladies had filed in and taken seats the men came and sat on the opposite side of the room. On the stage was an orchestra. When the orchestra started to play the men rushed over to the women. There was no time wasted in selection. A man bowed to the first lady he came to. It was odd to see a very young man bow to a very old woman.

Virginia had chosen a seat in the back row and she had kept on her leather jacket. She had borrowed a needle and thread from Miss Vance and sewed the buttons back on. Now she sat with the jacket buttoned up to indicate that she was here only to watch.

"Hey, Cunningham," a man called to her.

She shook her head. Had he learned her name from one of the nurses? Hearing your name gave you an unpleasant notion that you might have attended a dance before. No telling what all Dr. Kik had shocked out of your memory. "I'm not dancing, thank you," she said.

"Come on," he said.

He came toward her. Virginia looked for a nurse. The nearest was one she did not know. The nurse smiled and said to go on and dance with the gentleman. Do they really say Good Morning Gentlemen on the men's side? I should think they would be chummier and call them Boys. But this one waiting for her was no gentleman, nor was he a boy. He was a trembler. He wasn't such an old man and he was not bad-looking, but he was a trembler. His hands trembled; his whole body trembled. It was horrid to have to dance with him. He danced badly but at least he held her very loosely and showed no interest whatsoever in her. The dance was brief.

When the orchestra stopped playing he bowed to her and went back to the men's chairs. When the music started he came for her again. "All right, Cunningham," he said. There was no way out of it.

During the next intermission there was an announcement. The orchestra leader said he had been asked to say that no one was to dance more than three times with the same person. "And," he added, "I have been asked to say there musn't be any cheek-to-cheek stuff." He was a fat moronic-looking young man and he laughed loudly when he said this last. His players joined in his laughter and a few of the guests made laughing sounds.

Then Virginia's trembler came back. Now it was simply a case of which of them was the sicker. "I can't," she said. "I've already danced with you three times."

"Two times," he said. "Come on."

I know I'm not as sick as he is. "Three times," she said. He had to believe her; she did not shake.

The poor man looked dazed but he went away. Then another one came. This one was small and sleek with a shining bald head and a party smile. He was several inches shorter than Virginia but he danced fairly well and he did not shake. He made a small attempt at conversation and said that it was not quite so cold today as you might have expected at this time of year. Virginia agreed with him. He said that at this time of year you might expect several feet of snow. Virginia said indeed you might. She danced twice with him and at the end of the second dance he presented her with a handkerchief. It was a hideous cheap handkerchief and rather worn, but it was washed and ironed neatly and she needed a handkerchief. He said his mother had given it to him.

"I couldn't take it from you," said Virginia. "You keep it."

But he wanted her to take it as a party favor. He was around fifty and of the party-favor vintage and so she accepted it.

During the dancing she had been watching a handsome young man who did marvelously complicated steps. He danced the entire time with one of the colored nurses. Perhaps she was the only one who could follow his steps or perhaps he was one who could not be trusted. Anyhow it was wonderful to watch him and the pretty nurse with whom he danced. Once he noticed Virginia and smiled at her. She would have loved to try to dance with him. He was the only one who appeared to enjoy the ball. In general the patients plodded around as if this was another therapy they had got to endure. It made you think of stories about people dancing heroically as the ship sank. The music was atrocious, so bad that you decided the appointment must be political or that the czar of the music world had foisted it upon the hospital out of spite. There was the possibility that the band was composed of patients but undoubtedly the Maestro of American Music would not have permitted this. Anyway, you had always heard that insanity helped in the matter of music and this orchestra had had no help of any musical kind.

A half dozen or so women who were strangers to Virginia hailed her by name. One woman was especially effusive. "But I'd thought you had gone home long ago," she said. "You always seemed so well."

Virginia thanked her and made appropriate remarks and they parted with the usual Juniper Hill formula for the best possible taste. "I hope I won't see you again . . ."

You knew, after this dance, that you would never go to another. You had a certain status now. You were eligible to attend dances but you did not have to go. They would not urge you. They hadn't enough time.

There wasn't enough of anything at Juniper Hill. Not enough doctors, not enough nurses, not enough toilet paper, not enough food, not enough covers for cold nights. When the laundry did not get around to the wards in time there were not enough sheets and not enough pillow cases. As Virginia knew from her past experience, there were not even enough beds. There wasn't enough of anything but patients.

"There's no middle ground," Robert had said recently. "I fought this. I investigated private places all over while you were in the hospital in town. I couldn't find a single private sanitarium that charged as little as my entire salary. Here at Juniper the white-collar pays a percentage. It's fair enough. You pay what you can afford. If you have nothing you pay nothing and you get the best medical treatment in the country. Everyone knows that. But the surroundings . . . The public acts as if mental illness did not exist. They leave it entirely to the politicians. There's a lot of whoopla for tuberculosis and cancer and infantile paralysis, but to hell with the increasing number of mental cases. . . . Yes, I know they were right when they told me Juniper Hill has the best doctors and all, but there just aren't enough of them."

Robert was very bitter about Juniper Hill and Dr. Kik these days. Robert had been responsible for having her transferred to Building Five. "I didn't say I wanted you taken out of Reception, but I did make it clear I wanted you to come under the jurisdiction of another doctor. Kik was too busy. . . . I suppose Five isn't as nice as Reception, but I'm sure it's better for you."

"Yes, I'm sure it is," said Virginia. Robert had never seen the dayroom of Ward Thirty-three. He had never seen the cafeteria. He had never eaten one of the Juniper meals. He had never even got much of a whiff of paraldehyde. And he was bitter!

iii

Although she wasn't always as able to follow Robert's conversation as easily as he seemed to think, the periods of relaxed concentration were increasing. Often her share in their visits came without self-consciousness; it was something like playing a piano piece you hadn't played in years. If you didn't think about it you could tear through the piece without faltering, but if you began to wonder about what was coming next you were sunk. Robert's face had lost the strained look and he spoke to her as if they were two normal persons who were conspiring to break through the red tape of the hospital.

"It was hard to get you in," he said, "but nothing to getting you out. I think I've got the answer, though. I just happened to mention that we'd be going back home and did they perk up! I've been harping on that ever since."

"But what's that got to do with it?"

He laughed as if he had a delicious joke on the dignitaries of Juniper Hill. "You'd be in another state and they wouldn't be responsible any more. They like that."

After a moment Virginia laughed too, not just to please Robert but because she thought it was a joke. It had been a long time since she had thought anything was really funny.

"Of course I don't know a damn thing about psychology," said Robert after a while, "but I'd stake my life on Kik being wrong. Maybe he's right according to a book of theories, but he still doesn't know you. Why, you hear about psychoanalysis lasting over a period of years and he just had a few months of it with you."

"Months of what!"

"Psychoanalysis. I suppose it's important but anyhow he came out with the wrong answer."

"You mean he psychoanalyzed me? You mean when he was hiding somewhere in the bushes and asking those silly questions about did I hear voices. . . . It's sort of vague now. . . ." There was a stream, I think, and his voice. Or was it a girl's voice? There was a black couch. "I don't think it's fair to ask a person questions when the person doesn't know what's going on."

"It's part of a theory," said Robert. "They want to know what your subconscious has been up to. But I can't see this business about Gordon."

"Gordon?"

"Dr. Kik talked to you about that, didn't he?"

"It seems to me I do remember him saying something about Gordon. How did he ever know about Gordon?"

"Darling, it's not his fault if there's anything about you he doesn't know. He went all through your life and he decided you had a subconscious feeling of guilt on account of marrying me and that's what gave you a breakdown."

"Well, I'll be darned," she said. Gordon's been dead sixteen, no, seventeen years. She shook her head. "It's the sort of thing that would be nice in a book, but don't you think I waited rather long?"

"Seems that way to me."

Gordon had died just before Virginia and he were to have been married. From the start of it his illness had been recognized as incurable and so his death had brought a mixture of sorrow and relief. In those days Virginia hadn't heard much about people losing their minds— perhaps it had not been so fashionable then to have a breakdown; she had been surprised not to turn white but she hadn't thought to be surprised about remaining sane. "It's embarrassing," she said. "I mean, for Dr. Kik. I always think of him in connection with that little room with the electricity, always the man of science. This changes the picture. I'll have to think of him as a man of romance as well. Gee, I thought you had to be rich to get a doctor to listen to the story of your life. I thought you hired a doctor when no one else would listen to you. . . . Of course I think about Gordon. Why, of course I do. Often. Something will remind me of what he said or did—you think about him sometimes, don't you?"

"He was my friend," said Robert.

"Dr. Kik doesn't understand us," she said. "He just doesn't understand how we felt about Gordon or how we feel about him now. He's kind of young, isn't he?"

"Yes."

"Well, the hell with my subconscious. What I'm interested in is getting the old conscious to working again. You know, maybe my subconscious did cook up something like Dr. Kik said, but if it did I'm sure it was for a novel. I always did have a secret, anyhow I hoped it was secret, ambition to write tripe. Oh, tripe . . . You remember that Polish restaurant where they had tripes-in-cream on the menu and I ordered it because I thought it would be exotic?"

"And it was so white," said Robert, "and those slimy little white strips . . ."

I do not like thee, Dr. Kik—now that I am not so sick. Oh, I like you, but I think you are rather silly and maybe you have a secret taste for tripe—tripes-in-cream.

CHAPTER FIFTEEN

"You go to Staff today," said Miss Vance. "So you won't have to go with the Cafeteria Ladies."

The confidence Virginia had gained in the past few weeks vanished and again she was a shivering invalid. She could not remember the name of Robert's new employer; she could not remember his present address. He had told her but she had not written it down. And I forgot to have him note down the address of that apartment we had last and I still can't even remember the name of the street. . . .

After breakfast Miss Vance took her to a dressing room. "That old thing you are wearing isn't so hot, is it?" said the nurse. "I think you might wear your gray suit. It's real cute and about the only thing you wouldn't swim in." She shook the gray skirt and frowned at it. "You just sit there while I give it a little press. You want to look good when you go to Staff."

"Does it help?" asked Virginia weakly.

"Well," said Miss Vance as she plugged in the iron, "it sort of bolsters you up to know you look good. That was one of the things Sommerville was always harping on. She was always saying if the ladies were given better clothes and makeup and so on . . ."

"You mean—*our* Miss Sommerville?"

"Yes."

"The one who keeps the b.m. record?" You could not imagine Miss Sommerville ever making a sound remark.

"She used to be a nurse," said Miss Vance shortly.

"Oh."

The nurse wet a finger and touched the iron. "Here in this hospital," she said. "She felt things too much, though. In this business you got to have a hide like a rhinoceros."

"I've wondered about her. She worries about that record she has to keep. Isn't that responsibility too much for her?"

Miss Vance shook her head. "It's her own idea. She was a good nurse. She and I took our training together. I never would have come to Juniper if it hadn't been for her always pestering me about it. See, she came here right from training and she kept writing me about how they were always so short of nurses and how something had to be done and all . . . Once you get here it's sort of hard to get away. . . ."

"That's been my experience," said Virginia.

Miss Vance smiled. "Don't worry. It won't be long now. But I'm telling you it's even worse for a nurse. There's not a darn thing to stop you from leaving, except for what made you take up nursing in the first place. Oh, I don't want to make us out missionaries or anything holy, but there's easier ways to make a living. Take me, for instance. I got a little chicken farm in Jersey. Inherited it. I have a couple on the place now but always in the back of my mind I keep thinking I'll get out of nursing and go to that little farm. Pretty place and good money in it. But it's hard when you know there isn't anyone to take your place here. Of course if you died. . . . But you couldn't help that. That's what I keep telling my girl friend. But she doesn't understand. She doesn't know anything about it. She keeps saying suppose I died, then they'd have to get along without me, wouldn't they? Sure. But I couldn't help it if I died and I can help it about the chicken farm. I wouldn't feel right about walking out, especially now when nurses are scarcer than ever."

Virginia watched the pressing for a few minutes. "Is Miss Sommerville going to get well?" she asked finally. The question was not good form, but she couldn't keep from asking it.

Miss Vance slapped the iron down on the skirt. She was not using a pressing cloth but at least she was ironing on the wrong side of the material. "She's been sick a very long time."

"What a shame."

"Yes. She was a good nurse. But she felt things too much. She tried to get some changes made. It was like beating her head against a stone wall. Worse. The damage was more permanent. But maybe she wasn't such a good nurse. Look at it another way. A good nurse can't be any reformer and that's what Sommerville was. A good nurse has got to take orders and get along with what she has at hand. You aren't supposed to get any ideas. . . . Well, I guess that will do."

"Going to Staff, eh?" said Ruth, when Virginia went back to the dayroom. "All fixed up, aren't you? I suppose you think you're going to pass."

ii

Virginia was the only Thirty-three patient who went to Staff that day. She and Miss Vance met another nurse and several patients in the hall and Miss Vance turned her over to the other nurse. The terrified troop marched to a building where Virginia may or may not have been before. She had no memory at all today. They went to a room and sat on folding chairs and waited. She and three others were not called.

The nurse finally said it was time for dinner and that would be all until this afternoon.

On their way back to the home building they stopped to let a group of children run past. "They surely don't have children in this hospital," said Virginia to her marching partner. It's a nursery school that cuts through the Juniper grounds when it lets out. I cannot bear it if children have to live here.

But a nurse was shouting to the children.

"Yes," said the marching partner. She looked at Virginia and then added, as if to make it easier, "Some of them are above average in intelligence. Genius type. But they are better off here than they would be at home."

"So I've been told," said Virginia. "So I've been told."

She especially remembered having been told so by a Mrs. White a long time ago. "We had another child," said Mrs. White, confidential after a cocktail, "but he wasn't quite normal. Nothing hereditary, of course. It was a birth injury. We were very sensible about it and put him into an institution before our second child came. It wouldn't have been fair otherwise. Anyhow, he's much happier than he would ever have been at home. With his own kind. He's really quite remarkable in many ways. They cultivate special talents, you know. He's grown up now and they say he's one of the best they have in their handicraft work. Very artistic. So many of them are, I guess. Well, after so many years he really doesn't seem like a part of our family. We did everything we could for him. Spent hundreds and hundreds . . . We used to go to see him but it wasn't advisable. It upset him so. You see, he always knew us and that made it hard. We keep sending him money so he can have little extras and every Christmas he sends us a basket that he's made. . . ."

The shouting children had passed. No one could say they did not look happy and they certainly were making as much racket as normal children would make. Maybe the building they live in is pretty and gay and perhaps the nurses love them and don't mind being recognized by them.

Strange to be on the guest side of the cafeteria counter. "What's wrong?" whispered May. "I was afraid you'd been transferred. Aren't they going to let you . . . ?"

"I went to Staff," said Virginia.

"God!" said May.

"They didn't get to me. I have to go again this afternoon."

May shuddered.

After dinner Virginia went again to the little room of folding chairs. She had stopped shaking. You can shake just so long and then you become numb. While she was sitting there and staring out into the corridor a young man passed. He was the one who had come into the washroom of House Nine back in the scrubbing days.

When she went into the Staff room she noticed immediately that the young man was there and she wondered if he would remember her and hold it against her that she had been working in the washroom when he desired to use it.

This Staff was unlike the other one. Of course she recalled little about the other one but she was sure today's gathering was much less formal. The doctors were sitting around a table that was over by the windows. You had to walk across the room to them. They watched you. The room seemed very wide. Perhaps this was a part of a deep psychological plan. Perhaps they simply sat near the windows on account of the light.

"Mrs. Cunningham?" said a dark man who had a pipe in his mouth. "Sit down, please."

There was a chair beside him. Virginia sat down. The other doctors, including the washroom man, picked up papers and looked at them. The doctor with the pipe studied Virginia briefly and said he understood that her husband planned to take her home, out of the state.

"Yes," said Virginia. How emphatically he said that "out of the state."

He took his pipe from his mouth. "Well," he said. He looked at his colleagues. "Are there any questions? I believe we have sufficient information. That will be all, Mrs. Cunningham. I'll see you before you leave. Is there anything you would like to say?"

She swallowed. "No," she said. "I can't think of anything. Should I?"

"No, no," said the doctor quickly. "That will be all then."

"Thank you," she said.

She went back to the waiting room.

When she returned to the ward Ruth collared her. "Did you pass? Did you pass, huh?" the woman asked. There was a nasty glint in her eyes.

"I wouldn't know," said Virginia.

"Come on now. Give."

"I don't know."

After the days in the cafeteria the ward was unbearable. The next day Virginia asked Miss Vance if she might go back to work and the nurse said it would be all right. During the first day back in the cafeteria Bianca got word that she had passed Staff. This news caused quite an uproar and for a while it looked as if Joe might lose his control. Bianca kicked off her shoes and whooped and hollered and May looked questioningly at Virginia, but Virginia pretended not to understand. No one had come to inform her that she had passed but she was sure the man with the pipe would work it. She had never seen him before but she knew he was her friend for life. She did not know why, but he had made a decision about her and he had had no intention of discussing the case with the other doctors. It isn't that I don't appreciate all you did, or tried to do, Dr. Kik, but there is a sympathy in this other man that you lacked. You had pity and interest but this new one has an intuitive understanding and a willingness to admit that a problem is solved even when he does not understand what the problem was or how it was solved. Or this is what I think; this is what I hope; this is what my intuition told me. . . .

There was a new nurse in the cafeteria that day. Gracious, she was excited when Bianca went into her war dance. Bianca laughed in her face. "I'm going home," she said to this grand new nurse. "You think I shouldn't yell a little?"

The grand new nurse was young and beautiful. She did not assist with the scouring of the pans. She stood by and watched. Once she made a suggestion but Rachel scoffed at her. "This is the way we do it," said Rachel. Virginia could tell that the nurse did not like this at all but you could also tell that the nurse was frightened. When Jack brought in the boiling water did he try to make himself look more sinister than usual? He glowered at the new nurse and then turned and winked at Virginia.

When it was time for dinner the new nurse stood at the steam counter to supervise. May told her how to hold a tray in front of the food but the nurse did not seem to understand. She took the tray and held it in back of the pans of dessert; she did not get the idea.

The smell rushed into the large room and then the ladies. They jostled and shoved up to the counter and began to grab. The new nurse did not understand at all that you had to hold a tray upright in front of the food and to pass the dishes over the top of the tray. Virginia was standing beside the nurse and she held her own tray up to show the nurse how to do it. But that new nurse was not going to learn anything from crazy people. Not her. She stood there behind the desserts and looked down her pretty nose and of course it was not long before one of the ladies grabbed two desserts. Now that was all right. Frequently a patient grabbed around the trays and when this happened you just said sternly to give you back the extra helping. Usually the patient handed the extra serving back. If not, one of the nurses on the other side could handle the situation. It was nothing tragic; nothing to get into a lather about.

But the new nurse raised the tray she had in her hands and slammed it down hard on the wrists of the thief. Both pans of dessert went flying and the patient stared at her injured arms. The crash of the tray against the metal of the counter had made a noise loud enough to attract the attention of everyone in the cafeteria. For several seconds it seemed that no one was breathing. The workers at the counter stared down at the food.

It was a very frightening silence. Suddenly the new nurse whirled around and ran from the kitchen. Behind the dish-washing machine rail Joe stood with a large crate raised up in his arms. Jack, coming in with more boiling water, looked after the new nurse, shrugged, and poured a bucket of water into the coffee urn.

"All right, girls," said May. "Let's get going. Virginia, watch the desserts too."

The line moved on. After the meal one of the old nurses came back to the kitchen and she helped with the scouring. No one mentioned the new nurse. Why mention some one you'd never see again? Why bother with instability in a nurse when you had so much other instability to think about? That girl was scared to death. She was scared before she came in here. She will always think she was lucky to get out alive and maybe she was. Maybe she was. You can't tell. Jack and his boiling water. Joe and his heavy crates. Treva, even Treva who is always so aloof. Out of the corner of my eye I saw that she had picked up a chair. We, the almost well ones, were the dangerous ones just now. Those dumb creatures on the other side of the counter, they just looked and wondered why.

iii

"Your husband's coming today," said Miss Vance.

"But it's Sunday, isn't it? He works Sundays."

"His name's down, that's all I know. He must have a drag."

Could it be The Day? Don't count on anything; they have fooled you before. It wasn't so long ago that Dr. Kik promised you Robert would come and then later Miss Vance said he was flying, or something that sounded like "flying." Wouldn't your nurse know if you were to be released?

The man with the pipe was sympathetic and he hustled me on my way for fear I would betray myself to the rest of the staff—though he might have been fearing I'd bite him. . . . The washroom man? Did he speak against me after I left? But even had he remembered, would he hold my scrubwoman presence against me? You make a mountain, Virginia, out of what is after all only a juniper hill.

"You won't go with the Cafeteria Ladies, of course," said Miss Vance. "Sort of nice to have a rest?"

Sort of. "But I'll go tomorrow?"

There was no flicker in the nurse's eyes. "Sure, unless you want me to try and get you out of it. I thought you liked it, though."

"I do." I mean I did. I can't ever like it again, not after thinking maybe today . . .

"Cafeteria, ladies," cried Miss Vance, and Virginia caught a glimpse of May and after a while Breakfast Ladies Tunnel was announced.

A week or two of bad weather had kept the tunnel in steady use and the dim passage hung even heavier now with the stench. I wonder how it is in summer—but I don't wonder too much.

"My husband's coming," she explained to May over the counter.

"Oh," said May. "I was scared." She wouldn't have thought of a pleasant reason. "I thought maybe you'd been sent to tubs or pack."

You think I'm that sick? Perhaps I will be sent to pack, May, pack in the outside sense.

It was egg morning and there were admonitions about

Not Throwing Ladies, admonitions that made you ache to hit someone. Virginia peeled her egg and then the lady next to her snatched it away and, without bothering to take aim, threw it. Stupid, if you'd half tried you could have knocked her cap off. Don't scowl at me, nurse, I wouldn't throw an egg at anyone this morning—but watch out for me next egg morning, if I'm still around.

Remember the days when night followed morning without interval and you moaned in terror at the loss? Be thankful for the creeping seconds of this morning. One, two—sixty will make a minute.

In the dayroom the doll-maker demonstrated her clever wares and the Cat's Cradle Society held a meeting and the opera singer obliged with snatches of Wagner and the dancer danced and the vegetarian preached and Louise argued with her brother about the mortgage. "Fired from the job?" asked Ruth.

Could this one whose cradles were swift and untangled, know? "I guess my husband's coming," said Virginia.

"He doesn't come on Sunday."

"All I know is what Miss Vance said."

"Come on, give. Are you going home?"

Virginia shrank away from the tormenter. "I wouldn't know," she whispered. "I wouldn't know."

Before the noon rush, Miss Vance put Virginia into the gray suit and told her she looked swell. Swell enough to get on the bus for town? Swell enough and well enough?

See the fat one who crawls between the railings. Laugh and be reassured. Someone just now said there will be ice cream and that means it really is Sunday. And there is Flo, sure enough, presiding over the little round pans.

"I forgot to return your thimble," said Flo as she reached into her apron pocket.

"Keep it," said Virginia. "I have another one." At home. At home. Bianca kicked off her shoes and danced around the cafeteria when they came to tell her she was going home; she whooped and hollered, but she knew for sure.

Flo put the thimble on and held up her hand as if to admire a precious ring. "Gee, Virginia, you mean for keeps?"

Beyond Flo was Joe, already working at his dishwasher. Virginia waved when he glanced in her direction but he seemed not to recognize her. He was busy, of course, remembering how hot the water should be and how much soap powder to use.

"I don't think much of those gloves for a day like this," said Miss Vance when V. Cunningham was in hat and coat. "It's awful cold out."

If it's The Day, I'll have my muff. . . . But Robert stood in the hall with empty hands. Smile, smile. Don't let him know.

"We've got to see three people first," he said. "Button your coat. It's almost zero."

Three people before going to the store for hot chocolate or coffee?

In the lower hall was a checkroom for the convenience of visitors and Robert stopped there and asked for the package he had just left. "You might as well have it now," he said to Virginia. It was the muff, of course.

Of course? "It was even colder in the tunnel," she said when they went out of the building.

"Gifford first," said Robert. "He's the important one. I talked to him on the phone this morning and he said everything was set for today."

"I can't believe it," she said.

"Well, I can," said Robert.

They went into the building where the staff had met, but it was different now. "You will stay with me, won't you?" she asked in a sudden panic.

"You bet I will," he said. "Chin up. This isn't anything but a matter of routine."

God, make me look intelligent, she prayed. Don't let me bite anyone. That's much more important than looking intelligent.

Gifford was the man with the pipe. He laid it aside to shake hands. "Well, Mrs. Cunningham," he said, "you are leaving us?"

You are asking me? "I hope so," she said.

He waved them to chairs. "A very comprehensive history," he said, and he slapped a thick manuscript that was on the desk.

Robert said nothing and since the doctor seemed to expect some comment, Virginia spoke up. "History of what?"

"Er—you."

"All that?"

"Dr. Kik is very thorough," said Dr. Gifford.

"Oh, dear. I mean, yes, I know."

"We American-trained men can learn a great deal from men like him." Dr. Gifford glared at them as if daring them to deny this.

Robert said nothing. Was he already easing into his old-time habit of letting his wife do the talking? Robert hadn't much small talk and he had done none at all, any more, when the subject was distasteful to him. Years of curtain lectures had accomplished that much. When Robert P. Cunningham realized that speaking his mind would distress his wife, he maintained silence. That, he often said, was what she wanted, wasn't it? He said it was beyond him. When he did talk, she said it was wrong and when he didn't, she said it was worse. If Dr. Gifford was waiting for Robert to fabricate white lies on the subject of Dr. Kik he might as well settle back in his chair.

"He was always so kind," said Virginia. Yes, that's true. Robert probably camped on his trail, pestered him to death, and yet Dr. Kik remained a gentleman. He continued to be a gentleman even after he no longer considered me his little joking Jeannie. And behold the case history and think of the many many histories he's had to prepare. "We are so grateful to him."

Dr. Gifford nodded. "A sound man and very thorough."

You sound dissatisfied. Do you fish? I think I know what you fish for, but the bait is still out of reach.

"I'm fully in accord with Dr. Kik's findings," said Dr. Gifford, "but I hope you won't get any—sentimental ideas. Often the layman misinterprets the doctor."

"I'm sure they usually do," said Virginia. Robert, say something!

"It would be unwise if you were to deduce, from Dr. Kik's findings . . ." Dr. Gifford coughed and he transferred his glare to his pipe. "Damn pipe."

"Of course I don't understand psychology," said Virginia, "but if you mean about the boy who died, I'm sure Dr. Kik was mistaken." There, I took the bait. I hope you are satisfied.

Dr. Gifford knocked his pipe sharply against the ash tray. "Oh, you are, are you?"

Robert, if you'd spoken I wouldn't have got into this mess. Now he'll get so mad that he won't sign our paper. I wonder if we could make a run for the gate. "I was tired," she said. "And I suppose I was scared about money.

It was my fault, really, that Robert gave up his nice job at home, and so I kept trying to write something that would make up for it. It's bad when a writer begins to think more about the check than the story. It makes you awfully nervous. And Robert was working such terrible hours and having to do part of his sleeping in the daytime, and I knew that wasn't good for him. And after he started working I got so homesick. I'd never lived anywhere but Evanston before, you know, and I missed the family and our old friends and the trees and the familiar streets. At home I could go places without worrying about how to get there, but in New York! I went to a lot of meetings here and the people were cordial and all, but it was different. And I never once got on the right subway the first time. I can't understand the subway."

"Who can?" asked the doctor. "Are you going to start this meeting-chase all over again?"

"No, I certainly am not." She had relaxed now. Dr. Gifford hated to let them know what a pushover he was, but she knew it now and she realized that Robert had known it for a long time. Robert wasn't taking any chances. For once in his life he would have lied. Had it been necessary he would have spoken hours in praise of Dr. Kik and everything else about Juniper Hill, but it was not necessary.

"Don't do anything you don't want to do," said the doctor.

"That's a nice prescription."

"Cast down the gavel, Mrs. Cunningham." And then, in case they had missed his literary allusion, the doctor repeated the phrase.

Robert's social poise wasn't so horrible; he laughed. Then he asked about parties and Dr. Gifford shook his head and said only the family at first. "And if I know families, that's going to take a lot out of her. Later on you can have a friend or two in and after a while go to a party or so. Talk to that Chicago man I told you about. He'll know. But then you'll know too. She will tell you." He turned to Virginia. "Frankly, Mrs. Cunningham, I don't think you are entirely well yet."

"Goodness," she said, "I know I'm not."

For a minute or two the doctor was busy with his pipe. Virginia could have told him, as she had often told Robert, that he stuffed it too full. "Nearer well than you think," he said when the matter of lighting had finally been finished. "Always were. But don't crowd it. Plenty of time."

"What about writing? I used to do a little."

"What did I tell you? Already you're wanting to rush back."

"No," she said. "Even my kind of writing takes a little thinking."

The doctor grinned. "I read a review of your last book."

"But that was several years ago."

"*A Little Night Music,*" he said triumphantly. "And a picture almost as bad as the one Kik's got here." He thumped the case history.

"What a remarkable memory," said Virginia quite as effectively as a lush blue-eyed blonde would have said it.

The doctor glowed. "I always read the reviews," he said. "No time for anything else."

"I like the reviews better too," said Virginia. "Unless it's a mystery. I love mystery stories."

"Me, too," said Dr. Gifford. "They always turn out with everything tied up neatly. You aren't left wondering."

"What about the possibility of recurrence?" asked Robert. It was an abrupt question that no one but Robert would have asked in the presence of the patient.

Dr. Gifford threw the pipe down. "Since we don't know the cause," he began.

Had he slipped? Dr. Kik thinks he knows the cause and you said you were in accord with him. And yet Virginia was convinced that the slip was deliberate and that Dr. Gifford had planned, from the start, to inform the Cunninghams that his accord with Dr. Kik was not brimming.

". . . and when you don't know the cause, you can't say definitely. Sometimes we know exactly why; sometimes we can make a satisfactory guess. The confusion of city life? Thyroid? The thyroid trouble in this case seems minor and yet . . . I'm inclined to think the cause or the combination of causes entirely physical and yet I can't put my finger on it. I honestly don't know. . . . Why recovery? Shock was indicated but did shock do it? Was it rather a matter of time? And a sheltered life?" Here he shot Virginia a glance which she could not translate. "I'll put my neck out on the recurrence angle, though, and say in my opinion there will be none."

And did you insert "in my opinion" because here again you and Dr. Kik are not singing in the same key? But I'll not take your word for it nor Dr. Kik's word; I'll take my own. If this be shelter, give me storm away from the hills.

"A balanced diet of work and rest and play," said Dr. Gifford, "and no more than an hour a day when you begin to write again."

"You can't get started in an hour," she said.

"I'll see to that part of it," said Robert.

The doctor got up. "Fine," he said. "Well, here's the paper."

"You had already signed it," said Virginia.

"I signed it right after the staff meeting," he said. "I've been in this field a long time and although I may not know many of the answers, I think I know when it's time for a patient to get out."

They had left Dr. Gifford before Virginia began to think about what the paper meant. Until now she had concentrated upon getting the release and hadn't thought much beyond. Bianca danced, but was there fear under her gaiety? Did she, even while shouting her joy, suddenly realize that Juniper Hill, the shelter patients devoted their sane moments to hating, was indeed a shelter?

Terror of a world no longer familiar shook Virginia and she had to clutch her hands together to keep from snatching the paper from Robert. How can I go outside? I won't know what to say to people or how to look when they are talking. I won't know when to sit down, when to stand up. . . . I've forgotten the simplest of the social amenities and it's been so long since I've had to use my own judgment that I've lost the capacity. "Oh, Robert," she moaned.

"Just think," he said, "only a few more minutes." How happy he sounded! "It won't be long before we're on the train and the folks will be waiting at the station in Chicago, and we'll drive out along that old lake and pretty soon we'll be in Evanston. It's all over, darling. The doctors can beat their brains trying to figure out why you got sick and why you came out of it, but all we care about is that it's over. And it's never going to happen again. I'll see to that."

He wasn't afraid. He knew her better than anyone else did and yet he wasn't afraid. Her hands, hidden from him

275

by the muff, relaxed a little and presently she had calmed down to the extent of wondering what on earth they would do without her in the cafeteria. I was good in there. Maybe I never knew too much about mops, but I was really very good help in the cafeteria.

iv

She didn't catch the names of the other two doctors. One was the washroom man. He signed rapidly. The other man, not so eager to be rid of them, absorbed a little time by telling them of his misery with sinus trouble. When they neared Thirty-three, Miss Vance was looking for them.

"Sent to pack," said Virginia.

"Kid," said the nurse, "you slay me."

Robert asked if he could come into the ward to help with the packing, but Miss Vance said he knew better than that. "But we won't be long," she said.

The drab ladies of Thirty-three had seen Virginia's hat and coat often enough to be fairly calm about them, but the muff created a stir. "Ladies," shouted Miss Vance to the crowding admirers, "every last one of you will be sent to pack!"

"Sheared lamb," hissed Ruth.

Virginia turned to deny this, but when she saw the look in Ruth's eyes she nodded. "S. Klein's," she said.

Ruth shook her head. "No. I know fur. It's beaver, all right. And you're going home. I knew it this morning."

"I'm so sorry, Ruth. . . ."

"So what kind of a dope are you, you and your S. Klein?"

"One side or a leg off," said Miss Vance.

When she had dismissed the junior nurse who had started the packing, Miss Vance said she had taken the liberty of throwing the blue dress away. "I hope you didn't want it for a memento."

Virginia had taken off her coat and now she was ripping out the upper of the two labels. V. Cunningham. Under the hospital's name was a long string of numbers. All but the 33 were crossed out. "I've got plenty of mementos," she said. She dropped the label into the wastebasket and admired the remaining tag that meant nothing except that this coat had been purchased at a certain shop. The label didn't even give away that the coat had been bought off a Greatly Reduced rack.

On the table was a pile of her very best handkerchiefs. Robert must have worked hard to pick out the nicest ones to send along with her. Every handkerchief was stamped with that India-ink identification and yet Virginia had never once got to use one of her handkerchiefs here. But can you blame a nurse who has fifty noses to count?

The packing was nearly finished when Miss Sommerville came into the dressing room. The junior nurse had left the door slightly open. "I've been looking all over for you, Mrs. Cunningham," said Miss Sommerville. "I don't have your record for . . ."

"The patient is checking out," said Miss Vance. "She is leaving the hospital."

"That will make room for another one," said Miss Sommerville, "but they'll send us more than one. They always do. And we're so crowded already. I just don't know where it's all going to end."

Miss Vance snapped the large suitcase shut. "I'll tell you where it's going to end. When there's more sick ones than well ones, by golly the sick ones will lock the well ones up."

Miss Sommerville frowned. "I'm not sure they'll like it here," she said doubtfully. She raised her right hand and stared into the empty palm. "Where's my key got to? How can I let her out?"

"Just draw a line through her name," said Miss Vance.

"I've tried that before," said Miss Sommerville, "but it doesn't work." But then her expression of distress vanished. "I know. I'll erase it." She laughed a little as she scrubbed at the notebook. "There." She held the book out to Virginia. "See. You're gone."

"Thank you very much," said Virginia. She picked up her muff and Miss Vance said she guessed they had everything.

"I should have said good-bye, but it's too late now, of course," said Miss Sommerville. "It would be silly to say good-bye to someone who isn't here." And again reaching for the ghost of her key, the former nurse unlocked a private door.

El poder de la inocencia

Lee Wilkinson

Bianca™

HARLEQUIN™

Editado por HARLEQUIN IBÉRICA, S.A.
Hermosilla, 21
28001 Madrid

I.S.B.N.: 978-84-671-4920-3
Depósito legal: B-20114-2007
Editor responsable: Luis Pugni
Composición: M.T. Color & Diseño, S.L.
C/. Colquide, 6 - portal 2-3º H. 28230 Las Rozas (Madrid)
Fotomecánica: PREIMPRESIÓN 2000
C/. Algorta, 33. 28019 Madrid
Impresión y encuadernación: LITOGRAFÍA ROSÉS, S.A.
C/. Energía, 11. 08850 Gavá (Barcelona)
Fecha impresion para Argentina: 10.12.07
Distribuidor exclusivo para España: LOGISTA
Distribuidor para México: CODIPLYRSA
Distribuidores para Argentina: interior, BERTRAN, S.A.C. Vélez
Sársfield, 1950. Cap. Fed./ Buenos Aires y Gran Buenos Aires,
VACCARO SÁNCHEZ y Cía, S.A.
Distribuidor para Chile: DISTRIBUIDORA ALFA, S.A.

Capítulo 1

VALENTINA Dunbar estaba sentada en su despacho, situado en la primera planta de la empresa Cartel Wines, y desde allí, a través del cristal azotado por la lluvia, veía el aparcamiento y, un poco más allá, el río Támesis.

Estaba comenzando a anochecer, acababan de encender las luces de la calle y su reflejo reverberaba en las oscuras aguas mientras el cielo se teñía de naranja y de violeta.

La mayor parte de la plantilla salía pronto los viernes por la tarde y, en aquellos momentos, un montón de coches estaban saliendo del aparcamiento para unirse al tráfico de la hora punta de Londres.

Tina se había tenido que quedar a trabajar un rato más, pues la campaña de Navidad estaba a la vuelta de la esquina y tenía que organizar los eventos sociales y repasar los textos que siempre acompañaban a las campañas de Cartel Wines.

Sin embargo, por una vez en su vida, no tenía toda la atención en el trabajo. Aquel viernes trece, había estado marcado por la mala suerte. Por la mañana, se había torcido el tobillo al resbalar saliendo de la ducha.

Apretando los dientes, se había secado haciendo equilibrios sobre la otra pierna y se había recogido la melena rubia en un moño.

Para cuando terminó, el dolor había disminuido y pudo pasar al comedor a desayunar tostadas y café. Allí estaba también Ruth, su amiga y compañera de piso.

—¿Por qué cojeas? —le había preguntado.

Cuando Tina estaba terminando de contárselo, sonó el teléfono.

—Ojalá sea Jules —comentó Ruth, apresurándose a descolgar el auricular.

Efectivamente, era él.

Al novio de Ruth lo habían destinado seis meses en París, y lo echaba terriblemente de menos.

—Viene a pasar el fin de semana a Londres —anunció tras colgar el aparato—. Llega esta tarde y se irá el lunes por la mañana. Eh... da por hecho que vamos a tener la casa para nosotros... —añadió.

Eso quería decir que Tina tenía que buscarse otro sitio donde dormir aquellas tres noches. Su casa, situada en un antiguo edificio victoriano, estaba siendo reformada y, encima de que su amiga Ruth se había ofrecido a hospedarla durante las diez semanas que aproximadamente iba durar la obra, no podía fastidiarle el fin de semana con su novio.

—Mira a ver si puedes pasar el fin de semana en casa de Lexi o de Jo —sugirió Ruth.

—Sí —contestó Tina—. No te preocupes por mí, ya me las arreglaré. Tú pásatelo bien.

—Gracias —contestó Ruth, yendo a vestirse.

Tanto Lexi como Jo vivían con sus novios y Tina no quería molestar, así que había decidido pasar el fin de semana en un hotel. Tras meter en una bolsa de viaje unas cuantas mudas, un par de pantalones y la bolsa de aseo, se había ido, despidiéndose de Ruth desde lejos pues estaba en la ducha.

Al bajar las escaleras, había mirado el correo, había encontrado una carta para ella y la había metido en el bolso.

Hasta aquel día, el otoño estaba siendo maravilloso pues los días eran cálidos y ligeramente soleados y las noches frescas pero agradables. Sin embargo, aquel día había amanecido gris y frío y estaba empezando a llover.

Tras abrigarse bien, se había dirigido al aparcamiento para comprobar con desesperación que tenía una rueda delantera pinchada. El mecánico no tardó en arreglársela, pero para entonces ya llegaba tarde al trabajo.

La mañana se le había pasado volando y, cuando habían llegado las doce, se había dado cuenta de que, con las prisas, se le había olvidado hacerse un sándwich para comer.

Menos mal que había un delicatessen a la vuelta de la esquina que hacía comida para llevar. Tina decidió ir cuanto antes para no coincidir con todo el mundo. Al colgarse el bolso del hombro, vio la carta que había recogido al salir de casa y, al fijarse, vio que en la esquina superior izquierda del sobre había algo escrito en rojo.

La había dejado sobre la mesa con la idea de leerla cuando volviera, se había puesto el impermeable y había salido por la puerta de atrás. En pocos minutos, estaba de vuelta con un sándwich de jamón con lechuga y un yogur de frutas.

Estaba cruzando el aparcamiento, con la cabeza metida entre los hombros para resguardarse de la lluvia cuando, al mirar hacia arriba, había visto que un hombre la estaba observando.

Se trataba de un hombre alto, de pelo oscuro y muy atractivo que estaba en el área de carga y descarga y que no le quitaba ojo de encima.

Desde que lo había dejado con Kevin, completamente desilusionada, se había mantenido alejada de todos los hombres. Sobre todo, de los guapos.

Aunque de aquel hombre no se podía decir que fuera guapo como una estrella de cine, era muy guapo, pero de una manera dura y muy masculina.

Tina sintió que se le aceleraba el pulso, y se preguntó quién sería.

Al acercarse, sus miradas se encontraron.

Algunas miradas eran como colisiones. El impacto de aquellos ojos oscuros la paralizó, y Tina sintió que el corazón le daba un vuelco.

Estaba allí, detenida en mitad del aparcamiento, mirándolo fijamente cuando la parte inferior de la bolsa de papel que llevaba, que se había mojado, cedió y el sándwich y el yogur que se había comprado para comer cayeron al suelo.

Tina recogió la comida, completamente inservible, y la tiró en la papelera más cercana. Tras limpiarse las manos con una servilleta de papel, no pudo evitar volver a mirar hacia donde estaba el desconocido.

Por desgracia, había desaparecido.

Estaba segura de que no había pasado a su lado y tampoco había oído ningún coche, lo que significaba que se había metido dentro.

¿Quién sería?

Tina conocía a todo el personal de la empresa, y a aquel hombre no lo había visto nunca. Desde luego, no era del personal de almacén porque iba demasiado bien vestido.

En cualquier caso, el hecho de que estuviera allí significaba que tenía algún tipo de conexión con Cartel Wines.

Tal vez fuera una visita.

No, las visitas siempre utilizaban el aparcamiento de visitantes y entraban por la puerta principal, no utilizaban la salida de atrás y atravesaban el almacén, que era lo que él debía de haber hecho...

Al sentir una gota de agua en la nuca, Tina se dio cuenta de que estaba bajo la lluvia como una idiota y se apresuró a entrar en el edificio. Mientras atravesaba el almacén, lo buscó con la mirada, pero no lo vio.

Al subir las escaleras, se dio cuenta de que se

había dejado la puerta de su despacho abierta con las prisas. Mientras se secaba el pelo con una toalla, volvió a pensar en aquel desconocido. A pesar de que solamente lo había visto durante unos segundos, en su memoria habían quedado grabados su altura, la anchura de sus hombros y sus rasgos masculinos y firmes.

Aunque había intentado dejar de pensar en él, no había podido olvidarlo en toda la tarde. En aquellos momentos, mientras miraba por la ventana con sus preciosos ojos violetas, seguía preguntándose quién sería, qué haría allí y si volvería a verlo.

Tina se dijo que tenía que dejar de pensar en él y concentrarse en cosas más prácticas. Por ejemplo, eran casi las cinco de la tarde, hacía mal tiempo y todavía no sabía dónde iba a dormir.

Desde luego, después de haber convencido a Didi, su hermanastra, para que aceptara la plaza que le ofrecían en la prestigiosa Escuela de Arte Dramático de Ramón Bonaventure, asegurándole que ella pagaría los gastos, iba a tener que ser un hotel no demasiado caro.

Tina era consciente de que le esperaban dos años económicamente duros, pero merecía la pena por ver feliz a Didi.

El teléfono la sacó de sus pensamientos.

—Señorita Dunbar, el señor De Vere quiere verla —le dijo Sandra Langton, con su característica voz nasal.

—Voy ahora mismo —contestó Tina.

Preguntándose qué querría su jefe de repente, Tina salió de su despacho y, con cuidado porque todavía cojeaba un poco, bajó a la planta inferior, donde se encontraba el almacén de vinos y el despacho del dueño de la bodega.

—Pasa —le dijo la secretaria, mirándola de manera extraña.

Tina frunció el ceño y llamó a la puerta, esperando el acostumbrado «adelante». Los franceses tenían fama de ser hombres muy educados, pero Maurice De Vere debía de ser la excepción que confirmaba la regla.

Se trataba de un hombre de poca estatura, seco, canoso y enjuto que se iba a jubilar en menos de un mes. Lo cierto era que no era mal jefe, pero no le gustaba nada la tecnología moderna y se había negado a instalar ordenadores y cualquier otro equipo que hubieran hecho la vida laboral más fácil.

Además, siempre había sido más partidario del palo que de la zanahoria, así que, lo sustituyera quien lo sustituyera, casi seguro que sería para mejor.

El señor De Vere la hizo pasar y le indicó que se sentara.

—Me temo que tengo malas noticias para usted, señorita Dunbar... cuando decidí jubilarme y le vendí esta bodega al grupo Matterhorn, me dijeron que no habría muchos cambios. En general, han mantenido su palabra, pero esta tarde me han dicho que John Marsden, el hombre que llegará el lunes para hacerse cargo de Cartel Wines, tiene ideas muy claras de cómo llevar a cabo las campañas de ventas.

–No hay problema –contestó Tina–. Las sugerencias que he hecho se pueden cambiar o adaptar y...

De Vere negó con la cabeza.

–Me temo que Marsden se quiere traer a su equipo, lo que significa que usted sobra.

Tina se quedó mirándolo anonadada.

–No se puede ni imaginar cuánto lo siento. Su trabajo siempre ha sido impecable...

Aquello, viniendo de un hombre que jamás hacía cumplidos, era impresionante, pero ¿de qué le servía si había perdido su trabajo?

–Por supuesto, me aseguraré de que tenga usted buenas referencias.

–¿Y cuándo...? –preguntó Tina con voz trémula.

–Parece ser que Marsden quiere instalarse inmediatamente, así que tendrá que irse usted hoy mismo –contestó su jefe, visiblemente incómodo–. He dado orden a mi secretaria para que le haga una transferencia a su cuenta del equivalente a seis meses de sueldo.

Aquello era muy generoso. En su contrato, especificaba solamente un mes.

–Por supuesto, le enviaremos por correo las referencias y cualquier otro documento que necesite –dijo De Vere, poniéndose en pie y tendiéndole la mano–. Que le vaya bien.

—Gracias —contestó Tina, estrechándole la mano y saliendo del despacho.

Una vez fuera, la secretaria la miró con cara de pena, y ella se encogió de hombros y subió las escaleras con piernas temblorosas. Llevaba trabajando en aquella empresa dos años, desde que había terminado la universidad. Le encantaba aquel trabajo y se le daba bien, pero, por lo visto, eso daba igual.

Estaba en el paro.

Tina sintió que el pánico se apoderaba de ella.

Seguramente, cuando volviera a su casa, el casero le habría subido el alquiler después de la obra y, además, tenía que pagar la escuela de su hermana.

Desde luego, no la podían haber despedido en un momento peor.

Llevaba un año bastante malo y parecía que el despido venía a ser como tocar fondo. Bueno, de ser así, sólo quedaba ir hacia arriba.

Tina tomó aire, echó los hombros hacia atrás y comenzó a recoger sus cosas. Fue entonces cuando recordó la carta que había dejado sobre la mesa, pero no fue capaz de encontrarla, y se dijo que ya la leería más tarde.

Cuando tuvo todo recogido, decidió dejar las plantas que había comprado para alegrar el despacho, se puso el abrigo, se colgó el bolso tipo bandolera, agarró la caja en la que había metido sus pertenencias, apagó la luz y cerró la puerta por última vez. No había nada de valor en el despacho, por lo que dejó la llave puesta.

Las únicas luces que estaban encendidas eran las de seguridad. Eso quería decir que los compañeros se habían ido a casa y que ella era la única persona que quedaba en aquella parte del edificio.

Sin embargo, mientras bajaba las escaleras, se dio cuenta de que alguien la precedía, alguien que acababa de cruzar las puertas dobles del almacén y que también se dirigía hacia el aparcamiento.

Sin embargo, el almacén estaba desierto. Tina miró confusa a su alrededor y no vio a nadie. Aunque aparentemente estaba sola, su sexto sentido le decía que alguien la observaba desde la oscuridad.

Tina sintió que el vello de la nuca se le erizaba y que la piel se le ponía de gallina. Miró hacia atrás.

Nada.

Retomó el paso cuando, de repente, oyó otro ruido y se volvió parar en seco. Pensó que sería George Tomlinson, el guarda de seguridad nocturno.

—¿George, eres tú? —preguntó, sintiéndose como una tonta.

No obtuvo contestación.

Volvió a preguntar.

Nada.

Si no era él, ¿quién sería? ¿Se habría colado alguien en el almacén? ¿Para qué? Cualquier ladrón que se preciara sabría que, siendo viernes, día de pago, la caja estaría vacía.

Tina recordó que en el almacén había un par de

gatos. Claro que los gatos se movían sigilosamente, y las puertas no se movían cuando ellos pasaban.

Sintió un escalofrío por la espalda, y se dijo que tenía que emplear la lógica. Así, decidió que había encontrado las puertas dobles moviéndose porque George habría empezado su ronda poco antes de que ella bajara y por eso, cuando ella había llegado, todavía se movían.

Sí, muy lógico, pero aquella justificación no la dejaba más tranquila.

Decidió moverse porque le estaba empezando a doler el tobillo otra vez y la caja pesaba. Tenía la sensación de que alguien la observaba, esperando su reacción, pero Tina decidió apartar aquel pensamiento de su mente y seguir en dirección al aparcamiento.

Haciendo un gran esfuerzo para no correr, se obligó a caminar tranquilamente hasta la puerta de salida. No sentía las piernas, y tenía la respiración entrecortada y los músculos tensos, y no podía parar de mirar hacia atrás.

Una vez fuera, cerró la puerta y respiró tranquila. Sin embargo, pronto observó que el aparcamiento estaba prácticamente en penumbra. Al haber llegado casi una hora tarde aquella mañana, había tenido que aparcar muy lejos, cerca del río.

Mientras avanzaba hacia su coche, tuvo de nuevo la sensación de que alguien la observaba y sintió miedo. Vio que en uno de los edificios anexos todavía había luz, y pensó en ir para allá porque, obviamente, había gente. Pero ¿qué les diría, que le daba miedo cruzar el aparcamiento sola? Pensarían que estaba loca.

A lo mejor, era cierto. A lo mejor, se había vuelto paranoica.

Teniendo mucho cuidado porque no veía bien, avanzó hacia su pequeño Ford azul marino. Tras dejar la caja en el asiento trasero, se colocó al volante y respiró tranquila.

¡Sana y salva!

Mientras ponía el motor en marcha, se dio cuenta de que no había decidido dónde iba a dormir. Tendría que haber buscado un sitio barato y haber reservado antes de irse de la oficina, pero, con las prisas, se le había olvidado, y ahora el tobillo le dolía cada vez más, así que la prioridad era encontrar un sitio cercano además de barato.

Le parecía recordar que a un par de manzanas de allí había un pequeño hotel... ¿cómo se llamaba...?

De repente, vio unos faros en el retrovisor y sintió un impacto por detrás que hizo que su coche se diera contra el muro de ladrillo que tenía delante.

Momentáneamente paralizada por la sorpresa, Tina se quedó sentada. De repente, su puerta se abrió y le habló un hombre.

—¿Está usted bien?

—Sí... sí, estoy bien —contestó Tina.

El coche se había calado cuando Tina había soltado el embrague de golpe por el susto, pero, aun así, el desconocido metió la mano debajo del volante y le dio la vuelta a la llave.

—Entonces, quédese donde está mientras yo miro a ver qué le he hecho —le dijo.

Aunque estaba un poco mareada, Tina se dio cuenta de que el desconocido tenía una voz agradable. Había dicho que iba a ver qué le había hecho, pero ella creía que, aunque le había dado por detrás, la culpa había sido suya. Si hubiera estado concentrada en conducir y no pensando en dónde dormir, aquello no habría sucedido.

Tina se disponía a desabrocharse el cinturón de seguridad y a salir, a pesar de que estaba lloviendo, cuando la puerta se volvió a abrir.

—¿Es grave?

—No, yo no me he hecho nada... —contestó el desconocido.

—Menos mal —comentó Tina porque el coche de aquel hombre parecía de los caros.

—Sin embargo, me temo que su coche está bastante mal por el lateral. No creo que pueda llevárselo.

Aquélla fue la gota que colmó el vaso.

Después del día que había tenido, Tina no hizo ningún esfuerzo por controlarse y dio rienda suelta a la risa.

—¿Seguro que se encuentra bien? —le preguntó el hombre.

—Sí... es que estoy intentando ver el lado divertido de todo esto —le explicó—. He tenido un día de perros y he llegado a un punto en el que o me río a carcajadas o me pongo a llorar.

—Entonces, ha elegido usted bien.

Tina se dio cuenta entonces de que el desconocido se estaba mojando, y pensó que, de no haber sido por ella, estaría volviendo a casa para reunirse con su esposa, lo que la hizo salir a toda velocidad del coche. El desconocido dio un paso atrás y la agarró del codo para ayudarla.

—Siento mucho lo que ha sucedido —se disculpó Tina.

—He sido yo el que la he golpeado por detrás, así que soy yo el que le pide disculpas.

—No, ha sido culpa mía. Estaba pensando en otras cosas, he dado marcha atrás y no me he dado cuenta de que había alguien.

—Por favor, en lugar de ponernos a discutir bajo la lluvia, deje que yo cargue con la culpa de momento y luego ya decidiremos —insistió el desconocido, abriéndole la puerta de su Porsche todoterreno—. De momento, ¿qué le parece si la llevo a casa?

—Muy amable por su parte, pero...

De repente, Tina se interrumpió porque, al verlo a la luz de una farola, reconoció el rostro que creía que no iba a volver a ver.

—¿Algún problema? —le preguntó el hombre.

Tina no contestó.

—¿No confía en mí?

—No, no es eso.

–¿Entonces?

Tina contestó lo primero que se le pasó por la cabeza.

–No sé... a lo mejor tendría que intentar mover mi coche.

–Déjelo donde está –le dijo el desconocido con decisión–. Ahí no molesta a nadie, y le prometo que mañana a primera hora llamaré a la grúa y me encargaré de que lo reparen. ¿Necesita algo de dentro?

–Sí, una caja que hay en el asiento de atrás.

–Suba, que ya voy yo a por ella.

Tina subió a su coche. Jamás había estado en un coche tan lujoso y confortable. Una vez instalada, se encontró preguntándose qué haría aquel visitante en el aparcamiento de la empresa tan tarde.

En cuanto dejó la caja de Tina en el maletero, el desconocido se puso al volante del vehículo, se ató el cinturón y se quedó mirándola.

Avergonzada al suponer que tendría el pelo aplastado y la cara mojada, Tina se ruborizó. Al darse cuenta, el desconocido se apartó y desvió la mirada.

–¿Adónde la llevo?

–Eh... pues no lo sé –contestó Tina.

–¿Amnesia?

–No –contestó Tina, molesta.

–Bueno, bueno, no se enfade conmigo.

Tina dudó un instante entre sentirse molesta o divertida. Al final, decidió sonreír, lo que hizo que el desconocido sonriera también.

–Así está mucho mejor –observó.

Cuando sonreía, aquel hombre, que ya de por sí era guapo, se ponía guapísimo. Tina se preguntó cuántas mujeres lo encontrarían irresistible. De repente, se dio cuenta de que le había preguntado algo.

–¿Perdón?

–Le he preguntado por qué no lo sabe.

–Bueno, me están arreglando la casa y estoy temporalmente en casa de una amiga –le explicó Tina, intentando ser concisa–. Su novio va a venir a pasar el fin de semana y, como la casa es muy pequeña, tengo que buscarme un hotel.

«Una oportunidad de oro», pensó Richard.

–Bueno, en Londres hay muchísimos hoteles. ¿Alguno en particular?

–No, cualquiera me sirve... siempre y cuando no sea muy caro –contestó Tina.

A juzgar por su ropa y su coche, aquel hombre no se debía de preocupar mucho por lo que era caro o no, así que seguramente no conocería ningún hotel barato, y Tina no quería tenerlo dando vueltas por la ciudad.

–No sé si seguirá abierto, pero me parece que cerca de aquí, en Mather Street, había un hotel que se llamaba Fairbourn o algo así... –recordó.

El desconocido enarcó las cejas.

–Si es el que yo creo, no parece un sitio muy bonito –comentó.

–Sólo es para tres noches, así que me da igual.

Tres noches, ¿eh? Las cosas no podían estar saliendo mejor. Aunque había tenido que realizar un viaje que no estaba previsto, la había localizado mucho antes de lo que esperaba.

Tenía que actuar con rapidez, pero con cuidado a la vez porque se jugaba mucho.

—Yo creo que, tal y como usted ha dicho, ese hotel está cerrado, y no hace una noche como para estar dando vueltas por la ciudad, así que la invito a que se quede en mi casa.

Capítulo 2

TINA se quedó mirándolo fijamente, preguntándose qué estaría pensando.

—La invito a mi casa —repitió el desconocido.

Richard sabía qué tipo de mujer era Tina, así que esperaba que aceptara la invitación, pero no fue así.

—No puedo.

—¿Por qué no? Tengo una habitación de invitados que está vacía.

Aunque el hecho de que hubiera mencionado la habitación de invitados la dejó más tranquila, había otras consideraciones que hacer. Para empezar, que aquel hombre que tenía veintimuchos o treinta y pocos años, podía estar casado.

—Gracias, pero...

—Quédese por lo menos esta noche —insistió—. Mañana, si quiere, se va a un hotel. Tendrá todo el día para buscar uno que le guste.

—¿Y a su mujer no le importará?

—No creo, porque no tengo mujer.

No estaba casado. Tina sintió una gran ilusión. No tan rápido, no tan rápido. Seguramente, tendría novia.

–Bueno, pero... seguro que hay alguien...

–¿Se refiere a una mujer?

–Eh... sí.

–Sí, claro que hay una mujer en casa.

–Ah –comentó Tina, intentando ocultar la desilusión–. Bueno, muchas gracias, pero no me gustaría molestarla con mi presencia...

–A Gwen no le importará –le aseguró él.

–No creo que le haga gracia que...

–Gwen no es mi novia, es mi asistenta, una mujer muy seria y muy creyente.

Tina frunció el ceño pues tenía la impresión de que se estaba burlando de ella.

–¿Qué pasa? ¿Tiene algo en contra de las mujeres religiosas?

–Por supuesto que no –contestó Tina, dándose cuenta de que, efectivamente, le estaba tomando el pelo.

–Entonces, ya está –anunció Richard, poniendo el coche en marcha.

Lo había dicho con tanta naturalidad, que Tina no había reaccionado y ahora tenía la sensación de que se le estaba yendo la situación de las manos. Aunque aquel hombre le gustaba, se sentía profundamente atraída por él y quería estar con él, Tina se dijo que aquello era una locura.

El hecho de que fuera bien vestido, hablara correctamente y tuviera un coche caro no quería decir que fuera de fiar. En palabras de su madre, aquel hombre podía tener «segundas intenciones con ella».

Tina era una mujer alta y delgada de piel preciosa y rasgos claros, pero no se tenía por ningún bellezón. Los hombres no se volvían locos por ella, vamos.

Era obvio que un hombre de su atractivo y su carisma tendría a todas las mujeres que quisiera. Claro que también tenía una especie de integridad que la tranquilizaba y que la llevó a pensar que aquello podía ser la única oportunidad que tuviera de conocerlo. Si insistía en que la dejara en un hotel, lo más seguro era que no volviera a verlo.

La mera idea la llenaba de zozobra.

Tina no entendía cómo era posible que una mujer tan tranquila y controlada como ella sintiera algo tan fuerte por un hombre al que acababa de conocer, pero así era.

—¿Dónde vives? —le preguntó.

—En Pemberlye Square, cerca del St. James's Park.

—Ah...

Desde luego, nada que ver con Mather Street y el hotel Fairbourn.

—Ya que vamos a... iba a decir que íbamos a dormir juntos, pero eso podría llevar a malos entendidos, así que voy a decir debajo del mismo techo —sonrió—, creo que no estaría de más que nos presentáramos. Me llamó Richard Anders.

—Yo soy Tina Dunbar.

—¿Tina? —se sorprendió Richard.

—Sí, de Valentina.

—¿Es un nombre de familia?

—No.

–¿Naciste el 14 de febrero?

–Exacto.

–Lo normal sería que me hubieran llamado Valentine, que se puede utilizar tanto para niño como para niña, pero, desgraciadamente, a mi madre le gustaba más Valentina.

–¿Por qué dices desgraciadamente?

–Porque es un nombre kilométrico.

–A mí me gusta.

–Oh... –se ruborizó Tina.

–Así que trabajas en Cartel Wines... ¿y a qué te dedicas, Valentina?

–Soy directora de Relaciones Publicas y de Promociones –contestó Tina–. Bueno, más bien, era.

–¿Lo has dejado?

–No, me han despedido. Esta tarde me han dicho que Matterhorn, el grupo que ha comprado la empresa, tiene un equipo de promociones propio y que, dado que desembarca la semana que viene, yo sobraba.

–¿Llevabas mucho tiempo trabajando ahí?

–Desde que terminé la universidad.

–Ah, pero ¿has terminado la universidad? Lo digo porque parece que tienes dieciséis años...

–¡Tengo veintitrés! –se indignó Tina.

–Ah, bueno, usted perdone... ¡Qué mayor eres! Tina se rió.

–Dentro de unos años, cuando me digan que aparento dieciséis, me parecerá todo un cumplido –recapacitó–. ¿Y tú? Tú no trabajas en Cartel Wines, ¿verdad?

–No.

–Ya me parecía a mí. Tampoco me parecías una visita. Por lo menos, no te pareces a las visitas normales.

–¿Eso es una queja o un cumplido?

–Un comentario. Las visitas normales utilizan el aparcamiento principal, entran por la puerta delantera y siempre se van antes que el personal.

–Culpable.

Tina se dio cuenta de que, aunque le acababa de decir que no era una visita y ella ya sabía que no trabajaba en la empresa, seguía sin saber qué hacía por allí.

–Te he visto antes –comentó Richard.

Así que se acordaba de ella, ¿eh?

–Sí, he salido a comprar algo para comer.

Richard no quería darle oportunidad de que le hiciera más preguntas, así que prefirió seguir preguntado él.

–Una pena que se te haya caído. ¿Estás sin comer?

–Sí.

–Supongo que estarás muerta de hambre. Menos mal que Gwen tendrá la cena lista para cuando lleguemos.

–Ya, pero ella no sabe que yo voy y...

–No te preocupes. Gwen siempre cocina de sobra porque tiene seis hijos y está acostumbrada a hacer siempre comida de más –la tranquilizó Richard, eligiendo un tema de conversación neutro–. Lo que sobra se lo lleva a un comedor social que lleva su iglesia.

Justo cuando estaba acabando de contarle las actividades de beneficencia de su asistenta, llegaron a Pemberley Square, y Richard aparcó el coche ante una casa porticada. Tras sacar la caja de Tina del coche, la acompañó escaleras arriba hasta un vestíbulo bien iluminado donde los esperaba una mujer menuda y delgada muy bien vestida.

–Hola, Gwen –la saludó Richard–. Tenemos una invitada –añadió, presentándole a Tina–. La señorita Dunbar trabajaba en Cartel Wines.

La asistenta sonrió.

–Encantada de conocerla, señorita Dunbar.

Tina sonrió también.

–Espero que mi presencia no le cause mucha molestia.

–Claro que no. La habitación de invitados siempre está preparada. ¿Quiere ponerse cómoda antes de cenar?

–¿Me da tiempo?

–Dispone usted de todo el tiempo que quiera –le aseguró la asistenta–. He preparado un guiso para cenar, así que es fácil mantenerlo caliente.

–En ese caso, mientras la señorita Dunbar se cambia, yo voy a consultar mi correo electrónico. Tomaremos un aperitivo en el estudio –intervino Richard, consultando el reloj–. No quiero que tenga que hacer esperar a la gente del comedor, así que déjenos la cena en la cocina, que ya nos la servimos nosotros.

La asistenta asintió, agradecida.

–Una cosa más, la señorita O'Connell ha llamado varias veces. Me ha dicho que llevaba usted el móvil apagado y que no ha podido contactar con usted en todo el día. Parecía muy enfadada.

—Ya veo que Helen le ha hecho pasar un mal rato. Lo siento.

—Me ha dicho que quiere un anillo.

—Ya, gracias, Gwen.

A continuación, la asistenta tomó la bolsa de viaje de Tina y la acompañó escaleras arriba hasta la primera planta.

—El señor Anders es un hombre amable y considerado.

—¿Cuántos años lleva usted trabajando aquí? —le preguntó Tina, haciendo un gran esfuerzo para subir las escaleras sin cojear a pesar de que cada vez le dolía más el tobillo.

—Más de seis años, y en todo este tiempo siempre ha sido amable y educado conmigo.

—Qué bien.

—Es una de las personas más generosas que conozco. En los últimos dos años, el centro con el que colaboro ha podido salvar unas cuantas vidas, sobre todo en invierno, y gran parte de la labor ha podido ser hecha gracias a él porque, además de donar un gran almacén que hemos convertido en un albergue, paga todos los gastos de su propio bolsillo y compra la comida y todo lo que se necesita. Incluso les ha dado trabajo a unas cuantas personas que no tenían donde caerse muertas.

Tina estaba a punto de preguntar a qué se dedicaba Richard Anders cuando la asistenta le abrió la puerta de una habitación y se vio en una estancia preciosa, decorada en tonos pastel que daba a la plaza y desde la que se veía el jardín central.

–Hace una noche de perros, así que me voy a ir ya, no vaya ser que necesiten ayuda en el centro –se despidió Gwen–. Cuando baje, el estudio está justo al otro lado del vestíbulo.

Una vez a solas, Tina decidió darse una ducha en el lujoso baño que había dentro de la habitación. Mientras el agua caliente resbalaba por su piel desnuda, se encontró pensando en Richard Anders.

Por lo que le había contado Gwen, podía estar tranquila. Era obvio que Richard era un hombre de fiar.

Tras secarse, Tina se puso ropa interior limpia y se cambió de ropa, eligiendo un vestido de punto en color marfil. Tenía el tobillo bastante hinchado, así que eligió zapato plano. Tras ponerse un poco de maquillaje y cepillarse el pelo, bajó de nuevo a la planta inferior.

La idea de pasar la noche a solas con Richard Anders la llenaba de excitación y de nervios. Por primera vez en su vida, se encontró deseando ser una mujer inteligente, guapa y encantadora, lo que fuera necesario para interesarle a aquel hombre.

Pero no lo era. Era una chica normal y corriente que no era capaz de mantener el interés de un chico normal y corriente como Kevin, así que era imposible que un hombre como Richard Anders se fijara en ella.

Cuando llegó al estudio, llamó a la puerta y entró. Se trataba de una estancia llena de libros en la que había una alfombra color burdeos y cortinas a juego, una chimenea y frescos en el techo.

La luz era tenue e íntima, y un leño ardía en la chimenea, ante la que había una mesa de centro y un par de butacas de cuero. Richard, que estaba junto a la chimenea, se acercó a ella, y Tina sintió que el corazón se le aceleraba.

Él también se había duchado y se había cambiado de ropa. Ya no llevaba traje sino ropa de calle, se había peinado el pelo hacia atrás y se había afeitado.

–Hola de nuevo. Pasa y acomódate –le dijo, rozándole la cintura e indicándole una butaca.

Tina intentó mantener la calma y se sentó.

–Vaya, ahora aparentas dieciocho –bromeó Richard al ver que se había puesto un poco de maquillaje.

Al verlo sonreír, Tina sintió que el cuerpo entero le temblaba.

–¿Qué quieres tomar? –le preguntó Richard, indicándole el carrito de las bebidas.

Teniendo en cuenta que no había comido nada desde el desayuno, Tina pidió zumo de naranja. Mientras Richard se lo servía, Tina se dio cuenta de que estaba todavía más atractivo con aquella ropa que con el traje, y sintió que el corazón se le aceleraba. No quería que la sorprendiera mirándolo, así que desvió la mirada.

—Aquí tienes —anunció Richard al cabo de unos segundos, yendo hacia ella y entregándole un vaso de zumo de naranja recién exprimido.

A continuación, se acodó en la chimenea con un vaso de whisky con soda en la mano y se quedó mirándola.

Hubiera pensado que la vida que había llevado habría dejado huellas en ella, pero observándola de cerca se veía que estaba sana y que no parecía que nadie la hubiera tocado, a pesar de que él sabía muy bien qué tipo de mujer era.

Había sabido desde el principio que era rubia y de ojos azules porque había visto fotografías suyas, lo que lo había llevado a pensar que se trataba de una mujer atractiva. Sin embargo, cuando la había visto en carne y hueso, se había dado cuenta de que las fotografías no le hacían justicia, ya que era una mujer preciosa.

Tenía los ojos violetas y rasgados hacia arriba, un pelo rubio sedoso y maravilloso que parecía natural, cejas estrechas, pómulos altos, nariz recta y una boca que Richard se moría por besar.

Aquella mujer era realmente guapa. No, era mucho más que eso. Era espectacular y contradictoria a la vez porque, a pesar de tener una boca de pecado, también tenía un halo de inocencia y de vulnerabilidad que, aunque Richard sabía que era falso, le había llegado al alma desde la primera vez que la había visto.

Aquello podía resultar peligroso.

Richard apartó aquellos pensamientos de su mente.

Sentirse atraído por ella no era ningún problema siempre y cuando tuviera claro su objetivo y no permitiera que aquella atracción lo apartara de él.

Durante las últimas semanas, había considerado diferentes planes de actuación. Al final, había decidido que lo mejor sería elegir uno cuando la hubiera conocido.

Las cosas habían ido tan deprisa, que no le había dado tiempo a decidir nada, y ahora Tina estaba ante él. Era obvio que llevársela a la cama no iba a ser ningún sacrificio. Más bien, todo lo contrario.

Por supuesto, si conseguía que Tina sintiera algo por él, que se enamorara de él, todo sería mucho más fácil. Era evidente que se sentía atraída por él, pero Richard estaba extrañado porque estaba intentando disimularlo, nada propio de una mujer como ella.

Por los informes que le habían hecho sobre ella, sabía que era una mujer moderna que, a pesar de parecer inocente, no tenía ningún tipo de escrúpulo ni de inhibición. Claro que, para curarse en salud, Richard decidió asegurarse de que así era.

—¿Te pasa algo? —le preguntó Tina al ver cómo la miraba.

—No, claro que no.

Tina se dijo que la expresión salvaje que había visto en su rostro debía de haber sido a causa del juego luces de las llamas.

–¿Quieres beber algo más? –le preguntó Richard.

–Sí, por favor.

–Te sugiero que, esta vez, le pongas mi ingrediente secreto.

–¿Y cuál es tu ingrediente secreto?

–Un toquecito de Cointreau, tampoco te creas que soy muy original –sonrió Richard.

Tina se rió y aceptó el zumo de naranja con Cointreau que Richard le entregaba. Mientras la miraba, ella se fijó en que tenía los ojos pardos tirando a verde y unas pestañas larguísimas.

De repente, Richard se acercó, le tomó el vaso de entre las manos, lo dejó sobre la mesa con mucha tranquilidad y la besó.

Por supuesto, la habían besado otras veces, pero jamás así. Richard no la estaba abrazando, la única parte de sus cuerpos que estaba en contacto eran los labios. Aun así, aquel beso encerraba todo lo que Tina siempre había querido... calidez, ternura, pasión y dulzura.

Cuando Richard se apartó, Tina se sentía radiante y encantada.

–He querido besarte desde que te he visto esta mañana bajo la lluvia –declaró Richard muy satisfecho.

Aunque, después de haber visto su casa, Tina tenía muy claro que no podía aspirar a tener una relación seria con aquel hombre porque jugaba en otra liga, aquella declaración la llenó de placer y de excitación.

Lo importante era que Richard había sentido por ella la misma atracción instantánea que ella había sentido por él. Aunque aquello no los condujera a nada y pudiera resultar peligroso porque, tal vez, Richard quisiera seducirla.

Tina no era mujer de tener aventuras de una noche, ni sexo por sexo, así que, si Richard intentaba seducirla, iba tener que mostrarse fría y poco interesada.

¡Fría y poco interesada! ¿Pero a quién pretendía engañar?

Iba a tener que fingir. Tina se dijo que siempre se le había dado bien mantener las distancias con los hombres. Claro que eso había sido cuando no había tenido ningún interés de verdad en ellos.

Aunque parecía ridículo en los tiempos que corrían, a ella la habían educado para creer que el amor y el compromiso iban de la mano, y que el sexo sólo se practicaba dentro del marco del matrimonio.

No quería decir aquello que Tina criticara a los demás o se mostrara estrecha de miras, simplemente era un principio que ella había aplicado a su vida. Algunos de sus amigas la habían tildado de loca, otras se habían reído y otras la admiraban por ello.

Ruth le había dicho que había conseguido mantenerse virgen porque realmente nunca se había sentido tentada por un hombre.

—Ya sé que has salido con Kevin, que es muy guapo, pero obviamente a ti no te ponía. Menos mal que no te has casado con él –le había comentado su amiga.

–Mi reino por saber lo que estás pensando –comentó Richard.

Aquello sacó a Tina de sus recuerdos.

Tina se sonrojó.

–Estaba... estaba pensando en lo que me dijo una amiga una vez.

–No te habrás enfadado porque te he besado, ¿verdad?

Tina negó con la cabeza.

–Espero que no tengas novio...

–¿Y si lo tuviera, qué pasaría?

–Que tendría que luchar por ti –bromeó Richard.

Tina no contestó.

–¿Tienes novio?

Tina negó con la cabeza.

–Pero no te ha gustado que lo diera por hecho.

–Lo que pasa es que lo dejé con mi prometido hace unos meses.

Richard enarcó una ceja. No se esperaba que hubiera tenido una relación tan seria.

–¿Cuánto tiempo llevabais prometidos?

–Tres meses.

–¿Oficialmente?

–¿Te refieres a si tenía anillo de pedida?

–Sí.

–Sí.

–¿Quién lo dejó?

–Yo.

–¿Por qué?

–Porque lo sorprendí ligando con otra mujer.

–¿Sigues enamorada de él?

–No –contestó Tina sinceramente.

–Pero sigues disgustada por todo aquello.

Sí, era cierto que Tina seguía disgustada, pero no por lo que había sucedido, sino por cómo había sucedido.

–La verdad es que ya no me importa –contestó al ver que Richard esperaba una respuesta por su parte.

Richard se sentó frente a ella y cambió de tema.

–Me han comentado que el verano y el otoño que han tenido en el continente han hecho que la cosecha de este año sea maravillosa...

Mientras hablaban del clima y del vino, Richard le rellenó la copa una vez más.

–¿Quieres que cenemos? Supongo que estarás muerta de hambre –comentó, echando otro leño al fuego–. El comedor está al otro lado del vestíbulo. ¿Podrás llegar?

–Sí, claro.

–Me he fijado en que tienes hinchado el tobillo y cojeas un poco.

–Sí, pero estoy bien, gracias.

En el elegante comedor, decorado en dorado y marfil, encontraron la mesa puesta con una cristalería preciosa y una vajilla de porcelana. Una botella de vino los esperaba en el centro de la mesa. La cena, aunque sencilla, resultó muy agradable. Richard se comportó como el perfecto anfitrión, atento en todo momento a las necesidades de Tina.

Para alivio de Tina, Richard eligió temas de conversación impersonales. Mientras cenaban, hablaron de libros, música, arte y teatro. No tardaron mucho en darse cuenta de que sus gustos eran muy parejos. Por ejemplo, ambos preferían leer a ver la televisión.

—Yo creo que la televisión es la ruina de nuestro siglo —comentó Richard—. ¿Te has fijado en que en casi todas las casas el televisor ocupa el lugar protagonista del salón y toda la vida gira en torno a él?

Tina estaba completamente de acuerdo, y así se lo hizo saber.

Para cuando terminaron de cenar, Tina se había tomado dos copas de vino blanco y, dado que comenzaba a sentir la cabeza demasiado ligera, decidió tomarse un café solo y rechazó el licor que Richard le ofrecía.

Cuando terminaron de tomar café, se había hecho tarde, pero Richard sabía que no debía tener prisa, así que volvieron al estudio. Una vez allí, avivó el fuego y preparó dos copas de coñac.

—¿Qué te ha pasado en el tobillo? —le preguntó, sentándose y brindando con ella.

—Me he resbalado al salir de la ducha esta mañana.

—Menuda manera de empezar un viernes trece —comentó Richard—. Por lo que me has contado, las cosas no te han ido muy bien hoy.

—No, desde luego que no —contestó Tina, contándole lo del pinchazo que le había hecho llegar tarde al trabajo—. Resulta que, a la hora de comer, me he dado cuenta de que no me había llevado nada...

Richard sacudió la cabeza.

—Así que, además de terminar el día sin comer, también lo has terminado con el coche estropeado y sin trabajo.

—Podría haber sido peor. El señor De Vere me va a dar buenas referencias, así que no creo que tarde mucho en encontrar otro trabajo.

—Supongo que entenderás mucho de vinos.

—Bastante —contestó Tina sinceramente—. Es mi trabajo.

—¿Sabes de dónde procedía el vino de la cena?

—De Francia —contestó Tina sin dudar—. Yo diría que del valle del Loira.

—¿Sabes de qué bodega es?

—Sí —contestó, diciendo correctamente el nombre del vino y la añada a la que correspondía.

Richard la miró, sorprendido, pero Tina no se dio cuenta porque estaba tan cansada que se le estaban cerrando los ojos.

—Tienes sueño, ¿eh? —dijo Richard, poniéndose en pie.

—Lo siento...

—No tienes por qué sentirlo. Ha sido un día muy largo en el que te han pasado muchas cosas.

—Sí... —admitió Tina, poniéndose en pie con dificultad.

–¿Te ayudo?

–No, ya puedo yo –mintió Tina, cojeando hacia la puerta.

¿Por qué demonios había aceptado el coñac?

–Creo que sería mejor que te llevara en brazos.

–¿Cómo?

–Te voy a llevar en brazos –repitió Richard.

Tina se sonrojó de pies a cabeza.

–No hace falta, de verdad.

Ignorando su comentario, Richard la tomó en brazos y la levantó sin esfuerzo.

–Por favor, bájame –protestó Tina levemente–. ¿Qué va a pensar tu asistenta si nos ve?

–No nos va a ver. Ni ella, ni nadie.

–¿Por qué estás tan seguro?

–Porque Jevis, el chófer, vive en la parte de atrás, y Gwen se queda hoy a dormir en del albergue porque Tom, uno de los de siempre, está pachucho.

–Ah.

–Así que estamos solos –sonrió Richard, comenzando a subir la escalera.

Capítulo 3

SOLOS.

Durante un segundo, Tina tuvo la absurda sensación de que había caído en una trampa. Había habido algo en el tono de voz de Richard... ¿satisfacción? ¿amenaza?... que hizo que el corazón le diera un vuelco y que se estremeciera de pies a cabeza.

—No hay motivo para que te asustes —comentó Richard, dándose cuenta—. No te he traído a mi casa para encerrarte en el sótano ni en el desván.

—No, claro que no —contestó Tina, sintiéndose como una tonta.

—Aunque admito que tengo planes para ti —bromeó Richard.

—¿Qué tipo de planes? —se inquietó Tina.

Aquello lo hizo reír.

—No te preocupes. Te van a gustar.

Tina se dio cuenta de que le estaba tomando el pelo y, como le daba vueltas la cabeza, decidió no seguir con aquella conversación. Al llegar a lo alto de la escalera, Richard ni siquiera tenía la respiración entrecortada, lo que demostraba que, aparte de fuerte, estaba en forma.

Viril fue la palabra que se le ocurrió a Tina, una palabra que hizo que inmediatamente su mente se llenara de imágenes eróticas.

Sorprendida por sus pensamientos, se dijo que todo aquello debía de ser fruto del alcohol porque, normalmente, ella no solía beber, y aquella noche había bebido más de la cuenta con el estómago vacío.

Tina sintió que la cabeza le daba vueltas y cerró los ojos.

Richard la depositó sobre la cama, se sentó a su lado y le quitó los zapatos. Allí tumbada, parecía una muñeca preciosa, con los ojos cerrados, las larguísimas pestañas sobre las mejillas, los labios un poco abiertos y su precioso cuello de piel sedosa expuesto y vulnerable.

Evidentemente, el alcohol la había dejado fuera de juego.

Aquello hizo que Richard frunciera el ceño. Por lo visto, no estaba tan acostumbrada a beber como él creía. Tenía intención de emborracharla un poco, pero no de dejarla completamente K. O.

En cualquier caso, no podía permitirse el lujo de tener escrúpulos. Se jugaba demasiado. Si pudiera estar seguro de que Tina se mostraría razonable... pero no tenía manera de saber si sería así. Dependía por completo del tipo de mujer que fuera, y eso no lo iba a saber hasta que la conociera más.

Y, para entonces, sería demasiado tarde.

Por eso necesitaba ir hasta el final cuanto antes.

Mientras él tomaba la decisión, Tina abrió los ojos. Richard le sonrió y comenzó a desabrocharle el vestido. Tina se dio cuenta y se incorporó.

–Ya puedo yo...

–¿Seguro?

–Sí.

–Pero quieres que me quede –declaró Richard, muy seguro de sí mismo.

La verdad era que sí.

A pesar de que estaba borracha, se daba cuenta de que Richard sólo quería una aventura de una noche, y negó con la cabeza. Craso error. Al instante, todo le empezó a dar vueltas y tuvo que volver a cerrar los ojos.

–Preferiría que te fueras.

–Muy bien. ¿Me das un beso de buenas noches? –contestó Richard, inclinándose sobre ella y besándola.

Tina se dejó caer sobre las almohadas y, mientras Richard la besaba, le pasó los brazos por el cuello sin saber muy bien lo que hacía, aferrándose a él como si fuera lo único estable que hubiera en su vida...

Tina se despertó lentamente.

Con los ojos todavía cerrados, se dio cuenta de que estaba calentita y cómoda, lo que no era muy normal en el sofá cama que ocupaba en casa de Ruth.

Además, tenía el pelo suelto cuando ella, normalmente, se hacía una trenza para dormir, y estaba desnuda y sin camisón.

De repente, escuchó el ruido del agua, y se dijo que su amiga debía de haberse levantado muy pronto aquella mañana porque ya se estaba duchando. Normalmente, a Ruth le gustaba ducharse después de desayunar, incluso los días de trabajo.

Pero hoy era sábado, ¿no? Sí, el día anterior había sido viernes. Viernes trece. Tina recordó brevemente todo lo que le había sucedido el día anterior y, de repente, se paró en lo más importante.

Había conocido a Richard Anders.

Aquello hizo que se despertara por completo y que lo recordara todo con detalle. El golpe en el coche, la invitación a su casa, el trayecto hasta Pemberley Square, el beso en el estudio, la cena juntos, el coñac frente al fuego, Richard llevándola en brazos escaleras arriba y diciéndole que estaban solos, Richard entrando en su dormitorio, depositándola sobre la cama y dándole un beso de buenas noches...

Tina recordaba vagamente que, como quería que se quedara, ella también lo había besado y le había pasado los brazos por el cuello.

De repente, se incorporó de un respingo. Al hacerlo, sintió una descarga en las sienes que hizo que se llevara las manos a la frente.

—¿Te duele la cabeza?

Tina abrió los ojos y vio que Richard salía del

baño completamente desnudo. Aquel cuerpo mas-
culino, musculado y delgado, tonificado y fuerte,
era digno de observación, y Tina se quedó mirándolo sin contestar.

Richard se acercó a ella y la besó con naturalidad, como si fueran amantes. Obviamente, lo eran.
De no ser así, ¿qué demonios hacía él en su habitación completamente desnudo?

Tina se quedó helada.

Richard se percató y la miró. Aunque sabía qué
tipo de mujer era, no se estaba comportando como él
esperaba. Aunque lo deseaba, no lo había reclamado
a la cama de nuevo, como habían hecho casi todas
las mujeres con las que había tenido relaciones.

No, la estrategia de aquella mujer era muy diferente. Para resultar seductora, se hacía la inocente
y avergonzada, fingía que no estaba acostumbrada
a irse acostando por ahí con todo el mundo.

Si hubiera reaccionado como las demás, Richard habría aceptado la invitación porque, recién
levantada y con una buena resaca, seguía siendo
una de las mujeres más guapas que había visto en
su vida.

Era Tina una mujer de cuello largo, pechos pe-
queños y firmes y pezones sonrosados que Richard
se moría por lamer. Al darse cuenta de que no pa-
raba de mirarle los pechos, Tina sintió pánico y se
tapó con el edredón.

—Voy a buscarte algo para el dolor de cabeza
—comentó Richard en tono divertido.

Una vez a solas, Tina sintió una extraña sensación en la boca del estómago. Se dio cuenta de que era vergüenza. Se quedó sentada en la habitación, mirando la puerta por la que Richard acababa de salir.

Era obvio que la noche anterior se había olvidado de sus principios, había disfrutado de lo que Ruth denominaba «una de las mejores experiencias del mundo» y no se acordaba absolutamente de nada.

No debería haber bebido tanto.

Sabía que aquel tipo de aventuras no eran extrañas, pero nunca hubiera creído que le iba a suceder a ella.

Tina se mordió el labio inferior.

Si se hubieran querido, habría sido diferente. Si, por lo menos, hubiera habido algún tipo de relación entre ellos...

Pero no, sólo había sido una aventura de una noche.

Por lo menos, por parte de Richard.

Debía de pensar que era una mujer fácil que siempre se comportaba así. Tina se preguntó cómo iba a mirarlo a la cara. Estaría a punto de volver. Tina se dijo que lo mejor que podía hacer era ducharse y vestirse cuanto antes. Sí, después de una buena ducha, se sentiría mejor, más segura de sí misma.

Se levantó a toda velocidad de la cama. Al hacerlo, sintió que la cabeza le daba vueltas y tuvo que cerrar los ojos un momento y agarrarse a una butaca para recuperarse. A continuación, se recogió el pelo y, andando más lentamente, tanto por la cabeza como por el tobillo, que aunque estaba mejor no estaba del todo bien, se metió en el baño a ducharse y a lavarse los dientes.

Mientras el agua caliente resbalaba por su piel y disfrutaba del delicioso aroma del gel de lavanda, Tina repasó su cuerpo y se dio cuenta de que estaba exactamente igual.

Sin embargo, todo había cambiado.

Nunca nada volvería a ser ya lo mismo.

Richard le había prometido llevar a reparar su coche, así que, con un poco de suerte, dándole la dirección de Ruth, el mecánico se encargaría de avisarla cuando estuviera terminado. Mientras tanto, tenía que salir de allí y buscar un hotel.

Aunque se le encogía el corazón ante la idea de separarse de Richard, tenía que hacerlo. Si se quedaba por allí y le daba la impresión de que quería prolongar lo que había sucedido entre ellos, lo único que iba a conseguir era que la despreciara en silencio.

Acababa de volver a la habitación en busca de ropa limpia cuando un golpecito en la puerta la hizo meterse en la cama a toda velocidad.

Era Richard, que llegaba con su desayuno en una bandeja.

—Veo que te has duchado —comentó al ver que tenía algunos mechones de pelo mojado.

Tina se sentía entre avergonzada y excitada de nuevo, pues Richard estaba guapísimo.

–¿Qué tal tienes el tobillo?

–Mucho mejor, gracias –consiguió contestar.

Richard se acercó a la ventana y corrió las cortinas.

–Ha vuelto el buen tiempo –comentó–. Es maravilloso, aunque la lluvia también puede crear recuerdos maravillosos... –añadió, acercándose y besándola en los labios–. ¿Tienes hambre?

Tina se estremeció ante aquella caricia, se colocó el edredón por debajo de las axilas y miró al horizonte mientras Richard dejaba la bandeja sobre su regazo. En ella, había zumo de pomelo recién exprimido, tostadas, mermelada y café.

–Me encanta cocinar, pero no tengo ocasión de hacerlo porque Gwen se encarga de ello, así que esta mañana me he explayado contigo. Te he preparado incluso huevos revueltos, pero no sé qué tal tendrás el estómago... ¿Te atreves?

Tina asintió, encantada de que se hubiera tomado todas aquellas molestias por ella.

–Además de preciosa, eres encantadora. Ya verás, en cuanto hayas desayunado y te hayas tomado esto, te sentirás mucho mejor –le dijo Richard, entregándole un vaso con un líquido un poco viscoso que resultó ser un medicamento para el malestar general.

A continuación, se puso la servilleta en el regazo y se sentó junto a Tina en la cama. Tina pensó que aquella escena tan íntima era propia de una pareja que llevaba muchos años junta o de un matrimonio.

Al tenerlo tan cerca, todos sus sentidos estaban alerta. Tina sentía que el corazón le latía desbocado y que su temperatura corporal estaba por las nubes. Lo cierto era que se le había quitado el hambre, pero no quería hacerle un feo, así que tomó los cubiertos y comenzó a comer. Al cabo de un par de bocados, comprobó que su apetito había vuelto.

—¿Te gusta? —le preguntó Richard.

—Está todo buenísimo. Los huevos revueltos están deliciosos —contestó Tina sinceramente.

—Me alegro —sonrió Richard—. Deseo hacer todo lo que esté en mi mano para complacerte.

Tina se preguntó si aquella frase aparentemente inocente no escondía un segundo significado, y no pudo evitar sonrojarse.

—¿Te encuentras mejor? —le preguntó Richard, dejando los platos en la bandeja y pasándole las tostadas.

—Sí —contestó Tina sinceramente, pues el dolor de cabeza había remitido y las náuseas estaban desapareciendo.

Tina comenzó a untar mantequilla en su tostada. Le estaba costando horrores no mirarlo, así que decidió concentrarse en la mermelada. Se disponía a chuparse el dedo índice de la mano izquierda, porque se le había quedado un poco de mermelada, cuando Richard le agarró la mano y le chupó el dedo.

Tina sintió que la respiración se le entrecortaba y que se le formaba un nudo en la boca del estómago. Richard no pareció percatarse de su reacción y un segundo después, como si no hubiera pasado nada, le soltó la mano.

—Mientras preparaba el desayuno, he llamado al mecánico. Van a ir a buscar tu coche para repararlo en cuanto puedan.

—Gracias. Eh, estaba pensando que... si les doy la dirección de mi amiga, me podrían mandar a mí la factura...

—No, de eso nada, te di por detrás, así que lo mínimo que puedo hacer es arreglarte el coche —sonrió Richard—. ¿Más café?

—Sí, por favor.

—¿Tienes planes para el fin de semana?

—Tendría que buscarme un hotel porque ya he abusado bastante de tu hospitalidad...

Richard apretó las mandíbulas. De nuevo, aquella mujer no estaba reaccionando como él esperaba. No podía permitir que se fuera de su casa.

—También quiero acercarme a un par de agencias de trabajo para ver qué hay.

Richard tampoco podía permitir que hiciera aquello.

—¿En qué consistía exactamente tu trabajo en Cartel Wines? —le preguntó.

—Me encargaba de hacer las catas, de describir

y catalogar los vinos, de mandar los folletos promocionales, de organizar los eventos sociales y las fiestas que forman parte de las campañas de ventas y de asegurarme de tener la mayor cobertura posible por parte de los medios de comunicación.

–Madre mía, así que no parabas. ¿Te gustaba?

–Sí, mucho –suspiró Tina.

–¿Y dónde aprendiste tanto de vino?

–Bueno, estudié tres años.

–¿Tres años? –se sorprendió Richard.

–Sí, uno en la universidad y otros dos de prácticas en Château de Renard. Allí aprendí la composición de los suelos, los métodos de plantación, los factores que tienen que darse para obtener una buena cosecha, cómo mezclar diferentes tipos de uva... –Tina se interrumpió, preguntándose si no lo estaría aburriendo.

–¡Entonces, eres justo la mujer que necesito! –exclamó Richard–. Mi familia tiene un castillo, Castle Anders, a poco más de un ahora de Londres. Tenemos unos cuantos viñedos que hace años que no producen, y yo llevo años queriendo ponerlos en marcha...

–¿Y quieres que yo te aconseje?

–No sólo eso. Lo que estoy haciendo es ofrecerte trabajo.

–¿Un trabajo? –se sorprendió Tina.

–Sí, te has quedado sin trabajo y decías que necesitabas uno, ¿no?

—Sí... bueno... no sé...

Richard había previsto que se tomara la noticia con entusiasmo, pero decidió disimular su decepción y no presionarla demasiado.

—Por supuesto, no me tienes que dar una respuesta ahora mismo. Te propongo que vayamos y que lo veas. Así podrás juzgar y decidir.

Tina pensó que tendría que decir que no, pero lo cierto era que se moría por pasar unas cuantas horas más con él.

Richard vio que Tina dudaba, y se dijo que no podía permitirlo. Aunque él se había puesto en pie, Tina no se había movido.

—¿Te pasa algo? —le preguntó Richard.

—Bueno... tengo la bata en la bolsa...

—Ah... —dijo Richard, acercándosela—. ¿Y ahora? ¿Te da vergüenza? —añadió al ver que Tina no se levantaba a por ella.

Tina bajó la mirada.

—Después de lo de anoche...

—No me acuerdo de nada —interrumpió Tina.

—¿De nada?

—No.

—Ah, entonces, a lo mejor quieres que te refresque la memoria... —murmuró Richard.

—¡No! —exclamó Tina aunque, en realidad, lo deseaba con todo su corazón—. No, quiero decir que no hará falta... lo único que quiero es vestirme.

Richard no contestó. Se limitó a acercarse y a darle la bata. Tina se levantó y, de espaldas a él, se la puso. Richard se acercó por detrás, la abrazó y comenzó a besarla por la nuca.

Tina sintió que se estremecía de pies a cabeza, pero no se atrevió a moverse. Sentía los labios de Richard por el cuello, y sus dedos, sobre los pechos. Sentía el calor que irradiaban las palmas de sus manos, y el corazón comenzó a latirle aceleradamente. Cuando Richard comenzó a trazar círculos con los pulgares sobre sus pezones, Tina no pudo evitar ahogar un grito de placer.

Era consciente de que debía parar aquello antes de que fuera demasiado tarde, pero estaba clavada en el suelo, disfrutando de las caricias. Richard la giró y la besó en la boca. Tina sintió que la necesidad que tenía de aquel hombre la superaba.

Cuando Richard la despojó de la bata y la tumbó de nuevo en la cama, loca de deseo, no dijo nada.

Richard se quedó mirándola unos segundos, medio arrepintiéndose de lo que tenía intención de hacer, deseando que las circunstancias fueran diferentes, pero no tardó en despojarse de la bata, en tumbarse desnudo a su lado, murmurándole palabras bonitas al oído y besándola de nuevo con pasión.

Capítulo 4

MIENTRAS la besaba, sus manos viajaban acariciando su cuerpo, llenándola de deleite, una sensación que se intensificó hasta un límite insoportable cuando, tomando uno de sus pezones con el dedo pulgar y el índice, se metió el otro en la boca y comenzó a juguetear con él.

Cuando deslizó la otra mano hasta el triángulo de vello de la entrepierna y exploró la delgadísima piel interna de los muslos, Tina comenzó a emitir sonidos de placer, y Richard sonrió, satisfecho.

Había llegado el momento, ahora que tenía el control.

De repente, Tina sintió que Richard se apartaba diciendo algo que no acertó a escuchar y abrió los ojos. Richard la tapó con el edredón, se puso el albornoz y la dejó allí tumbada, sorprendida y excitada.

Aunque era inexperta en los asuntos sexuales, Tina tenía muy claro que Richard la deseaba. Entonces, ¿por qué había cambiado de parecer repentinamente?

—Gwen ha vuelto antes de lo previsto –le explicó Richard, besándola.

Tina no había oído nada, pero tampoco le extrañó porque estaba completamente concentrada en las caricias de Richard. En aquellos momentos, el mundo no había existido.

–Podría subir en cualquier momento, así que me voy a llevar las pruebas del delito –añadió, tomando la bandeja del desayuno y yendo hacia la puerta.

Mientras lo veía alejarse, Tina pensó que no parecía en absoluto molesto. Más bien, era como si hubiera tenido planeado irse en algún momento.

Pero aquello no tenía sentido, así que Tina apartó el pensamiento de su mente. Evidentemente, Richard estaba más acostumbrado que ella a aquel tipo de encuentros, pero Tina se sentía como una persona que hubiera estado a las puertas del paraíso y que no hubiera conseguido franquearlas.

Por supuesto, ella tampoco quería que Gwen la sorprendiera desnuda, así que se puso en pie y se vistió a toda velocidad mientras pensaba que, durante la época en la que había estado sola, ignorando su vida sexual, había sido muy fácil negarle a su cuerpo las necesidades que tenía, pero ahora que había despertado a la vida...

Intentando ignorar la necesidad física y la frustración que sentía, se peinó y se maquilló, recogió la ropa, se colgó el abrigo del brazo y bajó a la planta inferior, diciéndose que de nada le valía arrepentirse o desear que las cosas hubieran sido de otra manera.

En el vestíbulo de entrada, no encontró a nadie. Lo cierto era que volver a ver a Richard después de todo lo que había ocurrido se le hacía un tanto vergonzoso. Tina deseó ser una mujer completamente libre, como cuando el día anterior había abandonado Cartel Wines, pero no era así.

Todo había cambiado.

Ya no era dueña de su destino, no era capaz de irse sin decir nada ni de separarse de Richard, era como si la hubiera hechizado, como si estuviera unida a él por hilos invisibles que no entendía, pero de los que no podía escapar.

Aquella sensación le producía miedo, pero también, aunque se le hacía raro, un secreto placer.

Era imposible que se hubiera enamorado. Imposible que hubiera sucedido tan rápido. Lo cierto era que había pasado en una sola noche de ser una mujer solitaria a sentirse más viva que nunca. No se había sentido así ni siquiera estando prometida con Kevin.

En cualquier caso, cuando volvieran de Castle Anders, tenía que irse a un hotel.

Por dignidad.

Al no encontrar a nadie, se dirigió al estudio. La puerta estaba entreabierta. Richard estaba hablando por teléfono.

–Sí, lo siento, pero... tal y como están las cosas... –estaba diciendo–. Tengo que actuar inmediatamente... no me puedo arriesgar a esperar... confío en ello, desde luego... Bueno, te dejo... Sí, muy bien... adiós.

En un abrir y cerrar de ojos, la puerta se abrió y apareció Richard con la cara un tanto desencajada.

–Iba a subir a buscarte –anunció–. ¿Lista para que nos vayamos?

–Sí –contestó Tina.

Richard sonrió y la agarró de la cintura. Aquella simple caricia hizo que Tina sintiera un tremendo calor por todo el cuerpo.

–Supongo que, siendo sábado por la mañana, habrá tráfico, así que podemos ir tranquilamente y comer en algún sitio... –sugirió Richard.

Al ver la bolsa de viaje de Tina, se interrumpió.

–Me he traído mis cosas porque, cuando volvamos, me gustaría que me dejaras en un hotel –le explicó ella.

–Por supuesto. Si eso es lo que quieres...

Hacía un día precioso, el cielo estaba completamente despejado y el sol brillaba con fuerza mientras una suave brisa traía el olor de las últimas rosas y los pájaros cantaban haciendo que la ciudad pareciera el campo.

Al salir, los estaba esperando Jervis al lado de una impecable limusina azul marino.

–He decidido que voy a conducir yo, así que meta la limusina del garaje y tómese el día libre –le dijo Richard, dirigiéndose a su Porsche.

–Muy bien, señor –contestó el chófer–. Gracias.

–Esta noche juega su equipo, ¿eh? –sonrió Richard.

–Sí, y tenemos muchas posibilidades de ganar.

–Se me ocurre que, cuando vuelva Gwen, podríamos cenar pronto y verlo juntos –propuso.

¡Así que Gwen no había vuelto!

¿Por qué le había mentido?

Tina se dijo que no debía imaginar cosas, que normalmente era una persona equilibrada y que Richard no tenía motivo alguno para mentirle.

Tras despedirse del conductor, Richard se puso al volante de su coche y salieron a la carretera. Definitivamente, había bastante tráfico aunque, cuando consiguieron salir de Londres y tomar las carreteras locales, mejoró enormemente.

—¿Dónde está exactamente Castle Anders? —quiso saber Tina.

—A unos diez kilómetros de Anders Cross y a tres o cuatro de Ges Anders —contestó Richard.

Por lo visto, Anders era el nombre que llevaban todas las poblaciones de la zona.

—¿Cuánto hace que tu familia vive allí?

—Uf, más de seiscientos años. Mi madre, que perdió a sus padres en un accidente de avión cuando era muy pequeña, creció allí con sus abuelos. Cuando se enamoró de mi padre, Richard Cavendish, mis bisabuelos no tuvieron problema en que se casaran, pero con la condición de que mi padre renunciara a su apellido y se convirtiera en un Anders, lo que hizo sin problema. Cuando mi bisabuelo murió, a los noventa y tres años, me dejó su imperio empresarial y le dejó el castillo a mi madre con la idea de que pasara a mí cuando ella faltara...

—¿Así que tus padres siguen viviendo en el castillo?

–No, han muerto los dos. Mi madre murió a principios de año.

–Lo siento. Supongo que la echarás de menos.

Richard asintió.

–¿Tienes hermanos?

–No. Soy el último heredero de esta rama de la familia... hasta que me case y tenga hijos, claro.

Tina sintió celos al imaginar que algún día alguna mujer ocuparía el corazón de aquel hombre, sería su amiga y su confidente, su amante y su esposa, la madre de sus hijos. Intentando apartar aquel dolor de su pensamiento y de su cabeza, se quedó admirando el paisaje que se veía a través de la ventanilla.

–Dentro de un par de kilómetros, hay un lugar que me gusta mucho. La comida es muy buena, ya verás –comentó Richard al cabo un rato.

–Muy bien –contestó Tina.

Al llegar. Tina comprobó que se trataba de una antigua posada llena de alegres flores y, al entrar, el aroma de la miel y de las manzanas la embriagó. Una vez instalados en una preciosa mesa cerca de un ventanal, nerviosa, se puso a leer la carta, dándose cuenta de que no tenía demasiada hambre.

Al final, pidió un sándwich de jamón casero y una ensalada.

–¿Y de beber? –le preguntó Richard–. Tienen buenos vinos.

–No, la dueña me ha dicho que hacen ellos la cerveza, y me gustaría probarla –contestó Tina, sorprendiéndolo–. Quiero media pinta.

–Lo mismo para mí –le dijo Richard al camarero.

El hombre les llevó la debida inmediatamente y, tras probarla, ambos estuvieron de acuerdo en que era realmente buena.

–Háblame de ti –le dijo Richard–. ¿Eres de Londres?

–No, soy de un pueblecito. Me fui a vivir a Londres cuando me contrataron en Cartel Wines.

–¿Y qué prefieres, la ciudad o el campo?

–Me encanta Londres, pero prefiero el campo –sonrió Tina.

–¿Tienes hermanos?

–Tengo una hermanastra que se llama Didi –contestó Tina–. Mi madre murió cuando yo tenía siete años, y después mi padre se casó con una viuda que tenía una hija de mi misma edad.

–¿Y os llevabais bien?

–La verdad es que no demasiado. A pesar de que sólo nos llevábamos tres días de diferencia, porque incluso habíamos nacido el mismo mes y el mismo año, éramos muy diferentes de carácter.

–¿Ella sigue viviendo en el campo?

–No, Didi se fue de casa a los diecisiete años y vive en Londres.

–¿Y tus padres?

–Hace un par de años, un familiar le dejó a mi padre un hotel en Melbourne y se fueron para Australia. Antes de irse, me hicieron prometer que me encargaría de Didi porque había estado enferma y había tenido problemas. En aquel momento, yo ya trabajaba en Cartel Wines y tenía alquilado un piso de dos dormitorios, así que, cuando me enteré de que no podía pagar la habitación en la que vivía y estaban a punto de echarla, le dije que se viniera a vivir conmigo.

—Pero no vive contigo, ¿no?

—No, se fue cuando la admitieron en la Escuela de Arte Dramático de Ramón Bonaventure.

—¿Quiere ser actriz?

—Sí. Aunque su madre siempre se ha opuesto, ella siempre ha querido ser actriz.

En aquel momento, les llevaron la comida, y durante un buen rato se mantuvieron en silencio. Aunque Tina quería controlarse y parecer relajada, no podía dejar de sentir que lo tenía muy cerca.

—¿Y cómo es que el castillo tiene viñedos? —le preguntó para romper la tensión.

—Mi bisabuelo, que era banquero, pasó una temporada en el valle del Loira y se interesó en la producción de vino. Cuando volvió a Anders, hizo plantar cepas en las laderas que dan al sur y construyó una pequeña bodega. Cuando murió, el negocio del vino iba muy bien, y mi padre se encargó de ampliarlo todavía más. Sin embargo, cuando él también murió, la bodega se cerró. En aquellos momentos, yo estaba en Oxford y, cuando terminé la carrera, aunque mi madre me pidió que volviera a Castle Anders, decidí no hacerlo.

—Así que tú prefieres la ciudad.

—No, en absoluto.

—Ah...

—Mi padre murió cuando yo tenía dieciocho años, y mi madre se volvió a casar dos años después. Mi padre y ella habían tenido una relación maravillosa y se encontraba muy sola. Conoció a Bradley Anders, que era quince años mayor que ella, y se casó con él.

Tina lo miró, sorprendida.

—Sí, se apellidan igual, pero no eran parientes. Bradley fue adoptado cuando tenía cinco o seis años por Jonathan Anders, un miembro de la rama de la familia de Wiltshire cuya mujer no podía tener hijos. Por desgracia, Bradley y yo no nos llevamos bien. Yo no confío en él, y él me odia porque me opuse a que se casara con mi madre. Por eso, cuando terminé la universidad, decidí que sería mejor para todos que me quedara en Londres, me compré la casa de Pemberley Square y me limité a ir sólo de vez en cuando al castillo.

—No creo que te resultara fácil estar apartado de tu hogar.

—La verdad es que no. Sobre todo, cuando me di cuenta de que mi madre no era feliz. Para hacer honor a la justicia, admitiré que Bradley fue un buen administrador, pero era un hombre con el que resultaba difícil vivir y, aunque ella nunca lo dijo, yo creo que se arrepentía de haberse casado con él y se sentía culpable por ello. Poco después de que a mi madre le diagnosticaran una enfermedad terminal, a él le dijeron que tenía una dolencia cardiaca y que le quedaban como mucho uno o dos años de vida. Le prometí a mi madre que, si moría ella antes, no lo echaría, pero a él no le pareció suficiente. Pidió que pusiéramos un codicilo en el testamento de mi madre para que pudiera continuar viviendo en Castle Anders hasta que muriera, y yo estuve de acuerdo.

—¿Y sigue viviendo allí?

—No, murió de un infarto hace poco.

—Así que el castillo ahora es tuyo y sólo tuyo.

—Sí, mío y sólo mío —contestó Richard con una expresión extraña en el rostro.

En aquel momento, el reloj del comedor dio las dos y media.

—¿Nos vamos? —le preguntó Richard a Tina, recuperando la normalidad.

—Sí —contestó Tina, pensando que, al ritmo que iban, se les iba hacer muy tarde para volver a Londres.

Lo cierto era que la comida había sido maravillosa y le había dado la oportunidad de aprender muchas cosas sobre él y su familia. Por supuesto, nada de lo que había averiguado le hacía hacerse ilusiones porque era imposible encajar en su vida, pero conocerlo un poco más le hacía entenderlo, y eso le gustaba.

Cuando abandonaron la carretera comarcal para tomar un camino de tierra perfectamente pavimentado, Tina pensó que no debían de estar muy lejos. Efectivamente, no tardaron en llegar a unas imponentes verjas de hierro custodiadas por dos enormes leones de piedra.

—Se está haciendo tarde, así que, antes de enseñarte el castillo, me parece que sería mejor que bajáramos a los viñedos —propuso Richard.

—Muy bien.

Lo cierto era que a Tina le interesaba realmente verlos. Si las cosas hubieran sido diferentes, aquel trabajo habría sido ideal.

Tras recorrer un par de kilómetros hacia el sur, Richard paró el coche.

—¿Tienes el tobillo bien como para andar un rato?

—Sí, no te preocupes.

Richard se bajó del coche, lo rodeó y le abrió la puerta. A continuación, la tomó de la mano, gesto que a ella le encantó.

Mientras paseaban entre las viñas, Tina se iba fijando en los racimos de uvas.

—Supongo que habría que arrancar muchas cepas —comentó Richard.

—No necesariamente. Si están bien, no. A lo mejor habría que replantar algunas, dependiendo del vino que quieras producir —contestó Tina.

—Entiendo. Bueno, ya hablaremos de eso más tarde, cuando hayas considerado exactamente la propuesta.

—No creo que...

—A lo mejor, ahora que has visto que los viñedos están completamente abandonados, ya no te interesa el trabajo.

–No, no es eso –contestó Tina sinceramente.

–¿Entonces?

–El trabajo me interesa, pero...

–¿Pero?

–Dadas las circunstancias, se me haría un poco raro...

–¿Quieres decir después de lo de anoche?

Tina dio la callada por respuesta.

De nuevo, no se estaba comportando como Richard hubiera esperado, pero tampoco importaba demasiado. Le había ofrecido el trabajo sólo para conseguir que fuera con él al castillo, así que tampoco importaba demasiado que no lo aceptara.

Lo importante era que estaba allí, y allí tenía que quedarse por si intentaban ponerse en contacto por teléfono con ella. Richard frunció el ceño al pensar en que, si intentaban ponerse en contacto con ella en Cartel Wines, no lo conseguirían, pero, si llamaban a casa de su amiga, ella les daría su teléfono móvil.

El lunes, aquello podía convertirse en un problema.

Ante el silencio de Richard, Tina lo miró, incómoda.

–Lo siento –se disculpó.

Richard salió de sus pensamientos y sonrió.

–No te preocupes, no pasa nada –le aseguró–. ¿Te apetece que subamos al castillo?

En el trayecto hacia el castillo, se encontraron con un torreón derruido, y Richard le explicó que se trataba de una torre, la Torre Daland, que databa del siglo XI. Poco después, Tina vio un castillo de muros de piedra gris rodeado de colinas y se quedó con la boca abierta.

Era pequeño, un castillo en miniatura, pero toda una joya. Parecía sacado de un cuento.

—No me sorprende que te guste porque es una maravilla —comentó Richard.

El entusiasmo de Tina era tan genuino y espontáneo, que Richard se encontró confuso.

—Por supuesto, ha sido reformado varias veces para adaptarlo a las comodidades modernas, pero la estructura es la original. Eso significa que los gastos de mantenimiento son impresionantes.

—Pero seguro que merece la pena por tener una casa así —sonrió Tina.

—Desde luego.

Viendo cómo Tina observaba el castillo, Richard pensó que parecía una chiquilla mirando algo extraño y mágico. Al instante, sintió una punzada de dolor. Ojalá las circunstancias hubieran sido diferentes. Ojalá aquella mujer hubiera sido tan dulce e inocente como parecía, pero era imposible.

—Ahí abajo están las cuadras, los invernaderos y los huertos —le informó Richard a medida que avanzaban—. Ahora sólo tenemos dos caballos, Júpiter y Juno. A Bradley no le gustaban demasiado los caballos y quería que mi madre se deshiciera de ellos, pero ella se quedó con estos dos. Cuando venía a verla, solíamos dar paseos juntos. ¿Te gusta montar a caballo?

–Me encanta, pero hace años que no lo hago –contestó Tina–. Anda, tenéis patos y cisnes –observó, señalando a los animales.

–Sí, viven en lo que hace siglos era el foso de defensa del castillo.

–¡Y qué puente tan bonito!

–Ése se construyó hace ciento cincuenta años o así –le explicó Richard mientras avanzaban en dirección hacia el castillo–. El que había antes era de madera –añadió–. ¡Qué romántico!, ¿verdad? –se burló.

Tina se sonrojó.

–Perdón, creo que mi reacción ha sido exagerada.

Richard paró el coche, le tomó la mano y se la llevó a los labios.

–Soy yo el que te pide perdón a ti. Perdona por comportarme como un gruñón. En realidad, debería sentirme agradecido de que alguien exprese tanto entusiasmo al ver este lugar.

A pesar de las disculpas, Tina parecía incómoda, y Richard se recriminó a sí mismo su falta de sensibilidad. Para empezar, nada de lo que estaba ocurriendo era culpa de ella y, además, no le interesaba estar a malas con Tina porque podía dar al traste con sus planes.

Al ver que Tina se había quedado mirando al frente, Richard le giró la cara hacia él.

–¿Me perdonas?

–No tengo nada que perdonarte.

–Amable y generosa, además de bonita –murmuró Richard.

Sus bocas estaban a pocos milímetros.

Tina no se movía.

Tenía miedo de que la besara.

También de que no lo hiciera.

A pesar de que Richard le dio un beso tierno, Tina se estremeció de pies a cabeza, y el deseo insatisfecho de aquella mañana volvió a apoderarse de ella.

Richard deslizó una mano por dentro de la cazadora de Tina y le acarició los pechos. Al sentir sus pezones erectos, sonrió, satisfecho. Obviamente, Tina era una mujer apasionada y de respuesta rápida, tal y como había descubierto aquella mañana.

El único problema era que excitarla deliberadamente tenía el mismo efecto en él, que se sentía tan frustrado como ella por no poder llegar hasta el final.

Richard se dijo que no era aquél el momento de llevársela a la cama y se recordó que, cuando las cosas se hubieran solucionado, ya habría tiempo para el placer.

Capítulo 5

SERÁ mejor que entremos antes de que Hannah se pregunte por qué no lo hacemos. A pesar de que tiene casi ochenta años, no se le escapa nada –comentó Richard, apartándose con dificultad de Tina.

En aquel momento, se abrió la puerta de madera del castillo y apareció una mujer increíblemente menuda y de pelo canoso recogido en la nuca.

–¿Qué te estaba diciendo? –murmuró Richard, saliendo del coche y abriéndole la puerta.

Tina agarró su bolsa de viaje y siguió a Richard a través de la gravilla de la entrada hasta donde los esperaba el ama de llaves.

–Señor Richard... –lo saludó la anciana, sonriendo feliz–. ¡Todo está preparado para su llegada! ¡Bienvenido a casa! Me ha parecido que hacía un poquito de frío y, como sé que le gusta, le he encendido la chimenea del salón. Me alegro mucho de tenerlo de nuevo aquí.

–Yo también me alegro mucho de estar aquí, Hannah –contestó Richard, tomando a Tina de los hombros–. Ésta es la dama de la que le hablé por teléfono.

El ama de llaves inspeccionó a Tina de arriba abajo y asintió, aparentemente satisfecha.

–Es un placer conocerla, señorita Dunbar. Por favor, si necesita una doncella, hágamelo saber –le dijo, dando por hecho que se iban a quedar a pasar la noche–. La cena se servirá a las siete y media. Faisán con uvas. ¿Quieren tomar una taza de té antes?

–Sí, excelente idea –contestó Richard–. Dígale a Milly que se encargue de todo.

–Menos mal que la tengo a ella. Aunque me encuentro muy bien, gracias a Dios, estas piernas mías ya no son las de antes –contestó Hannah avanzando pasillo adelante y perdiéndose tras una pequeña puerta al fondo del vestíbulo.

Tina estaba anonadada ante la belleza del interior del castillo, pero no se atrevía a comentarlo, y Richard se dio cuenta.

–Siento mucho haberte estropeado el momento –comentó.

–No te preocupes, estoy disfrutando mucho.

–Pero no te atreves a decirlo.

–Estoy siendo prudente.

–Por favor, comenta lo que quieras. Mira, estas habitaciones de aquí forman la zona principal del castillo. El comedor de diario, el salón de estar, el comedor de invitados... –le fue explicando Richard a medida que iba abriendo puertas para enseñarle las diferentes estancias–. La biblioteca es el único lugar del castillo en el que no se nota en absoluto que estamos en el siglo XXI –añadió, guiándola hasta allí–. Aquí está el salón principal –continuó, mostrándole una preciosa habitación de grandes ventanales que daban a un jardín maravilloso.

Los muebles que había en ella eran antiguos y tenían la maravillosa pátina del tiempo, pero los dos increíbles sofás de cuero que había alrededor de la chimenea eran de vanguardia.

Efectivamente, el fuego estaba encendido, un reloj antiguo contaba los minutos desde un rincón y había flores y fotografías que hacían que el salón pareciera hogareño y acogedor.

–Qué sitio tan bonito –comentó Tina sin dudar.

–Me alegro de que te guste.

–Y no hay televisión –remarcó Tina, recordando la conversación que habían mantenido la noche anterior.

Richard sonrió.

–Lo cierto es que no fue fácil compaginar la tecnología moderna con el ambiente antiguo, pero... –dijo, abriendo un gran armario de madera maciza.

Al hacerlo, quedaron al descubierto una pantalla de televisión enorme y plana, un vídeo, DVD y una increíble cadena de música.

–Si no se utilizan, no molestan a la vista –concluyó, satisfecho, cerrando de nuevo.

Acababan de sentarse frente al fuego cuando, tras llamar a la puerta, entró una joven doncella con una bandeja.

–Gracias, Milly, ya nos servimos nosotros –le dijo Richard.

A continuación, le sirvió a Tina una taza de té y un pedazo de bizcocho de frutas casero. Mientras se lo tomaba, Tina se dijo que el ambiente era de lo más cómodo. Aun así, había entre ellos una tensión sexual que no le permitía relajarse completamente. Al mirar a Richard, que estaba sentado frente al fuego con las piernas estiradas y parecía completamente a sus anchas, lo envidió.

Richard levantó la mirada en aquellos momentos y la pilló mirándolo, lo que hizo que Tina se sonrojara.

–Si no tenías intención de aceptar el trabajo, ¿por qué has aceptado acompañarme? –le preguntó Richard.

–Porque quería ver el castillo –confesó Tina.

–Ah –murmuró Richard.

–Lo siento, supongo que te habré hecho perder el tiempo.

–En absoluto. Hemos pasado un día maravilloso.

–Yo también lo creo así, pero tendría que volver a Londres cuanto antes para buscar un hotel.

–Después de lo que pasó anoche, tenía esperanzas de que quisieras quedarte conmigo.

–Lo que pasó anoche fue error. Si no hubiera bebido tanto...

–¿Y lo de esta mañana?

–También ha sido un error. No debería haber permitido que sucediera.

Tina parecía sincera, y Richard no pudo evitar suspirar. Le interesaba que se quedara en el castillo y, aunque estaba seguro de que seguía interesada en él, por alguna razón, había decidido hacerse la dura.

¿Por qué? ¿Acaso querría algo más que una aventura? ¿Acaso querría algo serio con él? Richard estaba acostumbrado a que las mujeres corrieran tras él, creyendo que iban a poder cazar a un marido rico.

De ser ésa la intención de Tina, no le venía mal para sus planes, pero las cosas tenían que ir más deprisa. Lo único que no podía concederle era tiempo.

—Si tú tienes intención de quedarte aquí a pasar la noche, no tengo problema en pedir un taxi —le dijo Tina a pesar de que sabía que le iba a costar una fortuna.

—Querida Valentina. Jamás lo permitiría. Si quieres volver a Londres, yo te llevo.

—¿Seguro que no te importa?

—Por supuesto que no. Estoy a tu disposición. Sin embargo, me parece una pena que, ya que estamos aquí, no veas el castillo. Te propongo que nos demos una vuelta y que cenemos antes de irnos. ¿Qué te parece?

—Me parece muy bien —contestó Tina sinceramente.

—Entonces, vamos. Va a anochecer dentro de un rato, así que, antes de hacer la visita interior, yo creo que podríamos ir a la casa de los guardeses, desde donde hay una vista preciosa del lago.

Tina asintió y lo siguió escaleras arriba. Cuando llegaron a la casa de los guardeses, se quedó fascinada, imaginando cómo habría sido cuando hubiera estado habitada. Al darse cuenta de que todavía quedaba mucho por ver, siguió a Richard hasta la planta superior, desde la que accedieron a la azotea a través de una pesada puerta de madera.

Efectivamente, desde allí había una vista maravillosa. Richard la puso delante de él y la abrazó.

—Mira, ya se ve la estrella polar —comentó—. ¿Quieres pedir un deseo?

—No creo que el que quiero se me cumpla —contestó Tina—. Es un poco difícil.

—Inténtalo. Nunca se sabe.

Sintiendo que las piernas le flaqueaban al tenerlo tan cerca, Tina deseó gustarle de verdad a Richard.

Mientras Tina permanecía en silencio mirando al horizonte, Richard pensó si sería aquél el momento correcto para dar un paso más en su plan, pero decidió que no.

—Sigamos con la visita, que se nos va a hacer tarde para cenar —le dijo.

Tina lo siguió escaleras abajo.

Para cuando terminaron de visitar el castillo, Tina estaba convencida de que era un lugar especial.

—¿Quieres refrescarte un poco antes de cenar?

Tenemos tiempo –le dijo Richard, consultando el reloj al dar por finalizado el tour.

–Oh, sí, por favor.

Richard la acompañó a una suite maravillosamente decorada y le explicó que era la habitación de invitados. Tina se fijó en que en una butaca estaban su abrigo y su bolsa de viaje. Richard también lo vio, pero no comentó nada.

–¿Un cuarto de hora te parece bien?

–De sobra, gracias –contestó Tina.

–Yo voy a ducharme y a afeitarme mientras, y te espero en el vestíbulo –dijo, girándose y saliendo de la habitación.

Tina se sintió decepcionada porque se había ido sin besarla ni nada, pero se dio cuenta de que el cambio en su actitud había sido lo que había cambiado la actitud de Richard. Ella había cambiado las cosas al negarse a que su relación fuera a más.

Tina se mordió el labio y se dirigió al baño, una estancia lujosamente equipada. Desde luego, nada que ver con el baño que compartía con Ruth.

De repente, a Tina se le antojó que no iba bien vestida para la ocasión y, ya que su maleta estaba allí, sacó un vestido de seda violeta y unas sandalias de tacón alto, pues el tobillo había aguantado bien hasta aquel momento.

Mientras se miraba al espejo y se recogía el pelo, se fijó en la cama de dosel y pensó en todo lo que le tendría que contar a Ruth el lunes.

Claro que había cosas que ni siquiera le contaría

a su amiga porque eran demasiado íntimas y personales.

Tras ponerse un poco de colorete y de brillo de labios, bajó al vestíbulo y vio que Richard ya la estaba esperando allí. Además de ducharse y de afeitarse, se había cambiado y ahora lucía un traje impecable.

Desde luego, estaba increíblemente guapo y Tina sintió que se derretía por dentro. Lo cierto era que le habría apetecido muchísimo quedarse a pasar allí la noche y no tener que volver a Londres.

«No, después de cenar, me voy», se recordó a sí misma.

–Estás preciosa –le dijo Richard, dando un paso hacia ella–. Ese vestido te queda de maravilla. Es exactamente del mismo color que tus ojos.

–No sabía si tú te ibas a cambiar... –confesó Tina.

–Lo cierto es que no lo habría hecho, pero Mullins me había dejado todo preparado, y no he querido herir sus sentimientos. ¿Te parece que nos tomemos una copa en el estudio antes de cenar?

–¿Una copa? –exclamó Tina, horrorizada.

Aquello hizo reír a Richard.

–¡Madre mía, qué cara has puesto! ¡Te tendrías que haber visto! Te aseguro que nada fuerte. Como mucho, un jerez. Mañana no tendrás resaca, te lo prometo.

–Menos mal –contestó Tina, pensando que estaba increíblemente irresistible cuando se reía.

–¿Qué quieres tomar? –le preguntó Richard una vez en el estudio.

—Ese jerez del que hablabas no tiene mala pinta.

Richard le sirvió una copa y se sentó frente a ella.

—¿Tú no vas a tomar nada? –se extrañó Tina.

—No, como tengo que conducir en un rato, sólo me voy a tomar una copa de vino durante la cena –contestó Richard.

—Vaya, lo siento mucho, me siento culpable.

—No digas tonterías. Desde un principio dijiste que te querías ir a un hotel. He sido yo el que ha insistido. La verdad es que tenía la esperanza de que, cuando vieras Anders, cambiaras de opinión. Aunque no quieras compartir cama conmigo, podrías dormir sola en la habitación de invitados.

Tina se sentía de lo más tentada, pero no se fiaba de sí misma. Si se quedaba a dormir y las cosas se volvían a poner calientes entre ellos, no estaba segura de poder controlarse.

Mientras esperaba su contestación, Richard decidió que, si aquello no le salía bien, iba a tener que utilizar otra táctica para que se quedara en el castillo.

—¿Has dormido alguna vez en una cama con dosel?

Tina negó con la cabeza.

—¿Y no te apetece probar? Es toda una experiencia –intentó convencerla.

—No, prefiero volver a Londres –insistió Tina a pesar de que le costaba cada vez más mantenerse firme en su decisión.

–Muy bien –contestó Richard, sorprendiéndola al no insistir–. Entonces, te sugiero el hotel Rochester, que está en Crombie Street. No es muy lujoso, pero está bien. Es céntrico y no es demasiado caro.

–Muy bien –contestó Tina–. Como vamos a llegar un poco tarde, a lo mejor debería llamarlos para reservar.

¡Maldición! Richard pensó que el plan no estaba yendo bien. Tina se estaba poniendo en pie. Tenía que actuar rápidamente.

–Ya te hago yo la reserva. Tú tómate el jerez tranquilamente –le dijo, acercándose al teléfono.

A continuación, fingió que realizaba la llamada y la reserva.

Mientras tanto, Tina se preguntaba cómo era posible que hubiera cedido tan rápidamente, y se dijo que a Richard le debían de sobrar las mujeres. Si ella no quería estar con él, otra querría.

Ella no era mujer de aventuras pasajeras. A diferencia de muchos hombres y cada vez más mujeres, no era capaz de tomarse el sexo a la ligera. Si Richard hubiera sido un hombre normal y corriente y hubieran estado enamorados, las cosas habrían sido diferentes.

–Ya está todo arreglado –anunció Richard, colgando el auricular y volviendo a su butaca junto al fuego.

–Gracias –contestó Tina.

–Espero que no te arrepientas de haber venido –le dijo Richard.

–No, por supuesto que no. Me ha encantado conocer el castillo. Lo único de lo que me arrepiento es de haberte hecho perder el día.

–Te aseguro que yo no me lo tomo como un día perdido. Además de disfrutar de tu compañía, me ha hecho muy feliz que te haya gustado tanto el castillo.

Cuando Tina se terminó el jerez, Richard la acompañó hasta un comedor de paredes blancas en el que les esperaba una mesa impecablemente dispuesta. Durante la cena, para que no se encontrara incómoda, Richard le contó la historia del castillo y de su familia.

Cuando terminaron de tomar el café, Tina comenzó a plantearse cómo decirle que se quería ir ya. Richard pareció leerle el pensamiento.

–¿Nos vamos?

–Sí, voy a buscar mi abrigo y mi bolsa.

–Mientras tanto, yo voy a buscar a Mullins porque ha guardado el coche y tiene él las llaves –le explicó Richard.

Tina acababa de recoger sus cosas cuando apareció Richard de nuevo.

–Me temo que mi mayordomo ha salido. Me ha dicho su esposa que volverá dentro de una media ahora.

–Oh...

–No me he traído el juego de repuesto, así que sugiero que, aprovechando que hace una noche preciosa, salgamos a dar un paseo mientras tanto

—sugirió, ayudando a Tina a que se pusiera el abrigo—. Con un poco de suerte, a lo mejor, vemos al fantasma.

—¿Cómo?

—¿Has visto alguna vez a un fantasma?

—No. ¿Y tú?

—Yo, tampoco.

—No sé si creo en ellos.

—¿Estás segura? A Mag la ha visto mucha gente.

—¿Mag?

—Sí, hoy en día el diminutivo es Maggie, pero en la Edad Media era Mag —le explicó Richard, sacando una linterna de un cajón y guardándosela en el bolsillo—. Venga, vamos. Mientras paseamos, te contaré todo lo que sé sobre ella.

Preguntándose para qué necesitaría Richard una linterna en una noche de luna llena, lo siguió hasta la torre este. Una vez allí, subieron hasta las almenas.

El cielo estaba despejado y parecía de terciopelo, y la luna era un enorme disco de plata que iluminaba todo.

—Cuéntame lo del fantasma —dijo Tina.

—Cuenta la leyenda que Mag era la única hija del mayordomo de Lord Anders. Era una chica casta y pura, además de guapa, que se enamoró del hijo de un noble que vivía cerca de aquí. El chico le había dicho que también estaba enamorado de ella y le había prometido que, cuando muriera su padre y heredara, se casaría con ella. Solían verse en la torre Daland, lejos de los ojos de los demás, y siempre en noches de luna llena. Mag subía a las almenas y, cuando desde allí, veía llegar a su amado, bajaba por una escalera secreta hasta la bodega y, desde allí, tomaba un pasadizo secreto que la llevaba fuera de la torre.

–¿Y el foso?

–El pasadizo va por debajo del foso. Cuando yo era pequeño y me quería escapar y salir del castillo, solía utilizarlo –sonrió Richard.

–¿Y sigue existiendo?

–Sí, si quieres, te lo enseño...

–Sí, por favor –contestó Tina, entusiasmada.

–¿Vas a poder con los tacones?

–¿Es un camino difícil?

–Yo creo que si has podido subir hasta aquí...

–Seguro que puedo.

–¿Tienes claustrofobia?

–No.

–Entonces, vamos.

Richard la condujo hasta la torre oeste.

–No hay luz, así que voy a pasar yo delante –anunció, encendiendo la linterna.

A continuación, guió a Tina por unas escaleras de piedra que descendían hasta un túnel de techo bajo.

–Ten cuidado aquí –le advirtió.

El pasadizo por el que avanzaban era muy estrecho y estaba tan sucio, que Tina iba pensando que tenía ganas de llegar al final.

De repente, la linterna se apagó, sumiéndolos en la más absoluta oscuridad.

Tina no pudo evitar dar un grito y alargar la mano para tocar a Richard, pues se había puesto nerviosa, pero no lo encontró, y aquello le hizo pensar, angustiada, que se había ido y la había dejado allí.

Capítulo 6

INTENTANDO controlar el pánico, Tina se dijo que no debía pensar cosas ridículas.

—¿Richard? —dijo con voz sorprendentemente serena.

—Estoy aquí —contestó Richard, tomándola de la mano—. ¿Estás bien?

—Sí.

—Estaba mirando la linterna. Se ha quedado sin pilas.

—¿Qué hacemos?

—Estamos a medio camino, así que yo creo que deberíamos seguir hacia delante.

—Muy bien.

—Lo único que tienes que hacer es avanzar lentamente y con cuidado. Mantén la cabeza agachada —le indicó, apretándole los dedos—. Durante un rato el camino es bastante llano y, luego, comienza a subir de nuevo.

Durante el trayecto, que a Tina se le antojó una eternidad, anduvieron a paso de tortuga y, efectivamente, al final, el camino comenzó a subir. Tina notó que el esfuerzo le estaba haciendo que le doliera el tobillo de nuevo.

–Ya casi hemos llegado –anunció Richard–. Es-
pérame aquí un momento –anunció al cabo de unos
metros.

De nuevo, Tina se quedó sola en mitad de la oscuridad y tuvo la sensación de haber sido abando-
nada. Entonces, oyó pisadas en un suelo de piedra,
un ruido metálico y una puerta de bisagras viejas
que protestaba al abrirse. Momentos después, la
luz de la luna lo inundó todo, y Tina vio que tenía
ante sí unas escaleras que subían.

Richard volvió a buscarla, la tomó de la mano y
juntos subieron por las escaleras, que les conduje-
ron a una torre en ruinas que no tenía tejado y estaba bañada por la luz de la luna.

–Así que aquí era donde se encontraban –comentó Tina.

–Sí. En aquella época, aquí no había nadie, pero
la torre no estaba en ruinas. Aunque ahora sí lo
esté, este lugar está lleno de historia y merece la
pena venir a verlo.

A continuación, Richard se giró y cerró la puerta
de hierro por la que habían salido, se sacó un pa-
ñuelo impoluto del bolsillo y le limpió a Tina las
mejillas. Luego, se limpió la mano que había utili-
zado para seguir el muro del túnel.

–Supongo que, después de lo que ha pasado, te
estarás arrepintiendo de haber venido –comentó.

–No, en absoluto –le aseguró Tina–. Ha sido
toda una experiencia.

Después de leer el informe que Grimshaw le había hecho sobre ella, Richard no había creído que

Tina fuera capaz de tener tanto autocontrol, y el hecho de que se hubiera tomado la situación con tanta calma lo sorprendía y lo intrigaba.

–Creía que te iba a dar un ataque de histeria, pero obviamente había subestimado tu valor –le dijo, besándole la mano.

También había subestimado su belleza.

Sin soltarle la mano, se quedó mirándola a los ojos, unos ojos que lo tenían fascinado y que a la luz de la luna le gustaban todavía más.

Temerosa de que la fuera a besar y no pudiera controlarse, Tina se dio la vuelta.

–Bueno, yo no estaba sola, como Mag. Y ella sólo tendría una vela o, a lo mejor, nada.

–Sí, pero a lo mejor le funcionaba mejor que a nosotros la linterna –contestó Richard, girándola y mirándola a los ojos antes de besarla.

Tina no tuvo más remedio que abrir la boca y dejarlo entrar, lo que hizo que reviviera el deseo de aquella mañana y sintiera que un placer le recorría el cuerpo como si se tratara de un río de lava incandescente.

Perdida en un mundo de pura complacencia sensual, Tina se encontró incapaz de controlarse durante un rato, pero la alarma terminó saltando en su cabeza.

Richard se sentía excitado ante la noche que tenía por delante y no le estaba resultando fácil mantener la calma, pero, al sentir la resistencia de Tina, dejó de besarla y levantó la cabeza.

Tina tomó aire y se dijo que había sido una suerte que Richard dejara de besarla. De no haber sido así, si la hubiera tumbado sobre la hierba, se habría dejado tomar.

Y Richard habría pensado que era una mujer fácil.

—La torre es más grande de lo que yo creía —consiguió decir—. ¿Cuántas habitaciones tenía?

Richard procedió a contarle dónde habían estado los diferentes pisos, las chimeneas y las columnas de piedra. Cuando terminó, se giró hacia ella y la tomó de la mano. Temerosa de su caricia, temerosa de su propia debilidad, Tina la apartó.

Sin mediar palabra, Richard inició la marcha a través de un agujero que había en el muro, y Tina lo siguió, intentando no cojear demasiado.

Richard no volvió a intentar agarrarle de la mano. Mientras volvían al castillo, parecía sumido en sus pensamientos.

—No has terminado de contarme la historia de Mag —le dijo Tina.

—Me temo que no tiene un final feliz. Una noche, por lo que cuentan, esperó a sir Gerwain en vano, y al día siguiente se enteró de que...

Tina lo estaba mirando, completamente concentrada en lo que le estaba contando, cuando se le torció el tobillo herido y gritó de dolor. Richard se calló al instante y la agarró de la cintura para que no perdiera el equilibrio.

—Desde luego, no tendría que haber insistido en que viniéramos.

–Y yo no tendría que haberme puesto estos tacones.

Richard se quitó la cazadora y la tendió en el suelo. A continuación, se arrodilló ante ella y le examinó el tobillo.

–Mira, en este estado es imposible que vuelvas a la ciudad. Lo mejor que puedes hacer es meterte en la cama ahora mismo.

–Pero...

–No puedes andar –dijo Richard, poniéndose en pie–. Te vamos a poner una compresa fría y ya veremos cómo estás mañana por la mañana después de haber descansado toda la noche.

Richard tenía dos objetivos, y el primero lo había conseguido más o menos por casualidad. Ahora, con un poco de suerte, podía conseguir también el segundo.

–En estos momentos, nuestra prioridad es volver al castillo –insistió.

Haciendo gala de su valor una vez más, Tina intentó caminar.

–No te muevas –le ordenó Richard–. Voy a llamar para que nos vengan a buscar. ¿Tienes por ahí tu teléfono? Me he dejado el mío en la habitación.

Tina le dio su móvil.

–Mullins, mire, la señorita Dunbar se ha hecho daño en un tobillo, y me gustaría que nos viniera a buscar. Estamos en la torre Daland –le dijo Richard a su mayordomo–. Ya viene –añadió, mirando a Tina tras colgar–. Te estaba contando la historia de Mag, ¿no? ¿Dónde me había quedado?

—En que una noche sir Gerwain no acudió a la cita —comentó Tina.

—Ah, sí... al día siguiente, Mag se enteró de que se iba a casar con una noble con la que estaba prometido desde que eran niños. Embarazada y sola, se tiró desde la almena y se ahogó en el foso. Cuenta la leyenda que las noches de luna llena viene por aquí a esperar a su amado.

Tina suspiró.

—Ya te dije que era una historia triste.

—Me lo esperaba. Nunca he oído que un fantasma se quede en un sitio en el que ha sido feliz.

Aquello hizo reír a Richard.

—Y yo que siempre había creído que los hombres éramos más pragmáticos, y las mujeres, más románticas.

—En general, puede que así sea.

—Pero tú eres una mezcla fascinante de ambas cosas —dijo Richard, mirándola a los ojos—. Nunca he conocido a una mujer que me intrigue tanto como tú.

La estaba mirando con tanta intensidad, que era como si la estuviera acariciando. Tina se estremeció de pies a cabeza. Sin dejar de besarla, se inclinó sobre ella y la besó. A continuación, la tomó de la nuca y siguió besándola con pasión hasta que Tina se olvidó del resto del mundo.

Sólo existía él y lo que le estaba haciendo sentir.

—Mullins estará a punto de llegar —dijo Richard, apartándose cuando Tina ya había aceptado que estaba perdida.

Efectivamente, un par de segundos después oyeron que se acercaba un coche por el césped. Richard la ayudó a subirse y se sentó a su lado.

–Si no voy a volver a Londres, tengo que llamar al hotel –comentó Tina.

–No te preocupes por eso, ya me encargo yo en cuanto lleguemos al castillo –contestó Richard.

A llegar al castillo, el mayordomo los dejó en la puerta principal. Richard se bajó del coche y ayudó a Tina.

–Ponme los brazos alrededor del cuello –le dijo.

Tina así lo hizo, y Richard la levantó sin esfuerzo y la llevó en brazos al interior del edificio.

–Buenas noches, Mullins, y gracias –se despidió.

–Buenas noches, señor. Señora.

–Buenas noches –dijo Tina.

Estaba intentando mantener la calma, pero encontrarse en brazos de Richard se le antojaba de lo más excitante. El corazón se le había acelerado y notaba la respiración entrecortada.

Tina se dijo que debía controlarse, que no debía mostrar su debilidad. Si lo hacía, Richard se aprovecharía de ella y perdería el poco orgullo que le quedaba.

–Supongo, por lo que has dicho antes, que preferirás dormir aquí –comentó Richard, llevándola a la habitación de invitados.

–Sí, gracias –contestó Tina.

Richard la llevó al baño y la ayudó a quitarse el abrigo.

–¿Quieres que llame a una doncella?

–No, gracias. No hay necesidad de molestar a nadie tan tarde. Puedo yo sola.

–En ese caso, voy a por tu bolsa –dijo Richard, volviendo casi al instante con la bolsa de viaje de Tina–. ¿Estás segura de que estás bien?

–Sí, gracias.

–En ese caso, voy a cancelar tu reserva y a buscarte algo para el tobillo.

En el estado en el que estaba, Tina tardó más que de costumbre en ducharse, lavarse los dientes y ponerse el camisón. Lo último que hizo fue cepillarse el pelo y, aunque normalmente se lo recogía en una trenza para dormir, le dio vergüenza parecer una cría y se lo dejó suelto.

Cuando salió del baño, se encontró con que Richard estaba sentado en una butaca, esperándola y, al verla aparecer, se puso en pie.

–El botiquín de primeros auxilios está listo.

–Perdón por haber tardado tanto –se disculpó Tina.

–Teniendo en cuenta cómo estás, me parece que has tardado poco. Anda, métete en la cama y déjame que te mire el tobillo.

Tina se tumbó en la cama y se subió un poco el camisón, rezando para que Richard fuera rápido y se marchara cuanto antes.

Richard le tomó el tobillo entre las manos y se lo examinó.

–Te dolerá mucho menos cuando te lo haya vendado –dijo al verla hacer una mueca de dolor.

Y así fue cómo procedió a vendárselo.

—Ya está –anunció al terminar–. ¿Qué tal?

—Mucho mejor, gracias –contestó Tina.

—Con un poco de suerte, por la mañana estarás como nueva –dijo Richard, poniéndose en pie con intención de irse.

Tina suspiró aliviada pero, de repente, vio que se volvía a sentar.

—Estás un poco pálida. ¿Quieres que te traiga una infusión caliente y un par de aspirinas antes de irme a acostar?

—No, gracias. No me duele si estoy tumbada, así que no necesito analgésicos –contestó Tina–. Sólo me duele cuando intento caminar.

—Bueno, entonces, si no necesitas nada más, me voy –dijo, rozándole la boca con los labios–. A no ser que hayas cambiado de opinión y prefieras venirte a dormir conmigo –añadió, besándola por el cuello.

Tina se sentía como si se estuviera ahogando en miel, y pensó que, aunque no se acordaba, ya no era virgen, así que, ¿qué tenía que perder?

¡El respeto por sí misma, nada más y nada menos, lo que para ella era muy importante! La noche anterior había estado borracha y no había sido capaz de controlarse, pero ahora estaba completamente sobria y era responsable de sus actos.

—Quiero hacerte el amor –murmuró Richard mientras sus manos encontraban las suaves curvas de sus pechos–. Quiero dormir abrazándote, despertarme mañana a tu lado y volverte a hacer el amor... dime que tú quieres lo mismo...

Tina no dijo nada.

—Anda, dímelo —insistió Richard.

—No puedo —dijo Tina—. No puedo.

—¿Por qué? Sé que me deseas. Tu cuerpo te delata.

—Yo nunca he... —contestó Tina, tragando saliva—. Nunca he tenido aventuras de una noche ni he sido partidaria del sexo casual, y no quiero empezar ahora.

Richard frunció el ceño.

—¿Y quién está hablando de una aventura de una noche o de sexo casual? Ni lo que siento por ti ni mis intenciones son casuales.

Aquellas palabras hicieron que a Tina le diera un vuelco el corazón. Si de verdad hablaba en serio, aquello lo cambiaba todo.

Entonces, el sentido común le dijo que no se dejara engañar. ¿Cómo iba a sentir Richard algo por ella cuando hacía solamente veinticuatro horas que se conocían?

¿Y por qué no?

Lo que ella sentía, tanto si era encaprichamiento como si era amor, tampoco era casual. Más bien, era tan fuerte que, a su lado, lo que había sentido por Kevin era insignificante.

Confusa, Tina se quedó mirando la colcha.

—Que duermas bien —dijo Richard, poniéndose en pie—. Hasta mañana.

Tina se quedó mirándolo mientras Richard iba hacia la puerta, y se preguntó si iba a permitir que se fuera, si iba a ser capaz de no estar con él por orgullo o por miedo a lo que el futuro le deparara.

Entonces, decidió que si todo salía mal y aquello terminaba en un mar de lágrimas, por lo menos, se llevaría el recuerdo de lo que habían compartido.

Richard tenía la mano en el pomo de la puerta cuando Tina pronunció su nombre.

—Por favor, no te vayas —susurró.

Richard sonrió satisfecho y volvió a su lado.

—¿Nunca has dormido en una cama de dosel bajo un edredón de plumas?

—No —contestó Tina.

Tampoco había dormido entre los brazos de un hombre.

Richard apartó la colcha y se tumbó a su lado.

—Siempre hay una primera vez.

Tina no podía dejar de mirarlo. Tenía la sensación de que se estaba derritiendo por dentro. Se moría por poseer a aquel hombre.

—Cuando me miras así, me haces sentirme como Superman —comentó Richard con voz apasionada y divertida.

Por lo visto, le había leído el pensamiento.

En un abrir y cerrar de ojos, Tina sintió sus manos por todo el cuerpo, y aquello la hizo ponerse a temblar.

Richard le estaba chupando un pezón y acariciándole la entrepierna. Tina no quería que todo terminara antes de haber siquiera empezado, e intentó apartarse, pero Richard no se lo permitió.

Tina gritó de placer, dejando que las sensaciones se apoderaran de ella. Cuando el orgasmo hubo pasado, suspiró. Aunque Richard le había dado un placer maravilloso, le hubiera gustado compartir la experiencia con él.

—Muy bien, ahora pasemos a cosas más profundas —dijo Richard, besándola y acariciándola de nuevo.

Tina, que creía que había quedado saciada, se encontró excitándose de nuevo ante sus caricias. Cuando Richard se colocó entre sus piernas para poseerla, le dio la bienvenida encantada, pero la primera embestida le causó dolor.

—¿Te he hecho daño? —le preguntó Richard.

—Sí... no... no importa —contestó Tina.

Dejándose llevar por la intuición, levantó las caderas, y Richard comenzó a moverse dentro de su cuerpo con cuidado.

—¿Vas bien? —le preguntó.

Atrapada en una espiral de placer, Tina no contestó con palabras, pero, al verla con la cabeza echada hacia atrás y jadeando satisfecha, Richard se dio por contestado.

Satisfecho, llevó a ambos a un clímax maravilloso que los dejó extenuados más allá del tiempo y del espacio.

Las sensaciones habían sido tan profundas e intensas, que Tina se sentía confundida hasta lo más profundo de su ser. Al mismo tiempo, se sentía exaltada, omnipotente e invencible con aquel hombre a su lado.

De repente, se dio cuenta de que era feliz porque aquel hombre era suyo, era su compañero, su amor. Así que aquél era el amor de verdad, aquel amor al que cantaban las canciones y los poemas.

Si el amor eran dos personas juntas a todos los niveles en un encuentro tanto espiritual como físico, Tina estaba contenta de no haberse entregado a nadie, de haber esperado a Richard.

Cuando Richard consiguió recuperar la respiración, se incorporó y se apoyó en el cabecero de la cama. A continuación, le pasó a Tina el brazo por los hombros y le dio un beso tan tierno, que Tina se encontró rezando para que Richard compartiera alguno de sus sentimientos con ella.

De repente, se dio cuenta de un pequeño detalle muy importante.

—Anoche... anoche... no hicimos el amor —comentó, confundida.

—No —contestó Richard.

—¿Pero no me habías dicho que habíamos dormido en la misma cama?

—Sí, dormimos en la misma cama, pero no pasó nada.

—Pero esta mañana me has dicho que...

—Si haces memoria, verás que yo no te he dicho nada. Tú lo has dado todo por hecho, y yo, lo admito, no te he sacado de tu error.

Tina comprendió que, al no hacerlo, seducirla le había resultado mucho más fácil.

—¿Estás enfadada? —le preguntó Richard.

—No —contestó Tina sinceramente.

Aunque, tal vez, debiera estarlo, ¿cómo se iba a enfadar con un hombre que le había dado tanto placer y tanta ternura?

A la mañana siguiente, Tina se despertó feliz.

Cuanto se giró esperando encontrar a Richard a su lado, se dio cuenta de que estaba sola. El sol entraba por la ventana y, al mirar el reloj, comprobó que eran casi las nueve menos cuarto.

En algún momento de la noche, Richard la había despertado con un beso y le había vuelto a hacer el amor. Aunque sentía ciertas partes más sensibles de lo normal, Tina sentía el cuerpo saciado y gozoso.

Tras estirarse cómodamente, se dijo que estaba eufórica. Había encontrado al amor de su vida. Richard había llenado su corazón, su soledad se había evaporado, había satisfecho un apetito que Tina tenía hacía mucho tiempo.

Era el hombre perfecto para ella. Era fuerte, tenía sentido del humor y era tierno y comprensivo. También era reservado, lo que estaba muy bien porque, así, siempre tendría pensamientos y sueños con los que sorprenderla, elementos con los que mantener su relación fresca y lozana.

Su relación.

Tina se preguntó si podía decir que tenían una relación. ¿Por qué no? Aunque acabara de empezar, era una relación en toda regla. ¿Acaso no había dejado Richard muy claro que sus sentimientos y sus intenciones no eran meramente casuales?

Aunque los entornos de los que procedían y sus estilos de vida eran muy diferentes, Tina confiaba en que Richard llegara a amarla algún día.

Era todo lo que le pedía a la vida.

¿Y si no era así?

Se apresuró a apartar aquel pensamiento de su mente.

¡Por lo menos ahora sabía lo que era estar enamorada! ¡Era lo más maravilloso del mundo! Tina estaba tan contenta, que tenía ganas de gritarlo a los cuatro vientos, y decidió que, en cuanto se hubiera duchado y vestido, llamaría a Ruth para contárselo.

Se levantó con cuidado, apoyó el tobillo en el suelo y comprobó que ya no le dolía, así que se quitó el camisón y se metió en el baño. Tras ducharse, se puso unos pantalones color crema y una camisa de seda color caramelo.

Cuando se disponía a llamar a su amiga, se dio cuenta de que Richard le había pedido el teléfono la noche anterior. Suponiendo que lo encontraría en su chaqueta, metió la mano en un bolsillo, pero lo único que encontró fue la linterna.

Al tocarla, se encendió. Vaya, si Richard lo hubiera intentado con un poco más de calma, se habrían evitado el difícil trayecto a oscuras.

Tina no encontró su teléfono móvil ni en la chaqueta ni en el pantalón de Richard, así que decidió bajar a buscarlo para preguntarle qué había hecho con él. Mientras bajaba las escaleras, iba pensando en él, en la sonrisa que le dedicaría al verla y en que, sin duda, le desearía buenos días con un maravilloso beso.

Una vez en el vestíbulo, se encontró con Hannah, que llevaba un misal en la mano.

—Buenos días, señorita Dunbar. Espero que haya dormido bien.

—Sí, muy bien. Gracias, Hannah —contestó Tina, sonrojándose levemente—. ¿Va usted a la iglesia?

—Sí, es costumbre que todos los empleados vayamos a misa los domingos por la mañana en la capilla del castillo.

—Debe de ser una maravilla contar con su propio sacerdote.

—Desde luego —contestó Hannah con orgullo—. El reverendo Peter lleva toda la vida con la familia. Ha bautizado, casado y enterrado a todos los miembros tanto de la familia como del personal de servicio. Es ya muy mayor, pero antes de que Dios lo llame a su presencia le gustaría oficiar el matrimonio del señor. Cuando la familia de la señorita O'Connell se vino a vivir a Farrington Hall, todos nos preguntamos si sería ella la elegida, pero, después de la muerte de la señora, el señor Richard dejó de venir por aquí, y la señorita O'Connell dejó de llamar... menos mal que, a pesar de que el señor insiste en que todavía no es oficial, parece que, por fin, el reverendo va a poder oficiar ese anhelado matrimonio —sonrió Hannah de manera radiante.

Así que Richard se iba a casar.

—Bueno, la tengo que dejar, que no quiere llegar tarde —se despidió el ama de llaves, alejándose apresuradamente.

Capítulo 7

TINA sentía náuseas y no era capaz de moverse.

«¿Y quién está hablando de una aventura de una noche o de sexo casual? Ni lo que siento por ti ni mis intenciones son casuales».

Las palabras de Richard resonaban en sus oídos, y Tina se dijo que, como una tonta, se había creído sus mentiras.

Cuando, por fin, consiguió reaccionar, lo primero que se le pasó por la cabeza fue salir corriendo de allí. No quería volver a verlo jamás, pero iba a tener que verlo una última vez porque tenía que recuperar su teléfono móvil para llamar a un taxi.

Tina decidió que quería irse de allí con la cabeza bien alta, así que iba a tener que ocultarle cómo se sentía. Sintiendo que las piernas le temblaban, se dirigió al estudio y, al pasar por el salón, oyó a través de la puerta entreabierta la voz de Richard y se encontró escuchando una conversación telefónica ajena.

—El tiempo es un factor muy importante —estaba diciendo Richard—. No puedo perder ni un solo momento.

Tina se dio cuenta de que no era una conversación telefónica al oír la voz de una mujer.

–Ya es demasiado tarde. No hay tiempo.

–Claro que sí –insistió Richard–. Lo tengo todo controlado.

–¿Y no hay otra manera de hacerlo? No te falta dinero. ¿No podrías...?

–Eso fue lo primero que se me ocurrió, pero no sé si el dinero serviría para arreglar la situación. Lo cierto es que no sé a lo que me estoy enfrentando y, para cuando lo sepa, será demasiado tarde.

–Pero Richard... –se lamentó la mujer.

–No sigas, Helen, tengo que hacerlo así.

Helen... Helen O'Connell... la mujer con la que se iba a casar... Richard estaba hablando con su futura esposa.

–No quiero arruinarme. En cuanto esté en una posición de fuerza, podré utilizar mi dinero para otras cosas.

–Pero es tan... drástico.

–Le he dado muchas vueltas, y estoy seguro de que ésta es la opción mejor.

–¿Y qué crees que pasará cuando...?

–Por supuesto, se va a montar una buena, pero ya lidiaré con ello cuando llegue el momento –contestó Richard.

–A mí me parece que te estás equivocando por completo. Podrías ir a juicio –añadió Helen, esperanzada.

–Ya lo he pensado, pero podríamos estar años, y no tengo garantías de ganar.

–¿Te has parado a considerar la ética de todo esto?

–Por supuesto –contestó Richard, apesadumbrado–. He considerado los principios éticos de lo que voy hacer. Estoy dispuesto a hacer lo que sea necesario. Para mí, el fin justifica los medios. Tengo demasiado que perder como para ponerme a jugar a ser sir Galahad...

Tina se estremeció al oír el tono de voz tan rudo y frío con el que hablaba Richard. Era aquél un aspecto de él que no conocía, pero se dijo que, como hombre de negocios, tal vez, necesitara ser así también de vez en cuando.

–Sigo insistiendo en que estás cometiendo un gran error, en que tiene que haber otra manera de arreglar las cosas –insistió Helen al borde de las lágrimas–. A no ser, por supuesto, que sea eso lo que quieres en realidad...

En aquel momento, Tina oyó que Helen se aproximaba a la puerta y, temerosa de que la sorprendieran espiándolos, se apresuró a apartarse y a esconderse en el estudio de al lado. Desde el ventanal vio cómo Helen salía en dirección a su coche deportivo rojo seguida de cerca por Richard.

Ella iba llorando, y él la agarró del brazo, pero Helen se zafó de su mano y se montó en su coche, no sin antes cruzarle la cara de un bofetón. A continuación, puso el descapotable en marcha y salió del castillo a tanta velocidad, que el coche iba derrapando.

Richard se quedó allí plantado, tocándose la mejilla. Al cabo de unos segundos, reaccionó y volvió al interior del castillo. Temerosa de que la viera, Tina se apresuró a apartarse de la ventana.

Fue entonces cuando decidió entrar en el despacho a llamar un taxi. Estaba descolgando el auricular cuando la puerta se abrió de repente.

Era Richard.

—Ah, estás aquí —le dijo, sonriendo—. Como no estabas en la habitación... ¿qué tal tienes el tobillo? —añadió, acercándose a ella y besándola.

Tina no reaccionó inmediatamente, pero, cuando consiguió hacerlo, apartó la cara.

—¿Qué te pasa? —le preguntó Richard, enarcando las cejas.

Tina negó con la cabeza.

—A ti te pasa algo.

—Que no encuentro mi teléfono y quiero llamar a un taxi.

—¿Y para qué quieres un taxi?

—Para irme.

—¿Qué te ha ocurrido para que te quieras ir?

—Nada —mintió Tina, desesperada—. Simplemente, me quiero ir, así que, si no te importa...

—Claro que me importa. Después de lo que hemos compartido, me importa mucho que te vayas sin darme una explicación.

—No tengo por qué darte ninguna explicación —contestó Tina, apretando los dientes—. Simplemente me quiero ir y ya está. Por favor, devuélveme mi teléfono.

–No sé dónde está –contestó Richard con expresión inocente.

–No te creo.

–Y yo no te creo cuando dices que te quieres ir sin una buena razón.

–Me da igual lo que creas, pero no me puedes impedir que me vaya.

–No estés tan segura de eso.

Repentinamente asustada, Tina pasó a su lado en dirección a la puerta. Al hacerlo, sin querer tiró un sobre que había sobre la mesa. El contenido del sobre cayó al suelo, y Tina se fijó en que varias de las hojas que contenía tenían un logo en una de las esquinas.

Se disponía a abrir la puerta cuando Richard la agarró del brazo y la giró hacia él. A continuación, en un abrir y cerrar de ojos, cerró la puerta con llave, se la guardó en el bolsillo y se apresuró a recoger los papeles.

–No me puedes retener aquí en contra de mi voluntad –lo desafió Tina.

–Desde luego, no puedo hacerlo durante mucho tiempo, pero sí durante un rato –contestó Richard.

–Insisto en que me dejes marchar.

–Aunque te dejara salir de aquí, te resultaría muy difícil irte del castillo porque no tienes medio de transporte, así que cuéntame la verdad.

Tina se mordió el labio inferior y no dijo nada.

–Supongo que tu enfado tiene que ver con la visita de Helen –aventuró Richard–. ¿Has oído algo de lo que estábamos hablando?

–Una pena que ya no haya potro de tortura en el castillo, ¿eh?

–Hay otras maneras de hacerte hablar –contestó Richard.

Tina se estremeció.

–Por cómo te has apartado cuando te he besado, entiendo que prefieres que no te toque –añadió Richard.

–Efectivamente –contestó Tina, levantando el mentón en actitud desafiante.

–Pues anoche no te comportabas así.

–¿Y qué? Ahora, sí.

Richard sonrió y, con deliberada lentitud, comenzó a desabrocharse la camisa y a sacársela de los pantalones.

–¿Qué haces? –se sorprendió Tina.

–Me estoy desnudando. ¿No te apetece desnudarte a ti también?

–No.

–Bueno, entonces, ya te desnudo yo. Por otra parte, lo cierto es que no he hecho el amor completamente vestido desde mi época de adolescente. A lo mejor, me gusta y todo.

–Yo no quiero hacer el amor contigo –gritó Tina–. No quiero que me toques.

–Eso dices, pero... si no quieres que te toque, dime por qué te quieres ir de repente –dijo Richard.

Al ver que Tina no contestaba, con una rapidez que le impidió reaccionar, la tomó entre sus brazos, la tumbó en la alfombra y se colocó sobre ella.

Tenía la camisa abierta y, al encontrarse con su torso desnudo justo delante, Tina sintió que el estómago se le encogía.

—Suéltame —le dijo con toda la calma que pudo.

Richard se limitó a besarla en el cuello.

—Si no me sueltas, me pongo a chillar —le advirtió Tina.

Richard sonrió.

—¿Te crees que te lo voy a permitir? Además, no te va a oír nadie. Están todos en misa.

A continuación, le agarró ambas muñecas por detrás de la cabeza con una mano y, con la otra, comenzó a desabrocharle los botones de la blusa. Cuando estuvo abierta por completo, comenzó acariciarle el escote, justo donde terminaba el sujetador.

Tina sintió que se le entrecortaba la respiración.

Richard deslizó el dedo un poco más adentro y observó satisfecho cómo a Tina se le endurecían los pezones bajo la delicada tela.

Aun así, Tina no decía nada. Sin embargo, al sentir el calor y la humedad de su boca a través del raso y del encaje, comenzó a temblar y ya no pudo aguantar más.

—No —murmuró, desesperada—. No hagas eso...

—¿Por qué no? Anoche te gustó mucho.

—Eso fue antes de...

—¿De qué?

Tina decidió tirar la toalla.

—Antes de enterarme de que te vas a casar.

—Ah, así que es todo por eso —suspiró Richard—. ¿Cómo sabes que me voy a casar?

—Me lo ha dicho Hannah.

—¿Cuándo?

—Hace un rato, me la he encontrado cuando iba a misa.

—Así que por eso te has puesto así.

—Ni se te ocurra decirme que no es cierto...

—No pienso decirte nada parecido.

—Oh...

—Ya que sabes que me voy a casar, a lo mejor también sabes con quién —se burló Richard.

—Sí, claro que lo sé. Con Helen O'Connell.

Richard la miró con una ceja enarcada.

—¿Qué te hace pensar eso? ¿Es porque la has visto aquí?

—No, es lo que Hannah me ha dado a entender.

—¿Estás celosa?

—Por supuesto que no.

—Si no estás celosa, ¿a qué viene tanto enfado?

—¡A que eres un bruto, un bestia y un diablo sin sentimientos! ¿Cómo se te ocurre traerme aquí? ¿Y si se entera tu prometida?

—¿Se lo vas a decir tú? —le preguntó Richard con ironía.

—No, claro que no. Yo lo único que quiero es irme de aquí y no volver a verte jamás.

—Me temo que nuestros planes no coinciden porque yo tengo intención de tenerte siempre cerca —contestó Richard, inclinándose sobre ella y besándola.

Tina se revolvió, pataleó e hizo todo lo que pudo para zafarse de él, pero, aunque era joven y fuerte, Richard podía con ella.

—Por favor, suéltame —imploró, exhausta.

Percibiendo su desesperación, Richard la soltó, la ayudó a ponerse en pie e incluso le abrochó la blusa. A continuación, se abrochó él también la camisa, se la metió por dentro de los pantalones y se quedó mirándola.

—Quiero que me escuches bien —le dijo, muy serio—. Estás en lo cierto. Tengo intención de casarme.

Vaya, y ella que había albergado esperanzas de que lo negara...

—Sin embargo, te equivocas si piensas que es con Helen con quien quiero hacerlo.

—Yo sólo repito lo que me ha dicho Hannah.

—Es cierto que hubo una época en la que todo el mundo creyó que nos íbamos a casar, pero te has equivocado al dar por hecho que Hannah se refería a ella. Hannah lleva tantos años con nosotros, que la considero un miembro de la familia y le he contado mis planes... La verdad es que hubiera preferido que no hubiera dicho nada hasta que yo hubiera tenido ocasión de hablar con la mujer con la que me quiero casar.

Tina no dijo nada.

—¿No me vas a preguntar de quién se trata?

Tina negó con la cabeza. ¿Qué más daba la identidad de la mujer? El mero hecho de que Ri-

chard se quisiera casar con otra reducía su felicidad a cenizas.

—¿No me lo preguntas porque no te interesa o
porque el orgullo te lo impide?

—No te lo pregunto porque no creo que tenga derecho a hacerlo —admitió Tina, mirando hacia el
suelo.

—Después de lo que ha habido entre nosotros,
tienes todo el derecho del mundo a preguntar —la
corrigió Richard, levantándole el rostro—. Conse-
guí que vinieras al castillo ofreciéndote un trabajo, trabajo al que renunciaste porque dijiste que
te sentirías rara trabajando para mí después de ha-
bernos acostado. Eso demuestra que eres una persona sensible, algo no muy común en estos tiempos que corren en los que muchas mujeres no se
lo habrían pensado dos veces o les habría parecido que el interés sexual que había por mi parte
era un plus al trabajo. Ahora te ofrezco otro tipo
de trabajo, un trabajo en el que el interés sexual
no es solamente un plus sino algo absolutamente
vital.

Tina lo miraba con los ojos como platos.

—Quiero que seas mi esposa.

—¿Cómo? —se sorprendió Tina.

—Quiero que seas mi esposa —repitió Richard—.
Sí, ya sé que es un poco precipitado, pero creo que
desde el principio te dije que mi interés por ti no
era nada casual...

—Sí, bueno, pero... nunca creí... nunca soñé...

¿de verdad que quieres casarte conmigo? —le pregunto Tina, atónita ante lo que estaba sucediendo.

—Sí —contestó Richard con seguridad.

—Lo siento, pero me cuesta creerlo.

—Pero espero que mi propuesta no te parezca una locura —sonrió Richard, acariciándole la mejilla—. ¿Qué deseo pediste ayer por la noche cuando estuvimos viendo las estrellas?

Tina no contestó, y Richard sonrió, satisfecho.

—Tú eres mi deseo —dijo, besándola—. Lo único que tienes que hacer es casarte conmigo para que mi deseo se cumpla. Lo cierto es que habría preferido esperar un poco, pero ya que Hannah se ha ido de la lengua... Me habría gustado hacerlo de forma más romántica y en un lugar más apropiado, pero... Espero que esto no influya en tu respuesta...

El lugar y la forma era lo de menos para Tina. Lo importante era que Richard la amaba y se quería casar con ella. Ella se habría conformado con su amor, pero el hecho de que quisiera casarse con ella le llenaba el corazón de alegría y de gratitud.

Ante la expresión radiante que reflejaba el rostro de Tina, Richard estuvo casi seguro de que iba decir que sí, pero necesitaba oírlo de su propia boca, así que la puso en pie y la miró a los ojos.

—Estoy esperando a que me contestes. ¿Te quieres casar conmigo?

—Sí —contestó Tina, dedicándole una sonrisa gloriosa.

Aquella sonrisa hizo que Richard se sintiera fatal y, durante una milésima de segundo, dudara de lo que estaba haciendo, pero se dijo que no podía permitirse el lujo de flaquear a aquellas alturas.

–¿Estás seguro de que no necesitas más tiempo para pensártelo? No me conoces de nada...

–Te conozco lo suficiente.

–El otro día, cuando llegábamos al castillo, dijiste que querías que tu esposa y tus hijos vivieran aquí. ¿Y si no me gustaran los niños?

–¿No te gustan?

–Me gustan mucho, pero...

–Entonces, insisto en que sé de ti todo lo que necesito saber –la interrumpió Richard, besándola.

–¿Cómo puedes estar tan seguro cuando sólo hace un par de días que nos conocemos?

–Desde que te vi por primera vez, supe que eras la mujer de mi vida.

Aunque su respuesta había sido dulce y romántica, Tina no acababa de estar convencida.

–¿Sabes lo que es el flechazo? –dijo Richard al verla dudar.

–Por supuesto, pero...

–Llevo cruzando los dedos desde que te conocí para que hubiera sido mutuo.

–Lo fue –admitió Tina.

Richard la tomó entre sus brazos y comenzó a besarla con pasión. Durante un rato, se entregaron a los abrazos y a los besos, olvidándose del resto del mundo. Cuando, al cabo de varios minutos, Richard le propuso que fueran a dar un paseo, Tina accedió, encantada, sintiéndose la mujer más feliz sobre la faz de la Tierra.

Salieron con los dedos entrelazados por la puerta de la cocina, donde previamente tomaron un café. Hacía una mañana soleada y preciosa, y decidieron bajar a las cuadras y dar una vuelta a caballo.

Cuando llegaron, Josh, el mozo, les dijo que Juno había perdido una herradura el día anterior. Entonces, a Richard se le ocurrió que Júpiter, un magnífico ejemplar, podría con los dos, y así lo hicieron.

Al cabo de un rato galopando y riendo, pararon junto a un arroyo y se bajaron para dejar que el caballo bebiera agua y descansara. Ellos se sentaron sobre el tronco de un árbol caído, y Richard tomó a Tina entre sus brazos.

—Me gustaría que nos casáramos cuanto antes —comentó al cabo de un rato, mirando el agua en silencio—. Sí, ya sé que parezco un impaciente, pero es que no puedo más. Quiero que seas mía —añadió al ver que Tina lo miraba extrañada.

Tina sintió que el corazón le daba un vuelco. Obviamente, Richard sentía algo muy fuerte por ella.

—Si quieres una boda por todo lo alto con muchos invitados, siempre podemos hacer una segunda celebración —sugirió Richard.

—Yo no necesito una boda por todo lo alto en absoluto —contestó Tina.

—Bien dicho —suspiró Richard, abrazándola con fuerza—. ¿Qué te parece si nos casamos entonces mañana por la mañana?

–Muy bien –contestó Tina, creyendo que estaba bromeando.

–Como tenemos sacerdote y capilla en casa, lo único que tenemos que hacer es decírselo al reverendo Peter y buscar dos testigos.

Tina se dio cuenta de que Richard no estaba bromeando en absoluto.

–¿Y no necesitamos una licencia o algo así?

–Ya la tenemos.

–¿Cómo es posible? Supongo que tendrás tus contactos, pero es imposible que hayas conseguido una licencia tan rápido.

–Ya te he dicho que, desde la primera vez que te vi, supe que eras para mí.

–Pero si la primera vez que me viste fue el viernes, que fue el día que nos conocimos.

–En eso, te equivocas.

Capítulo 8

TINA lo miró, confusa.

—No te entiendo.

Richard le apartó un mechón de pelo de la cara.

—La primera vez que te vi fue hace más de tres semanas. Fui a Cartel Wines y te vi saliendo del despacho de De Vere. Me pareciste la mujer más guapa del mundo, y me dije que quería hacerte mía. Por desgracia, al día siguiente me tuve que ir de viaje a Oriente Próximo por un negocio increíblemente importante. Para entonces, ya había hablado con el reverendo para que lo tuviera todo preparado.

—Pero si ni siquiera habías hablado conmigo —se sorprendió Tina—. ¿Cómo podías estar tan seguro de que iba a querer casarme contigo?

—Por supuesto, no estaba seguro al cien por cien, pero, normalmente, consigo lo que quiero —contestó Richard con cierta arrogancia—. El viaje me retuvo fuera de Inglaterra más de lo previsto y me encontré con que no podía concentrarme en los negocios. No podía parar de pensar en ti, en qué iba a hacer para conocerte a la vuelta.

–Y yo que creía que nos habíamos conocido por casualidad...

Su sexto sentido le dijo que era imposible que hubiera sido por casualidad. Un hombre como Richard no dejaba nada a la casualidad. Si era cierto que estaba tan desesperado por conocerla como le acababa de contar, ¿por qué no había aprovechado la oportunidad cuando se habían visto a la hora de comer en el aparcamiento? Había sido la oportunidad perfecta. Seguramente, habría pensado que la próxima vez que visitara la empresa podría encontrar una excusa para...

Pero no, ella no hubiera estado allí la próxima vez que hubiera ido. Claro que él no tenía manera de saberlo. ¿Verdad? En algún lugar, en lo más profundo de su mente, un recuerdo, una impresión, intentó salir a la superficie, y Tina se dio cuenta de que, si pudiera recordar lo que era, tendría la respuesta a su pregunta.

–Deberíamos volver ya –dijo Richard de repente, interrumpiendo sus pensamientos–. Supongo que estarás muerta de hambre y, además, nos casamos mañana y tenemos muchas cosas que hacer.

Aunque se moría por casarse con él, Tina estaba un tanto inquieta. Tenía la sensación de que algo no encajaba del todo bien.

–¿Por qué tienes tantas prisas? ¿No podríamos esperar a...?

–Nos queremos casar los dos, tenemos cura, iglesia y licencia –la interrumpió Richard, un tanto molesto–. ¿Por qué esperar?

—Por ejemplo, porque no tengo nada que ponerme —contestó Tina—. Tendría que volver a mi casa a por algo...

—Yo te prefiero sin ropa —murmuró Richard, besándola para distraerla.

—Sí, ya lo sé, pero no tengo nada que ponerme para casarme.

—Podrías ponerte el vestido de ayer.

—Me lo manché en el túnel.

—Le diré a Hannah que lo lleve a la tintorería y, de todas formas, sacaremos tiempo para ir de compras antes de irnos de luna de miel.

—¿Nos vamos a ir de luna de miel? —exclamó Tina, encantada.

—Por supuesto. Vete pensando adónde quieres ir para que se lo pueda decir a Murray.

—¿Quién es Murray?

—Mi piloto. ¿No te había dicho que tengo un pequeño avión privado?

Tina negó con la cabeza y pensó que se iba a casar con un hombre increíblemente rico. De todas formas, aunque no hubiera tenido tanto dinero, se habría casado con él porque no era su dinero lo que le gustaba de Richard Anders.

—Vamos a volver porque Matthew Caradine, mi abogado, va a venir a las dos —dijo Richard.

—¿Un domingo?

—Sí, es que tenemos que arreglar un par de cosas antes de la boda —contestó Richard como quien no quiere la cosa.

Tras montarse los dos a lomos de Júpiter, se dirigieron al castillo. Durante el trayecto, Richard pensó que, aunque le había costado más de lo que había previsto, por fin había conseguido su objetivo.

Al día siguiente, sería el marido de Tina y estaría en una posición mucho más fuerte en cuanto ella hubiera firmado el contrato de matrimonio que su abogado había redactado.

Después de comer, Richard pidió al servicio que les sirvieran el café en su suite. Una vez allí, le entregó a Tina el anillo de boda de su madre tras sacarlo de un cajón secreto situado detrás de la cómoda.

Al cabo de un rato, ya cerca de las dos de la tarde, Milly llamó a la puerta y anunció la llegada de Matthew Caradine.

—¿Vamos? —le dijo Richard a Tina.

—¿Yo también? —se sorprendió ella.

—Sí, hay una cosa que te concierne.

—¿A mí?

—Sí, tenemos que dejar las cosas arregladas por si nos divorciamos.

—Pero yo... —se estremeció Tina.

—No te preocupes, es sólo una formalidad, pero hay que dejarlo hecho —la tranquilizó Richard.

El abogado los estaba esperando en el estudio. Se trataba de un hombre de mediana edad que era casi tan alto como Richard, pero más robusto.

—Cariño, te presento a Matthew Caradine —dijo Richard—. Matthew, ésta es Valentina Dunbar, mi prometida.

—Encantado de conocerla, señorita —la saludó el abogado amablemente—. Richard, he recogido todos los puntos de los que hablamos. Como a Tina sólo le atañe uno, si queréis podemos empezar por ése.

Richard asintió, y el abogado sacó un documento de su maletín y se lo entregó a Tina.

—Léalo y, si está de acuerdo, fírmelo.

Tina lo tomó entre las manos, se sentó en una butaca y lo leyó bajo la atenta mirada de ambos hombres.

En el documento se dejaba muy claro que, en caso de divorcio, Richard le compraría una casa y le pasaría una pensión mensual de lo más generosa a cambio de que ella renunciara al castillo.

También decía que, en caso de tener hijos, su padre se haría responsable de ellos y estarían bajo su custodia.

—Lo siento, pero no lo voy a firmar —dijo Tina tras haberlo leído dos veces.

Richard apretó los dientes.

—¿Por qué no?

—En lo que respecta al castillo...

Richard la miró con tanta frialdad, que Tina no se atrevió a seguir.

—¿Qué pasa con el castillo? —le preguntó Richard más calmado.

–Yo... iba a decir que por supuesto es tuyo y que yo nunca...

–Entonces, ¿cuál es el problema?

–El problema es que no estoy de acuerdo con entregarte a los niños si nos separamos.

Una emoción que no acertó a descifrar cruzó el rostro de Richard.

–¿Qué te parece si tuviéramos la custodia compartida? Vivirían contigo, pero yo tendría acceso ilimitado a ellos y las decisiones que tuvieran que ver con su educación dependerían de los dos. ¿Qué te parecería?

–Bien –contestó Tina–. Espero no tenerme que ver nunca en esa situación...

–Claro que no –dijo Richard, acercándose y besándole la mano.

–Como veo que se han puesto de acuerdo, voy a corregir el documento ahora mismo –dijo Matthew, procediendo a hacerlo.

Un rato después, Richard y Tina lo firmaron, y Tina los dejó a solas para que hablaran del resto de cosas que tenían mientras ella se iba a pasear por las almenas.

Mientras paseaba, recordó la conversación que había tenido lugar en el estudio, y se preguntó por qué a Richard le habría parecido necesario insistir en que renunciara al castillo.

¿Cómo se le habría pasado por la cabeza que iba a querer quedarse con él? Aquello era absurdo. Aunque hubiera querido hacerlo, no habría tenido derecho. El castillo pertenecía a la familia de Richard desde hacía muchas generaciones.

Diciéndose que aquellas cuestiones ya no tenían importancia, siguió paseando. Estaba llegando al final cuando se dio cuenta de que había algo que le rondaba la cabeza y que la tenía en ascuas.

Era lo mismo que se le había ocurrido aquella mañana en el río, pero, al igual que en aquella ocasión, no fue capaz de identificarlo. Tina se dijo que era inútil, que cuando tuviera que acordarse, lo haría.

Al ver que el Jaguar del abogado había desaparecido, decidió bajar a buscar a Richard. Al entrar en el estudio, comprobó que estaba vacío. Sobre la mesa habían quedado varios documentos.

Al girarse para irse, Tina vio por el rabillo del ojo el mismo sobre que había tirado al suelo aquella mañana, y se dijo que en aquel sobre estaba la clave del enigma.

Sin pensárselo, dejando la puerta abierta, se acercó y lo abrió.

Dentro encontró varios correos electrónicos y documentos y un sobre marrón con varias fotografías. Al sacarlas, Tina se encontró mirándose a sí misma. Todas las fotografías eran de ella y habían sido tomadas en Cartel Wines.

Sin su consentimiento.

Tina se sintió incómoda, expuesta, espiada.

Sin embargo, se dio cuenta de que las fotografías no eran la solución a lo que le rondaba la cabeza. Un par de segundos después, al fijarse en el logo de uno de los documentos, todas las piezas encajaron.

Aquello era lo que había visto aquella mañana y su cerebro había registrado inconscientemente. Se trataba de la representación estilizada de una montaña que rápidamente reconoció como el símbolo del grupo Matterhorn.

En aquel momento, se abrió la puerta por completo y entró Richard.

—Perdona por hacerte esperar. He ido a acompañar a Matthew al coche, y Hannah me ha dicho que el nuevo administrador quería hablarme de...

Al ver que Tina había abierto el sobre y estaba leyendo el contenido, se interrumpió y se quedó mirándola a los ojos.

—¿Has encontrado lo que buscabas? —le preguntó con sarcasmo.

—Sí —contestó Tina, decidida a tomar al toro por los cuernos—. ¿Qué conexión tienes con el grupo Matterhorn?

—Soy el propietario —contestó Richard.

Aquello explicaba su presencia en Cartel Wines.

—Cuando te dije que a mi empresa la había absorbido Matterhorn, no me dijiste que ese grupo fuera tuyo.

—No —contestó Richard con calma.

—¿Por qué?

—Me acababas de decir que te habían echado del

trabajo precisamente por esa compra, y no me pareció buena idea —contestó Richard.

—Deberías habérmelo dicho.

—¿Habría marcado alguna diferencia?

Lo cierto era que no. Richard no le había ocultado que era el propietario del grupo Matterhorn. En cuanto le había preguntado, había respondido sin dudar. Entonces, ¿por qué se sentía engañada? ¿Por qué le daba la sensación de que le había ocultado aquella información adrede? ¿Qué interés podría tener en hacerlo?

Tina recordó las dudas que se habían apoderado de ella aquella mañana junto al río. ¿Y si el accidente no hubiera sido un accidente? A lo mejor, Richard había ido aquella tarde a la empresa, se había enterado de que la habían echado y, para no perder la oportunidad de conocerla, había decidido provocar el accidente.

No, imposible.

Para empezar, era de noche, y era imposible que supiera que aquél era su coche. A menos que la hubiera estado vigilando, claro. Tina recordó la sensación de estar siendo observada y se estremeció.

No, todo aquello era ridículo.

Si Richard se hubiera enterado en el último momento de que la acababan de despedir, le habría bastado con incluirla en su nuevo equipo, y todo solucionado. Así, habría tenido todo el tiempo del mundo para conocerla.

—Tú sabías que me habían despedido.

–Me lo dijiste tú.

–No, lo sabías antes –lo acusó.

–¿Por qué lo iba a saber?

–Como propietario de Matterhorn, tenías que saber que, al tener tu equipo de promociones propio, yo sobraba en la empresa.

–Soy el propietario de Matterhorn, pero no me encargo de todo. Yo me limito a presidir el grupo y a tomar las decisiones ejecutivas. No tengo tiempo de encargarme de todo, para eso tengo empleados.

Tina se sintió como una estúpida.

–Por supuesto... lo siento.

Tina se dijo que se estaba comportando como una imbécil y que ya iba siendo hora de que dejara de hacerlo. Debía controlar su imaginación. Sin embargo, las fotografías no habían sido imaginaciones suyas.

–Veo que has visto las fotografías –comentó Richard como si le hubiera leído el pensamiento.

–¿Por qué me las hiciste? –le preguntó Tina.

–No te las he hecho yo.

Tina lo miró, confusa.

–Como te he contado esta mañana, después de verte por primera vez, me tuve que ir de viaje. Lo único que sabía de ti era tu nombre y que trabajabas en Cartel Wines. Eso me lo había dicho De Vere. Quería saberlo todo sobre ti, así que contraté a un detective para que averiguara todo lo que pudiera. Las fotografías las hizo él.

La idea de haber sido vigilada e investigada no le hacía ninguna gracia, y así se lo hizo saber.

–Sí, siento tener que haber recurrido a ello, pero, dadas las circunstancias...

–¿Y por qué tenías tantas prisas? –se indignó Tina.

–¡Soy un hombre muy impulsivo! –exclamó Richard, tomándola entre sus brazos y besándola con pasión–. ¿Nos vamos arriba?

–¿Y si alguien te necesita? –contestó Tina, intentando no caer en la tentación.

–La que me necesitas eres tú –le dijo Richard al oído.

Tina sintió que comenzaba a flaquear.

–¿No teníamos que ir a hablar con el reverendo Peter?

–Sí, tienes razón... menos mal que me lo has recordado... bueno, cuando tengamos todo organizado, podremos seguir con esto –añadió, besándola en la mejilla–. ¿Has hecho alguna vez el amor al aire libre con el sol poniéndose y una maravillosa brisa acariciándote la piel?

–No –contestó Tina.

–Pues ya va siendo hora de que lo pruebes –dijo Richard–. Es maravilloso. Cuando hayamos hablado con el reverendo, te propongo que lo hagamos. Al otro lado de la colina hay un prado soleado y solitario que es ideal... –añadió, besándole el cuello.

Tina se estremeció de placer, y Richard aprovechó para desabrocharle los dos primeros botones de la blusa y encontrar uno de sus pechos.

Haciendo un gran esfuerzo y no queriendo ir a hablar con el reverendo excitada, protestó y se zafó de él. Richard se apartó a regañadientes y le volvió a abrochar los botones.

–No me extraña que los recién casados se vayan de luna de miel –comentó–. Es la única manera de olvidarse del mundo y concentrarse el uno en el otro. Hablando de luna de miel, ¿has decidido dónde quieres que vayamos?

–No, la verdad es que me da igual –contestó Tina sinceramente.

Cualquier lugar del planeta se le antojaba el paraíso siempre y cuando estuviera con Richard.

–Vamos, mi amor –le dijo él.

Así que de verdad era su amor. Tina sintió que el corazón le daba un vuelco. Era feliz.

–Estaba pensando que yo preferiría que la ceremonia fuera por la mañana –comentó Richard mientras, agarrados de la mano, iban en busca del reverendo.

–Como quieras –contestó Tina.

–Así, después de comer, podríamos acercarnos a Anders Cross a comprarte ropa.

Tina pensó que, si se casaran por la tarde, podrían ir de compras por la mañana y así tendría un vestido nuevo para la ceremonia, pero a Richard no parecía importarle aquel detalle, y Tina no se atrevió a decir nada.

El reverendo Peter resultó ser un hombre bajito y regordete de cara alegre y pelo blanco. Cuando le dijeron que se querían casar, el cura los acompañó a la capilla, un lugar pequeño y tranquilo que a Tina se le antojó perfecto para celebrar su matrimonio.

Como si le hubiera leído el pensamiento, Richard suspiró y le apretó la mano.

—Me alegro mucho de que vayas a utilizar los anillos de tus padres —comentó el reverendo cuando tuvieron todo organizado—. A tu madre le habría encantado la idea. Por cierto, hablando de tu madre. He estado pensando en el segundo testamento, aquél del que fuimos testigos Hannah y yo...

Richard le hizo una mueca de advertencia con la cara, pero el reverendo no se dio cuenta y continuó.

—Se me ha ocurrido que podría haberse mezclado con los documentos eclesiásticos que estaba leyendo en aquellos momentos tu madre, así que si tuvieras un rato para mirarlo...

—Sí, en cuanto tenga tiempo lo miraré —lo interrumpió Richard, agarrando a Tina de la cintura—. Ahora, teníamos intención de irnos a dar un paseo.

—Si tenéis algo que solucionar, me puedo adelantar yo y luego tú te reúnes conmigo —le dijo Tina.

—¿No te importa? —le preguntó Richard.

—Por supuesto que no.

—Muy bien, toma el sendero que rodea el foso y asciende por la colina, y nos vemos dentro de un rato —le indicó Richard, besándola.

Tina sintió que aquel beso contenía promesas

inequívocamente sexuales, y se estremeció de placer.

Tras despedirse del clérigo un tanto sonrojada, salió de la capilla. Una vez fuera, se fijó en que el anillo de compromiso que le había entregado Richard refulgía bajo los rayos del sol.

Al imaginarse la cara que iba a poner Ruth cuando lo viera, no pudo evitar sonreír. Al pensar en ella, se dio cuenta de que su amiga esperaba que volviera el lunes, así que iba a tener que llamarla y contarle lo que estaba sucediendo para que no se preocupara.

Tina cruzó el puente y se quedó un buen rato mirando las nubes. Había pasado un cuarto de hora, y Richard no se había reunido con ella, así que decidió seguir andando. Tras haber avanzado durante un buen rato, decidió sentarse a esperarlo.

El cielo estaba despejado, y el sol le daba en la cara. La falta de sueño de la noche anterior y el agradable calor hicieron que se tumbara sobre la hierba y cerrara los ojos. Se estaba quedando medio dormida cuando oyó que se acercaba un caballo.

Al incorporarse, creyendo que podría ser Richard con Júpiter, vio que se trataba de una mujer. Helen O'Connell.

HELEN desmontó de su caballo, se acercó a Tina y se sentó a su lado. Tras quitarse el sombrero, lo dejó sobre la hierba y se presentó sin preámbulos.

—Me llamo Helen O'Connell.

Al tenerla tan cerca, Tina percibió que era una mujer de treinta y pocos años, de cabello oscuro y enormes ojos azules.

—Tú debes de ser Valentina Dunbar, la mujer con la que Richard se quiere casar —comentó, mirando el solitario que Tina lucía en la mano izquierda—. Te he visto y me he acercado a hablar contigo. ¿Cuándo se supone que os vais a casar?

—Mañana por la mañana —contestó Tina sin dejarse intimidar por la rudeza de la otra mujer.

Helen se rió con amargura.

—Desde luego, cuando me dijo que no había tiempo que perder, no creí que fuera a ser tan rápido. Supongo que tendrá intención de llevarte de luna de miel después de la boda, ¿no?

—Sí, pero no entiendo...

—Te lo advierto, no te cases con él. Si lo haces,

cometerás un grave error –le dijo Helen–. Ya sé que es un hombre muy rico, pero...

–No me voy a casar con él por el dinero.

–Bueno, yo lo único que te digo es que si, te has enamorado de él, me apiado de ti por qué tú a él no le importas un pimiento. Supongo que no te lo habrá dicho porque no le conviene, pero hemos sido amantes durante muchos años y, si todo esto no hubiera surgido, se habría casado conmigo.

–Lo siento –le dijo Tina–, pero yo...

–Tú no tienes la culpa de nada –le dijo Helen–. Eres la víctima de todo esto. El que se ha vuelto loco es Richard. Por lo visto, cree que casarse contigo es la única manera de arreglar las cosas. No dejes que te engañe. En cuanto haya conseguido lo que quiere y volváis de la luna de miel, se divorciará de ti –le advirtió.

Entonces, al levantar la vista, vio que se acercaba alguien y se apresuró a ponerse en pie, a colocarse el casco y a montar en su caballo de nuevo.

–Te lo digo en serio, te iría mucho mejor si no escucharas nada de lo que te dice. Haz el equipaje y vete lo más pronto posible de aquí –le dijo antes de azuzar al caballo y alejarse galopando.

Tina se quedó mirándola. Cuando Richard llegó a su lado, muy tenso, la encontró nerviosa y confusa.

–¿Qué te pasa? –le preguntó, sentándose junto a ella en la hierba.

–Nada...

–No me mientas –le dijo con sequedad–. He visto irse a Helen. ¿Qué te ha dicho?

–Me ha dicho que no me case contigo –contestó Tina.

Richard maldijo a Helen en silencio.

–¿Y qué razones te ha dado para que no lo hicieras?

–Ninguna, sólo me ha dicho que cometería un grave error si lo hiciera.

–¿Qué más te ha dicho?

–Que te importo un pimiento, que habéis sido amantes durante años...

–Continúa –le ordenó Richard.

–No mucho más.

–Continúa –repitió Richard, muy serio.

Tina bajó la mirada.

–Me ha dicho que, en cuanto volvamos de la luna de miel, te divorciarás de mí.

–Ya. Bueno, espero que no te hayas creído ninguna de esas tonterías.

Tina no contestó.

–Ya veo que sí te las has creído –suspiró Richard.

–No sé qué creer –contestó Tina, desesperada–. Lo que me ha dicho no tiene sentido, pero me pregunto qué gana diciéndomelo si no fuera...

–¿Se te ha ocurrido pensar que puede estar celosa?

–¿Me estás diciendo que es verdad que habéis tenido una relación durante años?

–Sí, pero eso ya es agua pasada. Seguimos siendo amigos, pero nada más.

–¿No sigues enamorado de ella?

–Nunca estuve enamorado de ella. Y ella de mí, tampoco. Nuestra relación fue siempre muy superficial, algo temporal y sin futuro.

–Por lo visto, ella no piensa lo mismo. Me ha dicho que, si no hubiera surgido lo que ha surgido, te habrías casado con ella.

–Pero no te ha dicho lo que ha surgido, ¿no? –quiso saber Richard.

–No.

Richard parecía más tranquilo.

–Será alguna de esas cosas que se inventa. Siempre ha sido muy dada a tener mucha imaginación. En cuanto a lo de casarme con ella, lo ha debido de soñar porque yo jamás le he dicho que tuviera intención de convertirla en mi esposa. Por favor, no le hagas caso, no pienses en lo que te ha dicho. Está celosa. Es a ti a quien quiero. Es contigo con quien me quiero casar –le aseguró, pasándole un brazo por los hombros–. Espero que mis palabras te tranquilicen –añadió, besándola.

Tina se dijo que lo importante era que Richard estaba allí, junto a ella, besándola. La amaba y se quería casar con ella. ¿Por qué iba a dejar que los celos de otra mujer le estropearan su felicidad?

–Anda, vámonos a casa inmediatamente –le dijo Richard al ver que estaba temblando–. Es cierto que una cama no tiene tanto glamur, pero está calentita, y estar a gusto también es importante –añadió, queriendo mantener a Tina distraída para que no pensara en lo que Helen le había dicho–. Nuestra cama tiene siglos de historia, ¿sabes? En ella han nacido muchos miembros de la familia y otros muchos han pasado sus noches de boda.

«Ha dicho nuestra cama», pensó Tina, encantada.

Durante el resto del trayecto, hablaron de muchas cosas y, al llegar al castillo, los estaba esperando Hannah.

–El reverendo Peter me ha dicho que la boda va a ser mañana por la mañana.

–Así es.

–La cocinera y yo hemos pensado que nos gustaría mucho organizar un desayuno nupcial si nos dicen cuántas personas van a ser.

–De momento, solamente seremos nosotros, el personal de servicio y los trabajadores de la finca. Más tarde, cuando volvamos de la luna de miel, haremos otra celebración con invitados, banquete y todo lo demás.

Hannah sonrió.

–Han traído todo lo que me pidió. Lo he dejado en su suite. La señora Diomede lo ha traído personalmente y me ha dicho que, si hay el más mínimo problema, la llame y vendrá inmediatamente –añadió, girándose hacia Tina–. Si necesita ayuda para vestirse mañana, no dude en llamarme.

–No creo, gracias –contestó Tina, visualizando su sencillo vestido violeta–. No creo que vaya a necesitar ayuda.

–Muy bien –dijo el ama de llaves–. ¿Van a tomar el té en el salón de abajo o en su suite, señor Richard? Me ha parecido que había vuelto el frío y he encendido todas las chimeneas.

–Entonces, lo tomaremos arriba.

Cuando llegaron a su suite, encontraron la chimenea encendida y se sentaron frente al fuego. Al instante, apareció Milly con el servicio de té y, tras dejarlo sobre la mesa e inclinar levemente la cabeza, se fue.

Además del té, había magdalenas, mantequilla, miel y un tenedor largo.

–¿Quieres que tueste yo las magdalenas en el fuego o lo haces tú? –preguntó Richard.

–Me apetece hacerlo a mí –contestó Tina–. Hace años que no lo hago, y de pequeña me encantaba.

–Muy bien, aquí tienes –dijo Richard, pasándole el tenedor de trinchar.

Mientras Tina se concentraba en las llamas para no quemar las magdalenas, Richard se quedó mirando cómo se le sonrojaban las mejillas por el calor.

Al instante, le entraron unas tremendas ganas de golpear algo; estaba furioso. Aunque tenía muy claro que Tina no era la mujer dulce e inocente que parecía, también sabía sin ningún género de dudas que era la mujer a la que había estado esperando toda la vida, la única mujer que de verdad le había llegado al corazón.

Además de belleza externa, tenía una fuerza interna y un cerebro curioso y, sobre todo, tenía una integridad que le hacía preguntarse si no podría haber hecho las cosas de otra manera.

Imposible.

Ya no podía echarse atrás.

—¡Ya está! —exclamó Tina—. Dos magdalenas perfectamente tostadas...

—Me has dejado el listón muy alto —sonrió Richard.

Tras tomarse el té con magdalenas, Tina suspiró, encantada.

—Creo que no voy a comer en una semana.

Richard se rió.

—Ya me lo dirás dentro de unas horas. Por ejemplo, a las ocho, cuando esté la cena preparada —le dijo.

A continuación, retiró el servicio de té de la mesa, se puso en pie y sacó de detrás del sofá un montón de cajas azules.

—Mientras esperamos a que llegue la hora de la cena, supongo que te apetecerá ver tus cosas.

—¿Mis cosas? —se sorprendió Tina—. ¿Pero no me habías dicho que íbamos a ir de compras mañana por la tarde?

—Sí, pero eso será para comprarte la ropa de la luna de miel, pero también vas necesitar un vestido con el que casarte, ¿no?

Richard se sentó en el brazo de uno de los sofás y observó a Tina, que estaba encandilada por el contenido de las cajas.

Se trataba de un precioso vestido de novia de seda en color marfil y escote y mangas estilo medieval. Iba acompañado de una diadema de fantasía y de un velo de tul, zapatos a juego, medias de seda y ropa interior de cuento de hadas.

Todo lo que una novia podría soñar.

¿Cómo había podido creer que Richard iba a ser tan insensible como para no comprarle un vestido de novia?

—Gracias —le dijo, mirándolo a los ojos.

—Espero que te guste.

—Me encanta —contestó Tina, besándolo impulsivamente.

Richard se apresuró a secarle una lágrima que le resbalaba por la mejilla y a besarla.

—¿Cómo has podido comprarlo si hoy es domingo?

—La dueña de la tienda es una de mis mejores amigas, así que no ha habido problema. Por desgracia, no te lo ha podido hacer a medida porque no ha tenido tiempo y te ha tenido que traer uno de los que ya tenía hechos, pero...

Tina le puso un dedo sobre los labios.

—No digas «por desgracia». Te aseguro que es el vestido más bonito del mundo.

Richard sonrió, encantado.

—Supongo que habré acertado con la talla, pero

quizá sería mejor que te lo probaras –sugirió–. Mientras, voy a ver si acabo un par de cosas que tengo pendientes. Cuando termine, voy a hablar con Murray para organizar la luna de miel –se despidió, besándola.

Una vez a solas, Tina se dio cuenta de que las palabras de Helen no se le iban de la cabeza.

«Supongo que tendrá intención de llevarte de luna de miel después de la boda, ¿no?».

Tina hizo todo lo que pudo para apartar aquellos recuerdos tan desagradables de su mente. Para mantenerse ocupada, se probó el vestido de novia y todos los complementos. Aunque todo le quedaba de maravilla, su felicidad se había evaporado.

¿Qué habría querido decir Helen cuando le había dicho que Richard parecía creer que casarse con ella era la única manera de arreglar las cosas? ¿Qué cosas?

Confusa y nerviosa, atrapada en un laberinto de dudas y conjeturas, Tina se sentó junto al fuego, y allí la encontró Richard cuando volvió casi a las ocho de la tarde.

–Perdona, me he entretenido más de la cuenta –se disculpó–. Ya veo que te has estado probando el vestido. ¿Y qué tal?

Tina no contestó.

–¿Me he equivocado de talla?

–No, no... Es mi talla. El vestido me queda de maravilla...

–¿Pero no te gusta?

—Me encanta. Es precioso.

—¿Entonces qué te pasa?

Tina dudó si compartir con él sus dudas. Necesitaba respuestas. Sin embargo, decidió no hacerlo, pues sabía que Richard le diría que no pasaba nada, que era simplemente que Helen estaba celosa.

Tal vez, fuera cierto.

—No me pasa nada —le aseguró, intentando sonreír.

—¿Seguro? —insistió Richard.

—Seguro.

Richard tenía muy claro que lo que Helen le había dicho la tenía preocupada, y volvió a maldecirla. Para intentar normalizar las cosas, se acercó a Tina y la tomó entre sus brazos.

—Me voy a ir a duchar —anunció ella—. No quiero que la cena se retrase por mi culpa.

Richard asintió y apretó los dientes mientras Tina se retiraba al baño.

Aquella noche, la cena resultó un tanto complicada. Tina intentó comportarse con normalidad, pero lo cierto era que estaba apesadumbrada y preocupada y le dolía la cabeza.

—No has comido nada —le dijo Richard.

—No debería haber merendado tanto —se defendió Tina.

—¿Qué quieres hacer? —le preguntó Richard cuando terminaron de tomar el café.

–Estoy muy cansada y me parece que me voy a acostar pronto –contestó Tina, poniéndose en pie.

Necesitaba estar sola.

–Buena idea –contestó Richard, poniéndose en pie también–. Nos acostaremos pronto –añadió, mirándola de manera inequívoca.

Tina negó con la cabeza.

–Es por Helen, ¿verdad? –suspiró Richard

–No...

–No me mientas –se impacientó Richard.

–Me duele la cabeza.

–Entonces, no haremos nada, pero quiero dormir contigo.

–Prefiero dormir sola –le espetó Tina.

Richard apretó los dientes.

–Muy bien –concedió, besándole la mano.

–Buenas noches –se despidió Tina, corriendo escaleras arriba.

Aunque era cierto que estaba cansada y que le dolía la cabeza, una vez en la cama, Tina fue incapaz de dormir. Durante lo que se le antojó una eternidad, estuvo dando vueltas y preguntándose si Richard la querría de verdad. Al final, decidiendo que no debía dudar de él por lo que le había dicho una mujer a la que no conocía de nada, se levantó y se dirigió al dormitorio principal.

Al abrir la puerta, y aunque la luz estaba apagada, vio que Richard estaba tumbado en la cama, con las manos entrelazadas bajo la nuca y mirando al techo.

Tina se estremeció y se preguntó si seguiría enfadado con ella por haberlo rechazado. No se atrevía a moverse.

Al ver que Richard extendía el brazo, se acercó a la cama y se metió bajo las sábanas, acurrucándose rápidamente junto al cuerpo desnudo de su amado.

Al sentir su torso, el deseo se apoderó de ella y esperó a que Richard hiciera algo, pero no hizo nada. Tina comprendió que, al haber dicho que le dolía la cabeza, Richard no iba a hacer nada.

Si quería que ocurriera algo, lo iba a tener que provocar ella.

Tras dudar un momento, comenzó acariciarle los pectorales y la pierna. Richard no se movía. Tina continuó por las costillas, la cintura, el estómago...

–Ten cuidado –le advirtió–. No sigas jugando si no estás preparada para las consecuencias.

–¿Qué consecuencias? –bromeó Tina con fingida inocencia.

–Sabes perfectamente de qué consecuencias estamos hablando –contestó Richard, apartándole la mano.

Tina se dijo que al día siguiente aquel hombre sería su marido, se dejó llevar e hizo lo que le apetecía hacer en aquellos momentos, que era acariciarle la erección.

Al instante, oyó que Richard tomaba aire y apretaba los dientes.

–Creía que te dolía la cabeza.

–Me dolía.

–¿Se te ha pasado?

–Sí.

–Qué oportuno –comentó Richard con sarcasmo.

Tina se mordió el labio y se apartó, pero Richard la agarró.

–Demasiado tarde. Ya te he dicho que no jugaras si no estabas preparada para atenerte a las consecuencias.

–No estaba jugando. Quería que... quería que me hicieras el amor.

–¿En pasado? ¿Has cambiado de parecer?

–No, sigo queriendo.

–En ese caso... –dijo Richard, tumbándose sobre ella–. Vamos a ver qué puedo hacer para darte gusto.

A continuación, le quitó el camisón y lo tiró al suelo. Segundos después, Tina temblaba de placer mientras Richard la besaba y la lamía desde los dedos de los pies hasta la parte interna los muslos y más allá.

Aquella noche, hicieron el amor varias veces de manera muy creativa y prolongada, y Richard la hizo tener sensaciones tan dulces y exquisitas, que Tina se encontró saciada y feliz antes de quedarse dormida.

Cuando se despertó a la mañana siguiente, aunque era bastante temprano, comprobó que estaba sola en la enorme cama.

Al incorporarse, suspiró.

A pesar de que había intentado arreglar las cosas entre ellos, las dudas e incertidumbres que las palabras de Helen O'Connell habían sembrado en su cabeza habían abierto una brecha entre Richard y ella.

Aunque habían hecho el amor de manera apasionada y experta, Tina se daba cuenta de que Richard se había dejado llevar más por la rabia que por el amor.

Aquello la hizo suspirar de nuevo.

Aquél era el día de su boda. Se suponía que tendría que ser el día más feliz de su vida. Lo hubiera sido si... ¿por qué demonios no hacía un esfuerzo y se concentraba en cosas más felices que el encuentro con Helen?

En unas cuantas horas, sería la esposa de Richard, y unas horas después emprenderían el viaje rumbo a su luna de miel.

Todo había sucedido tan rápido, que nadie sabía nada.

Excepto Helen O'Connell.

Tina no pudo evitar volver a recordar parte de su conversación.

«Desde luego, cuando me dijo que no había tiempo que perder, no creí que fuera a ser tan rápido».

De repente, recordó la conversación que había oído el día anterior entre Helen y Richard. En aquellos momentos, cuando había escuchado la conversación, no había sabido de qué se trataba. Ahora, sin embargo, sabía algo. Aunque no tenía todos los detalles, era obvio que Helen había intentado disuadir a Richard para que no se casara con ella.

Entonces, recordó que, finalmente, y desesperada, Helen le había preguntado si se había parado a considerar la ética de todo aquello, y Richard le había contestado que tenía mucho que perder.

Aunque no sabía qué era exactamente lo que Richard quería de ella, lo que estaba claro era que, hasta que no supiera la verdad, no se podía casar con él.

Evidentemente, preguntárselo a él no le iba a servir de nada. Tal vez, hablar con Helen la sacara de dudas. Tenía que encontrar la manera de hablar con ella sin que Richard se enterara.

¿Cómo hacerlo? ¿Por teléfono quizás? No, el asunto era demasiado serio. Quería tratarlo cara a cara.

Entonces, se le ocurrió que podía acercarse a los establos sin que nadie la viera y, fingiendo que quería dar un paseo, llevarse a Juno e ir a Farrington Hall.

Y eso fue exactamente lo que hizo.

Capítulo 10

TINA no sabía exactamente dónde estaba la casa de Helen, pero sabía, más o menos, la dirección, así que no le costó encontrarla.

Al llamar a la puerta, la atendió una mujer mayor vestida de servicio y, tras presentarse, Tina le dijo que quería hablar con la señorita O'Connell.

—Espere aquí un momento, señorita Dunbar, voy a avisar a la señorita Helen y le voy a decir a Tom que venga a hacerse cargo de su caballo —le dijo la mujer.

Un par de minutos después, apareció un joven que, efectivamente, se hizo cargo de Juno. Al mismo tiempo, apareció Helen, que le indicó a Tina que la acompañara.

—Estaba terminando de desayunar —le dijo, conduciéndola a un acogedor invernadero bañado por el sol—. ¿Quieres un café?

—No —contestó Tina—. No quiero entretenerte. Sólo quería hacerte un par de preguntas. Ayer me dijiste que, en cuanto volviéramos de la luna de miel, Richard se divorciaría de mí. ¿Por qué me lo dijiste?

—Pregúntaselo a él.

—¿Crees que me lo diría?

—Lo dudo mucho.

—También me dijiste que, si no hubiera surgido el problema que había surgido, se habría casado contigo. Por favor, dime qué problema es el que ha surgido y qué quiere Richard exactamente de mí.

—¿Y si no quiero decírtelo?

—Entonces, seguiré adelante con la boda. Si estás tan segura de que se va a divorciar de mí...

—No creo en el divorcio —gritó Helen con dolor.

A Tina le daba pena la otra mujer, pero necesitaba saber.

—Entonces, más te vale contármelo todo.

—Si lo hago, Richard jamás me perdonará.

—Lo hará si te quiere.

Helen permaneció en silencio, y Tina se puso en pie, creyendo que había perdido la batalla.

—Está bien, me arriesgaré —dijo Helen—. Si se casa contigo, lo habré perdido de todas maneras... Todo comenzó cuando Bradley Sanderson murió. Resultó que había hecho testamento dejando el castillo a su hija.

—Creía que no tenía hijos y, además, el castillo no era suyo, ¿no?

—Sí, sí era suyo. Resultó que era suyo. Sorprendió a Richard dejando el castillo a una hija ilegítima de la que nadie tenía noticia. Por lo visto, no había tenido contacto con ella nunca y no sabía dónde estaba. Lo único que sabía de ella era su nombre, más o menos su edad y dónde había vivido después de ser adoptada, así que les dijo a sus abogados que la encontraran. Y la encontraron sorprendentemente rápido.

—No entiendo qué tiene que ver esto conmigo.

—Mucho, porque tú eres la hija de Bradley Sanderson.

Tina se quedó mirándola con los ojos como platos.

—Richard pensó que, en cuanto los abogados del marido de su madre se hubieran puesto en contacto contigo, sería demasiado tarde. Temía perder el castillo, y decidió que lo mejor que podía hacer era casarse contigo antes de que te enteraras de que habías heredado. Por eso tiene tantas prisas.

Desde luego, la historia tenía sentido, pero había un detalle que no encajaba.

—Es imposible que yo sea hija de Bradley Sanderson.

—Pues sus abogados están convencidos de que lo eres. Te han mandado una carta y todo. Richard me ha dicho que consiguió interceptarla.

Tina recordó aquella carta que había desaparecido de encima de su mesa y sintió que el corazón le daba un vuelco.

Ella tenía muy claro que era imposible que fuera hija de Bradley Sanderson, pero era evidente que Richard sí lo creía. Por eso tenía prisa por casarse con ella y le había hecho firmar un documento por el que renunciaba a sus derechos sobre el castillo en caso de divorcio.

Todo lo que le había contado de que se había enamorado de ella nada más verla era mentira. No la amaba en absoluto. Lo único que quería era salvaguardar su herencia.

Tina sentía un intenso dolor en el pecho que la había paralizado. La agonía era insoportable. Tras unos segundos, el dolor cedió un poco y se sintió como anestesiada, como si la fuerza vital la hubiera abandonado.

—Gracias por contármelo —se despidió de Helen.

A continuación, buscó a Tom, se montó en Juno y volvió al castillo. Al llegar, y tras dejar al caballo en las cuadras, se dirigió a buscar a Richard, pero con quien se encontró fue con Hannah.

—Ah, menos mal que la encuentro. Richard la está buscando —le dijo el ama de llaves.

—¿Dónde está?

—Buscándola. Le voy a decir a Mullins que usted también lo está buscando... Si ha cambiado de opinión y quiere que la ayude a vestirse...

—No, gracias, no he cambiado de opinión. Por favor, dígale al señor que lo espero en el estudio —dijo Tina, alejándose y dejando al ama de llaves perpleja.

Tan sólo llevaba unos minutos en el estudio cuando apareció Richard. Llegaba vestido con un precioso traje gris y camisa y corbata de seda, pero su acostumbrado autocontrol se había esfumado.

—¿Dónde demonios estabas? —le preguntó—. Te he estado buscando por todas partes.

—He estado en Farrington Hall, hablando con Helen O'Connell.

—¿Y?

—Y he obtenido las respuestas que necesitaba.

—Bien, ya hablaremos de eso más tarde. El reverendo nos está esperando —comentó Richard, mirando el reloj.

—Ahora que sé por qué te quieres casar conmigo, no tengo intención de seguir adelante con la ceremonia —lo informó Tina con mucha tranquilidad, suponiendo que Richard iba a ponerse como un basilisco.

No fue así.

—Muy bien. Le voy a decir al reverendo que la ceremonia se ha pospuesto.

—Se ha cancelado.

—Por lo visto, Helen ha hecho un buen trabajo.

—Lo único que ha hecho es contarme la verdad, así que no le eches la culpa a ella.

—¿Estás segura de que lo que te ha contado es la verdad?

—Sí.

Richard se giró y se fue. Volvió al cabo de unos minutos, y Tina se fijó en que llegaba mucho más calmado.

—Cuéntame exactamente lo que te ha dicho Helen —le dijo, sentándose frente a ella.

—Al principio, no me quería contar nada, pero la

he presionado y ha terminado contándome que el marido de tu madre te engañó y le dejó el castillo a su hija ilegítima. Me ha contado que tú crees que yo soy su hija y que querías casarte conmigo cuanto antes, antes de que yo descubriera que había heredado Anders.

—¿Y tú la crees?

—Es la verdad, ¿no?

—Sí —admitió Richard.

—¿Y qué tenías pensado hacer cuando descubriera por qué te habías casado conmigo? Lo más normal es que no hubieras podido ocultar la razón durante mucho tiempo.

—No lo tenía muy claro —contestó Richard—. Al principio, mi idea era lidiar con ese asunto cuando ocurriera. Luego, cuando empecé a conocerte, decidí contártelo todo cuando volviéramos de la luna de miel con la esperanza de que, una vez que supieras la verdad, decidieras permanecer a mi lado.

—Helen está convencida de que tenías intención de divorciarte de mí y, dado que me hiciste firmar un documento en el que renunciaba a mis derechos sobre el castillo...

—Eso no fue porque tuviera intención de divorciarme de ti, sino por si tú querías divorciarte de mí.

—Lo tenías todo pensado, ¿eh? —le espetó Tina con acidez.

—De verdad, no estoy orgulloso de lo que he hecho. Estaba desesperado —se disculpó Richard.

–Lo que no entiendo es por qué creías que tenías que casarte conmigo –comentó Tina con dolor–. Seguro que había otras maneras de arreglar la
cuestión. No es que no tengas dinero...

–Sí, tengo mucho dinero, pero no tenía manera
de saber si tú ibas a querer vender el castillo. Aun
en caso de que hubieras querido, no sabía el tipo
de mujer que eras, y la verdad es que no quería
quedarme sin un penique.

–Yo nunca te hubiera pedido más de lo que vale
en realidad.

–Ahora que te conozco mejor, comprendo que
es cierto lo que me dices, pero entiende que no tenía tiempo para descubrir qué tipo de mujer tenía
ante mí –dijo Richard, tomándola de la mano–. No
me quedaba más remedio que actuar de manera
drástica para conservar el castillo. Además de que
me encanta este lugar, es mi herencia y el lugar en
el que he nacido. Por favor, entiéndeme...

–En cierta manera, te entiendo –contestó Tina,
retirando la mano–. Lo que no entiendo es cómo
pudo Bradley dejarle el castillo a nadie.

–Ya te dije que me había parecido bien añadir un
codicilo al testamento de mi madre en el que se decía que Bradley podía quedarse viviendo aquí hasta
que muriera –suspiró Richard–. Al principio, se
conformó con eso, pero, cuando mi madre ya estaba
muy enferma, comenzó a presionarla. Le dijo que le
haría muy feliz ser el dueño del castillo durante la
poca vida que le quedaba y añadió que estaba con-

vencido de que se lo debía. Al final, mi madre terminó accediendo con la condición de que él hiciera también testamento. Por supuesto, a mi favor. Ambos testamentos fueron recogidos por Alexander Fry, el abogado de la familia. Unas cuantas semanas después, Alexander llamó a mi madre para preguntarle si sabía que su esposo había vuelto a su despacho para hacer otro testamento. Mi madre no tenía ni idea, y su abogado le advirtió que el segundo testamento de su marido invalidaba el primero. Aunque mi madre sabía que su marido no tenía a nadie a quien dejarle nada, se preocupó mucho. Habló con Hannah y con el reverendo Peter, que fue quien me lo contó a mí, y ante el temor de que Bradley hubiera hecho algo perjudicial para mí, hizo ella también otro testamento. Para entonces, estaba demasiado enferma como para salir a la calle y no quería levantar las sospechas de su esposo haciendo que su abogado viniera aquí, así que lo escribió en una hoja de papel normal y corriente y les pidió a Hannah y al reverendo que fueran los testigos. Según ese testamento, me dejaba a mí todo.

—Entonces, no veo dónde está el problema —suspiró Tina, aliviada.

—El problema es que ese segundo testamento no aparece por ninguna parte. Yo creía que iba estar en el cajón secreto de su cómoda, pero no es así. Lo hemos buscado por todas partes, pero no aparece. Supongo que Bradley lo encontraría y lo haría desaparecer.

–Oh.

–Yo sé que mi madre tenía intención de dejarme el castillo a mí, así que doy por hecho que es mío hasta que se demuestre que el testamento de Bradley es el válido. Cuando eso ocurra, a no ser que vayamos a juicio, el castillo será tuyo.

–No –le dijo Tina.

–¿Cómo que no?

–Yo no soy hija de Bradley Sanderson. Es imposible que lo sea. Yo nací cuando mis padres llevaban un año casados, y te aseguro que mi madre no tuvo ninguna aventura con el marido de tu madre. Además, soy el vivo retrato de mi padre. Lo único que se me ocurre es que haya habido un error de identidad.

Richard frunció el ceño.

–Dunbar no es un apellido muy común, y estoy seguro de que los abogados hicieron bien su trabajo.

–Hablando de abogados, Helen me ha dicho que le habías contado que se habían puesto en contacto conmigo a través de una carta que tú me robaste.

–Sí –admitió Richard–. Lo siento, en aquellos momentos me pareció necesario hacerlo –añadió, explicándole que había entrado en su despacho en Cartel Wines y se la había llevado de encima de su mesa–. Cuando vi que no la habías abierto, di gracias al cielo. Lo cierto es que se me pasó por la cabeza hablar contigo, pero decidí esperar a que tu jefe te hubiera dicho que estabas despedida.

—Así que fuiste tú. Supongo que formaba todo parte de un plan para dejarme cada vez más vulnerable.

—Así es.

—¿Y el accidente fue provocado?

Richard asintió.

—Necesitaba conocerte, así que no dudé en hacerlo. Mi intención era llevarte a casa y ver cómo eras para ver si podía hablar contigo. Lo de que no tuvieras dónde dormir me vino caído del cielo, y el resto de la historia ya la conoces...

Tina sintió que la angustia le oprimía el pecho y que no podía hablar ni moverse. Todo lo que había ocurrido entre ellos había sido una farsa.

—¿Sigues teniendo la carta de los abogados de tu padrastro? Podría darnos una idea de por qué me han confundido con otra persona.

—Lo dudo, pero aquí la tienes —contestó Richard, poniéndose en pie, abriendo un cajón de su mesa y entregándosela.

El sobre iba dirigido a la señorita V. Dunbar y procedía del bufete de abogados Barnard, Rudge y Fry.

Estaba sin abrir.

Tina la leyó y se quedó helada.

—Ahora lo entiendo todo —anunció.

—Pues explícamelo, por favor —le rogó Richard.

—Esta carta va dirigida a la señorita Valerie Dunbar.

—¿Valerie?

—Sí, Valerie, mi hermana. ¡Mi hermana es la hija de Bradley Sanderson!

—¿Pero no me habías dicho que se llamaba Didi?

—Didi la llamamos en familia, y Val la llaman sus amigos, pero su nombre es Valerie —le explicó Tina—. Ahora que recuerdo, mi madrastra me contó en alguna ocasión que ya había tenido a Valerie cuando se casó con su primer marido.

Richard se dijo que, por lo visto, los abogados habían encontrado a la mujer adecuada y que había sido su detective quien había cometido el error de confundir a las hermanas. Aquello le hizo preguntarse si el informe que le había hecho Grimshaw sería sobre Valerie o sobre Valentina.

—Háblame de ella. ¿Cómo es?

—Muy guapa, alta y morena.

—Bradley también era moreno.

Tina asintió.

—¿Y de carácter? Me dijiste que erais muy diferentes, ¿no?

—Sí. Yo siempre fui más introvertida que ella. Didi es mucho más atrevida y temeraria que yo. Hasta el punto de que en el colegio se juntó con gente poco recomendable. Su madre estaba muy preocupada porque tuvo problemas con...

—Drogas, alcohol y sexo —dijo Richard.

—¿Cómo lo sabes?

—Me lo dijo mi detective.

—¡Y tú creías que ésa era yo!

–Sí –admitió Richard–. Pronto me di cuenta de que había algo que no encajaba. No te parecías en absoluto a la imagen que mi detective me había dado de ti. La mujer que me había descrito ya tenía relaciones sexuales con apenas dieciséis años y, desde entonces, habían pasado por su vida muchos hombres. Tú, sin embargo, sólo me has hablado de tu prometido –recapacitó–. Me dijiste que tu hermana había vivido una temporada en tu casa, ¿no? ¿Y no me dijiste también que rompiste el compromiso con tu prometido a causa de otra mujer? –añadió Richard, frunciendo el ceño.

Tina asintió, apesadumbrada.

–Una noche, volví a casa antes de lo previsto y me los encontré en la cama.

–A él le dejaste. ¿Y a ella?

–Me dijo que lo sentía mucho, que había ocurrido de repente, y la perdoné porque siempre me ha parecido que no era inmoral, sino amoral.

–¿Y tiene novio en la actualidad?

–Que yo sepa, no hay nadie especial en su vida. ¿Por qué? ¿Estás pesando en seducirla para ver si te puedes casar con ella?

Richard apretó las mandíbulas.

–Me dijiste que estaba en una escuela muy buena de arte dramático, y me estaba preguntando quién se la paga.

Tina permaneció en silencio, y Richard comprendió que era ella.

–No te preocupes, a mi hermana nunca le ha gustado el campo, no creo que tenga problema en venderte el castillo. Didi tiene defectos como todo el mundo, pero te aseguro que no es una persona ambiciosa. Si le haces una buena oferta, la aceptará.

Richard suspiró, aliviado.

—Bueno, ahora que hemos dejado todo esto claro, me gustaría que me devolvieras mi móvil —dijo Tina, poniéndose en pie.

Richard abrió el cajón superior de su mesa y se lo entregó.

—Gracias —dijo Tina, encaminándose a la puerta.

—¿Adónde vas?

—Vuelvo a Londres. Tengo que buscar trabajo. Te sugiero que despidas a ese detective porque, si no hubiera sido por él, tú no habrías perdido tanto tiempo y tanta energía, y yo no habría perdido mi trabajo.

—Valentina, yo...

En aquel momento, llamaron a la puerta y entró Hannah.

—Señor Richard, la cocinera quiere saber qué hacemos con la comida, y la señorita O'Connell quiere verlo. Parece histérica.

—Muy bien —contestó Richard tras dudar un momento—. Por favor, dígale que me espere en el salón.

Hannah se fue, y Tina abrió la puerta con intención de seguirla, pero Richard la agarró del brazo. Tina se zafó de su mano y abrió la puerta.

—Espera, necesito hablar contigo.

–No tenemos nada de lo que hablar. Voy a llamar a un taxi y me voy en cuanto haya recogido mis cosas.

–Valentina, por favor, escúchame –le dijo Richard con desesperación.

Tina negó con la cabeza, cruzó el vestíbulo y subió las escaleras con los ojos arrasados por las lágrimas. Por fortuna, Richard no la siguió. Una vez en su dormitorio, llamó a un taxi y se puso a hacer la maleta, intentando ignorar el precioso vestido de novia que reposaba sobre la cama.

Mientras terminaba de meter su ropa en la bolsa de viaje, se fijó en que todavía llevaba puesto el anillo de compromiso, y se preguntó qué debía hacer con él. Obviamente, lo mejor que podía hacer era dejarlo en su sitio, así que se acercó a la cómoda de la madre de Richard y abrió el compartimento secreto.

Tras dejar el anillo, se dispuso a cerrarlo, pero no pudo. Después de haberlo intentado varias veces, metió la mano y, para su sorpresa, encontró una hoja de papel muy arrugada. Aunque estaba en mal estado, la fecha y el contenido eran perfectamente legibles.

Se trataba del segundo testamento de su madre.

Tras ponerse el abrigo, bajó a la planta inferior. Justo en aquel momento, Richard y Helen salían del salón, y se quedó mirándolos mientras se despedían como buenos amigos.

Richard salió a acompañarla al coche y, cuando

volvió a entrar con la intención de volver al salón, la vio al pie de las escaleras.

—Supongo que habrás visto que Helen se acaba de ir.

—Sí.

—Hemos hablado y lo hemos arreglado todo. Volvemos a ser amigos.

—Me alegro mucho por vosotros —contestó Tina—. Yo me voy ya, mi taxi debe de estar a punto de llegar, pero antes de irme quería darte esto —le dijo, entregándole una hoja de papel.

Richard la aceptó y la leyó. A continuación, la miró, conmovido.

—Gracias —le dijo, profundamente agradecido.

—Bueno, ahora que ya tienes lo que querías... —se despidió Tina, yendo hacia la puerta.

—No, no tengo lo que quería —dijo Richard, guardándose el papel en el bolsillo y yendo tras ella.

En un abrir y cerrar de ojos, la tomó en brazos y la condujo al salón, donde sin ninguna ceremonia la dejó sobre el sofá.

—Suéltame, mi taxi tiene que estar a punto de llegar —protestó Tina.

—Ya ha llegado. Estaba en la puerta esperándote cuando he salido a despedirme de Helen, y le he dicho que se fuera.

—¿Cómo te atreves?

—Ya te he dicho que teníamos que hablar.

—Y yo ya te he dicho que tú y yo no tenemos nada que hablar. Deja que me vaya inmediatamente.

Richard se inclinó sobre ella y la besó.

—Puede que tú no tengas nada que decirme, pero yo sí, pero antes de nada me gustaría hacerte una pregunta. ¿Por qué me has entregado el testamento de mi madre?

—¿Por qué tipo de mujer me tomas? Obviamente, te lo he devuelto porque no creo que mi hermanastra tuviera derecho a aprovecharse de la perfidia de tu padrastro.

—Muy bien —sonrió Richard—. En contestación a lo que me acabas de preguntar, te tengo por una mujer honrada, leal y valiente, el tipo de mujer que cualquier hombre querría a su lado porque puede sentirse orgulloso de ella. Quiero compartir mi vida contigo.

—Si te crees que...

—Tienes todo el derecho del mundo a estar enfadada conmigo —dijo Richard, poniéndole los dedos sobre los labios—. Te he tratado fatal, te he engañado y te he mentido, pero no en todo. Cuando te dije que me había enamorado de ti a primera vista, era cierto. Me daba miedo que, cuando descubrieras la verdad, me dejaras. Aunque no tenía buen concepto de ti, me quería casar contigo, quería que fueras mi esposa y la madre de mis hijos. Si no te hubiera amado y no hubiera tenido intención de casarme contigo para siempre, jamás habría sugerido que utilizáramos los anillos de mis padres. Este castillo significa mucho para mí, pero tú significas más.

Tina sintió que la ira y el resentimiento se desvanecían de su corazón, que quedó repleto de amor y de gratitud.

—Por favor, perdóname. Te propongo que empecemos de nuevo. Te prometo que esta vez iré más despacio —le dijo Richard.

—Yo no quiero volver a empezar —contestó Tina.

Richard la miró, desolado.

—Te quiero —dijo Tina, acariciándole la mejilla con ternura—. Tenemos cura, capilla, vestido de novia y alianzas. ¿Por qué vamos a esperar? Además, no quiero decepcionar a...

Richard la tomó en brazos y la besó.

—¿A quién no quieres decepcionar? ¿A Hannah?

—No —rió Tina.

—¿Al reverendo?

—No, iba a decir que no quería decepcionar a nuestra cama —rió Tina.

—Cariño, con lo mucho que nos queremos, nuestra cama va a estar muy satisfecha —le aseguró Richard.

Bianca™

**Se había casado por venganza…
pero se había acostado con ella por placer**

El millonario Andreas Trigliani buscaba venganza. La mimada heredera Gemma Landerstalle, que tanto daño le había hecho en el pasado, ahora necesitaba un marido… ¡urgentemente! Andreas estaba encantado de ayudarla porque, por muchas mujeres que cayeran rendidas a sus pies, a la única a la que quería ver suplicar era a Gemma.

Pero Gemma había cambiado. Un terrible accidente la había dejado traumatizada y la había convertido en una mujer tímida, inocente y vulnerable, algo que Andreas descubrió con sorpresa y placer…

De pronto, Andreas se dio cuenta de que sus deseos de venganza habían desaparecido…

Venganza placentera

Melanie Milburne

Acepte 2 de nuestras mejores novelas de amor GRATIS

¡Y reciba un regalo sorpresa!

Oferta especial de tiempo limitado

Rellene el cupón y envíelo a
Harlequin Reader Service®
3010 Walden Ave.
P.O. Box 1867
Buffalo, N.Y. 14240-1867

¡Sí! Por favor, envíenme 2 novelas de amor de Harlequin (1 Bianca® y 1 Deseo®) gratis, más el regalo sorpresa. Luego remítanme 4 novelas nuevas todos los meses, las cuales recibiré mucho antes de que aparezcan en librerías, y factúrenme al bajo precio de $3,24 cada una, más $0,25 por envío e impuesto de ventas, si corresponde*. Este es el precio total, y es un ahorro de casi el 20% sobre el precio de portada. !Una oferta excelente! Entiendo que el hecho de aceptar estos libros y el regalo no me obliga en forma alguna a la compra de libros adicionales. Y también que me puedo devolver cualquier envío y cancelar en cualquier momento. Aún si decido no comprar ningún otro libro de Harlequin, los 2 libros gratis y el regalo sorpresa son míos para siempre.

416 LBN DU7N

Nombre y apellido	(Por favor, letra de molde)	
Dirección	Apartamento No.	
Ciudad	Estado	Zona postal

Esta oferta se limita a un pedido por hogar y no está disponible para los subscriptores actuales de Deseo® y Bianca®.
*Los términos y precios quedan sujetos a cambios sin aviso previo.
Impuestos de ventas aplican en N.Y.

SPN-03   ©2003 Harlequin Enterprises Limited